SILENT PAST

FRANCESCA PIERRE

SILENT PAST: A REFLECTION OF SHADOWS AND SECRETS

*S*ilent Past is not merely a story—it's an exploration of the psychological scars inflicted by childhood experiences. It delves into how the unresolved pains of the past can manifest in the present, influencing choices and relationships. The novel intricately weaves themes of betrayal, love, and redemption, underscoring the belief that true healing requires not just self-awareness but a willingness to confront emotions and actively seek resolution.

Through its characters, Silent Past reveals that secrets are seldom one-sided. Everyone carries their own burdens, often concealed behind facades. This intricate dance of hidden truths resonates deeply with Francesca's philosophy: life's struggles shape us, but they do not have to define us. Healing begins when we embrace our vulnerabilities and confront the shadows of past wounds.

CHAPTER 1

Cold Beginnings

Magda snapped her fingers to get June, the barkeeper, to refill her glass. She gulped down her third tequila shot and enjoyed the serene voice of the jazz singer in the background. She wore a pair of wide-legged pants matching her green-striped blouse. A beige headband kept her bangs in place. Makeup was not her strong point; a bit of face cream and nude lipstick would do. She crossed her legs and leaned her elbow on the counter.

"It'll be in your best interest to remain close to me. You're the only woman here," cautioned June, the barkeeper and Magda's cousin. He was bulky, around 6'7, with his arms as strong as a bull. No one would take the chance to approach Magda, even for a minute. She caught a few discreet eyes gazing at her petite silhouette from the stool. She turned her glance away to avoid drawing too much attention.

"You have to leave, Maggie." June took the bottles of Tequila out of her sight. He refused to allow her to get one more shot since she would be driving home.

She scowled at him. "I hate when you call me Maggie."

Magda was aware of June's intention to watch after her since the bar was unsafe. She would rather be in an uncomfortable place than be at home, waiting for her daughter to be released from school while watching the same reruns over and over. Life was boring when everything became routine. Living in a mansion with servants doing daily chores and caring for the household left her the minimum to keep busy. At least she had June's company and his dry sense of humor. He could make her laugh at anything, and that was what Magda needed. Someone to keep her joyful and bring the juvenile side out of her.

"That's what Richard used to call me," Magda said, her palm briefly touching her cheek, offering a fleeting warmth.

"Do you still hate him?" June asked, briefly pausing his task to read his cousin's face. "You're clearly not over his death."

"All I know is that he died a horrible death," Magda replied, her gaze dropping to the counter, where her fingers fidgeted aimlessly. A shaky breath followed as she rubbed her neck. June reached for her hands, but it was obvious. It was not comfort that Magda needed.

"And, has anyone ever mentioned Richard to you, or anything about the fire at all?"

"Hm… Not really," June replied, wrinkling his nose. "But I do wish his death was investigated more." June took a brief look around, as he signaled to the waiters to clear the prepared orders. "But why do you ask? You constantly bring up the fire as if you don't really believe that he's dead."

"I know that—" "He's not going to rise from his grave, Magda," June snorted, shaking his head. "Besides, why should you worry about it? It is not like you were still together at the time he died." "It's just—It's just a feeling I have, as if he's somewhere out there watching me. I don't know…" Realizing that she was saying more than she intended to, she stopped, easing her thoughts. She needed another shot of tequila, or to be in her painting room where she could paint Richard. That face of his, which reminded her of what love and hate felt like. "You know what? Let's talk about something else," June advised,

"I don't like to see you upset." "Y-Yes," Magda said, nodding slowly. "I agree."

"Do you remember when we used to do the groceries for aunt Allimair?" recalled June with a smile.

"Of course." Magda said, keeping her hands on her lap below the counter. "Mom could only afford a couple of items to make ravioli on Saturday nights."

"I was a fat kid," June said, as the vivid memories flooded through his mind.

Magda's laughter finally broke through. "Oh, please, you weren't fat. I loved that you could eat so much, so I didn't have to finish those ravioli bowls."

"They were salty too," June said with a snort.

Magda wheezed. "I bet she did it on purpose. More salt meant more water to knock us out."

"By the way, how's Helmer doing?" June asked, as he discarded a couple of empty whiskey bottles. "Are there any issues between you two?" A stream of tears threatened to run down her face again, at the mention of her husband's name. Magda looked away, rubbing her hands on her lap. "H-He is fine. You know... It's just that sometimes, he can be so possessive, overprotective, and aggressive—"

"Aggressive—" June snapped, stopping what he was doing, making sure he heard her right.

"No, no, not like that," Magda corrected quickly. "I mean... I can't stop thinking about what my dad used to say about him when we were about to get married."

"Like?" Urged June, wiping up the counter before starting new orders.

"That he's not as good as he seems to be," Magda replied. "Honestly, I think dad was looking too much into Helmer not having a great father figure. But living with him can be challenging."

"What are you talking about?" June frowned, trying to make sense of Magda's puzzling statements. "I thought you guys were okay."

"I thought so too," Magda replied. "It's complicated."

Three men arrived and greeted June. They scanned the bar menu for the various cocktails and wine choices. They rested their hands on the counter and ordered three cocktails, which June started pouring.

Magda was happy to see June doing what he had always wanted to do ever since he was a child. To be independent, carefree, and pursue a lifestyle he loved. Magda scanned June from head to toe and struggled not to pick on him for his odd taste in fashion. He had a pink-colored shirt, a blue tie, a green pair of pants, and brown shoes. She didn't say anything about his outfit, but he knew she did not like it.

"You smell like Margaritas." He handed her a pack of chewing gum. As protective as he was, he no longer entertained her staying there longer since more men started to walk in.

"It's already 4:00 pm," said Magda, checking her watch. "I must go. We'll catch up."

She waved to June before he could say anything and ran to the exit. She walked into the corridor to retrieve her car. While she pulled her keys, a male-looking shadow overpowered her. She slowed down and reached for her purse, making sure to have her pepper spray on hand. The person kept following her. Magda looked from the corner of her eyes but couldn't see the person's face. She gripped her phone, but her heart raced when the footsteps ceased. Her breath caught in the air, fragile like a candle's light dimming before vanishing into darkness. Her lungs refused to expand, realizing the ultimate betrayal. Her phone dying when she needed it most, leaving her stranded in silence.

Magda looked around the street and made it to the parking lot. Her trembling hands refused to let her get a firm grip on her car key to unlock the door. A feverish fear numbed her legs and even more when the shadow returned and loomed closer, unrecognizable in the chaos of her pounding heartbeat. Magda turned sharply, colliding with something solid—someone solid. Her keys fell, a sharp clink on the ground, now the familiar outline becoming clear. It was her husband.

She rested her elbows on the car to catch her breath. "Helmer? What are you doing here?"

"Come! We need to talk," he said. "I told one of our chauffeurs to take my car home."

His hazel-green eyes met hers and made her struggle to make any objections. Her brain tried to grip a few words to ask how he knew where to find her. She was a stubborn character, and being submissive was a challenge. She liked to do whatever was on her mind, go wherever she wanted, and get home when she pleased. It was a matter of time before these liberal habits ended.

Magda had to adjust to being a housewife and closing her flourishing painting business. Meanwhile, Helmer still had the leisure of spending extra hours at work, coming home late, and being out with friends whenever he wanted. He was tall, handsome, but he never gave Magda any reason to not trust him around other women. Although Magda never admitted it, this trait of his was her weakness.

Helmer stepped forward and laid a kiss on her lips, then placed his arm around her waist. He walked her to the passenger's seat and opened the door so she could get in. He asked Magda to put on her seatbelt and took a brief gaze at her hair. "It's beautiful! You didn't tell me you were going to cut it."

"I didn't get the time to tell you." She cleared her throat. "Or should I say you're never home?"

"June told me you were here," he said. "I judged it unsafe to let you drive home after those drinks."

"I should've known he'd snitched on me," she replied. "What did you want to talk about?"

"Us." He drove to a private park and rested his forehead on the wheel. "We should get Meg to live with your mom."

Magda gawked at him with unbelieving eyes and hopped out of the car. She stood about four feet away, her stance unstable, as she twisted her fingers. She burst into tears, staring at the ground. It was not the alcohol; she wished it were; but it was her husband making her cry. The soft breeze kissed her cheeks and danced into her ears. Its calming effect helped to keep her composure while she itched to confront him. Helmer got out of the car and leaned on the trunk.

"You want our daughter to leave our house. Is that your way to get revenge?" She eyed him. "Because I'm not ready to have a child with you?"

Helmer shrugged. "It could be."

He put his hands into his pockets and kept his distance, so the situation did not escalate. He could not help being honest, although the truth was brutal. "Just stop acting, Magda! You'll never be ready because we both know you don't want to build a family with me."

Magda listened carefully, wondering whether she had heard her husband right or whether the liquor was making up stories in her head. But whatever it was, she knew she wanted to get away from him. Magda staggered off, dragging her weight to a bench, then rested her hands on her lap, welcoming the tears tingling in her eyes.

Helmer couldn't watch her cry. He pursed his lips, swallowing the lumps invading his throat. He dashed into the car to process his agony, raising the radio's volume to smother Magda's sobs.

CHAPTER 2

Going Backwards

Magda decided to cook. She took the hot pot off the stove and poured the pumpkin soup into the ceramic bowl. Magda added a pinch of salt to the ravioli and stirred it before turning off the oven. She cooked baked chicken, ravioli, and creamy three-cheese spaghetti. Then, a fruit salad with green vegetables and guava cakes for dessert. Meanwhile, her daughter's absence was going to make the house lifeless since cooking together was a bonding moment for them. Besides, Allimair, Magda's mom, was too busy with her hair salon and talk show during the week to keep Magda company. For the very first time, Magda felt the need to escape the dependency on her husband and find something that could fill the void. Yet, her real enemy wasn't her lifestyle but her past.

Magda heard someone's footsteps from the hall, assuming it was her husband. Mr. Hens, the Butler, showed up and bowed to greet her. He crossed his hands behind him and straightened himself. He was the type to linger when he had something important to say. Mr. Hens was responsible for the daily menus, hosting the guests, and answering calls. He would also manage the staff's duties and pantry.

"Madam, your daughter told me she won't come down to eat." "Did she tell you why?" she asked, taking her oven mitts off. "No, Mrs. Dupris," answered Mr. Hens. "We have three choices for today's dinner. What would you like?"

Magda forced a smile and shook her head. "I'll leave the honors to you to pick what you want. Tell everyone we will have supper in the family dining room tonight."

Mr. Hens nodded and left the room. Magda watched his tubby figure run through the hall and giggle before grabbing a piece of cake. She couldn't swallow it, thinking about how her daughter remained in her room, not eating. Magda's mind was racing, thinking the worst when it came to her husband.

Helmer entered in silence while Magda was setting up the table. He hung up his keys and went to wash his hands before taking a seat. He wanted to offer his help, but he knew she'd refuse. As she reached for the tong to mix the vegetables, Helmer noticed a huge burn mark below her wrist. "You got burned!" His eyes flashed in horror. "Wait here! I'll get a burn relief cream to spread on it."

"I'll be fine," she replied. "It won't be necessary."

"Why do you always have to find something to argue about? I'm trying to be nice."

"Keep your false empathy to yourself," Magda said, aggressively placing the plates on the table.

Helmer flinched, fearing that she'd try to break one of the plates on his head. He walked away and headed to his room to get the burn relief cream. Meanwhile, Magda sat filling up her plate with fruits and guava cakes. Assuming Helmer left, her chest tightened, and her taste buds became bitter. She no longer felt hungry sitting in front of the table alone. Yet, she was the one who told Helmer to leave.

Her eyes glimmered when she saw his shadow from the dining room's entrance. Helmer came and pulled the chair next to her. "May I see the burn?"

"No." Magda reached for the steamed vegetables and filled her plate. "You may eat your food. Don't worry about me!"

"Is it because I'm sending Meg to live with your mom?"

Magda glared at him. Her face crimsoned with fury, and tears rolled down her eyelids, yet the sobs suppressed her voice. She was angry at herself for allowing him to see her sadness.

Helmer's empathy shell cracked, witnessing the pain he had caused his wife. "It's temporary. It's not healthy for our daughter to witness us growing apart." His voice broke. "We're sleeping in different rooms and keep fighting." His breath grew heavy as he watched her wailing. He reached for her hand, but Magda pushed back her chair.

"You know why I moved out of our bedroom! Don't try to make me the villain of our marriage." Magda pointed at him. The serene look on her husband's face kept tempting her to shove him off his chair. Magda played the fun scene over and over in her mind, but she didn't dare to execute it. Her marriage was suffering enough, and she was no longer that person to make herself heard. In the most profound chambers of her heart, Magda knew there was still that spark to create chaos around her. Helmer could not become one of the victims from her list, and out of all her relationships, she had to save this one to redeem herself, to prove she was able to love properly and commit.

"If you have ever endured half of the misery I went through." She sniffled. "You would've understood. Do you know how it feels to be used and—"

A wave of his hand cut her off. "Your mother used me to improve her social status, so I know the feeling."

"You're being unfair—"

"It was hard coming home and finding my wife with a baby that's not mine," Helmer spat out. "I deserved to know the truth about Meg. No matter how it'd affect us."

"What did you expect? You wanted me to call and say, 'Hey, Helmer! I got raped by my ex's brother, and I'm pregnant by him, and I want to keep the baby?' You wouldn't have forgiven me."

He sighed. "Listen, I can't say that I know exactly what it feels like to be in your shoes. I empathize with you. I really do, but... you had months to tell me."

"I found out I was pregnant with Meg a month after you traveled to France. I was afraid that you'd abandon me." Magda said, repelling the memories in her mind.

"Well, I didn't," Helmer whispered. "Because I cared about you." "Stop being a hypocrite! You cared, but you didn't love me enough to stick by my side as a normal husband would have. You left me behind for nine months right after leaving the courthouse. We didn't have a proper wedding, nothing! What was so important for you to leave me like that?" Magda inhaled, pushing the tears away. She didn't want him to catch her crying, but the pain was loud enough to be heard in her voice.

"I didn't have a choice!" He explained. "My dad needed me in Paris to oversee the construction of his new office. I had to be there."

"I understand you needed the opportunity to be with your father, but it wasn't the time. You didn't have to go to France and desert me. It was our time, and you made it about your father's company." Magda reached for a glass of water and swallowed the lump clogging her throat. She took a couple of breaths that slowly transformed into a heavy sob. "You hurt me just as much and don't even realize."

"I missed my father," Helmer said, his hand slowly reaching toward Magda's. "That's why I left. I was still that broken child who was desperate for a parent." His nose stuffed up, allowing a few drops of tears to run free. "I'm still not over what I've done to you! I know it was a childish thing to go to Paris for that long, and I'm sorry. But you kept your pregnancy from me. That hurt more than anything. More than finding out that my father didn't want anything to do with me. I'm broken, and that impacts our marriage despite this not being my intention."

"Being broken doesn't give you the right to wish my daughter away," Magda said. "That's not your decision to make; you should remember that."

"Now you feel the need to remind me that she's your child and not mine?"

"I was saying what was on my chest," spat Magda. "You should know how it feels to not have a father in your life. Why wish it on my child?"

Helmer leaned back, the words boring into his mind like a relentless drill. He refused the idea that his wife had accurately described his reality. He put the burn cream on the table and got up to leave.

His eyes reddened from the constant blinking and squinting to fight the tears. But tears were not something new to him. However, he was tired of letting his trauma get hold of him.

Magda watched him take a few swift steps away from the table. She knew he was hungry, exhausted from work, and probably craved some peace. A couple of thoughts settled in—was she ruining it for him? Was he really wrong about everything? Magda's eyes drifted over the table, and something woke in her, a tense feeling in her chest. Her heart was sinking. She'd have to eat alone, and he'd go to bed hungry. Magda stood, and just before Helmer fully disappeared, she cried out for him.

"Helmer, I'm sorry, I didn't mean it that way," Magda pleaded, taking the burn cream. "I need your help to apply it. Please, don't go."

Helmer turned, his eyes instantly softening at the sight of hers, and he walked back to the chair. He took her arm, gently applying the cream to the burn. They both needed to heal, and it took them 15 years to realize it.

"Did you ever wonder what broke us apart?" He lifted her chin. "The lies, the secrets, and..." He paused as a couple of shallow breaths escaped his lips. Tears gathered in his eyes, and he blinked them away. "The fact that you don't want to have a family with me."

"Helmer, that's not true—"

"It is, and it's obvious," he emphasized. "How is it so hard for you to be okay having a baby with me?"

"It's complicated."

"What's so complicated about it?" He dropped the cream on the table and leaned against his chair, eyeing her. "Tell me. Why is it such a big problem for you? Not to mention I raised and took your daughter as my own. Never have I complained about it, because I understand you went through a lot, and she's innocent from all of this." The words flew out, perhaps louder than he intended. Helmer drew his hands to himself, his fingers slowly curling into fists. His breath quickened, but he managed to continue. "So, tell me. What is the problem?"

"Helmer, my pregnancy with Meg was very traumatic. I simply find it hard to—"

"Imagine having a baby with me?" Helmer cut in, his breath shaky. Warmth pooled in his chest, radiating through his body as tension coiled in his muscles. If his eyes were matches, they'd ignite with the heat of his gaze fixed on his wife.

"That's not it," Magda objected, "And you're being selfish right now making it about you."

"It's been 15 years," Helmer said, gathering his thoughts, choosing them carefully, knowing how unhinged they were. "I'm just putting it out there. Maybe it's simpler than you think... You never loved me, and until now, you're struggling to prove otherwise."

"I am not going to continue with this conversation," Magda said, backing away. "I'll tell Mr. Hens to prepare the menu for tomorrow."

"Do you think avoiding this subject will help us fix our marriage?" A sarcastic laugh rumbled under Helmer's breath. "You always run away when we're trying to look for a solution."

Magda fumed. "Are you calling me a coward?"

"You are." Helmer pushed his chair and stood, the heat from his body increasing. He looked at the food, scanning each dish. "By the way, you keep forgetting that I'm allergic to cheese. We've been living together for fifteen years, and it's like you don't know me. Enjoy your meal!" He exited the dining room and took his car keys, leaving her at the table.

He drove back to work, the road emptier and quieter than usual. He could've brought his driver, or called a friend for a chat, but he didn't. The soft wind slipping through the cracked windows already felt like a hug. Th e tightness in his face loosened, and the tension in his body began to melt away. That's when he recognized it: peace. It distracted him through the half-hour drive.

Arriving at the company, he unlocked the doors and stepped inside, heading straight to the elevator. Once in his office, the familiar scent greeted him, his gaze landing on the whiskey bottle in the corner. A small smile curved his lips. He poured a glass and sat down, diving into the pile of papers waiting for him, grateful for the stillness around him.

CHAPTER 3

Friends

Helmer tried to ignore the cramps overtaking his legs below the chair. Even though his body kept telling him he was exhausted, he would rather be in his office than at home. He leaned forward and grabbed a handful of files from his desk. The documents felt like an army ready to attack him. He was burnt out, thinking about an important meeting scheduled for the next day. The FMCA—Furniture Manufacturing Company Associates—struggled to increase profits. Helmer had to find a budget that would help the Company survive among its competitors.

Helmer clapped, and the lights turned off. There he was in the darkness, losing track of time. He placed his elbows on the desk but struggled to find room to rest his head. A half bottle of vodka and an empty glass cluttered the surface. His unmotivated frame of mind made him blare out of annoyance, assuming no one would hear him. Besides, most of the employees clocked out. The janitors were the main ones staying to finish their shifts.

He heard his office door open. "I knew you'd be here," whispered Sonia, his colleague and childhood friend. She clapped to turn the lights back on and walked to his desk.

"What a mess!" That was the first thing that caught her attention due to her tendency to be a clean freak. Sonia liked having her belongings in place and sanitizing her office three times a day. She loved homemade foods and had a night out with Helmer and Bryant —their mutual friend—every other weekend. Red wine was her weakness, causing her to babble about her enigmatic relationship with Bryant.

"It's late, and your desk is—"

"Chaotic?" Helmer summed up, reading her judgy face.

"You picked the right word." Sonia said with a quick nod. "Are you alright though?" She grabbed a seat and looked through the documents to stack them in the right files.

"I'm fine, except for the part where I wonder why you travel to Paris so much," he said, his tone invasive. "It's almost like you have a whole another life I don't know about."

"For your information, I am not tied to this company," reminded Sonia, shaking her head. "A girl deserves some alone time, especially in Paris, where everything is beautiful and romantic."

"What's with the excessive alone time?" he asked, his eyebrows creasing into a frown. "And what about Bryant? Why not take him with you? At least it'd be safer."

"Helmer, we spoke about this," Sonia replied, opening one of the thick documents, as she felt Helmer's gaze on her. "I travel to visit my family. I mean, some of them!"

"Why have I never met them?" He leaned backward, crossing his arms. "What are you hiding?"

"I-I am not hiding anything," Sonia said, her voice cracking between each syllabus. She closed the documents and glanced back at him. "But what's wrong with you? You don't look good."

Helmer glanced down, his long eyelashes like gates to heaven, luscious, yet burdened with a weight that was impossible to ignore. "Magda and I argued over Meg today," he finally answered. He reached for the bottle of vodka, and Sonia grasped it away from him.

"Hey, give it back!" Helmer scowled at her, as his eyes itched with sleep.

"Not a chance. You're not drinking today." Sonia walked past his chair and placed the bottle on the shelf behind him. She tramped into the office break room and started to move some things around. Helmer waited, like a toddler craving to throw a tantrum but knew better. "Sonia!" he shouted with a head shake, presuming she wanted to make herself some coffee.

"Why don't you ever use your coffee pot? That's why I bought you one."

"Actually"—she peeked past the door—"I'm not making it for me, and it's not coffee." She stepped out after a few minutes and brought him the mug.

Sonia placed the hot, soothing tea on the desk and wiped the surface. Helmer stood and stretched, hearing every single bone crack in his body. The numbing sensation in his legs decreased while his eyes refused to stay open. He sat back down and blew on his tea.

"Thank you, Sonie." He rustled, noticing her wandering by the tiny library facing the window.

"You're welcome." Sonia plopped herself in the chair from the opposite corner. "I'm sorry you're going through this rough patch in your marriage. What happened to Meg?"

Helmer brought the mug closer to his lips and sniffed the tea's relaxing aroma. His heart pounded, recalling his wife's angry face earlier. He snapped his eyes open and was startled by Sonia's concerned stare. The feelings of guilt invaded his eyes, and Sonia could read right through them. Helmer placed the tea on the desk and crossed his arms. Sonia moved her chair closer to the desk, patiently waiting for him to open up.

"I asked Meg to go live with my mother-in-law."

Sonia's eyes widened. "If I remember correctly, you can't stand Magda's mom."

Helmer palmed his face and fought the impulse to defend himself. "That doesn't sound like something you'd do," Sonia said. "This won't be good for your marriage."

"That's the point!" Helmer slammed his hand on the desk and backed away from his chair. He walked across the shelf to avoid alarming Sonia, who covered her face in terror when he exploded.

"I'm sorry," he said, realizing he had frightened her, and it wasn't the first time. He had a sudden flashback of his past, picturing how much his anger had a hold of him. But one thing though about such temper, no one could fully break free from it. "My marriage is failing, and I am not happy. Everything is upside down in my home. I try to please Magda and obey her every command. Why is it so difficult for her to do the same for me? At least once in her life!"

"Wishing her daughter away is not the solution," said Sonia, curling her lips. She actually understood Helmer's side, but Magda's even more. The deep emotions relating to parenthood and wanting to have a child one may call their own.

"I know." Helmer leaned his forehead against the shelf and breathed through his rage. "I want to be a father and have a child...my child, you understand? Is that too much to ask?"

"No," Sonia answered, the gloomy expression in her eyes extending onto her face, exposing her discomfort with the subject. Sonia rubbed her cheeks and refocused on Helmer, still expressing his frustration. Sonia had to be there for him and listen to those same sentences over and over and hide the wave of melancholy she'd felt every time. "But—" resumed Sonia. "You already have a daughter who knows you as the best father in the world. Whether she's your blood or not, Meg loves you and is unaware of the vile conditions that introduced her into this world. Don't punish her for it."

"You know, sometimes I wish things worked out differently between us," Helmer spat out, his eyes awkwardly greeting Sonia's. "I shouldn't have ended things the way I did—"

"Don't!" Sonie interrupted, knowing where the conversation was going. They were friends, and it must've stayed that way. Helmer was married, and she was dating. There, that was the end of it. Whatever happened before shall forever remain in the past. "I really need you to make things work in your marriage. Helmer, you deserve to be happy, and so does Meg. She's your daughter, legally. Please, don't ever turn your back on her."

Sonia's gaze softened as she watched Helmer, his shoulders tense, eyes distant. "And I do believe that you have to give yourself some credit. You've been through so much. Maybe that's why you're so determined to keep everything together now, with Meg and Magda."

Helmer shook his head. "You think I'm holding it together? I'm doing everything I can, but sometimes it feels like it's slipping through my fingers."

"You've taken on more than most would," Sonia said, her voice softer. "I mean... taking in Meg, loving her as your own, despite everything—that's not something just anyone could do."

Helmer sighed, his hand dragging through his hair. "I didn't have a choice. I couldn't let her grow up like I did. My father... When my mom left, he took it out on me. The beatings, the punishments—they were relentless. He hated looking at me because I looked just like her. Same skin, same eyes... I was his punching bag because of it."

Sonia blinked, the sudden admission crushing her heart. "I... I remember."

"He isolated himself for months after my mom left, but that wasn't enough for him," Helmer said, his fists clenching at his sides. "Torturing me was his only relief. I guess I was the closest thing to her that he could hurt."

Sonia placed a hand on his arm, squeezing gently. "You're not him, Helmer. You've already proven that."

"That's why I can't walk away from Meg or Magda," Helmer continued, his voice strained. "I've seen what a divorce can do. My dad's destroyed him."

"I understand," Sonia empathized.

"I'll do whatever it takes to make this marriage work. I can't have a divorce, Sonie. I wish to expand our family, that's all." He brought his elbow toward his face. "I won't let Meg suffer because of someone else's selfishness. I know what that feels like."

"You're a wonderful person, Helms," Sonia said, crossing her legs. She rested her elbow on her lap, using her palm to cradle her chin for support, her posture sagging slightly. "I am sure your wife loves you in her way. It's hard to open up after enduring what she had gone through."

"I know." He took another sip of tea, taking another sip of tea and letting the steam rise, brushing gently against his face.

"Are you still taking your antidepressants?" Sonia asked.

"Why do you ask?" he retorted, placing the mug back onto the desk.

"To know if you're doing better," Sonia replied, briefly scratching her head. "Helmer, it's okay to be sad and go to therapy."

"And who exactly am I going to therapy to? Elvino? People like me can't trust anyone."

"Not if you make amends with Elvino—"

"If you truly want us to end this day on good terms, don't bring up that man ever again," Helmer interrupted sharply. "I don't ever want to see him in my life. And I hope to God you stay the hell away from him too. You hear me?"

Sonia hesitated, her lips parting to argue, but Helmer's face had hardened like stone.

"You told me in the past to steer clear of him, so what changed?" Helmer added, his eyes flaring, like embers on the verge of erupting into flames. "Tell me, has he contacted you?"

His scowl deepened as he leaned back in his chair, his arms crossed. "I know in the past I did say bad things about him, but now..."

Helmer rolled his eyes. "I don't want to talk about him! And I have tough skin, Sonie. I don't crack easily. Stop worrying about me."

Sonia glared at him, eager to object, but her lips did not dare. Elvino was a man she should have never mentioned, aware of his history with Helmer. Yet, she could not deny the shadow he cast over their lives— an unavoidable presence born of specific, unfortunate circumstances.

Sonia checked her phone, going through her missed calls. Bryant was downstairs, waiting for her to come down so they could go on a date.

Bryant and Sonia were Helmer's childhood buddies. They had known each other since middle school. Bryant and Helmer studied business and finance at the same university; meanwhile, Sonia preferred a fine arts school where she learned interior design. Helmer encouraged Sonia to join the business world by actively investing in big companies.

It massively increased their revenue, which inspired them to start their company.

Sonia dropped her phone in her purse. "I must go. Bryant is in the lobby waiting."

"Oh, alright." Helmer stood, offering to open the door for her. "And I apologize for raising my voice earlier. I got triggered..."

"It's okay."

"It was not okay," he emphasized. "But thank you for always bringing out the best in me."

His kind words tugged at her heart. Sonia glanced at him, wishing to run to the hallway and leave the conversation hanging. She would usually say something, but no words came to mind. She stared until Helmer broke out in laughter.

"C'mon! Don't make him wait. Otherwise, he'll show up here thinking I gave you extra work to finish."

She nodded and left.

CHAPTER 4

Nightmares

Droplets of sweat speckled the soft surface of Magda's skin. She panted, feeling a painful sting below her abdomen. She squeezed her eyes and lurched for the opposite side of the bed. A sizzling sound drummed in her ears. She tried to silence the storm in her mind until she saw a gust of smoke from the window. Magda shivered and tugged at the pillows around her as she rolled in a puddle of sweat. Feeling the excruciating ache from her abdomen moving down to her legs, she breathed slowly, almost as if someone was trying to suffocate her. She shouted Richard's name, and no one heard a sound. Her toes wiggled at the image of him dying, consumed by a blazing fire. Well, Magda knew someone had predicted his death. Claiming to be innocent was an overstatement.

A manly hand brushed her neck, then she threw her hands in the air and groped for the glass candle holder on the nightstand. She opened her eyes, yet everything appeared blurry. She saw two faces laughing with malice, which made her jolt out of bed, waddling in tears and swearing that her small weapon could drive her foes away. She swung the candleholder toward her targets. He caught her arm in time.

"Magda!" yelled Helmer, catching her sleepwalking in her bedroom. He took the heavy object from her hand and flicked the lights on. "Take it easy. You had a nightmare."

She was disoriented, blinded by the sudden light saving her from her disturbing dream. It wasn't the first time she had them, and it wasn't something she wanted anyone to know.

Her eyes twitched open after adjusting to the brightness. She was glad to see her husband there, ready to help her escape the dangerous figures she kept seeing in her sleep.

She buried herself in his arms and wept on his chest. Helmer caressed her hair and sniffed it. He missed doing this since she decided to sleep in a different bedroom. He wondered why she was shaking and clenching onto him as if her life depended on it. He still didn't ask any questions. He folded his arms tightly around her back; she felt safe and could ultimately catch her breath.

"Please, stay here tonight. Don't leave me."

She held onto the collar of his shirt. Every woman would agree that his height, broad shoulders, and muscular arms were distracting. Bewildered by her instant stares and begging eyes, he kissed her hands. Helmer took his shirt off, exposing the large tiger tattoo on his chest, to dry Magda's tears and sweat from her face. "My husband is so handsome," Magda told herself. She was not wrong.

"You're so perfect!" She cupped his clearly defined cheeks and snuffled. "I don't deserve a man like you. I'm not the person you think I am, Helmer..."

Her voice trailed away when he crashed his lips with hers. She mumbled, trying to form another sentence through the kiss, but Helmer's tenacious hunger for his wife was stronger than her. She tightened her arms around his neck as they wobbled toward the bed. In an abrupt second, a clear image of a fire startled her. She could never get used to these vivid memories she wished to erase.

"I can't! I'm sorry." She fixed her nightgown. "We have to stop."

"What's wrong?"

"One day, you'll leave me," Magda sobbed. "I'm not a good wife. I will never be able to make you happy."

"That's not true," Helmer disagreed. "I'll never desert you. But I do have to admit, there is some accuracy in your statement!"

He couldn't lie, even if he wanted to. She gazed at him, sank her face into her palms, and then walked past him. She glanced at the mirrored walls and straightened her posture. Her sins stared back at her, and she could no longer endure it. What if, one day, her past caught up with her? Would her husband keep his promise to stay by her side? Questions like these terrified her.

"Well," she said. "If ever one day you decide to hate me, it's the right call. This woman standing in front of you, I hate every piece of her."

"If this is about Meg, I'm sorry," Helmer blurted out. "I shouldn't have decided to send her away." He moved his thumb across Magda's back, and that was the call. An apology, but also a desperate need for her lips to greet his. For her to tell him that everything was forgotten. "I was angry at you, and it was wrong to use her to make you suffer."

Magda turned and lowered her hands from her face. Whenever she tried to reason with him, he missed the point. The issue was not her daughter but her past.

Magda's heart melted. His voice was soothing, sounding like a harp playing by a cozy fireplace. His kisses warmed her; besides, sleeping in a cold room alone was not fun. Magda wasn't trying to overwhelm him with her unexplained warnings to not love someone like her. It would be useless to tell him why anyway.

"Meg may stay. She's our daughter," he said.

"Do you mean it, or you're trying to get something in return?" she asked, noticing a smile forming on his lips.

Helmer approached and kissed her shoulder. "Perhaps I do want something."

His kiss sent shivers down her spine, causing her to let out a gasp. He looked into her eyes, his hands sliding across her back, pulling her closer. "You know what I want."

"No, Helmer, I can't," she said, trying to break free from his embrace, knowing it was too much of a temptation to have him so close. She was held against his solid physique, emitting his warmth and subtle demands for her to surrender. His breath blew on her neck, raising her anticipation for a kiss. She loathed that thought, knowing what it could've led them to, yet she fought through, not knowing how long her resistance would last.

"Just give in, please. I need you!" whispered Helmer, slowly biting her ear and reaching for her nightgown.

"I can't," she said, pushing herself away from him. "We talked about this, Helmer. I can't have a baby right now."

Helmer heaved a sigh, bringing both hands to his face. He rubbed his cheeks and stepped away. He was succumbing to the thought of never becoming a father, and the years of him waiting did feel like centuries. His heart couldn't wait anymore. Helmer's blood was boiling, and the urge to punch at something increased with every breath he took.

"You don't want to have a baby with me," he whispered, taking a quick look at the solid-painted wall, hoping that'd ease his anger.

"Helmer, I am trying—"

"You're not trying," he yelled. "You've been saying that for years. If you really wanted to have our baby, you would have had it a long time ago. You are so self-centered that you cannot see my side of it. I took your daughter as my own, which I did not have to do. I stayed married to you despite the feelings of betrayal and your lies. I gave you a good life."

"Which you don't have to remind me of every time we don't agree on something," said Magda, interrupting him in the middle of his sentence. "Goddamn it, you don't get the point," he raged. "I always give you whatever you want or ask, but that one time I do, I get a no. You refuse to grant me that one thing I have ever wanted in my life. I wonder if it is on purpose. What did I do to you? Tell me. What have I done to make you loathe me this much, keeping my dream at your mercy?"

Magda remained silent, watching him steam off. What really pulled her heartstrings was the sorrow in his eyes, knowing she'd caused it.

"I don't know what your heart is made of," continued Helmer, "but if you do have one, I am begging you to be honest with me. Do you want to have a baby with me or not? One day, you agree, then you change your mind the next, and I can't take it anymore."

His voice cracked, trying to let out his agony. It had been a while since he'd held it in, fearing it'd make him too vulnerable. No man liked to feel so fragile like this. His joy solely relied on her answer, hoping it would be a yes.

"I want to be a father, to watch my child take his first steps and drool as I rock him to sleep," he continued. "I want all of these, including you being lenient to them. Is this too much to ask? If so, starting today, I will never ask again."

Magda stared at him, her lips barely forming a word following his avid request.

"That's what I thought," he said, sharply turning away, as Magda's silence lingered. "You don't want to."

"I didn't say anything."

"You didn't have to." He turned, glancing at her.

"You're right," she said. "I wasn't trying, and neither did I mean it whenever I told you I was okay having a baby, but I will this time."

"What?" he said, wondering if his ears were playing tricks on him. "I will try to give you what you want."

A smile carved around Helmer's cheeks, receiving the affirmation he had asked for. But he stopped himself from succumbing to the assumption that his dream would finally come true after all those years of waiting. It did not feel real. What if she changed her mind again this time?

"I'm sorry. Can you repeat that?"

Magda nodded, walking up to him. "I said I am considering expanding our family."

"I feel so guilty for asking you this," he said. "It's not my intention to pressure you into having a baby with me. I want you to want it as much as I do."

"I know," she said, taking his hands. "But like you said, you have never asked me to do anything except for having a baby. Watching you beg me for it crushes my heart."

"If you need some time to think about it, that's fine. That way I won't feel like a monster who—"

"First off, you're not a monster," she interrupted, her voice wavering, as if she was trying to convince herself. "But..." Magda backed away, brushing the pieces of hair off her face. "I'm just... I'm thinking about what it'll be like. You know, with a child. Because it does change everything." She glanced at the floor, pondering about her own statement.

"Like what?" Helmer questioned; his gaze steady.

"Like us, Helmer. Life." She sighed, running a hand through her hair, searching for the right words. "You're barely home. How exactly are you going to help me raise our child if we do get one? We're barely managing as it is."

Helmer's eyebrows shot up. "What do you mean by I'm barely home? Haven't I been there to help raise Meg? What exactly are you getting at?"

Magda crossed her arms, her posture straightened. "My point is we don't know if we're in a good place to have a baby together—"

"I knew it," Helmer cut in, "It was too good to be true. That you'd agree so fast. Now, you're changing your mind again."

"I meant everything I just said to you," Magda replied, her tone defensive. Her words were slow, measured, like each one was a heavy stone in her mouth. "But we fight constantly. We don't even see eye to eye when it comes to raising Meg."

Helmer scoffed. "I think you should check your facts." Magda's voice sharpened. "My facts?"

"Damn right," he said, nodding vigorously, "check your facts. Most of those fights you're talking about, you start them. I mean, if anyone here doesn't know how to be a parent... it's you."

Magda's eyes flashed. "Excuse you?"

"You heard me. You do realize Meg doesn't always come to you when she needs something, right? She comes to me. Think about why that is."

"That's because she's a teenager, Helmer. That's what they do," Magda spat out. "What? You've never been young in your life? And I can't believe you're saying this to me. Judging my parenting like yours is perfect. You can be so unfair sometimes, always looking for other people's flaws so you don't have to face your own."

Helmer's face twisted. "You don't even know what you're saying." "Oh, I know exactly what I'm saying," Magda snapped back, stepping closer. "You act like you are on some pedestal, above everyone. But we're both in this mess. Don't pretend I'm the only one to blame."

Helmer snorted. "Are you sure about that?"

Magda palmed her forehead, a thick veil tightening in her throat. "You're so infuriating."

"Says the one making up excuses."

"It's not an excuse," she objected, bumping him with a light shove. "You're the one who won't listen. You push and push, and then you wonder why I never say yes."

"Oh please, Magda." Helmer let out a groan. "If you don't want this, just say it. Just tell me you never want to have a child with me, and I will stop asking."

"But I don't know," Magda said, her voice softening.

"You don't know what?" Helmer questioned.

Magda's hands trembled as she tried to find the words, something that would not tear them apart. But there was no right or wrong answer at that moment. Only one thing hung in the air between them—blame, and the unspoken question: What future could they possibly have after this?

Helmer's gaze softened, just for a second, as if he was silently pleading for her to say something that wouldn't shatter the fragile hope he held onto. But Magda's throat tightened, words crumbling before they could leave her lips.

"I am scared, Helmer." The admission slipped out before she could stop it. She wrapped her arms around herself as if she could shield her own heart. "I don't know if I'm ready. What if I'm not good enough? I'm not a good mother—you said it yourself. So, what if I fail at this too? What if we mess everything up and grow even more apart?"

Helmer's arms slowly dropped to his sides, his pulse quickening at the sight of Magda's face. One tear rolled down her cheek, then another, and another. A single question filled his mind: Had he just made her cry? Her cheeks, shaped like perfect, crisp apples, were now damp and flushed at the mention of his prior statement.

Helmer took a few steps toward her, hesitantly reaching for her arms, his fingers gently tracing down to her hands. He looked at her, appalled by the trembling in her fingers. The words knotted in his throat, unsure where to begin. Should he simply apologize? Acknowledge they both had valid points and let the topic rest? He wondered if he should kiss her but worried it might be inconsiderate. Maybe just holding her cheeks and waiting for her to speak was the best option.

"But... actually..." Helmer tried, despite the uneasiness growing within his body. "A-Actually, I never implied that you're a bad mother—"

"Yes, you did," Magda said quickly. "I try so hard to be a good mom, and you know that. Hearing you say that... it hurts."

"I... I'm s-sorry," Helmer stammered, his hands rising to her cheeks to brush away her tears. "I'm sorry. I'm sorry. I didn't mean it like that."

"It does not matter what you meant. What matters is that you said it."

"And you're right," Helmer nodded, cupping her face. He couldn't help but notice how small and delicate she seemed compared to him. As she tucked in her lips, his thoughts wandered— her lips looked soft, inviting, delicious, like her guava cakes. He wondered if his thoughts were even healthy, eyes trailing down to her chest before he snapped back to reality. "Again, I'm sorry. I wish I could take back what I said."

"Okay."

"Okay?" he asked, eager for confirmation, hoping she wasn't being sarcastic.

Magda nodded. "And... If I do agree to have this baby, will you be home? Will you truly make sure you're present for it? To look after us?"

"Of course," he said confidently. "I always look after you. You know how important our family is to me."

"Do you promise that no matter what happens between us in the future, you'll make sure we stay a family?"

"Yes, I promise," Helmer replied, his voice soft but steady.

"Okay," Magda whispered, tilting her head back, her eyes locking onto his.

"Okay what?" Helmer asked, his enthusiastic smile betraying his hope that she was not being sarcastic.

"I'll have a baby with you." "For real?"

"Yes," Magda replied with a sharp nod.

A feeling rushed over Helmer, like fireworks exploding in his stomach, heat blazing through his body. The urge to kiss her was overwhelming, but it was more than that—it was a primal hunger, like a tiger ready to ravage its prey. He gorged onto her lips, and before they knew it, they couldn't keep their hands off each other.

There she was, snuggled on him, leaving all quarrels behind and starting to get past their differences. Helmer placed his head in the crock of her neck, leaving a trail of kisses. Magda's eyes shut close as his warmth engulfed her half-bare chest. He kissed her left shoulder and tugged the strap of Magda's nightgown with his teeth. Then she was fully exposed and vulnerable to his vigorous appetite. Helmer seized her lips and lifted her up, her legs crossed around his waist.

***

Helmer's eyes snapped open. It was already morning. Helmer reached for the alarm clock to snooze, wishing he could sleep for another hour. He wanted to shake the stiffness out of his arm, but Magda was still sleeping on it. He placed a pillow under her head cautiously to avoid waking her but still allowed his arm to break free. He stumbled across her shoe closet and bolted out of the bedroom in his shorts. He carried his clothes along with him and went to his bedroom to freshen up. It was his routine to check on Meg first thing in the morning, so he went there to see if she was still asleep. Helmer wasn't expecting to run into anybody since it was early. None of the servants would come to the second floor unless it were time to summon him for breakfast. Or to do their chores scheduled at a specific time during the week.

Helmer turned the doorknob, and then the door swiftly opened. He stuck his head inside and saw Meg's mouth hung open, snoring as usual. He held back the urge to laugh and silently watched her roll on the bed, almost falling on the floor. He walked in and repositioned her to a more comfortable position. Helmer sat by the headboard and brushed Meg's hair away from her face. He spotted her uniform on the chair, which had lipstick stains on the sleeves. He tossed it in the laundry bin from the walking closet. He was running late, though he went to the door to leave after stealing a last glance at her.

"Dad?" Meg sat, rubbing her eyes.

Helmer paused and turned, surprised that she was already awake. "Hey, pumpkin!"

She sprung out of bed and ran to him.

He bent over, knowing that she'd hugged him. "How are you? I heard you didn't come down to dine with your mom."

"I felt angry at her. I know for a fact you two will get divorced anyway," Meg said. "It's a matter of time."

Helmer frowned. "Who put that in your head?"

"Marie Lisa, our laundry lady," Meg replied, "But c'mon, Dad, I'm almost 16. I saw it coming."

In a large household with small personnel, words spread quickly. Helmer loathed gossipers, yet he couldn't be angry at his employees. He was used to Marie Lisa being talkative and curious.

"Well, Marie Lisa is probably just worried about your mom and me. But there's nothing to worry about. Like every couple, we argue, we fight, then get reconciled."

"Oh, Dad, please!" Meg drew her mouth close to her father's ear. "You know I love you, but you and mom don't work."

"What are you trying to say?" he asked, leaning away.

"I want the truth. Are you getting divorced?" Meg demanded. "I need to know so I can start preparing my mind for it."

"That's the thing, pumpkin," Helmer said, his tone a bit unwavering. "You can't always prepare your mind for what's to come. Your best bet is to embrace whatever hits your way and fight to keep going."

Helmer's empathy toward Meg's concerns made him reflect on his childhood. He remembered when his mom divorced his dad and abandoned them. Helmer never found out all the details behind his parents' divorce except for the chaos and pain it had caused him. He never wanted the same to happen to Meg. Having her pay for the mistakes of two adults who potentially could fall out of love.

"I am not going to lie to you," Helmer added, cupping Meg's cheeks. "Marriage is a full-time job. You don't know yet what that means, but every day you wake up, you're going to have to commit, dedicate energy and time to it, find solutions for what's not working, and definitely hold on when it gets hard."

"What would you say makes you hold on then, Dad?" "You."

Meg's eyes widened, not expecting such a response. Knowing this calmed her heart like a sea wave brushing upon a shore. She learned that not only was marriage a lifetime commitment, but so was love, and they were supposed to make one feel safe.

She pulled Helmer into a hug, locking her arms around him. "I love you, Dad."

"I love you way more, pumpkin."

"Okay now, old man," Meg said, releasing him. "Don't let Marie Lisa know I told you. That way, I can find out what rumors she's up to spreading next."

"If you do, you'll end up getting her fired," Helmer whispered.

Helmer pushed Meg's hair behind her ears since some strands stuck in her mouth. Her curly hair was thick and heavy, looking like a lion's crown since she stopped letting her nanny, Gladice, comb her hair.

"I won't snitch, I promise!" Helmer said, masking the fury in his voice as he thought of Marie Lisa interfering in his family matters.

"Thanks, Dad!" Meg's smile faded. She walked to her hairdresser and grabbed a comb to tug through her stiff tresses. She sat on the bed and tucked her legs under her multicolored blanket.

Helmer knew what was on her mind before she even said it. "You're not going to your grandma's house anymore. It was meant to be temporary anyway."

"Really?" Meg dropped the comb on her lap and clapped. "That's fantastic!" She pulled the linens up to her chin and laid down. "I like grandma, but she always wants to babble about her talk show and prestigious name. It's exhausting."

"I agree, and she's the last person I'd want to talk about right now," Helmer said in an urgent tone, noticing the time. He was running late for work, and hearing about Allimair's talk show only grew his contempt for her. Helmer did not even want to let her visit or be near his family, and he never reached out to Allimair about his decision for Meg to go live with her. That story was only a way to make his wife feel his agony, which also failed as he couldn't watch her go through it. He didn't know if he was a villain for doing this or still the perfect guy he painted himself to be. However, in life, pain could make even the good ones bitter, and Helmer wasn't exempt.

"Okay, pumpkin, enough chatting. We'll meet at the golf court later." "I always beat you. Why not play tennis?" Meg bragged. "Maybe you'll beat me this time."

"Fair!" Helmer grinned. "I always let you win. This time, I will show no mercy."

Meg took her comb and threw it on the chair close to the bed. "Have a great day, Dad."

"Thanks, Pumpkin." Helmer pushed the door closed and went to his room to shower.

Meanwhile, Magda woke up, filling the empty side her husband slept in, only to realize he was gone. She wrapped the bed sheets around her naked body and staggered to the bathroom for a hot shower. Her cheeks hurt from smiling. The last memories of her husband left her daydreaming and humming every love song she knew.

She turned off the water and dried herself, then tramped through her wardrobe, which was congested with old clothes. Magda grabbed a skirt and a short-sleeved shirt to wear with a pair of flats. It was time to head downstairs to the kitchen for breakfast. Magda ran into Mr. Hens carrying a large bouquet of roses.

"Good morning, ma'am!" Mr. Hens handed her the beautiful gift with a note on it. "Someone sent these for you."

Magda curled her eyebrows and grinned nervously, wondering if Helmer would send her those so early in the morning. "Did my husband go to work already?"

Mr. Hens shook his head. "No, ma'am."

Magda dismissed him, sniffed the red roses, and read the card impatiently.

"Red. Every killer's favorite. We'll meet again!" R.

The roses dropped to the floor as dread filled her eyes. Did someone else know about this anonymous gift besides Mr. Hens? No one was supposed to see them, especially with a note like that. And who knew her well enough to send something like this?

Her heart pounded, loud and heavy. The flowers did not feel like a kind gesture, but a threat, or maybe a warning. Magda glanced down at her hands. They felt dirty, almost bloody, as if tied to something far bigger than anyone could imagine. But that couldn't be. She wasn't well-known, and she had no friends. And for good reason—why have friends when carrying a past like hers? Still, the question lingered, haunting her: Who sent those flowers?

Magda bent over and picked up the bouquet after sliding the card into her shirt pocket. There was no better place to hide the roses than her painting room, inside her dusty box. Heading to the drawings, Magda dropped to her knees on the wooden floor, inserted the card in the box and placed her bouquet on top of an old painting. Finally, her enemy had found her.

CHAPTER 5

Workplace

*H*elmer's driver dropped him off in front of the building and waved as his boss ran to the entrance for the closest elevator. Helmer tapped his foot as he waited. Dots of sweat covered his forehead, and his heart raced when he looked at his watch. Some of the employees made eye contact with him as they walked by. Seeing his unwelcoming stare, they plodded down to the elevator at the end of the hall.

His memories of the night before kept him in a good mood. He could still smell his wife's perfume lingering in his mind. When the elevator's door opened, he hurled himself in before it became full. As his elbow bumped into one of the individuals, he sighed, realizing it was Bryant.

"You're late," teased Bryant. "You're even too nervous to put in the floor number." He pushed the seventh-floor button and stepped back, giving Helmer a sly grin.

"Better to be late than not show up at all like you," Helmer shot back, finishing tucking in his shirt. The slight lilt in his voice, a product of the Creole he'd grown up hearing, revealed that he was of mixed descent.

"At least I'm beating the allegations," Bryant replied, glancing down at Helmer's shoes, noticing the untied laces. "I'm not trying to tell you how to live but do better. Those shoes are outrageous." He then eyed Helmer's hair, smirking. "And if you're aiming for the 'black guy' look, at least make sure your fade's on point. You should've come to me; I would've lined you up better."

"Are we really doing this right now?" Helmer muttered, bending down to fix his shoes, praying he'd finish before the elevator doors opened.

"No worries," Bryant said, stepping aside to stand next to his best friend, loosening his tie, revealing the small tiger tattoo on his neck. "I blame Elvino."

"Bryant, if you don't stop—"

The elevator opened, then Bryant sprinted out as Helmer followed him, continuing their banter as they made their way to the meeting room.

"I have to go to my office. Would you mind coming with me?" Helmer asked.

"I mind," Bryant jested, stroking his thick beard. "But I will go with you." He wore a black suit, looking fit, not as bulky as Helmer, who used to pick on him for his Canadian accent. He'd strutted around the hallway between breaks to bring some saltines for Sonia to snack on. It was a regular occurrence to see women fuss over him and troll around his department to get his attention. "I can't deny that it'll be awkward to run into Nina."

"Nina, my secretary?" Helmer stopped dead in his tracks. "I can't believe you always use me to fix your problems. Besides, you're dating Sonia. You shouldn't be worrying about other women."

"I'm not!" Bryant argued.

He couldn't play his innocent card on his best friend, who knew about his unbridled greed for women. The history of failed relationships he had in the past did not make him seem like his habits would change even after conquering Sonia's heart.

Helmer turned and tried to grab Bryant by the collar. "You better not hurt Sonie! She's a sweet woman. Even too good for you."

"What are you? A therapist? Did you steal Elvino's license or something? I figured you stopped seeing him for a while. Maybe that's why you look so unhinged." Bryant skirted Helmer's hand and shook his suit, which started wrinkling up. He gestured at one of the employees walking down the hall and pointed a finger at Helmer. "Please, help! This man is off his meds. Nurse, please save me. He's going to hit me."

The employees laughed, knowing he was usually the joker of the building. They glanced at Helmer, whose face instantly flushed.

His threatening look halted the employees' giggles as they darted to the elevator.

"Bryant, you may be an idiot, but you surely know how to hit a nerve!" Helmer said, motioning at everyone in the hall to clear the way. He had enough of their faces and surely of Bryant, who knew how to hit him where it hurt. "You're really bringing up Elvino? You know why I stopped seeing him."

"And do you want to know the reason why I'm pulling your leg so much?" Bryant said, his laughter fading out. "You never fail to remind me I'm not worthy of Sonia. It's like you're obsessed with her!"

"I've never said you don't deserve Sonie," Helmer objected. "However, it would be disappointing if you two went separate ways. I've done everything in my power to keep you guys together."

"Spare me from your sentimental speech! It's not like I'm going to fall for it, and I hate being the one bringing this to your attention. But our workplace is not a fight club." Bryant slapped Helmer's shoulder and then continued to walk.

"Did you really have to mention a fight club in our conversation?" Helmer snorted, spreading his arms. It wasn't what he expected to hear from his best friend, who knew he had closed this chapter of his life long ago.

"Well, I did mention it!" Bryant teased. "Because wearing a suit doesn't erase the kind of man you are, Helmer. You have one hell of a temper, and you're not perfect. Maybe remembering this can remind you not to judge anyone."

"Not you talking when you have an old addiction history," said Helmer, following Bryant along. "So, you do have a point. That makes the two of us!"

Bryant paused, taking in what his best friend had just said. "Finally, I did strike a nerve. Thought you wouldn't fold so quickly."

"Helmer—"

"And you're such a douche when it comes to women!" Helmer said, gesturing at Bryant to keep walking. "It pissed me off to find out that you have hooked up with Nina for almost a year, and I never knew a thing!"

"For what? To judge me like you always do?" Bryant replied. "Besides, you know what I really want? To take Sonia to Canada, extend our business there, and look after my parents. That way, I would be closer to them and the woman I love."

"But we both know she won't say yes," Helmer added, sighing.

"Or you don't want her to say yes," Bryant opined. "She keeps the company running, so you'd be damned if she leaves. Thus, you keep her here, increasing her salary every time I propose that we leave for Canada. I know what you're doing."

"You may assume whatever you want..." said Helmer, stopping in his tracks and poking a finger toward Bryant. "I have nothing to do with her saying no to your offer. Maybe you should change your strategies. Words are not enough to get her to agree. Have a better business proposal, and she might say yes. Now, let's go!"

They reached the office, and Bryant stopped by, spotting Nina answering a call. She saw him and jerked on the chair to avoid facing him. After she hung up, Helmer approached and greeted her.

"Has Mr. Will arrived yet, Nina?"

"Y-Yes..." She took a couple of deep breaths, scratching her forehead. Her fingers weaved through the cascade of thick locks adorned with golden shells that shimmered softly, a striking contrast against her radiant dark skin. The shells caught the light, as though whispering secrets of the sea, framing her in a quiet, regal beauty. "I mean...yes, sir. He's in the conference room, and Ms. Sonia is in the office, awaiting you." Her breathing increased, and her voice shook. It sounded frail and filled with distress. She couldn't tell whether it was the urge to cry or to curse Bryant. It wasn't something to wish for anyone, but she yearned for the day a car would run him over. The idea of making him have a brief taste of pain comforted her.

Bryant waved at her. "Not even a good morning?"

Nina stood and grasped a few documents, which she finished stapling. She dropped her pen on the small desk and stepped past him, her eyes searching for Helmer, as if he was an escape.

"Mr. Dupris, I'll go ahead and make some copies." Nina excused herself and lowered at Bryant. "I don't wish to talk to a liar and an immature bastard who promises a ring to every woman they meet."

Helmer's eyes widened, not expecting Nina's words. She was a respectable and amiable woman. She was still recovering from her breakup with Bryant. Silence reigned over as she left, and Bryant kept his head down.

"You promised her a ring?" Helmer rubbed his face, trying to digest the news.

"Can we forget about it?"

"Of course not!" Helmer hissed. "This girl had a breakdown because of you and took a month off work. I even had to convince her to go see a therapist. You told me the breakup was consensual."

"I dumped her! Happy? I'm sorry you came to find out this way." Bryant kept an eye around, so his secrets did not reach any wrong ears. "Please, don't say a word to Sonia."

"So, you were with Sonie while seeing Nina?"

Bryant shrugged and nodded after a long stare. "Nina and I are no longer together. We broke it off before it even became a thing."

"Goddamn it," said Helmer, struggling not to punch the words out of his best friend's mouth before he could finish. "You dirty bastard. How could you do this to Sonie?"

"It wasn't serious between me and Nina. We had a couple of drinks a few times; that was it."

"If what you're saying is true, how come Nina loathes you that much, stating you promised her a ring? These things don't occur in 2 weeks."

"It was a mistake; what else do you want me to say? Sonia is inside the office," Bryant whispered. "She could hear us!"

"Well, I hope she finds out about Nina," Helmer scolded, his voice rising.

Bryant glared at Helmer, a storm brewing behind his eyes. "How about you let me handle my life and my relationship for once?"

"Handle it?" Helmer snorted. "Like you're doing now?"

"And you're the one to talk?" Bryant spat, his words like venom. "With a marriage like yours, you don't get to lecture anyone about loyalty."

Helmer stepped closer, his pulse pounding in his temples. "I'm going to act like you didn't just bring up my marriage."

"Why? Because it's so perfect?" Bryant's shoulders tensed, the lines in his face hardening. "You're a saint? You've never done anything you regret in your life? Because I can remind you of a few things, if you've forgotten."

Helmer's nostrils flared as he leaned in, his voice dropping dangerously low. "You've got no shame—"

"Just like you." Bryant spat. "Mr. Helmer Dupris, the man with a history of anger issues, a criminal record that somehow stayed squeaky clean—though it shouldn't have—and the underground fighter nobody's supposed to know about."

"And you've got a past drug addiction. You can barely wipe your own behind without someone doing it for you." Helmer riposted, his voice tightening. "Don't even get me started on why you left Canada. You couldn't rely on Daddy and Mommy anymore because they disowned you. Don't act like they still care—they don't, because you're a lost cause."

Bryant's face tensed, but Helmer kept going.

"If it weren't for me, and this company, you'd be nothing."

"Since we're speaking of my parents," Bryant said, and paused, drawing in his last trail of thought. "At least, I know where to find mine."

Silence hung in the air, thick and tense. Each man stood, breathing heavily, the weight of their words settling between them. Helmer's resolve was unyielding, and he took a deep breath. "Well, Sonie is not some kind of fling. I care about her, and if you don't tell her, you can bet on it, I will."

Helmer pushed the door open and found Sonia eating some peanut butter crackers on his desk. He stared, assuming that she didn't get enough time to have breakfast yet ruminating over and over on Helmer's prior threats.

Sonia waved at him and straightened out a newspaper to hide from his tedious glare. Bryant approached her and pinned the journal on the desk to make fun of her.

"You're eating peanut butter before our meeting?"

"It's like eating a clove of garlic before kissing your date," said Helmer.

Sonia rumpled the newspaper into a ball and threw it at him. She gorged on the last piece of crackers and dusted the crumbs off her red blouse. Bryant poured her a glass of water and placed it on the desk. She looked at him while fixing her short afro, contrasting perfectly her deep ebony complexion. Bryant couldn't help gazing at it. He leered at her curvy figure as she stood from the chair.

"Bryant?" She sighed. "Are you staring at my butt?"

"Can you blame me?" Bryant crooned, shoving his hands into his pockets. Sonia blushed at his praise, brushing her hands on her skirt, smoothing out a few wrinkles. She was usually a confident figure, but there were times being strong and smart weren't enough, especially as a woman and minority in a high-end Company. Never have Helmer or Bryant made her feel lesser, but on the outside, some did due to feeling threatened by her outstanding competency in the business field. "Back in middle school," resumed Sonia, "I was bullied for having curves. They swore I was built like a duck. It's like you can't live life peacefully without someone hating on you when you're black."

"They were jealous," replied Bryant in haste. "You're gorgeous, baby! People tend to hate what they can't have."

Helmer watched the pair flirt and crack jokes, meanwhile keeping what he knew a secret already pained his soul. It was torture hearing Bryant laugh across the room, wondering how he was able to pretend everything was fine.

Helmer walked over to his desk and asked Sonia to clear the way. She smacked Helmer's shoulder in defiance and moved off his desk. "I don't want to be late for this meeting," urged Helmer, snatching Sonia's peanuts so she could hurry. "This deal might change our lives, and the company depends on it right now."

"He's right!" Bryant added, taking a box of tissue from the shelf across the desk to wipe some crumbs off Sonia's shirt.

"No need to baby me; just give me the tissue!" Sonia requested as Bryant took forever to tidy up her shirt.

"Okay, people. Let's get out of here," Helmer grabbed the box from Bryant and placed it back on the shelf. He headed to the door, motioning at them to follow along but they lingered even longer. He grabbed Sonia's hand and exited the office, scurrying through the hall.

"Can you let go of my hand now?" asked Sonia, realizing they were almost reaching the conference room. Helmer let go and stopped at the door, giving her a heads up for the meeting. They had to impress the client and get a good deal out of him. The least he'd wanted would be for anyone to piss off the client and make him lose that contract. He warned Sonia and Bryant to make sure the meeting was memorable and fair for all parties.

"We heard you, Helmer," Bryant said, nodding. "Can we go now? Lingering to enter that door and lecturing Sonia and me is only going to make you sweat more than you are now."

"Okay, okay, sorry," Helmer agreed, slowing down on the lectures and pep talks. He rubbed his hands and reached for the doorknob.

"We got this, and you will get that contract. I'm sure," Sonia reassured, seeing how nervous he was. She gave Helmer a pat on the back, then they proceeded together inside the conference room.

Nina was inside, keeping the associates and clients waiting. She was sitting on the hot seat, trying to keep everyone calm as Helmer's tardiness was quite a few minutes.

Helmer and Bryant greeted the client, and so did Sonia before taking a seat.

Mr. Will clicked on the first slide and introduced an overview of his business and offer. "I have ten restaurants in the country, each in a different state. I want to open one in Canada and the other in France. The furniture and all the equipment, I need them to be well designed, modern but with a special antique finish."

"What would the budget be?" Helmer asked, intrigued by the antique design request.

"$100,000 and extra profits, which we can discuss later on after you accept the deal," Mr. Will replied, knowing his offer was tantalizing. "Mr. Will, in those countries, the restaurants' designs are top- notch," Sonia pointed out, analyzing the proposal. "We can meet these requirements, but I hope you're aware that the costs for such negotiation have now tripled."

"On what ground?" asked Mr. Will, scoffing.

"The quality you're requesting us to provide," Sonia replied. "That's well-articulated input—"

"Well articulated?" Sonia interrupted, calling out Mr. Will's statement.

"Yes," Mr. Will replied. "It's rare to find someone as articulate who would boldly pursue a triple instead of accepting what I offered in the first place."

"Hm, articulate?" Sonia asked again, raising an eyebrow. "You mean for a black woman like me?"

"I never said that," objected Mr. Will, throwing a glance at the associates who anticipated a better response from him to shut off the abrupt tension.

"You didn't need to," Sonia said, putting her pen down.

The associates looked at Sonia and then at Mr. Will. It was uncomfortable to be in Mr. Will's shoes, knowing that it'd be hard to break the awkwardness with his chauvinistic side exposed in plain air. It was a complex subject at the workplace, and Sonia was an equal partner on the deal. However, Mr. Will wasn't worrying about her, since it was Helmer who was in charge of doing the closing.

"Mr. Helmer, I hope we can proceed," said Mr. Will, looking over Sonia's shoulder to talk to Helmer, as he moved to the next slide.

Sonia's urge to respond to Mr. Will's covert animosity almost got the best out of her. She thought of how important the deal was to the company and retreated from putting him on the spot. She was willing to sit through and watch Mr. Will, a client who had no chance of getting away with an easy deal if it was up to her.

Sonia lowered her head, hoping the meeting would end sooner, losing interest in proceeding with a presentation to impress that same man who passively questioned her competence.

Helmer looked at her and then at Mr. Will. Although he didn't want to interrupt, Helmer was utterly disgusted by his racist comment.

"Mr. Will," Helmer said, "We have been tapping through the slides and yet have found no specific approach for the deal. What do you propose?"

"I want that contract to be one hundred thousand as I mentioned earlier, where I get a discounted price on each piece of equipment. In return, you'll get ten percent of the profit in the first year of execution." "I'll go with what my partner proposed," Helmer said, "since the restaurants on the contract are overseas, the price will be tripled.

"We won't go any lower."

Mr. Will shut down the PowerPoint. "Am I wrong to infer that you're letting an unskillful woman's opinion overpower your judgment, Mr. Helmer?"

Sonia placed her notepad on the table and saw Helmer give her a subtle nod to take over. He smiled at her with discretion and switched on his serious face when Mr. Will's eyes locked with his.

Sonia walked to the board and turned on the PowerPoint, making everyone stare at Mr. Will. The associates murmured, concerned with the meeting's direction and wondered if she had the situation under control.

"How about we discuss your restaurants' demographics, Mr. Will?" said Sonia, pulling up the first slide of her PowerPoint. "You were brief about the statistics, but here at the FMCA, we're detail-oriented, and we work with numbers. When I looked at your reports, it seemed that your profits have dropped, which means your competitors have exceeded your expertise and, therefore, earned over thirty percent of your clientele. I wonder why that is?"

"T-To be frank, t-this PowerPoint has not been updated," Mr. Will objected.

"Then why present it? Or, I can pull off my research about your restaurants and estimated net worth. Funny enough, I am a dark-skinned woman pulling information up on our screen to expose a defamatory report of your company." Sonia laughed, grabbing her laptop to connect it to the projector.

Helmer was entertained by Mr. Will, whose eyes filled with constant regret when Sonia exposed the reviews his customers had written on the restaurants' social platforms.

"That's not a good look, is it?" Sonia sneered. "Your customers are complaining about the lack of accessibility for the handicapped and the stiffness of your furniture, excluding the other issues they've mentioned. But I'm sure there's no need to broadcast them; the reviews are awful enough. So, tell me, Mr. Will, why should we accept your deal?"

"I-I know my restaurants are currently struggling," Mr. Will stuttered, "but they're the best in town. The food—"

"I'm sorry, Mr. Will," Sonia cut in. "We're not talking about the food, but the furniture designs and their lack of accessibility to the handicapped. Their heights, bulky appearance, and the appalling experience of your customers. This leads me to infer that there is an increased demand for better equipment and design to ease the tension and save the clientele. Thus, you need us more than we need you, Mr. Will. The FMCA is not impressed by the numbers you've shown or your offer. And according to our policies, I have the right to turn down your deal, charge you for harassment, and put you on the blacklist so you don't get any business from us or our competitors now and in the future."

"Mr. Dupris, what did you think of my PowerPoint?" Mr. Will asked, still vexed at Sonia's detailed rundown of his restaurants' reports and everyone's silence. He sat and laid out his documents in front of

Helmer and took his pen, awaiting an answer. Helmer browsed through the files and pursed his lips.

"I loved the trajectory of the business proposal. It seemed stable, but after my partner has thoroughly gone through the statistics and reports, I won't accept anything less than five hundred thousand with twenty-five percent of the profits throughout two years of execution."

"Y-You can't be serious!" Mr. Will stammered, his smile faltering away.

"I think we are!" Bryant said, backing up Helmer's new offer. "Don't forget to keep your reports updated next time so there are no surprises. Friendly advice!"

"This is where our meeting ends, Mr. Will! Ms. Sonia has already mentioned everything that needed to be said," Helmer concluded, stretching his arm to Mr. Will for a handshake.

Mr. Will gathered his documents and bolted out of the conference room, leaving Helmer's hand hanging. Then Bryant followed him to pick up a call. Sonia grabbed her notepad and eyed Helmer, who drew closer to hug her. Everyone congratulated Sonia for handling the meeting and dismissed themselves.

"Thank you, Helmer, for backing me up," she whispered. "Always!" He embraced her.

"I didn't think the bullying and racist remarks would resurface. It hurts to see that I still have to fight to be accepted. I get frowned upon because of the color of my skin." She stretched out her arm and pointed at her skin with disgust. "I know you could've agreed with him if it weren't for what I said. The deal would've helped the company."

"Sonie, I'd never allow anyone to disrespect you, even if they had millions to offer."

Her eyes sparkled at his comment, and her cheeks rounded into a smile. "Thank you. I appreciate it!"

"And look at me," he said, snorting. "I'm Haitian, different complexion, yet people don't believe me when I say it. You know why? Because sometimes, for some people, we may never be enough, and that's okay." He drew a breath in before resuming. "The truth is the color of your skin has never been an issue; don't allow it to become one now." Helmer put his notepad in his briefcase and withdrew.

CHAPTER 6

Melancholy

Magda checked with the personnel, set the menu for the week, and asked them to move her belongings back to her former bedroom. The nights with Helmer and them reconciling put her in a playful mood. She hung around the kitchen, watching Gladice cook and Mr. Hens helping with the dishes setup. Magda reached for the apron hung by the large stove, starting to help Gladice by peeling the potatoes and carrots on the table.

"You don't have to, you know?" said Gladice, her accent unmistakably apparent, every word carrying a rhythm like the gentle waves lapping against the shores of Haiti, her sweet homeland.

She didn't like being helped since she wouldn't have all the credits for the dinner. However, she couldn't refuse, as the request came from the head of the house.

"No, please. I insist," said Magda, continuing to peel the potatoes. "And you're like a mom to my husband. That's the least I can do."

"Oh... that's good to hear that," Gladice said, reaching for the carrots. "Helmer is a good boy. Se ti cheri mwen wi." She paused, her eyes widening as she realized once again that Magda didn't speak Creole, even though she'd tried a few times. It was a common slip-up, but Magda just giggled.

"I wish you would tell me more about Haiti," Magda said. "I know my father-in-law is from there."

"It's a beautiful country," Gladice replied, a fond smile shaping across her face. "There are so many wonderful places, especially in the countryside. But like anywhere else, it has its challenges."

"I understand," Magda said. "It's just like my mom's side. Some are from Trinidad, others from Cape Verde. But I never got to know them, so you could say it's a lost heritage. So, telling me about Haiti always intrigues me."

"Ti pitit, you never know," Gladice said with a smile. "It's a small world, wi. Remember that."

"And of course Helmer is a good man," Magda added, giving Gladice a poke with her elbow. "I mean you raised him. There could've been no other outcome."

Magda offered for the personnel to have dinner with her and Helmer at the end of their shift. She was excited about making up with her husband, but her only worry was becoming a mom again. She didn't want to go through a pregnancy, reliving the moments that tormented her in the past—becoming pregnant with a baby she didn't plan for or wanted at the beginning. She had to learn to love her daughter as the years passed, and although the situation was sometimes tense at home, she still considered her family to be a happy one.

"I'm going to let Marie Lisa know about the dinner plans later so she can help," said Mr. Hens, leaving the plates ready and rushing out of the kitchen.

"He's so chubby; no wonder he's running instead of walking. He knows he needs to shred that excessive amount of fat," mocked Gladice after Mr. Hens left.

Magda looked at Gladice in confusion, noticing that she was the last person to talk about someone else's weight. Magda said nothing, carried on washing the potatoes, gathered the bowl of vegetables, and let Gladice rant about Mr. Hens's flaws, which slowly started to become a hobby.

"I guess you don't agree that he's a chubby mutt," added Gladice, side-eyeing Magda.

"I don't," Magda replied, taking a brief break from her task to give Gladice her full attention. "But you know? I have nothing against an enemy to lovers' romance. I think they make the most special stories. You and Hens give me hope!"

Magda refocused on her task, amused by Gladice's stupefied expression. She always had something to say. Always a comeback at hand, yet this time, Gladice was quiet. Her face was flushed, and she could do nothing but go back to focusing on the carrots. She looked at Magda and then gave her a nod, seeing how fast she was preparing the vegetables.

Cooking was one of Magda's best skills and hobbies. To her, cooking was like painting, mixing colors to create art and memorable memories. It was about getting others closer by clashing minds together, challenging different perceptions, and making life what we wanted. Cooking taught her that when life gets salty, it's up to us to make our own recipe. We are not always stuck; we always have a choice.

Magda noticed her daughter walking in, her AirPods snugly in place, a small book bag slung over her shoulder.

"Hey, honey," Magda greeted, waving, but Meg slid into a chair at the table without a word.

Gladice caught the eye roll and placed her wooden spoon on the tray from the counter. With hands firmly on her hips, she shot a glare at Meg. "Oh oh, rete! What's with the attitude? Your mom just talked to you. You didn't hear her?"

Meg glanced up, pulled a piece of chewing gum from her sweater, and popped it into her mouth with a defiant snap. She opened her bag, books spilling out onto the table, taking as much space as possible, a smirk creeping onto her lips.

"Please, stop smacking that gum," Magda sighed, setting the vegetables on a dry sheet to soak the water out. "It's driving me crazy."

"What?" Meg shouted over her music, her eyes still glued to her phone. "I can't hear you; I have homework."

"Oh Jezi, have mercy," Gladice mumbled, her patience fraying. She fought the urge to snatch the phone from Meg's hands, feeling the heat rise in her chest.

"Meg? Meg?" Magda pressed, leaning slightly over the table to get her daughter's attention. But Meg's indifference stung. Raising a teenager felt like navigating a minefield, and each silent moment felt like a failure. Magda left the uncooked food on the table and darted toward Meg, snatching the AirPods from her ears. Memories flooded back—her younger self, rebellious and overconfident, the very traits she saw in her daughter. "Now, you listen, young lady. I'm tired of you embarrassing me. When I'm talking to you, I expect your attention."

"For what?" Meg retorted, nonchalantly. "I don't want to talk. I have homework."

"Meg, I am tired of this whole ordeal," Magda said, her breath coming in quick bursts. "What's going on? You won't talk to me, won't cook with me anymore, and it's making me wonder if I did something wrong."

Meg looked up at her, hesitant to say what was on her mind. She closed her books and gathered them to leave. But watching the gloomy look on her mom's face, she reconsidered, hoping maybe saying what she felt could make things better.

"Well," Meg said slowly, her voice steady, and thudding the books onto the table. "I know you think I'm a child and I don't know much about grownups and life. But what I do know is when parents are growing apart and not trying, it makes everyone suffer."

Magda's expression softened, but she shook her head. "Whatever happens between me and your dad only concerns us; it has nothing to do with you."

"This is where you're wrong," Meg said, "because whatever happens hurts me. This is why I shut down, because I am scared. I don't want to become like those kids living in a broken home."

"We are not a broken home. We are trying—"

"Dad is trying," Meg interrupted, crossing her arms defiantly. "But you're not. Because we both know you only care about yourself. You don't care about Dad or what he wants. Things always have to go your way."

"What do you mean by that?"

"Simple, Mom. You're selfish," Meg replied, her voice rising. "Maybe you could include him more in our activities together as a family. Because of you, I am forced to spend time with him separately. How about you do what he likes sometimes? Maybe join us at the golf or tennis court, visit him at work, or go to dinners, not just you and me, so he knows you care about him."

"Has he told you any of this?"

"That's the thing, mom. Dad is not like you when things don't go his way," Meg said, her arms dropping on her sides. "He doesn't have to badmouth anyone or throw a tantrum. Actually, he rarely tells me anything. I just know because I care to know."

"If it was my kid, I swear it would have ended differently," Gladice chimed in, her voice sharp as she turned down the heat on the stove. "I wouldn't put up with that attitude."

"Gladice, please," scolded Magda, cutting her off. "I'm handling it."

"Handling what exactly? Your marriage?" Meg scoffed, leaning back in her chair. "Because that's what you need to focus on right now."

Gladice mumbled to herself, grabbing her cutting board to chop onions for the stew. "Mezanmi. Could never be me."

"Gladice?" Magda said, her tone firm.

"Yes, ma'am," Gladice turned, hoping it'd be the end of this charade.

"I put you in charge of the dinner later for the employees," Magda said, drying her hands and motioning to Gladice to take the potatoes from the table. "I'm not joining anymore."

Magda got a glass of orange juice and a plate of crackers from the fridge. She put them on the table by Meg's books, sitting across from her. "Eat something light. We are going to dinner later with your Dad.

He'll appreciate it if you tag along."

"And what's with this sudden change of heart? Let me guess, you know I'm right."

"No," Magda objected, shaking her head. "I think you're wrong about a lot of things. But your biggest problem with me is not listening and being compliant, so today, I choose to listen."

"I don't know, Mom," Meg said, straightening herself from the chair, and placing her elbows on the armrests. "You may be on good terms with Dad now. But one dinner won't fix everything."

"Why are you so difficult?" Magda sighed, her eyebrows knitting together, a frown deepening on her face. "I'm only asking you to join us." "Sorry, not interested," Meg clicked her tongue, stretching her arm out to her mom, asking for her AirPods back. "I have homework." "If I give them back to you, you need to come later," Magda said, her tone softening.

"Okay, I'll be there." Meg nodded quickly. "Now, can I have my stuff back?"

Magda handed her the airpods and stood, walking away from the table, the light on her face slowly dimming away.

She didn't have everything figured out yet about motherhood even though she's been raising her daughter for 15 years. She was still learning the do's and don'ts, the balance for healthy communication, and how to win her daughter through the chaos at home. Her insistence for Meg to spend time with her was a desperate cry to fill in her loneliness.

People couldn't understand being married didn't always make one feel accompanied and less lonely, especially when two individuals are falling apart.

"Mom, wait!" Meg said. "What are you doing? You don't have to leave and miss dinner, you know? I was only trying to express how I feel."

"No, it's okay. Tonight is family time. I'm just a bit tired."

Meg reached for the saltines and stuffed a few into her mouth. She took a sip of the orange juice and lifted a finger, asking Gladice to get her some peanut butter. "I might as well just stay and help you guys out."

"Didn't you have an assignment to do?" asked Magda. "Not really," Meg said. "I'm going upstairs to change." "So, you lied?"

"Oh please, Mom," said Meg. "You mean you have never lied in your life? I'll be right back."

Meg grabbed the books from the table and put them back in the bag. She sprinted out of the kitchen, taking everything upstairs with her so she could come to assist Magda and Gladice with the cooking.

Magda checked the hall, making sure no one was around. She approached Gladice and tapped her shoulder. "I know you meant well, but I did not appreciate you interfering in my conversation with my daughter. I would like to handle things myself next time."

Gladice, still stupefied and disappointed at how the interaction ended with no disciplinary action, nodded to not worsen the matter. "I'm sorry about my commentary earlier if that offended you."

"Meg is not Helmer," Magda added. "You may have raised him, but kids are different."

"Well, I'm sorry I overstepped," Gladice repeated. "I will try not to do that again; I got carried away because I know you love her."

"I do." Magda nodded, a melancholic expression plastering over her face, remembering Meg's first day as a newborn. "You have no idea."

FLASHBACK

There were things only a mother could understand. The precious bond that births between a child and a mother. The thrilled moments of holding a newborn for the first time. Magda experienced all of it, but the emotional suffering it had brought along the way made her not so confident to go through it again.

"Trust me. She will be fine," reassured Allimair as Magda nursed her newborn, watching her little hands curl around her breast.

Tears ran from Magda's eyes when she saw how beautiful her baby was. It was the first time she had to fight for two lives. She felt relieved to see the morning sickness and sudden cravings come to an end. The empty nights that the baby would keep her awake and not give her enough time to reach the bathroom to pee. These little habits became a part of her life and the best memories that she guarded in her heart.

Except, she couldn't imagine the price to pay for keeping this baby a secret from her husband.

Allimair was glaring at the newborn. She slouched in the chair next to Magda's bed and laid her head back. Her eyes looked red and swollen from lack of sleep since Magda spent 22 hours straight in labor. There were many complications before the doctors could relieve her.

She was close to undergoing a C-section, which Allimair opposed with persistence.

"Are you angry with me?" asked Allimair while Magda stroked the baby's hair.

"I don't know how you can ask me to abandon my baby," Magda said, gazing at the infant whose skin was soft as satin. Meeting her daughter made her overlook how difficult it was to make this decision. Although she was hesitant to change her mind, she knew that it wasn't the right thing to do to give her baby away, as Allimair requested.

"Magda, if you don't give this baby away, Helmer will find out, and you can say goodbye to this marriage," barked Allimair. "You hear me? We can't afford him walking out on you. I am not losing your father and everything else at the same time. You must make up your mind."

Allimair scowled at Magda and walked away from her seat. She turned, took a glance at her granddaughter, and summoned a young couple who originated from Cook County inside the room. They put on the proper garments to see the baby and rushed in to greet Magda, apologizing for their delay. They held each other's hands as they saw the infant sleeping on Magda's chest. They asked Magda if they could hold her for a moment. She nodded at them and handed her daughter to the friendly couple.

The couple caressed the baby's cheeks and complimented her dimples. The baby slept with her eyes half closed and twitched a couple of times.

"Meg," whispered Magda. "Name her Meg."

The couple looked at each other, puzzled at Magda's request. "We were planning to name her after someone very special..."

"My grandfather, to be exact," added the woman as she admired the baby. "I promised him that I'd named my daughter after him before he passed. It has been a year now, and we still can't conceive. So, I'd truly appreciate it if you allowed us to choose the name."

"I promise we'll be great parents to your daughter," the man said, following his wife's statement, trying to incite Magda to proceed with the adoption.

Each word felt like a violent stab in Magda's gut, and the urge to grab her baby away from the couple grew at each second. She breathed heavily when they finally asked her if she made up her mind to sign the papers to officially start the procedures. However, she was no longer certain that it was worth such a sacrifice. It was a decision that was about to impact her entire life and that altogether made her overwhelmed.

"I," Magda said, shaking and taking shallow breaths in between. "I-I can't. I can't do it. I'm sorry."

"I am so sorry about that," said Allimair, stepping toward the young couple, attempting to keep them engaged and hold on to the adoption paperwork. "These are the hormones speaking. It's a very emotional moment for my daughter, so that's why she sounds so hesitant. Right?"

She looked at Magda, flashing her eyes at her to reconsider. But it wasn't a mistake. Magda knew what she wanted, and that was to keep her baby.

"I want my child back now," Magda demanded. "Give her to me."

"You can't do this," said the man. "My wife has been preparing the baby's room and everything. The social worker meetings, the hours spent at our lawyer's office, and not to mention all the other requirements we had to make sure to meet would be for nothing."

"I'm sorry about that," Magda said, "but I am not giving my daughter away neither am I the person to blame. It was never my idea to give my daughter away in the first place."

Allimair's eyes flashed at Magda. "She doesn't know what she's talking about—"

"I do know what I'm talking about, Mom. Please, stop thinking so much about yourself. What about what I want?" Magda said, her voice swallowed by the sobs that followed.

"Let me tell you something," Allimair started. "In this life, you have to forget about what others want to get where you need to be. You might think it's selfish, but trust me, one day, you'll thank me."

"I'll take your advice then," Magda said. "I no longer give a damn about what you want. My daughter is staying with me whether you like it or not."

"And what do you think Helmer will do when he finds out you've been keeping your pregnancy from him this entire time while he's in Paris?"

"It has always been your idea to keep my pregnancy a secret, I wanted to tell him since day one," Magda riposted, gesturing at the couple to give her back the baby. "But I won't tell him it was you behind all of this. Because I was your puppet, and I'm done being so. I'll find a way to tell him before he finds out and this time, you better stay far away from my family."

The couple's faces flushed, the twinkle from their eyes fainting away. Their hearts were wrecked by the brutal change of events. They handed the baby to Magda and hugged each other for comfort.

"I'm sorry," Magda said, noticing the couple was upset and confused. "Please, forgive me. I assumed I could do it, but I was wrong. I'm realizing that I love her even more than I thought. It wouldn't be fair to deprive my daughter of the joy of being around her biological mother."

"We understand, but we have the right to be upset," fumed the husband, pointing at Magda. "We invested three months in that baby, followed her growth, and worked to keep our finances stable. We accompanied you to every medical appointment and then you do this to us!"

"I'll reimburse every penny you've spent, for that matter. However, it's out of the question to give Meg up for adoption. I am not sacrificing the privilege to be a mother..."

The woman clung to her furious husband's arms to appease him. She didn't want the situation to be more heated. She gazed at the baby and then at Magda and left without a word. They were indeed deceived by Allimair's false promises, who thought they had everything under control.

"I can lose a husband, but I never wish to lose a child. The scar of a mother never erases," Magda whispered, placing the baby on her chest, feeling her heartbeat and tiny body briefly squirming in her sleep.

Allimair, watching how the procedure turned out, stared down at the baby, deceived that she couldn't do anything about it. There were many words she could've said and yet came to no results. She leaned toward Magda and pointed a finger in Magda's face. "You will pay for that. No one who turns on me runs free with no consequences. You embarrassed me, Magda. You pretended to go along with our plan."

"How exactly are you going to make me pay?"

"Her." Allimair pointed at the baby. "I don't know how, but I'll make sure she hates your gut and that your home is never at peace."

"You're mad because I told Father about you working in a brothel while you told him you found a job at a modeling agency. That's what this is about. The adoption is only an excuse to get back at me, and I don't care anymore about what you will do. Meg will be loved and safe."

***

Magda took the peanut butter from Gladice and put it on the table for Meg as she waited for her. As she stretched her back, a pair of arms laced around her torso. She smiled and cocked her neck to the side, welcoming his kisses. "I'm so glad you're home."

"Me too," replied Helmer, smooching Magda's cheeks. "However, I have bad news."

Magda turned, knowing something was up following his apologizing tone. She was impatiently waiting for him to come home for dinner and to tell him she had changed their plans. It had been a while since they'd eaten as a family, so the night was expected to get them closer to each other and strengthen their bonds with Meg. "I hope it's not about work."

"Actually, it is."

Helmer walked up to Gladice and pressed a kiss on her cheek. He uncovered the pot from the stove and sniffed the stew's aroma. "It smells delicious. Make sure you save me some for tomorrow. I'll take it to the office."

"Wash your hands before you come over here, interrupting my cooking," scolded Gladice, covering the pot back. "And mezanmi, who gave you that haircut?" she started, noticing his head, shaking her head with a soft chuckle. "Even I with my old eyes could've done better. But you don't come to me anymore."

"I had to listen to Bryant joke about it all day," he said, leaning over and resting his chin on Gladice's shoulder. "I could really use a break."

Gladice smiled, grabbed a pastry from the counter, and held it up to his mouth. Crumbs fell onto her as he bit into it, both of them laughing. He stepped back, still chuckling, as she turned to brush the crumbs off his shirt.

"Thirty years of feeding this mouth, and it still feels like just yesterday," Gladice said, a soft smile playing on her lips.

"Are we still on for dinner tonight?" Magda asked, her voice barely rising above the interaction between Helmer and Gladice. It was clear that a nanny's job truly never ended.

"C'mon son," Gladice said, patting Helmer's cheek. "Your wife is talking to you."

"Oh yeah…" Helmer resumed, shifting his head to Magda. "I can't stay for dinner tonight."

"I-I told you this morning. So, why the sudden change?"

"It was unexpected, believe me. I must run to help Sonia with something—"

"Sonia?" Magda frowned. "What about Bryant? He can't help her?"

"He's taking care of some financial issues regarding the company. It'll probably take all night."

"What about Nina? Have you called her? I told Meg we'd go out tonight."

"Which I just found out about," Helmer said, stepping toward her. "But Helmer, she won't understand…"

"I'll talk to her, don't worry," he reassured. "She'll understand." "Of course she will," said Magda sardonically, giving Helmer a pat on the chest. "It's you."

"Magda, I didn't mean to cancel—"

"No, there's no need to apologize. Go! Work is calling." She stepped across from him and pulled a chair to sit, hoping her silence would make him dismiss himself.

"Are you sure we can't talk this through?" Helmer asked. "You can go."

The seething tone in her voice warned him to keep away. Helmer didn't want to taunt her more with his apologies nor ruin the night for everybody. He approached her slowly and leaned forward in an attempt to kiss her cheek and appease the tension.

"I said go." Magda jerked her head away and shifted her body toward the opposite chair from the table. She crossed her arms, facing the wall, hoping her patience wouldn't run low as he lingered to leave. But her heart sank as soon as she heard him step toward the kitchen entrance. She turned her head, stealing a glimpse at him. He stopped in his tracks, and her lips parted, tempted to beg him to stay. Her lips moved slowly, and if they weren't fast enough, he'd leave. But her mind was like a blank canvas, not a single ink of thought to form a word. Then she heard him reach outside. He finally left, and Magda felt the loneliness tugging at her soul all over again.

CHAPTER 7

Nerves

*H*elmer folded his arms and laid his head on the desk. He had reviewed tons of paperwork to sign, which Nina had dropped by in the morning. He thought of calling Magda, but they were still not on good terms after he had canceled their dinner plan the week before. Hearing Bryant walking into the office, he raised his head and greeted him.

"What's with that face?" said Bryant, rushing to grab a seat as he held onto a yellow folder. "I'm starting to believe you have not been getting laid."

"Bryant, I am not in the mood," Helmer warned. "Exactly! Because you're not getting laid."

"Not sure why you're so obsessed with my sex life but I hate to break it to you. You're not my type."

"Finally, something we can agree on," Bryant said, nodding. Helmer snorted, sitting up. "What do you have for me today?"

"A graph of our last sales." Bryant handed him the folder and urged him to open it. "The numbers are dropping, and we have serious competition."

"By competition, you mean?"

"There's a new furniture company; their designs exceed our expertise so far," Bryant explained. "They combine their inventions with high technology, which makes them impeccable."

"How do we beat them?" asked Helmer, analyzing the reports. "Well, I have an idea," Bryant said, standing up. He grabbed a paper from the stack at the corner of the office and drew a sale map to illustrate his idea. "Our new competition's prices are high, so if we upgrade our designs and set lower prices for ours, we can attract more clients and keep our consumers happy."

"We're already struggling," Helmer pointed out, pushing the sale map aside. "That will put a strain on our employees, requiring more work from them, so we would also have to give them a raise."

"Exactly," Bryant nodded excitedly. "No," said Helmer, firmly.

"That's the best option we have." "Absolutely not. We'll lose money."

"Helmer, with this new company out there, we are not only risking losing money but our workers as well. The pay is competitive, so we have to step up our game and give our people what will keep them here—a better wage."

"And losing our workers will cost more," Helmer concluded. "Yeah." Bryant nodded.

"Goddamn it. I didn't realize it was that bad." Helmer grabbed the sheet back, scanning through it, considering Bryant's sale plan.

"That's why I decided to do something that will benefit everyone tomorrow." Bryant sat, hesitant to utter his idea. "I called Mr. Will and set a meeting for tomorrow so we can discuss the contract."

"Bryant, he disrespected Sonie," fussed Helmer. "If we invite him into our home after demeaning our own, what do you think that will say about us? And Sonie, she agreed to this?"

"She asked me to," Bryant replied. "She's aware the situation is above all of us. We have to take the hit and call Mr. Will for help."

"There's no way in hell I would eat at the same table with that man and worse, sign a damn contract with him!"

"Helmer..."

"Sonie felt bad about me letting the contract go. That's why she asked you to call Mr. Will, and you should've disagreed with her request," Helmer opined, his face so full of rage that Bryant knew he wouldn't change his mind.

"Well, counter to you, I can put my own emotions aside to do what I have to do, and right now, the company is at stake. So, will you save it or not?"

"I will, but—"

"I?" Bryant cut in. "This is a team decision. You can't decide this on your own."

"You don't care about Sonie, do you?" Helmer sighed, his shoulders dropping forward.

"We're talking business here, not about my relationship issues," recalled Bryant, slowly losing his patience. He couldn't understand why it was such an issue to accept the contract. Business transactions weren't always for the faint of heart, that he knew really well. But also the importance of putting work above emotions and personal matters.

"I am not going to let you embarrass her," Helmer replied, his tone resolute.

"Is this about your parents?" Bryant said, slamming his palms onto Helmer's desk. "Because your mom left your dad, and she had cheated on him, so you feel like putting it on me too?"

"What did you say?"

"Exactly what I said!" Huffed Bryant. "To stop making everybody's situation about you. I know what happened between me and Nina is triggering for you, but it's my life!"

"I am not having this meeting," spat Helmer. "You are."

"I am not, and damn it, you're not going to change my mind," Helmer shouted, pushing his chair back and standing up. "Now, get out of my goddamn office."

"Because I told you the truth? You don't own Sonie, and you don't have a say in our relationship; neither should you act like you're the only one running this company."

"What is your problem?" Helmer snapped, his jaw clenched, fingers tapping impatiently against the table. He raised an eyebrow, his lips pressed into a thin line. "Has something gotten into you lately?"

"Not really, but don't forget we have the same shares in this company, and I say this meeting will take place whether you like it or not."

"Guess what, it won't. And next time you want to mention my parents, remember that you're somebody thanks to me, and every goddamn time your behind is in some mess, I am the one who comes to your rescue." Helmer grabbed the folder and tossed it at Bryant. The reports scattered over the floor, leaving a mess. "So, you may have the same shares in this company, but nobody, I repeat, nobody cares about it more than I do. Besides, you know damn well you haven't funded a penny in it. May it be the last time you say something like this to me."

Bryant glared at him and went ahead, picking up the sheets on the floor. He dropped them in his folder and pointed at Helmer. "You're not perfect either, and you owe me just as much. Counter to you, I won't remind you where you come from."

Bryant stormed out of the office and slammed the door behind him.

Remembering past mistakes always caused pain. They both wanted to conceal those memories. Helmer slumped in his chair, still absorbed in his fury, processing what Bryant had said. He grabbed a book and flipped a few pages, trying to divert his mind from his anger with no success. He closed the book and loosened his tie to get more air; then, he heard a knock on the door.

"Everything's ok, Mr. Durpris?" asked Nina, stepping into the office. She paused, her eyes flicking between Helmer and the cluttered desk.

"There's no need for these formalities, Nina. No one's in here." "I'm sorry," Nina said, sitting down. "I meant to tell you about the meeting, but Bryant had scheduled it without my knowledge. I found out when it was too late."

"He's crazy," Helmer whispered, attempting to let the steam cool off, but he couldn't ease down. His hands shook from the viscous urge to punch at something. Hearing his parents brought up in the conversation woke something in him that he thought he had overcome for years. That wound was tied to an indescribable anger he had tried to keep under the rug since his childhood.

"Are you angry at Bryant for the meeting or the affair?" asked Nina, lowering her head.

"Nina, it's not you," Helmer reassured. "It's him, you know? It's like he has no remorse for hurting the women I respect and care about. I wish I could pull his ears or something. I am so sorry for what he has put you through."

"Thank you for caring," Nina said, "I don't get that a lot." She couldn't smile through the pain. She made peace with the fact that her healing would take longer than expected. There was someone out there who was still seeing her in high regard and considered her side of the story, not automatically categorizing her as the villain. The women usually were, in every cheating scandal. And thanks to Helmer, the story had not reached further ears.

"By the way, how are you doing?" Helmer asked, easing down. "Are you ok? How do you feel seeing him every day?"

Nina thought of the question and brushed her arms, her eyes giving away her urge to cry. "Like my heart gets ripped out of my chest all over again. But what can I do? I have to live with the pain."

"It'll get better with time," empathized Helmer, recalling his own sorrow, the damaging relationship he had with his father. "And don't expect closure either. Sometimes, closure can be an excuse to tell ourselves the lies that broke us in the first place and make them our reality."

"Maybe, but I don't think it will get better." Nina shook her head. "Not everything heals with time. Believe it or not, closure is to accept what we can't change, whether it's the past or somebody else's behavior. But thank you."

Nina drew Helmer's attention to the document on the desk. She slid it to him to scan through, slowly switching the subject. She was done being reminded of her old sad tale, which was a wound that seemed to have no chance of ever healing.

"Tell Sonie, Nina," Helmer blurted out. "What?"

"Tell her what happened with Bryant," Helmer said. "I-I can't do that," Nina stammered, her heart racing. "She deserves to know."

"If this is about trying to sabotage the meeting using me to do it, I refuse," Nina said, shuffling through the document, trying to escape Helmer's request.

"I'm not."

"You are," lectured Nina, standing up. "What will Sonia think of me?"

"She'll see you like I see you. A victim of a womanizer who has no regrets for what he has done to you and her," Helmer replied. "You didn't know he was playing around with both of you at the same time. So, it is something you should bring up for your sake and Sonie's."

"But is this really about me—"

"Are you going to do it or not?" he interrupted, his voice clipped. "You understand it's not easy to do what you're asking, right?" Nina challenged, crossing her arms.

"Then find a way!" He said dismissively. "You're a smart woman, Nina. I'm sure you can handle it."

"You really want to hit back at Bryant that bad?"

"You damn right I do," Helmer said, shrugging nonchalantly. "So, tell Sonia. That way, all hell breaks loose, and nobody gets to meet anyone."

"You're picking a fight with him; I hope you're aware," Nina pointed out.

"Not if you do what I asked," Helmer replied, picking the document up from the desk and jerking his office chair back. He crossed out the appointment date with Mr. Will and handed the document back to Nina with a dismissing hand wave.

"You don't always have to get even, you know?" said Nina, walking out, aware that this feud could go horribly wrong.

Helmer stood, walked to the shelf, and grabbed his bottle of vodka; he poured himself a glass and chugged it down his throat. The piquant taste eased his nerves, but he couldn't stop thinking about his dad, leaving an anxious feeling in his chest. He took a short walk around the office, hoping to clear his mind, yet nothing helped. It had been months since he had talked to his father, and the last time they had, it went violent. He didn't want that to happen again. Helmer didn't want to become that person, the bitter and angry reflection of Mr. Jean.

Helmer went to his desk and pulled out a drawer, taking one of his prescriptions, but the bottle was empty. He had run out of his pills since he had stopped going to his therapy sessions. He sat, itching from the butterflies fluttering in his chest. He ran to take a couple more vodka shots and then grabbed his suitcase, sprinting out of the office for air.

"Hey, you ok?" asked Nina, seeing him sprinting past her desk. "Yes, I think so," he replied, through a shortness of breath. "Call my driver to meet me at the entrance."

"Okay, hm... By the way, Mrs. Durpris' cousin called. I think his name is June," Nina explained. "He said he's at the bar, to meet him there. I don't know why."

"I'll head there then. And not a word about today with anyone."

Helmer rushed to the elevator, heading down to the entrance to meet his driver, who was on lunch break. He signaled him to park by the road and hopped into the car, heading to June's bar.

Helmer put the windows down, letting the wind splash on his face, bringing him instant relief. With his heart racing, he patted the left side of his chest, taking in a few deep breaths repeatedly. He laid his head back and relaxed until they reached the bar.

"Thanks," said Helmer, getting off. "Wait here. I'll see if you need to drive my wife's car home."

The driver nodded and parked the car. Helmer hastened to get into the bar, putting on his best face so Magda didn't suspect he had an anxiety episode. He walked to June and greeted him, grabbing a stool next to Magda.

"Let me guess. June called you," inferred Magda, taking a sip of tequila. "No wonder he's nowhere to be found suddenly."

"I know you're still mad at me, but please, let's go home and have a chat. I'll make it up to you one last time."

"How exactly are you going to do that?" Magda asked, squeezing the side piece of lime into her tequila shot.

"Ask me anything, and I'll do it." "Are you sure?"

"Positive," Helmer replied, pulling her stool closer to his. He leaned over and stared into her eyes, placing one hand over her thigh. Even though she didn't know, her warmth gave him instant solace.

Magda was wearing a red dress with some ruffles on the side, but she had no makeup, or anything fancy on to match. And still, she looked perfect, like an appealing and mouthwatering dish, filling Helmer's mind with unholy thoughts.

"I want to do a painting exposition in the upcoming month in Paris," Magda said, sliding a few fingers under Helmer's sleeves for a close touch of his skin. "Maybe you could help me set it up."

"Ok," Helmer said, nodding hastily to Magda's request. "I don't know much about painting, but I'll definitely help."

"You realize I'm only asking you to be there, right?" Magda pointed out, gazing back at him.

"Of course, I'll support."

"Thanks." Magda pushed the empty shot glasses to the side and pecked a kiss on his lips.

However, their moment was interrupted by the waiter erupting through their conversation and bringing Magda a drink. It was a tequila-based cocktail decorated with olives and dried guava. The smell captured her senses and plunged her into a deep, happy memory, and Magda stood as soon as the waiter stretched it to her.

"What is this?" She asked.

"I'm not sure, ma'am. Somebody sent you this drink," the waiter replied.

"Somebody?" Helmer stood, his hands already forming a fist. "Who's that somebody?"

"The guy from over there—" The waiter stopped mid-sentence, pointing at the back. "Oh, I swear he was there. I guess he disappeared."

"So, I have an admirer," joked Magda.

"Or a stalker," Helmer opined. "Who would send that to you despite seeing us here together?"

"I don't know. A psycho, maybe," Magda said, curiously reaching for the drink.

"Is there a name or anything at all?" Helmer asked, taking the drink before Magda could. "Are you sure you can't tell us who it was? Did he give a name or something?"

"Can you help us out, please?" Magda inquired, placing one hand over Helmer's shoulder. "My husband is not going to let that go until you give us a hint."

"I don't know." The waiter shrugged. "The guy was here since you came earlier."

"He came in after me?" Magda asked. "Yeah." The waiter nodded.

"That's why I always insist you don't come here alone," spat Helmer, discarding the drink as he scanned through the bar. "I really need to know who sent this."

"The only thing I can tell you is that this guy is the scariest thing I've seen in my life," the waiter added, dismissing himself.

"All right," Helmer said, watching his back leaving. "Thanks for the input, even though it's not helping."

"Helmer!" Magda said, tapping his arm. "It's just a drink."

"I'm sorry," he apologized. "I had a bad day at work and this drink is pulling the frustration out of me."

"It's ok." Magda rubbed his arm. "You don't have to be so worked up about this. I don't know who sent it."

Helmer hugged her but was still distant, his eyes everywhere to see if he could at least get a hint to find the person, but the guy was nowhere to be found.

CHAPTER 8

Seek And Hide

There was a coffin out in the woods and a grieving man standing by it. He was in deep mourning, and the pain echoed in his voice as he let out a scream. Magda watched him from a distance, hiding and absorbing the man's agony. It was too much of a torture to witness a man cry, his heart wrecking like a ship on fire, sinking with no way out.

Magda approached slowly, barefooted, seeking to offer solace to the man, the leaves crunching under her feet. The clouds were gray. The air was thick, as if it was filled with gas, enough to suffocate a cat. The man had not turned nor stopped sobbing. His voice grew louder and hoarser the more Magda got closer. Crows croaked in the trees from across where she stood as if they were warning her to stay away. But Magda was curious. Although frightened, she stretched her arm toward the man, attempting to touch his shoulder.

"Hey, I know how it feels," said Magda, "I have grieved him too."

At that, the man stopped sobbing. There was silence, then a whisper from the trees. Magda startled, hearing different sounds and screams. Her instinct was commanding her to run but nowhere would've been far enough not to be found. She was a bird caught in her own nest, and for such death, one couldn't be innocent.

"Him? Who's him?" asked the man, slowly turning his head toward Magda, his eyes letting out a stream of blood.

Magda's heart pounded, each thud echoing in her ears as cold sweat prickled along her spine. Her breath hitched, coming in short, sharp bursts, her chest tightening. She had never seen such a thing before, and neither understood why this man wasn't in the coffin. He was supposed to be in there. Her hands trembled, fingers gripping the fabric of her dress as though it were the only thing grounding her in reality.

"I'm here now, Maggie," the man said, taking a step toward Magda. Every instinct screamed for her to look away, but her eyes were glued to the impossible scene, unable to comprehend how this could be happening. How did he make it out of his grave? The thought raveled through Magda's mind, turning her stomach.

A sharp scream came out of the woods, and a gush of wind hit them. As soon as Magda got distracted by the sounds coming from the trees, the man seized her arm. There was no time to react. He had her there, at his mercy.

"Richard," she whispered, noticing the coffin creak open. "No, no, I can't go in there. Please, I can't go in there. You have to let me go home." She couldn't scream anymore; Her voice was gone, and her legs turned unresponsive, as if the ground beneath her had shifted. The numbness crawled up her body, leaving her frozen in place, unable to move or react.

"Please…" Mouthed Magda, failing to release the scream lodged in her throat. Her heart hammered against her ribs, the only present sound filling the void.

"What home? You mean the one you burned?" The man pointed at a tiny old house, smoke coming out of it.

Seeing it, tears cascaded down Magda's face, her body growing rigid. Each drop of tear felt like lava, placing her soul in excruciating agony. She panted and screamed, staring into the man's dead eyes, showing malice and animosity. Magda was trapped, unable to move.

"You don't know what's happening. Do you?" The man laughed, quite entertained seeing her helpless. "Your time has come. This coffin belongs to you now." The left side of his face started to melt, exposing his bones, his flesh slowly falling away.

He grasped her neck and pinned her inside the coffin. Magda attempted to fight back, trying to remove the man's hands off her neck as he squeezed harder. But he wasn't willing to let go.

"Say you're sorry!" the man yelled, squeezing the last breath out of her. "Say it. Say you're sorry, murderer!"

Magda jumped, reaching for her face. She patted her body, making sure she was out of the coffin. It wasn't there. She felt a hand reaching for her and screamed, crawling away.

"Hey, you had a nightmare. It's ok," said Helmer, sniffling and putting his book on the nightstand. He leaned forward cautiously, making sure she was fully awake. "You're safe. You're ok, it's me."

"Where is he? I didn't do it," wept Magda, traveling her eyes around the room. What she couldn't explain was that her dreams were always close to reality. Something from them reminded her that no one can run forever.

"I didn't do it. I didn't..." she repeated. Helmer wrapped his arms around her on the bed, trying to calm her down. The man's melting face and the tiny old house were the last things she'd ever want to see in her dreams. Being caught up in such a predicament led her to wonder one thing. Was she running from her past or justice?

"What time is it?" she asked, her face buried in his shirt. "3:00 am," replied Helmer, kissing her forehead.

"And you're awake? You don't have work later?" asked Magda, rubbing her eyes. She glanced at the book on the nightstand. It was a psychological novel about mental health and how to cope. She sat up and cupped Helmer's face, seeing the despondent expression in his eyes. "You're alright?"

"Yes, I just couldn't sleep," he answered, nodding. "I had a bad day at work yesterday and have some things to sort out. That's all."

Magda stretched her legs, recovering from the tension in the dream. She usually took melatonin to help her sleep at night, but even her dreams weren't peaceful. Neither was her home. There was always something to fix, to do, or to bury in her secret box. And a husband who was dealing with his own nightmares, which he refused to share with her.

"You can tell me anything. You know that right?" she said, touching his hand. "Your eyes are swollen. What's wrong?"

"Nothing," he said. "What are you talking about?"

"I don't know," Magda said, "but you don't look fine to me." She rubbed her arms, her body still catching chills.

"I told you, I am fine," he said, but his gaze wandered away, thinking of something. His voice was breaking, and by the sound of it, he was the one falling apart. He couldn't put his own feelings into words, and he couldn't explain his own nightmares.

"Tell me what's wrong."

"Nothing is wrong," he said. "I'll go to the library to finish my reading." He kissed her forehead, grabbed his book, and darted out of the room before she could object.

The dread came upon Magda once again, reliving the images from the dream as she was left alone. The chills insisted, and her heart was pounding. She reached for the drawer beside the bed and took her melatonin bottle, tossing some into her mouth, hoping it'd help her sleep. However, neither sleeping nor staying awake would help escape from her torment. Her dreams were an abyss and an everyday reminder of Richard's screams before he died. He was gone, so he couldn't be a threat. However, some things do come back to bite us when we least expect them.

She pulled the huge comforter up to her head until she couldn't see anything. It was all dark again under the sheets, and after hours, her eyes shut until noon.

The glare of the sun filled the room with its beauty and greeted her. She rolled on the bed, sitting up in a jump, her mind still waking up. Patting her hands on the side of the bed, she didn't see Helmer, which made her head shift to the clock from the nightstand. It was indeed midday. But of course, what would be the rush for anyway? She was not an ordinary housewife. Her life was financially secure, with maids doing all the chores. It was only out of passion she'd choose to cook.

Magda slumped back into the bed, yawning and stretching. Light. Yes, the beautiful sunlight. That was what she needed. Because at night, her demons would resurface and haunt her. With such a conscience, Insomnia was just one of the side effects.

Magda turned her head and jumped at the sight of Marie standing there by her bathroom door, revealed by her shadow.

"Oh, I'm so sorry," apologized Marie. "I didn't mean to scare you, Mrs. Dupris. I was taking the dirty towels out of the bathroom."

"Well, you did scare me," said Magda, placing one hand over her rising chest. "You seem preoccupied. What happened? Did Gladice make breakfast?"

"Yes." Marie nodded, her head down, and took the dirty laundry out. She looked at the melatonin on the nightstand and then at the drawer, still left open.

"Don't," warned Magda, motioning at Marie to stay away from the drawer. "I got it." She reached for a bottle of pills and tossed one into her mouth. She pushed the drawer in, catching Marie peeking her head over to look. "I said I got it, Marie. You can go."

"I know," said Marie, lingering as she held on to the laundry baskets. "I wanted to say that Mr. Dupris seemed very upset this morning—"

"Upset how?" Magda asked, scooting off from the bed. She fixed her nightgown and brushed her hair off her face.

"He has not gone to work yet this morning. Usually, he leaves as early as 5:00 am, but he got dressed and sat in there, staring at the wall. I don't know; he looked very pensive."

"And how do you know that?" Magda frowned. "I would almost assume you were spying on him. Oh, Marie, Marie, Marie, Marie. What are we going to do with you?"

Magda walked past Marie and grabbed a dress, laid it on the bed and dropped a matching purse on the side. She had to go to June, for she could always confide her dreams with him. That was the only scary side of her life, it was safe to share, and being haunted every night wasn't for the faint of heart.

"Marie." Magda turned around. "Why are you still standing there? Are you trying to see me naked, or are you here to ask about June?"

Marie laughed nervously and brushed the tip of her nose. She indeed thought of asking about Magda's cousin but for a particular reason. After all, everyone had their little secrets; why would she divulge hers? "Actually, ma'am, I was going to."

"Aren't you dating my husband's driver? Last time I checked, you two were in a relationship. Or did that one fail as well?" Magda asked, going to the bathroom to wash her face.

"Me and Mr. Dupris's driver broke up. So, I'm officially single again."

"That's unfortunate," empathized Magda, drying off her face. She came out of the bathroom and watched Marie's face indulge in sorrow, somewhat with a wave of guilt. Magda couldn't put her hands on whatever it was, but her gut told her there was more to the story.

"Well, I'm sorry," added Magda, stretching an arm across Marie's shoulder.

"Mrs. Dupris..." sobbed Marie, seizing Magda into a hug and dropping the laundry basket on the floor. The clothes scattered all over, but her abrupt demand for comfort didn't leave Magda any room to think of it. "I am so broken! He left me for a model. I guess he doesn't like basic girls like me. I don't know what to do."

"Okay, hmm… Let's sit for a minute," Magda said, progressively freeing herself from Marie's firm hold. This latter rushed to the bed to sit but stopped following a scream of panic from Magda.

"There's a chair by the nightstand; let's, huh…sit there instead," Magda said, walking Marie to the chair across the bed.

"You know what? Stay here for a minute. I'll check on my husband and be right back. No rush!" Magda darted out of the bedroom, unsure if she was moved by empathy or pure discomfort by the situation. However, she could relate. She had a failed relationship years before meeting Helmer. However, that relationship wasn't meant to ever be talked about or remembered.

Reaching the library, Magda ran in and locked the doors. She stopped halfway, apprehended by the alarming scenery in front of her. "Helmer!"

He was sitting on the floor panting, his legs stretched out and his hands numb to his sides. His speeding heart made it hard to breathe and respond. His attempt to turn to look at Magda failed when a sob escaped his lips.

"Hey, what happened?" whispered Magda, kneeling next to him and securing her left arm behind his back for support.

He blinked repeatedly, drawing her attention to his tie to unloose it. He couldn't form a word nor snap out of his detriment. Being a man wasn't always easy, as there were always double standards about showing emotions. Showing too much would make one weak, and showing none would be careless. But in his case, there was a downfall of being too vulnerable. What if he revealed too much about his childhood? How he grew up, the things he had to do to survive his father's abuse, and the mistakes he's made that he could never be redeemed for. There was so much down the line, so he refrained from expressing himself.

"Here," said Magda, removing Helmer's tie and encouraging him to take a few deep breaths. "You're safe here. I'm here, you know? I'll always be here. Try to count to 20 this time."

His lips parted open, slowly forming his first count, then his second. Feeling Magda's body heat brought him back to his focus, shielded from his racing thoughts.

"Think of us, just us somewhere in a park with our future kids. Imagine our life in 5 years, walking our kids and telling them what a great father you are." Magda rubbed his arms, trying to keep him engaged.

He blinked again in response, and his face lightened up. "Y-Yes. Kids."

"Yes, our kids. I can't wait to have a baby with you."

She helped him count until he stopped shaking and his breathing came back to normal. However, the numbness kept his soul hostage, and his mind trapped in an intangible terror.

"Did you have a trigger? Did you get your medicine?" She sat beside him, allowing him to take his time to reply. She touched his hand and gave him a kiss, but he had not reacted to it.

"T-Today marks the date my mom left." He let out a sob, struggling to breathe through his agony. "The day she abandoned us, my father and I."

"I'm sorry," said Magda, brushing her knuckles on his chest. She placed her hand on his heart, hoping it'd slow down and release him from the anxious feelings.

"It's like that little voice inside, telling me it might happen with you," he revealed, shifting his gaze toward her. "You, Meg, and everybody. You all might leave just like she did. I just hope to never see that woman in my life again."

"Helmer…" whispered Magda, leaning over and cupping his cheeks. "We would never abandon you. We're here for you, and we're here to stay."

"What you said about the baby, it's true?" he asked. "Do you genuinely want to have a baby with me?"

"Of course," she nodded. "If anything, we can always adopt." "Thank you!" he said, his nervous system appeasing down.

"Are you sure you need to go to work today?" Magda asked. "I mean, some rest might do you good."

"What I need right now is to go far away with our family, and hopefully somewhere we can start anew," he said, sniffling. "But yes, I do have to report to work today. I have to!"

"I'll get you some water," offered Magda, getting up.

"No," he said, reaching out for her arm. "Please, sit with me for a few minutes. My legs are still numb."

"Okay." She sat with him, leaning her head on his shoulder, easing into the silence between them. But not every moment needed words anyway. Her being there told him he had someone to count on, even in his most vulnerable state.

His body progressively regained control and allowed him to move around. He kissed her forehead and held her hand, standing up. His heart dropped just at the thought of facing Bryant and telling Sonia about his cheating.

"I'll see you later." He kissed her on the lips and walked out of the library, heading to the stairway. His mind was filled with unliberated thoughts and the challenge of keeping them at bay seemed almost as impossible. He sprinted down the stairs and headed through the foyer, alerting his driver to take him to work. The ride was silent, and his face exposed his discomfort.

"Everything ok, sir?" asked the driver, throwing a glance at him from the rearview mirror.

"Just drive!" he replied, unbuttoning the top of his shirt. He lowered the windows down and enjoyed the breeze coming in. Then his eyes caught a woman walking a toddler in a stroller, striking his soul with an abrupt melancholy. He put the windows up, his body heating out of anger.

"Sir, are you sure you don't want me to stop for a minute?" the driver asked, worried. "There's a coffee shop nearby."

"No," declined Helmer, taking his seatbelt off. "The caffeine will make me worse."

"We can always get a decaf."

"I'm super late for work," he said. "Take me there instead. I got a meeting to attend."

The driver drove off while keeping an eye on him during the ride. The building was close by, so it didn't take long to reach. However, it felt like an eternity as the pressure to step out of the car rose by the minute.

Helmer hopped out of the car and entered the building. He rushed into the elevator and pressed the floor button. He had butterflies in his chest, but his stomach twisted up, giving him the urge to vomit. Drops of sweat formed on his forehead and hands. As the elevator's door opened, he attempted to close it, but only for him to be caught by Nina, darting in.

"We have a problem!" She pressed the button to close the door; she was too shaken up by her own worry to notice his panic.

"Whatever it is, don't tell Sonie about Bryant," Helmer spat out, twisting off his tie. No matter what he did, the heat flashes persisted. It was a matter of time before he collapsed. Perhaps he'd fight it. Except, it'd make him more exhausted trying to hide his malaise. "She won't be able to handle it. I changed my mind about the meeting. I'll find another solution—"

"She knows," interrupted Nina, the sobs forming in her throat. "I wasn't the one who told her. I am screwed!"

"Bryant," whispered Helmer as the realization hit him. "He told her. Stay put, I'll handle it."

He pushed the button to the seventh floor and rushed through the hall, perturbed by the screaming coming from the conference room. His heart raced, almost like a plane taking off, yet everything seemed to be moving at a slow pace. All the voices and murmurs from the employees hiding their discreet stares as he walked by sent an abrupt vibration to his brain. He pushed through and made it to the meeting room and melted at the sight of Sonia tossing a glass across the room.

She slumped in the chair, her arms limp at her sides, her eyes desperately looking for the sight of Helmer. "Tell me you didn't know."

"Sonie…" murmured Helmer, his eyes forming the tears he'd held back.

"So, everyone knew," she said, crying silently and staring at him, then at Bryant. Her heart was shrieking and cutting up in pieces, so little that she could barely feel anything. Her blood felt cold, and so did the room around her. Everything they said sounded like torture in her ears. Sitting through the apologies, the guilty pleas were tearing her soul, and for a moment, she wanted it all to end.

"I'm so sorry, Sonie," said Helmer, his voice barely audible. "I didn't know until a month ago."

"Reschedule the meeting," Sonia said, her voice faltering, brittle. "I need… I need a moment to myself. Actually, I might need to go home."

"I'm so sorry," lamented Bryant, getting up and heading toward her.

"I-I'll get you a ride. Please, allow me."

"No," Sonia declined, her body shaking as she stood up. "Stay away… Stay away from me."

"Baby—"

"No, don't baby me," she snapped, thrusting a finger toward him, to not get any steps closer as he attempted to. "You've done enough damage. You realize, I've never cried in this building before, and now I am because of you—someone I'm supposed to trust."

"I-I know that, and I'm sorry—"

"You're not sorry, Bryant," she spat. "You're ashamed you got caught. That's what guilt feels like."

She took the files from the conference table and secured them against her chest. Tears ran down her face, then she pushed out a shaky breath, her arms retracting from the sudden wave of the new reality. These two men—once her pillars—would never be the same to her again.

"I can't watch you like this," Helmer said softly, stepping forward. "I know, Helmer." She raised a trembling hand to stop him. "It wasn't your truth to tell, but I... I need to be alone right now."

Helmer stepped across from her, a clear attempt to stop her. "I'm so sorry, Sonie."

"Don't pity me," Sonia cut in, her voice sharper. "I don't need it.

What I need is for you to do what I said—get out of my way."

She turned on her heel, her body fragile and drained, and made her way to the door.

"You told her," Helmer said, shifting his head toward Bryant. "Withhold the false empathy, would you?" Bryant sniffled, his eyes exposing his taunting guilt over the matter. "I figured you'd want to tell her before I did. I know you, Helmer. You were ready to throw me under the bus over a stupid meeting that would have benefited all of us."

"Yet here you are, doing the same," Helmer riposted. "I never told you this, but I think you are as selfish as you are dishonest. You cheat your way in life, even in your relationship with others, and perhaps that's the main reason why you're always bringing up my mom whenever we have a downfall. You two are just the same."

"Though I dare to differ," said Bryant, walking past the desk. "Your mom does not only cheat, but she does not give a damn about you or anyone. But I do care, and if I didn't, I would've left this company a long time ago because as long as you're here, you'll never let anyone excel, fearing that they surpass you. Actually, you can't handle it. It's always about winning with you."

"You know it's not true."

"Oh, it is," Bryant said, his throat tightening. The lump rose higher with each breath, but he swallowed hard, fighting it down. "You are tied to this obsession of constantly proving your worth even when it's not needed. The problem is I can't help you unless you realize that you're using us, the company, and everything around you to either make up or cope with the things your parents have caused you. And Helmer, you sure know where to get that help. Until then, we'll always go through this." Bryant shoved past Helmer, his footsteps quick and uneven, storming out of the conference room.

CHAPTER 9

Hunted Rose

The traffic was heavier than usual due to the rainy weather. People crossed the streets, squeezing between cars and buses, some running with their coats on and others hurrying to find shelter in nearby coffee shops and subways. Then there were Magda and June, casually walking on the sidewalk, enjoying the slow pace of the city. It was a chill day for them, taking a break from their usual activities. No personal drivers, no customers calling June here and there for orders, and definitely no kids to take to school. Life was easy compared to most living in the city. There was no rushing to get back home, not even a pet to take care of.

Everything was simple, just as plain as a blank sheet of paper.

"Did you tell Helmer I'm stealing you today for a coffee?" teased June, gesturing at Magda to stay on the safe side of the road. "You can't walk in a straight line for nothing. You've been pushing me off on the streets the entire time."

"I'm sorry," Magda said, rolling her eyes. "Now that you've mentioned Helmer, being married doesn't mean you can't have your space sometimes. I need it, you know? Otherwise, it'd be like being married to my mom, monitoring my whereabouts and everything I do." "That's being protective," June opined, jumping to his aunt's defense. "You mean controlling?" Magda snorted. "However, I wouldn't put her and Helmer in the same boat. They're different, and Helmer has his reasons."

"I know he cares about you, but have you ever asked him why he's so afraid when you're out on these streets? I mean…anywhere you go. It's like he owes someone, or he's hiding from something."

"Sounds odd coming from you. You defend this man so much that I started to think maybe you're more related to him than me," Magda said.

"Can we blame him, though? The south side of Chicago is not the safest—"

A man erupted between Magda and June, slamming her shoulder with a heavy shove. He was wearing a black overcoat with a large fire design imprinted on the back, and the hood covered his head.

"Hey, watch where you're going, you punk," shouted June, trying to catch him. But the man was faster, as if he was prepared for this moment.

"Damn it, I lost him," whispered June in defeat as the man sprinted through traffic. He took a moment to catch his breath, resting his hands on his knees and bending down. Looking back and noticing Magda waving from the distance, he rushed back, fearing for her safety. He approached and checked her out, especially her shoulder. "You're okay?" Magda nodded. "My shoulder hurts a little, but it's nothing major."

"Now I see what Helmer was saying," June said, soothing Magda's shoulder. "There are lots of psychos running free on these streets. Let's go in."

They walked into the coffee shop and stood in line, waiting to order. The line was fast paced, so they didn't have to stay long. Then, as they were up next, June and Magda went back and forth about letting each other pay. But the cashier looked at them amused and said casually, "It's okay; it's already paid for."

"Paid for?" they said in unison.

"It's already paid for," the youngster repeated, barely keeping eye contact. His hands dropped by his sides, jerking his head and smiling. "It's already paid for."

"No," June said. "I didn't hand you my card yet."

"I am so sorry. He is one of our special kids," said a lady as she came and took the young boy away from the ordering counter. "It takes them some time to process what you're saying. We have partnered with a foundation supporting these kids so they can have a normal social life, such as getting jobs and becoming more independent..."

"I-I get it. I'm the one who should apologize," June said, taking a look at the boy, who was still smiling at him. He didn't know why he felt provoked, but he couldn't help it. The boy seemed fine. Maybe he was. Who knew really what was behind the behavior?

"Do you know who paid for us?" asked Magda, curious yet eager to order. She wasn't bothered by it. After all, maybe there were still lots more strangers who were kind enough to make such a nice gesture in the world.

"Red," the boy yelled from where he sat. "Red." Then he walked into the back.

Red.

Magda felt a sudden jolt, a memory surfacing like a ghost. Richard's laughter echoed in her mind, his boyish grin as he leaned in close to hear her favorite color. But then the roses crept back, their scent suffocating, mingling with the note that haunted her thoughts. The world around her blurred as blood rushed into her ears, drowning out everything else.

But out of all those memories, there was one she tried to silence—the one where Richard was screaming. His arms reaching out into the void for her, calling her name, and his voice able to slice through even the smoke in the air and the swirling dust.

"Oh my god, red. He said red."

A feeling sprouted in Magda's stomach, suffocating her, as if the weight of Richard's despair wrapped around her throat, choking off her breath. Magda brought her hands to her face, tracing the memory of him, every detail vivid—the way his eyes dimmed, and the sharp angles of his face in those final moments.

"Magda!" June said, giving her a tap on the forehead, bringing her senses back to the present. "Let's leave. They won't tell us who it was, and I'm not comfortable accepting charities from someone I don't know." Magda blinked, the bustling coffee shop swirling around her. The chatter felt like distant thunder, and her heart raced as she tried to steady herself.

"Wait..." Magda whispered, brushing past June and leaning on the counter, her palms pressed against the cool surface. She turned, her eyes darting to the customers glaring at her, murmuring, their mugged faces threatening her to hurry. "Do you have any hints for me? What did that person look like? Was it a man or a woman? Did he leave a note or anything?"

"Red," the lady replied, her brow furrowing as she looked between Magda and June. "That was the message he left."

"So, it's a man," Magda murmured, breath hitching. "What did he look like?"

"I don't know," the lady said, shaking her head, her eyes wide. "Please, I need to know..." Magda said, her voice rising. "I know you know!"

"Hey, stop harassing the lady; move out of the line," complained a couple of folks in the line.

Magda slammed her hand on the counter, her voice trembling. "Tell me! I need to know, please."

The lady, seeing Magda's face and hearing the complaints from the customers, leaned forward and checked around her before proceeding. "The man's face was covered; we didn't get to see it. However, he left that message, which we just told you, along with a generous amount of cash so you two can get whatever you want. Then he ran out of the coffee shop like a maniac."

"Alright, let's go," June said, his voice firmer than usual, fingers tapping impatiently against his phone. "Enough with the theories. I already texted Helmer to pick us up. I'm not dealing with any more of this foolishness." He grabbed Magda's arm, hurrying her out of the coffee shop, his grip firm as he pulled her along.

"Do you really have to call my husband for every inconvenience in my life?" said Magda, being dragged out of the coffee shop.

"Okay, let go!"

She yanked her arm free from June's grip and paced away. Her mind spun, reliving that chapter from her past which she managed to close off for years. Why come up now? Red. What did it mean? No matter how hard she tried, Magda couldn't wrap her mind around it, the answer slipping through her fingers like smoke.

"So, what do you want me to do?" June asked, wondering how to calm her. However, nothing could help. No one could save her from the guilt, the nostalgia, and the heartbreak. Richard represented all of these, and still, he was the orbit her heart—at one point—gravitated to. That, she could never forget.

Her eyes widened as they lay upon something on the ground. It was where she got bumped right before going into the store. Magda rushed to the spot as June followed her along. She bent over to take a close look at the red flower on the floor. It was a tiny rose, dried up and barely noticeable on the street.

"What is it?" asked June, as Magda stopped over the ground, her back facing him.

"It was the man." "What?"

Magda turned her head, bringing the rose to June's attention. "The man who bumped past me, he must've dropped this. He was probably the one who paid for the coffee."

"How exactly do you know that?"

"I don't know," she said, getting up and gazing at the rose. "The lady said he ran out of the coffee shop. His face was covered. And he left a message. The guy was coming from the coffee shop."

"It could've been anybody," June muttered, his eyes scanning the street.

"Maybe. But what if the rose means something?" "What do you mean?" June asked, his brow furrowing. "I'm thinking—" Magda started.

"Well, not for long," someone shouted, interrupting her trail of thoughts. She sighed, noticing Helmer park across from the sidewalk, making haste to open the door for her. The timing was not ideal. Only one thing ran through her mind: finding out who the man was.

"Are you serious?" Magda groaned, shifting her seething gaze toward June. "Don't tell me you called him to come here before you even mentioned it to me."

"I had to," June admitted, his voice low. "I can't pretend I didn't have a feeling about this guy, too, bumping into us like this on the street."

"But why call Helmer?" Magda asked. "Why not take me home yourself? I'm not some ob—"

"Sorry to interrupt," Helmer said, stepping in, his arm immediately arching behind Magda's back. He kissed her cheek, then glanced at June. "Thank you for calling. What was the trouble?"

"There was no trouble," Magda fussed, yanking away from Helmer's embrace. "I don't know why you're so obsessed, keeping tabs on where I go—"

"Because it's dangerous out here," Helmer replied, swiftly.

"It's not like you have anything to hide," she added, her voice rising. "So, stop acting like you're trying to shield me from a mob or something."

"It's Chicago we're talking about," Helmer pointed out, his tone firm.

"I know, Helmer," Magda scoffed, her eyes flashing. "I grew up here.

I know this city."

"No," Helmer insisted, taking a step closer, his gaze steady. "You may know some parts of Chicago, but not the city the way I do."

"Anyway," Magda said, her grip tightening around the dried rose, her gaze fixed on it as if it were the only thing anchoring her to reality. "You're not the only one going insane here."

"What do you mean?" Helmer asked, shifting his gaze toward June, who was silently scanning the street. "Something's happening?"

"No," June replied, feeling a knot form in his stomach. "We can go." June watched Magda's eyes dart from the rose to the street, her mind clearly racing with thoughts she wasn't sharing. June's jaw tightened, and he instinctively took a step closer, positioning himself between her and the bustling street, as if shielding her from something unseen.

"Are you guys sure everything's okay?" Helmer asked, noticing how June's hand hovered near Magda's arm, as though prepared to pull her back at any moment.

"Y-yeah," June stammered, his voice tight. "We're good."

"All right," Helmer said, reluctantly proceeding to hold the door for Magda. As he closed it behind her, June turned back toward him, his muscles tensing.

"You said you wanted me to come over, right? For the party?" June asked, his voice steady, though his mind was still racing.

"Of course," Helmer replied. "You must be there. But seriously, what's going on? You look stressed."

June swallowed hard; his throat dried. The bizarre turn of events clung to him like a shadow, a nagging reminder of how fragile their situation was. He knew Magda wasn't losing her mind; the circumstances felt undeniably strange. "Hm… Nothing. Honestly, it's nothing."

Yet, he couldn't shake the nagging thought that Magda was still entwined in her grief for Richard. He watched her often—how she clung to memories, how her eyes would drift off, lost in the past. This rose felt like another piece of him, a tangible reminder she couldn't let go of. And yet, June couldn't understand why she remained so obsessed with a dead man—a ghost she wouldn't let rest.

"Okay," Helmer said, still watching him closely. "But if something's up, let me know."

June nodded. "I will." He got into the backseat, directly behind Helmer, his eyes flicking over Magda as she clutched the dried rose. June leaned forward slightly, angling his body toward hers. His hands moved, but hesitant to reach out to hers. Helmer could pick up on it, and ruin Magda's cover.

"So, June, how did the day go?" asked Helmer as he stopped at the yellow light, enjoying the slow traffic since it meant enjoying it with Magda.

"It was good, man," June replied, "Interesting, though."

He noticed Magda still tracing her fingers over the edges of the rose absentmindedly. He could ask if she was okay, or better yet, pull the rose away from her, afraid that it was fueling her turmoil. But no— again, it was better to stay quiet.

"You won't regret stopping by the house. It'll be a fun day," said Helmer, as he glanced at his phone, scanning through the popped-up notification. He had to be home quickly, and he purposely took the day off for it. Of course, there was him needing a break from the office too, since Sonia being mad at him and all the chaotic controversies made his anxiety reach its peak.

"Why do I feel like something nice is about to happen?" June said, reading the excitement on Helmer's face.

"Let's wait and see." Helmer put on a jazz playing, knowing Magda liked the genre. He reached for her hand and brought it to his lips. "You're so beautiful."

She looked at him, her face gradually softening like a canvas being painted with warmer colors. A smile broke through, and she exhaled deeply. "Thank you."

Helmer felt the slight stiffness in her body as he rested his hand on her lap, his thumb gently brushing against her. At first, she didn't react, her gaze still distant, lost in the rose she held. But gradually, he noticed the way her shoulders softened, her breath easing.

They sat in silence for a while, admiring the slow drops of rain running upwards on the windshield, pushed by gravity. That was like a breath of fresh air, as June couldn't take the tiring silence inside the car any longer. He hummed a soft tune under his breath, although he was not a fan of jazz. It wasn't long before Magda joined in, her voice quiet but steady, as if testing the waters of her own calm. Before they knew it, they were laughing together, their voices mingling with the rain as it trickled upwards on the windshield, pushed by gravity. The karaoke went on and on until they reached the house.

***

Helmer got out of the car and moved ahead of Magda and June, leaving them midway to the gate. An unsettling quiet fell over them as June stepped through the entrance. The guards, unusually attentive, delayed him, asking questions they'd never posed before since he was a regular visitor. Magda, wondering what was happening, stayed there insisting to the guards that June was her cousin and ordering them to let him in. "I can't believe it," fussed Magda. "Helmer could've at least stayed here to tell security that it was a mistake. They should've never given you any issues coming in."

Grasping June's hand, she surged through the entrance, leading him into the foyer. They both stopped short, their eyes widening in awe.

"Happy anniversary!" shouted the staff personnel holding a huge banner of red heart balloons, their feet surrounded by wrapped gifts and bags. The foyer was surrounded by cardboard hearts and pictures of Helmer and Magda, including some portraits from their wedding. Candles led to the staircase, and Mr. Hens held a bouquet along with a cutlery tray, covered to add mystery.

Helmer walked to Magda and kissed her. "Happy anniversary." He gestured at Mr. Hens to come forward and removed the cover, exposing the ring box on the cutlery tray. The lights in the room reflected on the ruby stone and diamond studs around it. Showering her with diamonds was a habit, but that ring was special. The stone was, and the occasion it was given. There wasn't a time he could've been happier than this one, knowing that they would finally be a complete family, soon with a child of his own.

Helmer took the ring and Magda's hand. "I know today marks 16 years of marriage, and I had been angry at myself for not appreciating you enough." He kissed Magda's knuckles and then drew closer to her. "We got married at the court and I failed to give you a proper wedding. We didn't even have an enjoyable honeymoon after we said our vows because I went straight to Paris…"

"Helmer, it's okay," mouthed Magda, stroking Helmer's cheeks, feeling every word. She didn't want him to blame himself, for she had her own fallouts in their marriage, which he didn't even know about.

"No," Helmer resumed, "I abandoned you. I left for almost a year. I have no excuse. But now, I want to make it up to you. I've been saving to give you the greatest wedding of all time. And that's why I have to properly ask again…" Helmer knelt, taking the ring from Mr. Hens. "Magda Brooks Dupris, would you marry me again, committing to living an eternity with me despite my gregarious snores at night?"

Magda's smile faded, knowing she had something to tell Helmer. And the pressure was heavier since he had said it in front of everyone. Now, she was expected to carry their very first child soon, and that was a possibility for things to get either better or worse for their marriage. Seeing his worried face with her delaying answer, Magda hopped and nodded excitedly. "Of course, I'd marry you a million times over and over again, and I can't wait for us to plan—"

Helmer cut Magda's words short with a kiss and put the huge ruby stone on her finger. Everybody clapped, and each member of the personnel gave her a single rose and then the bouquet. But the experience with the dried rose prior to coming home reminded her of the man, though Magda asked for the flowers to be taken upstairs and placed in Meg's bedroom.

Magda's eyes kept roaming around for the sight of her daughter, her heart growing faint with the assumption that she wasn't present. "She's upstairs, helping Gladice to finish setting up the dinner. I told you I'd make it up to you for missing it last time."

"Thank you, and happy anniversary. All these gifts are for me?" she asked.

"Yes, and I also had something for June," Helmer replied, turning toward June to shake his hand. He asked one of the personnel to bring forward a box and remove the ribbons from it.

"This beer is from Haiti, where my dad's from," Helmer said, handing the box to June. "I had someone import it from there. It's prestige, the best beer you'll ever have. Happy second anniversary to your business."

"Man, you didn't have to," said June, astonished by the surprise. "You deserve it. Your bar is so well known, You're literally the spotlight of town," praised Helmer, bracing an arm around June's neck. "It's not easy to run a business and be so successful within two years." "I'm-I'm flattered. I don't really know what to say, man. Thank you." "Just accept the gift," teased Magda, urging June to open the box.

"My pleasure," Helmer replied, patting June's shoulder. "Now, you may all go upstairs to the ballroom for the party. I'll go ahead and check a few things out so there are no interruptions with work."

Magda reached for his arm and tiptoed for a kiss. "Thank you again for making the day so special."

"You're welcome," Helmer smiled. "Soon, we can plan our wedding together. It'll be the most beautiful wedding in the entire world. I'll make sure of it."

"I hope so." Magda kissed him again and allowed him to dismiss himself. Then she pressured June to open the box, excited to taste that special flavor Helmer was talking about. June allowed her to unwrap the bottle, only to find an unexpected present. A rose, but with a clear note this time. Magda looked up at June in horror and slowly took the rose out of the box.

June snatched the box from her and noticed a little scroll at the bottom. It was a note. He took it and read: "Hunted."

"Dried rose," Magda murmured. "What?"

"June…" Magda backed away, letting the flower slip from her fingers, its thorny stem scratching against her palm. "I am the hunted rose."

The words hung between them like a heavy fog. Magda's breath quickened, each inhale sharp and shallow. Images of her past loomed large, closing in on her like a relentless predator. She felt exposed, as if this rose was not just a gift but a sinister reminder of her darkest fears. The thought that someone might be watching, waiting, sent chills crawling down her spine.

Magda's mind spiraled into a haunting echo of memories—the guilt that had settled in her heart like a weight she could never cast off. She could almost feel the presence of that unknown figure lurking in the shadows, relentless and unforgiving. Who hunts a hunter?

"What if he's still out there?" Magda thought, her gaze darting around the room, searching for an unseen threat.

"Magda, there's no one here," June said, his fingers tightening as though trying to anchor her in place.

The room felt smaller, suffocating, each corner casting a long shadow that seemed to reach for her. Magda could almost hear something;

perhaps a faint rustling, the whisper of danger, or a chilling reminder that she was never truly safe.

"He's here. He's watching me," Magda whispered, her voice cracking into a whimper.

CHAPTER 10

Secret Admirer

Richard and Magda agreed to meet in his tiny house near the woods since Richard couldn't afford to live in the city. He was an ordinary guy, not as well-spoken, and definitely not Ms. Allimair's favorite. He wasn't welcome in the Brooks family, though he thought it was best to keep his relationship with Magda in the shadows. That was the problem from the beginning. "You didn't have to," said Magda, welcomed by a huge bouquet of roses. Red. The charming and taunting color. She loved it. "These probably cost you a fortune."

"You're worth it," Richard said, gesturing at Magda to join him on the couch. He placed a wooden bowl of popcorn on the coffee table, which could barely stand on its own.

"Wait!" said Magda, securing the bowl on her lap instead. She wanted to laugh, but she didn't want to risk ruining the moment or making him feel more insecure about his place. It was almost empty inside, the paint on the walls needing a fresh layer, and a retro TV that didn't have any sort of advanced features.

"It's comfortable," reassured Magda, seeing the uneasy expression in Richard's eyes. She scooted down and placed one hand on his chest, knowing he had a few things on his mind.

"I'll buy you a house one day," he said, rubbing his hands and facing down. He couldn't look at her, knowing that he couldn't offer everything she wanted. What was worst of it all, Magda had told him about her father months ago, which increased the pressure to improve his finances one way or another.

"How is Mr. Brooks holding up?"

The light left Magda's eyes, and she was hesitant to give a response. "He's…hanging in there, working hard," Magda replied. "But his health is deteriorating; I'm not sure yet how it will go months from now."

"Do you know why?" asked Richard, knowing how much Mr. Brooks meant to Magda.

"He hasn't told me anything."

Richard stood and walked to the bunk bed he had from the corner of the room. He lifted the mattress and grabbed an envelope from underneath, then handed it to her.

"What's that?" Magda asked. "You know what it is."

Magda opened the envelope, her eyes gleaming at the sum. It was the first time she'd seen such a heavy amount of money in her life, and she looked concerned, wondering how Richard could've got it.

"Richard, are these your savings? If so, I–I can't accept it…"

"Trust me, it's fine," he interrupted, smiling and stroking her cheeks. "I was saving it to help your father. I will earn more this week since I got more orders coming in. I met a guy who was kind enough to help my art get exposure. Since then, I have been selling my sculptures."

He uncovered a piece of art he had by the TV stand. It was a bare figure of her, her hair shaped like a flower. The white-painted piece accurately presented her porcelain skin. Richard waited for Magda's reaction, her chest tightening just at the thought that she might not be impressed.

"Is that really me?" Magda asked in awe, bending over and touching the art piece, letting out a few giggles. "Richard, this is beautiful. I-I don't know what to say."

"And I carved these stones yesterday," continued Richard, showing her more of his art pieces. His heart indulged in the moment, knowing he'd made her smile. "Aren't they great?"

"Richard..."

"Maggie, no need to talk me out of it. Your mom hates my guts; I understand. She probably won't ever accept me or my help, but I respect Mr. Brooks. Giving my support for his health is the least I can do. And I have to build the bridge if I need to reach him to ask for your hand one day."

"I agree, but I'm worried about you. You need that money."

"Not as much anymore. I told you I started selling my sculptures, and I am planning to paint more, so I can extend my portfolio."

"You should teach me your tricks, so I can be as amazing as you one day."

"I will, I promise. You'll be a great painter, better than me."

Magda cupped the side of his face and pecked a kiss on his nose and lips. She grabbed one piece of rose from her bouquet and pushed it behind his ear to tease him. Richard chuckled and removed the flower, amused yet disgusted.

"Now I look like I'm from a romance-drama. I hate it."

"And why is that? I thought some men loved flowers. My dad does."

"I already have a real rose." He kissed her hand. "No need for extra ones."

***

The memory of Richard slipped away, leaving a chill in its wake. Magda picked up the dried rose again, her knuckles whitening as she stared at it. June noticed her sudden stillness, also caught up in that nightmare—an unseen stalker turning his cousin's world upside down.

"Magda," he said, stepping closer, his voice low.

Magda flinched at the sound, her eyes darting around the room as if shadows held hidden dangers.

"Are you okay?" June asked, his hand slightly reaching out for hers. But Magda's silence deepened, creating a hollow pit in June's stomach. "You're scaring me. Magda. There's no one here with us."

"How do you know?" she blurted out, pulling away from him. "I just told you about that night we were together. He called me a rose. He always called me his rose, June."

"I don't under—"

"What if... What if it's him? What if it's—"

"Richard?" June interrupted, raising his arms toward the ceiling. "So, what you're saying is that Richard's ghost sent you a bouquet of roses, just like the ones he gave you the night you were at his house?"

"You're not understanding. I'm saying that I received a bouquet weeks ago. They're all dried up, as you can see, but it can't be a coincidence that I keep receiving them. Someone out there wants to hunt me down."

"And why would that be? You didn't kill him."

Magda paused, reliving the moment she had last seen Richard. He was in agony, screaming her name. His voice lived inside her head; she heard it even through her dreams. It was a lot for one to bear, especially for Magda, who had to keep this secret even from June, the person she could trust with her life. She was afraid of telling him what truly happened.

"Right?" Emphasized June, confident to make a point.

"Of course, I didn't," Magda replied, hesitantly shaking her head. "You know what you should do?" June said, sitting Magda down and massaging her shoulders. He felt the tension and pain in her voice and the shivers spiking up through her arms. "You need to go to his grave and make peace with it."

Magda hopped from the stool, shaken up by June's suggestion. She had never stepped foot in a cemetery ever since her father died. For Richard, going there and standing over his grave was like challenging God himself. What if she was finally punished for her sins? What if a bolt of lightning lost its way and purposely hit her? Or her demons followed her, exposing the darkness she tried to hide for so long? There were lots at play, especially her peace. Anyway, for such a person, peace was only a dream.

"I-I can't." Magda gasped, tramping around the painting room. She looked to her left; there stood a collection of dried roses and old portraits of Richard. The paintings were black and white, almost haunting, as if they were all tributes to him. She had never taken anyone to this room, keeping it hidden, away from prying eyes that might unearth what she had buried deep for a decade if not longer. This room was her sanctuary and prison, a taunting place of torment—where she could mourn Richard, the ghost she could never forget. So much that Magda held onto him tighter than she held onto her marriage itself.

"You need to," June insisted. "I can't continue watching you being haunted by this guy. He's gone, and if you refuse, I'll have to tell Helmer so you can get some help."

Magda let out a snort from disbelief. "So, you think I'm crazy?" "No, I think you're tormented, and it must stop. Have you tried to see a therapist?"

"Are you serious?"

"I don't know," shrugged June. "Isn't Helmer in therapy? You could use his doctor—"

"Shut up, June," Magda said, realizing her point not making it through. She went over the portrait collections and piled them into a box along with the roses. She placed all of them in the closet and sat back on the stool, knowing her day was going to be a hell of a struggle to focus on her marriage anniversary.

Magda wanted to enjoy the moment and be there with her husband. But how could she explain that her heart was too filled with agony over another man? Magda knew she could never fully escape Richard. It wasn't just the memories that lingered or the dried rose she kept hidden away; it was something deeper, more insidious, binding her to him. Magda wondered if that was what guilt was supposed to feel like. But it couldn't be just guilt; there was also rage simmering within her soul, whenever she thought of him.

"People are in the ballroom waiting for us," reminded June, hoping he'd make Magda leave, since she kept glancing at the closet, tempted to go and take a second look at the roses. "Besides, what if it's a secret admirer? Some random dude who got a crush on you and tried to play with your head?"

"No, it can't be." Magda sighed. "The day Richard and I broke up, he gave me a bouquet. I mean…when he decided to end our relationship. I never wanted to let him go, even though being together seemed impossible. But he never explained why he made that decision. He only sent that stupid letter and a bouquet. What was I supposed to do with a bouquet, June? What were those roses supposed to bring me?" Magda said, her eyes mirrored a storm, releasing streams of turbulent tears.

There were types of sorrows that could never leave one's soul, and Magda knew what that was like more than anyone. That lingering sorrow emerged in her heart and left no way for it to stay afloat. Magda was so accustomed to the pain in her soul—the anguish had made her life its home.

"I know it was cruel on his part," June empathized, sitting on a stool across from his cousin. "But I am not sure how you can forgive a dead person. You must find a way to do it for your own well-being."

"I don't want to forgive him," she replied, her voice steady. "He hurt me."

When Magda became pregnant, she was hoping that Richard would still follow through with their plan to leave the country and he'd marry her. He added colors to her life and everything she knew. He was her all, her happiness, and the main reason to look forward to living every day. However, that day, Richard sent a letter where he conveyed his goodbyes. He was going to leave the country without her, and Magda couldn't take it. It was such a betrayal and a stab in the heart that she couldn't be sane after that. Anyone going through such heartache knows the madness it's caused and the chaos it'd bring on. He did more harm to her heart than anyone else ever could, and for that, he became a scar in her memories, a wound that had no existent recovery.

Magda sat there in the painting room, her gaze fixed on the worn canvas in front of her. The soft strokes she'd once made now blurred together, lifeless and distant, like memories of Richard she couldn't fully hold on to—but couldn't let go of either. She ran her fingers along the edge of the canvas, her touch trembling, as if expecting to feel him in the rough texture beneath her hand.

How could someone she'd once loved so completely leave her with such emptiness? She could still hear his voice, soft but taunting, as if the walls of this room held onto every word he'd ever said.

But the sweetness of his memory twisted with each passing second. Did Richard deserve what happened to him? That question circled Magda's mind, though she never spoke it aloud. Maybe. Maybe not. But every time she tried to make sense of it, something told her that what was done to him had simply balanced the scales.

"Helmer is waiting for us. We must head back to the party," June reminded, his voice drifting in and out, a distant murmur that barely registered.

Magda wanted to respond, to tell him everything was fine, but the words stayed trapped on the tip of her tongue. How could she celebrate on a night when both her present and future felt threatened? And now her marriage—how could it survive with this stalker lurking in the shadows?

***

Helmer was there in the ballroom, helping Meg and Gladice finish setting up. He instructed them to keep the best part of the surprise for last, wanting to make Magda's night special. There were sets of fireworks and lanterns to shoot up to the air and a jazz musical show to welcome her inside the ballroom when she'd walked in. The personnel were busy doing touch-ups, so everything was perfect, as Helmer demanded.

"Tann mwen, what's with the tie? It's crooked!" said Gladice, approaching to fix Helmer up. "You have to look good, ti cheri."

"With the amount of Creole I've heard growing up, I'm surprised I still can't speak it," Helmer said, lifting Gladice's hand to his cheek.

"One day, son. One day," Gladice replied, rubbing his cheek gently, seeing how much he was blushing. He couldn't wait to show Magda the surprises of the night.

Helmer looked over to the ballroom entrance, wondering what might be delaying her arrival. He rushed toward the door, stopped by a 6-year-old boy who jumped at him for a hug.

"Mr. Helms!" shouted the boy, his huge gap showing as he smiled.

"Hello, little man," said Helmer, carrying the boy inside the ballroom, assuming that Jonathan, his bodyguard, was a few steps closer. "How are you doing, champ?"

"I am great," the boy replied, playing with Helmer's tie. "Mom is here, by the way, probably planning to hide the candies from me."

"If that's so, I'll ask your dad to give you some. That will be our little secret. Mom won't know a thing."

Jonathan walked in, his face showing annoyance at his son, who dirtied Helmer's shirt when he jumped at him. He rushed over, took the boy off Helmer, and stepped back. "I'm sorry, Boss. I told him not to do that."

"C'mon! You know we're family here," Helmer said, bumping Jonathan's shoulder. "You've been working here for a decade now."

Helmer had hired Jonathan as a bodyguard, valuing the safety of his family. Some people thought his ways of protection were extreme. No one knew why he wanted to make sure his house was surrounded by surveillance, nor why he never let his family go anywhere too far from his sight. But who knows? Maybe he was hiding from someone or something bigger than him. Who would ever dare to ask anyway? He was not an open book; neither did he give way to having conversations about how he grew up and his deepest fears.

"That's right," added a woman, stopping at the entrance door and caressing her huge baby bump. Her face looked worn out as if she didn't want to be there.

Helmer approached and placed both hands on the woman's belly. He couldn't help it, even though he wondered if it was appropriate to do so.

"Oh, wifey is here," Jonathan said, seeing his wife greeting Helmer with a side hug. "I insisted for her to join the party. She's been confining herself lately."

"Blame the baby," replied the woman. "This little man takes up all my energy. My back hurts like hell. It's not easy, I tell you."

"How many months already?" asked Helmer, holding Jonathan's wife's belly.

"Eight and a half," the woman replied, her cheeks finally shaping into a smile. She looked down at her bump and flinched, then giggled. "I just felt a kick. He must like you."

"I like him too already," Helmer said, excited by the continuous kicks and experiencing the joy of it. Parenthood, the miracle of feeling a tiny human's presence despite the walls keeping them apart—two different worlds, yet there still felt no difference.

"Soon, it'll be my turn," Helmer said, giggling to himself. "Enjoy the party and thank you for coming. I'll be back! I need to go find my wife now."

Jonathan and his wife nodded, and then Helmer left. He went out and stopped in the hall leading to the stairs and noticed Marie Lisa rushing to come to him.

"Marie? You okay?"

"Yes, I just can't find Mrs. Dupris. I think she dropped this." She handed him a bottle of tiny blue pills and dismissed herself. Helmer, curious about the pills, turned the bottle over, and read the label. A half-filled bottle of birth control pills.

CHAPTER 11

Aversion

Magda walked in, and the lights in the room dimmed away, exposing the reflections of stars from the ceiling on the marble floor. The bright light of the projector moved to where she stood, leaving her too amazed to say a word. The jazz's lead singer hit a note then the rest of the group followed, singing her favorite piece, Etta James, At Last, as Helmer approached to ask her to dance. Magda acquiesced and laced her arms around his neck, following the slow pace of the song. It was like there were only two in the room, their bodies greeting each other and their warmth interlacing, exporting them to their own world. However, Helmer's mind kept racing. He had questions or, perhaps, hoped that what he thought could be a misunderstanding. He didn't want to believe his wife could've lied to him and, worse, about something he'd wanted all his life: a baby.

"Helmer, you look distracted," said Magda, brushing her knuckles on Helmer's cheek, her eyes begging him to kiss her. She grazed her nails onto the nape of his neck, trying to bring him back to the moment.

"Magda…" he said, his tone harmonizing with the melody playing in the background. Helmer couldn't hold back his charm, although his mind was telling him to leave her standing there alone.

Candles surrounded the place, and the personnel stood on the side with fluorescent lights and tiny bouquets. The sheer curtains allowed the moonlight to steep inside, showing their shadows dancing. Magda placed her head on Helmer's chest and laced her arms around him, closing her eyes and absorbing the calm of the night. The peace found within Helmer's arms felt like heaven. She wanted to stay there, for it had been a long time since she had felt those tingles under her feet, those invisible butterflies that made their dance a fantasy. She giggled, hearing Helmer's heart racing, assuming he was just so thrilled to be there. But he was only taming the hungry beast inside of him to not eat her alive.

"Thank you," she whispered, looking up at him and smiling.

Magda tiptoed, her lips parting apart, begging for a kiss. Those buttery glossy lips of hers would tempt any man to surrender. Her eyes were inviting and enticing, withholding the power of a moissanite stone. That gaze made Helmer shiver from his very bones, and it was a matter of time for him to lose all power. But he refused to let himself be distracted from the taunting questions that were twisting his mind and turning him insane.

"Let's go to the balcony," he said, taking Magda's hand and walking away, aware that he had denied her invitation to kiss her. He motioned at the jazz singers to keep singing so no one suspected they were heading off to chat in private. Helmer took Magda there, his heart accelerating, anxious to find out whether his suspicions were true. Would he be able to detect or catch her in her lies?

"I'm so excited to be here with you," said Magda, brushing Helmer's shoulder to keep the wrinkles at bay. She readjusted his tie and laced her arms around his waist.

"Same," Helmer said sharply, turning his face away.

"What's wrong?" Magda said, seeing the rough look plastered onto Helmer's face. No smile, or a warm look in his eyes as earlier. "Did I do something?"

"I wouldn't know if you did," he replied, glancing down at her, his stare so cold that it could slice through her skin if she touched it.

"Why do I feel like you're upset about something?" she asked, her voice softening.

"I-I don't know," Helmer's voice wavered, his eyes darting away from hers. "But look, I got us the tickets for Paris." His fingers tightened slightly around the edge of the ticket envelope. "I thought it'd be a nice surprise... for us and your painting exposition." He paused, tapping the tickets against his palm. "I was also planning to take Meg along."

"Helmer..." whispered Magda, a laugh erupting out of her lips, "I can't believe you did that for me."

It was the first time she had planned to do an art event in another country. Besides, she was always self-conscious about her art, and she also hesitated to expose it to the world since every piece she painted was a reminder of Richard. Every trick and color science he taught her was seen in her paintings. So, there was not a day Magda would paint and not think of Richard's laughter, his piercing gaze connecting with her soul in a way not even her husband could. How does one run away from a stubborn heartbreak that purposely refuses to heal? How could someone get over a lover whose death was the only closure? Questions were hanging in the air for both Magda and Helmer, and both were afraid of those answers.

"I can't believe you got us these tickets. How many more surprises are left for the night? The party was enough," she said, pressing the tickets against her bosom. She threw a glance over Helmer's shoulder, and then a set of fireworks hurled to the sky and blew out in smoke, forming into a grand heart shape and a baby bottle, stealing the smile off her face.

"That's…"

"A baby bottle. It's silly but I thought it'd be cute," explained Helmer, turning his head toward her, his eyes filling with tears. "You-You know what? I was so looking forward to it."

A tremor ran through him, a sharp vibration settling in his chest. His heart raced, battling the thoughts he dared not to voice, fearing they would shatter the fragile moment. "Do you… I mean… I meant to ask you. Magda, do you truly want to have a baby with me? I know I put you on the spot a few minutes ago. Maybe I shouldn't have. But I really want to know. Do you want that with me?"

"Of course. With all my heart," she said, cupping his cheeks. "I had gone to see a doctor before I agreed to. I'm excited about it, and I am not changing my mind."

Helmer stepped back, circling, trying to make sense of what his wife said. Could he be wrong about his assumption that she was lying to him? There was no indication that would prove otherwise. There was not even a single drop of sweat on her face, no hesitation in her voice, not even one gesture that could indicate anything.

"I don't understand," Helmer mumbled, palming his face and leaning over the balcony's rail. He needed these answers fast, or he could explode any second. The risk of making the night a disaster was tremendous and gave him the haste to walk away. But could he? Would the personnel or Meg suspect that something was happening? For some reason, Helmer didn't want to make it obvious either that he was upset since, to find out the truth, one must play the game. The irony was that he knew how to play. He was great at reading through things, except he never showed it since he, too, had things hidden under the rug.

"What's wrong?" asked Magda, sliding her hands across Helmer's back. His body responded in shock from her touch, growing rigid in an instant. Her voice was like a plague clotting through his ears, leaving his mind exhausted and needing rest. "You know you can tell me anything, right? Helmer, I'm your wife."

"I know that!" he spat, bolting out of her embrace. Realizing that he had raised his voice, he threw a glance inside and noticed Meg looking at them. His head dropped, knowing that he couldn't hide his frustration, not even from his daughter, for the sake of the event. Helmer wanted everything to be perfect, but his favorite little person walked out of the ballroom, which left his heart in a towering loop of exasperation. "I'm sorry for snapping at you."

"Helmer, it's ok," replied Magda, showing empathy, unaware she wasn't helping by still standing there. "You can tell me the truth. Is it work? You seem so stressed..."

"Stop touching me, please," he said, his voice rising slightly. "What do you mean? I'm trying to help—"

"I said don't touch me!" he yelled, immediately regretting it, seeing the fear in her eyes and hearing the ballroom go quiet.

The jazz singers flinched, and the personnel turned their heads away, avoiding Helmer's frantic gaze. He couldn't go back to ignoring his feelings and acting as if nothing was happening. What troubled him was Magda's unawareness about what he could be so upset about. She couldn't even guess about anything besides work.

"I'm confused," Magda said, awkwardly gesturing at the singers to resume the party. She forced a smile, wondering if Meg was still in the ballroom.

"She left," Helmer said. "What?"

"Meg left."

"That's probably because she sees her father upset, blowing off steam, and not talking."

"I need a drink," he said. "Excuse me."

Helmer walked back into the ballroom, motioning at Mr. Hens to bring him a glass of rum. He needed something strong to wash the steam off and perhaps something to loosen his nerves.

Helmer grew up in a violent household; there were risks for him to adopt the same patterns. He didn't want to, just like many other kids who did not choose to end up being on drugs, drop out of school, and end up on the streets. Some of those things were forced onto him. Maybe he didn't turn to drugs to cope with his abusive father, but he did turn to some people to save him from Mr. Jean. And those people had a special mission to bring out the worst in anyone. One could not remain innocent, nor a peaceful soul being trapped in such a situation.

"Boss, do you have a minute?" said Jonathan, walking toward Helmer.

"Of course," Helmer replied, grateful that someone was there to bring his focus to something else. The liquor warmed him up, stopping his anxiety from overpowering him. He was silently fighting, but his main issue was the anger he had tried to tame for years. He didn't want to allow another relapse, nor ever go back to his Doctor, Elvino, the man the southside of Chicago worshiped.

"I wanted to bring something to your attention," Jonathan resumed. "I checked the security cameras the other day, and I noticed something strange."

"Strange as?"

"I saw someone deliver a bouquet of roses... I don't remember exactly when, but they were delivered to your wife—"

"And?" urged Helmer, gripping his glass, afraid he might throw it. Jonathan took a post-it from his vest pocket and handed it to Helmer. "When the mailman came and gave the rose to one of the guys, he dropped this note, so I picked it up, assuming it was meant for Mrs.

Dupris. Then I saw my name on it." "Your name?"

"Yes." Jonathan nodded. "I don't know if it was sent by someone who's playing a trick or who knows me personally..."

Helmer took the post-it, reading each word carefully. But the warning didn't seem to make sense. Would it be about his wife? And who would dare send such a daring note? Worse, flowers to his wife, which she has never mentioned anything about.

She's beautiful, but her thorns are deadly. Careful!

Warn your boss.

"Would someone you know send this?" Jonathan questioned.

"I'd say it's Bryant, but I doubt it's him. We're not on good terms right now, and Sonie would never say something like that." Helmer sighted Mr. Hens and requested another glass of liquor. His blood was boiling. He didn't know whether it was the haunting thought that his wife could be lying or that another man was out there trying to warn him about something. Could it be a warning about another lie? Could it be a secret admirer? Or perhaps, someone who knew his wife better than he ever has. Besides, the jealousy of a man was also dreadful and often deadly. Helmer hoped that his doubts would not end up pushing him to cross a line he could never come back from. He reached for a third shot, then another, before resuming the conversation. He was taking many things in, and the noises from the party became torture. He needed silence and a safe place to process his emotions, maybe a book or go to Gladice for advice. He wasn't sure what would be right at the moment; however, stopping the party sounded convenient. He wondered how long he could last pretending. Hopefully, long enough to make it to the end of the night.

"You know what? Leave the note with me and run the cameras to see who delivered the flowers."

"On it, Boss." Jonathan dismissed himself and went back to spend time with his family, enjoying the party dance. Everyone followed his steps, seeing him being the highlight of the night. Each house personnel got themselves a partner, which was perfect to divert attention from the tension between Helmer and Magda.

Helmer watched Jonathan interact and dance with his son. Hearing their laughter cracked his heart apart, leaving a profound tear—too huge to be healed with words. He reached for another shot, but the tray got pushed away from him.

"You had enough drinks," someone said.

"Oh my God," he groaned, realizing it was Magda trying to come to his rescue. Helmer moved past her and called Mr. Hens for a glass. He stretched his hand out from impatience and grabbed the bottle. "Please, move and let me go through."

"I am not moving anywhere," Magda said, her voice firm and apathetic. "You need to speak to me. Are you hiding something?"

"Hiding?" Helmer snorted. "I don't know how you manage to do this, Magda. I've never seen someone with so much audacity and lack of decency in my entire life."

"What did you just say to me?" Magda asked, confirming that her ears weren't playing tricks on her. There was no way her husband had said that; whether it was the drinks talking or him deliberately crossing a line. "Let me remind you, this is our marriage anniversary. Our daughter is upstairs, locking herself in her room after seeing us arguing. Does that ring a bell to get it together or not?"

Hearing about Meg being in her room and not even able to enjoy the party, Helmer gave the bottle back to Mr. Hens and walked away, heading to the ballroom's exit. No way, he had just walked away while Magda was still talking to him.

"What in the world is happening to him today? He was fine an hour ago," said Magda, glancing at Mr. Hens to see if he'd have any hints or answers. But he shrugged and dismissed himself from the spousal quarrel before he got dragged in. Besides, Magda wanted to inquire about the box with the roses from earlier and find out who imported it. From where, who? What friend, company, and if that box was a plan of her stalker. And June was too busy interacting with Marie Lisa to notice a thing.

"Mrs. Dupris, it's time for the other surprise," Gladice said while motioning at the girls to put a blindfold on her.

"Wait, what's happening?"

They took Magda's hand and led her out of the ballroom to the front of the mansion. It was the last surprise of the night and the best, just as Helmer wanted. The servants removed the blindfold from Magda's eyes, and there stood a Bugatti red car with a ribbon around it in front of her.

Mr. Hens approached and handed Magda a tiny box with the car keys, dazzling in the moonlight. "Is that…"

"Yes, ma'am," replied Mr. Hens, drawing Magda's attention to the ribbon from the car. There was her name on it, and a signature underneath. "Mr. Helmer made sure to keep it for last. He signed it right before you walked in."

Hearing those words left Magda's heart in absolute dismay. How could she do such a thing to her husband, who put so much effort into making her happy? After deliberately telling her he was happy that she finally changed her mind to have a child with him? Either way, she felt that it was the best way to go about things. How could she tell him she didn't want to after making a promise to him? Maybe she was trying to give him hope to fight his depression, something to keep him going. But at what costs? How would she get out of it if she ever told him why?

Magda couldn't even understand the reason for resisting the idea of being a mother again, whether it was her traumatic experience going through her pregnancy with Meg and her fights with Allimair. Or whether she simply didn't feel the desire to bear the fruit of her husband's seeds.

"I'll be right back," she told the servants, running back inside to find Helmer. She tramped up the stairs and went to their bedroom. The door was locked, which hit her with a violent wave of panic. "Helmer? Open up. You're acting strange. Are you okay?"

Magda pounded on the door, yet there was no response. She insisted, shouting his name, refusing to leave. Then she heard a sound, the door slowly unlocking. Magda walked in, finding Helmer bare-chested, standing in his boxers with a dismissive posture. Magda stepped closer and slowly slid her hand over his chest. Feeling his heart pounding, she soothed his arms and glued up against his skin. She knew how to calm him down, but it wasn't certain that her tricks would work this time.

"What's wrong, Helmer? The party is downstairs, and you're locked up in here alone. Talk to me!"

"I need to rest," he groaned. "I have work early tomorrow."

"I can help," offered Magda, digging her fingers into the crack of his back.

"Magda," he whispered, feeling the shivers and the blazing urge to reach for her waist. His eyes wandered and stopped track on her bosoms, hesitant to give in. He leaned in, his lips tempted to touch hers, and his body contracted from all the anger he'd stored. Helmer allowed his hands to move up Magda's dress, pulling her closer. She closed her eyes, expecting him to kiss her. Helmer lifted her but took her out of the room and shut the door.

Magda bolted back into the room. "What is wrong with you?" "Magda, honestly, you need to leave," warned Helmer, pained by the sight of her.

"I'm not moving!" Magda said, moving up to his space, not letting him walk away. She insisted, refusing to leave, unable to make him stay still. Feeling hopeless to make him talk, she pushed him. Realizing what she had done, her heart dropped, seeing the fury in Helmer's eyes. "I'm sorry," apologized Magda as Helmer stared at her. "But please, talk to me. It doesn't make any sense. You have gifted me my dream car and tickets for Paris. Then you start acting like a child."

The more words that came out of her mouth made Helmer wish for peace. He would've thrown himself down a window if there was one in sight. Hearing her, seeing her, put his soul in a taunting martyr. He didn't want to lose control, but it was almost getting there. Helmer walked away and headed to the bathroom to take some air. He was suffocating from all that pressure and resistance to not let the ugly side of him come out.

"Helmer," Magda said, following him to the bathroom. "Tell me what's going on. What did I do? For God's sake, stop being such a—"

"Stop! I said stop!" Helmer roared, his arm swinging toward Magda's face. His hand caught her arm, the grip tight, almost crushing.

"Helmer, wait. Please…" cried Magda, her skin burning beneath his fingers, and feeling the strength in his grasp. "You're hurting me, let go." Magda searched for a trace of the man she knew, but in front of her stood a wild beast showing no mercy at the sight of its prey. Helmer's once mesmerizing eyes had hardened into something unrecognizable, cold and distant. Her breath spiraled as his hands clamped down on her shoulders, the pressure growing with every heartbeat.

"Helmer, please, I'm begging you—" Magda squeezed her eyes shut, her muscles tensing, as his grip tightened, sinking into her skin. She could feel the raw force behind it, like he might break her if he pushed just a little harder.

CHAPTER 12

Triggers

It was the third time the copy machine had stopped working, and somebody had reported a lack of supplies. Due to the rising complaints, Sonia has voted for a new rule that all codes be revoked, and two employees be placed in charge of the copy room. Each person from the office would need to submit a copy request for the week before when it's needed, so the maintenance team wouldn't have to come on a weekly basis to fix the machines.

"It's nonsensical. All this," said one of the maintenance workers. "The machines are old, rules or not, they'll break anyway."

"Whether they'll break or not, you guys don't have to come for the next two weeks," Sonia riposted. "I want to test this new system at hand; then, if anything comes up, I'll call you."

"I was only suggesting that you replace the machines," suggested one of the men from the team. "What's a better way to make sure this new system works than starting everything anew?"

"I said they won't be replaced until I say so," Sonia emphasized, placing a notice on the copy room's door so no one walked in. It was a busy day, with new rules and reinforcements, including meetings with the personnel. Of course, where there are rules, there would also be complaints and enemies made.

"No need to get angry," the man said in a sarcastic tone. "We weren't trying to overstep."

"Maybe you are!" intervened Bryant, stepping beside Sonia and glaring at the men. "She said what she said. We'll call when we need your services again. As for now, we're testing this new strategy."

The men glared at him, grabbed their toolbox and gloves, and moved across the lobby. "Hopefully, we don't get too busy when you call. Have a great day."

Sonia took a pack of copy paper and dropped it down the desk in the corner of the room. She placed both hands on her hips, gathering her thoughts before unleashing her frustration. "Why did you do that?"

"Do what?" asked Bryant, genuinely trying to connect the dots. "Intervene?" Sonia replied. "Why did you have to defend me?"

"Because that's what we do," he replied, shrugging but wondering if he had said the right thing. "We got each other's back. We're a team." "I am not angry, Bryant," she said, her voice steady yet taut, like a wire ready to snap. She stepped closer, invading his space, her seething glare fixed on him. "I was just trying to make a point. I'm not incompetent. I don't know why everyone is treating me like an amateur. I was… just trying to keep the company together and everyone on task." "I know that," reassured Bryant, realizing she needed the space to vent.

"And I definitely don't need saving," Sonia snapped, crossing one arm tightly over her chest as if trying to shield herself. Her fingers pressed into her skin, a silent attempt to steady her heart in Bryant's presence. He wasn't her boyfriend anymore—just a coworker, a role they hadn't played in a long time.

"Of course you don't. I was trying to help, not because you couldn't handle things on your own," Bryant said, raising his hands in a placating gesture. "I just thought—"

"Then stop!" spat Sonia, the heat between them crackling and thickening the air. "I wouldn't want anyone to think I earned my place here because of your sympathy or Helmer's protection. I am okay. I don't need it."

"I get it," Bryant said, nodding, though the tension in his shoulders remained. "You're upset at me, at Nina, at Helmer, and at the fact that we're working so close together. You feel trapped—"

"I do feel trapped!" Sonia yelled, her voice starting strong but shattering like thin glass. "You're constantly in my face, and then there's Nina..." she paused, her breath catching in her throat, suffocating her. "I-I can't stop the thoughts swirling in my head—of you touching and kissing her while we were together..."

"Baby—"

"No!" She said, her finger pointed at his face. "You can be so selfish. There are no words for what you've done. You're so calm about it, I don't even think you care enough."

"That's what you think?" Bryant's voice softened, smoothing like honey. "Sonia, I can't imagine my life without you in it, and you're right.

I-I don't have the words. I don't know how to show you that I've repented for what I did. But I do know that what I feel for you will never change." He took a step forward. She stepped back. But Bryant didn't stop.

He kept closing the gap, his gaze locked on hers, until there was no space left between them.

"Each breath coming out of my lungs reminds me how much I need you," he whispered, his voice low and pleading. "I belong to you, flesh and bones. Please, forgive me."

"You hurt me," Sonia said, her voice breaking. Her eyes gave in to the tears she held back all the time hiding them. She didn't need to anymore. There was no point. She stayed in place, melting under the natural heat coming from his body, the chance of resisting his demand growing faint every second.

"No, you're wrong," Bryant whispered, nuzzling her face, leaning in close to get in contact with her lips. "I hurt myself."

"You?" sniffled Sonia, her lips fully exposed to his mercy.

Bryant's voice dropped to a plea. "My hands sweat when I hear you coming from afar, too eager to wrap around you. And my heart, you've trained it to love only you. I swear it can't love no other, not since I confessed its secrets to you."

"But Bryant—" Her words faltered, dissolving into silence as his hand gently rose to her face.

"Please, show mercy. I'm begging, baby. Please!" Bryant's voice wavered, his lips hovering just inches from hers, tightening as he fought to hold back. His breath became shallow, every part of him leaning in, aching to close the gap.

Sonia's gaze softened, the sharp edge of her anger slowly dulling despite her resistance. She could feel the warmth of his touch melting the wall she had so carefully built, even though every fiber of her being wanted to hold on to her anger. Her lips tingled, yearning for his, though she fought to keep them still. It was a battle—her heart pulling her toward him while her mind screamed to stay away. But the pull was as undeniable as a lightning bolt cutting through the sky. She couldn't ignore it anymore. Her lips quivered, ready to surrender to the moment, even as her mind resisted.

"I can't," she whispered, her voice barely audible. "I can't, Bryant."

Bryant's breath hitched, his body leaning in before he forced himself to stop. His lips hovered near hers, but with a heavy sigh, he slowly pulled away. "Then I won't kiss you. I won't touch you," he whispered, each word laced with restraint. It took every ounce of willpower to step back, his feet anchored to the ground, begging to stay. "But don't ask me to give up on us. That, I can't do."

Sonia's tears delayed him from leaving as he couldn't bear the thought that he'd caused them. He didn't know whether to offer comfort or walk away. Neither option seemed to make him look worthy of redemption, but for her peace, he commanded himself to leave. He headed to the elevator, cuddling himself and swallowing the tears clogging his throat. Who would want to look weak when you're the joker of the room? He liked being the attention in the building, the jerk, the one who cracked the most inappropriate jokes at the wrong time. It was almost addictive being the bad guy. Everything seemed easy for him, but being vulnerable was never on the list.

Reaching the hall leading to Helmer's office, he passed by Nina, whose face clearly showed her disgust toward him. He smiled and still waved at her, pushing his hands into his pockets, playing it cool. Yes, he liked to play the games of not caring and living life like there was no tomorrow.

"The boss is busy," Nina said.

"Yet, you're not," Bryant replied. "It wouldn't be the case if you were doing your job. And no need to escort me; I know the way."

He walked to the office and immediately started unleashing all his frustrations on Helmer about Sonia having too much on her plate with the copy room situation. As he kept lecturing Helmer, who did not say a word the entire time, he noticed something in the room was unusual. The window had a hole, making it obvious something had been hurled through it. There was broken glass on the floor, and some of Helmer's books were thrown off the shelf.

"What happened here?" Bryant asked. "I hope you're not throwing a tantrum because of that stupid meeting."

"I want to be alone," Helmer said, staring at the painting on the wall across from his desk.

"That's why you asked Nina to tell me you're busy?"

"Please," insisted Helmer, reaching for the pill bottle on his desk. He looked at it, and a wave of anger rushed through his body. He never liked the idea of losing his composure, as it could be dangerous if not retained.

"Honestly, I'm not walking out of here until you tell me what all this is about," said Bryant, crossing his arms, patiently waiting for an answer.

"She lied," Helmer confessed. "It felt so natural for her to do so that I wonder what else she has probably lied to me about. There was no hesitation. No remorse, nothing." With all this tension and anxiety he had been feeling in the past weeks, the least he could do was to let somebody know what he was going through. He wished that'd give him some relief. Besides, he had not slept or eaten since the day he had found out about the pills.

"What?" Bryant squinted, trying to get more clarification.

"Magda lied." Helmer stretched out the pill bottle to Bryant, motioning at him to take a look at the description.

"No way! These are birth control pills," Bryant realized. "I thought you guys were trying to have a baby."

"I thought so too," Helmer said, knocking his knuckles on the desk. There was nothing else to reach for to throw across the room as he normally would do when stressed. He had already torn everything down, but nothing seemed to be enough to appease him.

"Did you try to have a conversation with her lately?" asked Bryant.

Helmer shook his head, feeling the guilt churning in his chest. "The last time I did, it didn't end well."

"Did you hit her?" Bryant questioned, knowing his best friend was never sane when angry.

"Of course not! I'd never raise my hand on her," Helmer replied. "But... I was indeed very upset."

"I can't let you keep going like this though," said Bryant worried. "You have to see Elvino. You two may have to make amends now; it's been years, and he may have his flaws, but he cares about you."

"If you say that name again, I swear to God, you'll be the one I hit next," Helmer raged. "And you should stay the hell away from him, too, for your own goddamn good."

That name brought so many painful memories that he tried to push back from his mind, but he didn't seem ready to let go. Doctor Elvino was not a simple man, nor the one anyone would associate with.

"I was only trying to help," Bryant said, pursing his lips.

"I know..." Helmer paused, hearing the cracks in his own voice, fearing they'd unravel into a sob.

"It felt good by the way, picturing me as a father for a few seconds the last time she mentioned it," resumed Helmer. "To be honest, that's what got me going all this time. Now, I have nothing to hold onto. No dream, no baby, nothing. I'm crashing, Bryant. I am crashing."

"No," Bryant said, shaking his head and pulling a chair next to Helmer's. "This won't happen on my watch. You're needed here. I need you; Sonia needs you. The company and everybody in here do. If you crash, we all crash."

"No, you said it yourself. I'm not as good as I picture myself to be."

"I was only trying to convince you the hard way," Bryant said, recalling their last argument. Even though he meant it, he never wished to see his best friend willingly giving up on life. "You were right. I can be selfish and in my head at times. But you're my brother; nothing will change that."

"I wish I were like you," said Helmer, getting up. He went near the window, looking through the hole he made. Cars drove by, and busy crowds strolled on the sidewalks in the late afternoon, but that couldn't distract him from his disturbed thoughts. He wanted to talk things out with Magda. But what if the old him crept back in? It had been years since he had relapsed. Besides, his unresolved issues with his psychologist left him feeling alone. "You don't seem to care about anything," Helmer resumed. "How do you even do it?"

Bryant's eyes flicked to the ground, staying quiet for a moment. He couldn't bring himself to admit how he had been coping—the hollow distractions, the sleepless nights. "Trust me," Bryant muttered, forcing the words out, "you don't want to be like me."

Helmer stepped back from the window, brow furrowed, studying Bryant's rigid stance. Something wasn't right, but Helmer couldn't quite pin it down. "You're okay? What's with the face?"

"I'm good, but c'mon. I'm taking you somewhere," Bryant suddenly said, motioning toward the door.

"Where are we going?" Helmer asked, his forehead creasing, every instinct telling him to be cautious.

"I'm taking you to a friend of mine. He'll make your dream come true."

"Bryant, when you don't tell me stuff, it's always when we're about to call for trouble."

"Says the depressed guy who's getting played by his wife and who's probably not getting laid."

"I understand you got a crush on me, but let's keep my sex life out of it."

"Well, about your sex life… We're about to make your 3 inches do a better job than it ever could." Bryant took Helmer's suit and handed it to him, gesturing at him to hurry. "Are you coming or not?"

They sprinted past Nina's desk and took the elevator to the lobby. Heading out, Bryant suggested that they take a taxi to their destination, leaving Helmer more perplexed about his idea. It started to get dark, which made it ideal for them not to get caught in that neighborhood. It was on the south side, deep in the ghetto. Helmer recognized that place and became restless as soon as he realized.

"Bryant, where are you taking me?" he asked.

"I told you already," Bryant replied, motioning at the taxi driver to stop. He handed him a few bucks and poked Helmer to step out with him. "We're about to do what you should've done a long time ago."

Helmer followed Bryant through the dimly lit streets, the night air dense with the smell of sweat and gasoline. They stopped in front of an old, crumbling building. Its walls were covered in layers of graffiti—angry scrawls and a chaotic blend of obscenities merging with faded artwork from years past. At the entrance, heads of tigers were painted, snarling from the walls as if warning those who dared to step inside. Chewed-up bubble gum dotted the cracked pavement, littered with cigarette butts and discarded trash.

Stepping inside, the dim lights flickered above, casting uneven shadows over the gritty, makeshift space. A fight club. Men were sprawled on benches, gulping water and dabbing at bloodied faces, freshening up before returning to the cage in the center. Blood stained the floor of the ring cage, splattered across the ropes and puddled in the corners. It seemed to call out to the fighters, urging them to summon whatever strength they had left.

Across from where the men were loudly placing their bets, a group of women lingered, their shorts cut high, revealing far more than what should be private. "Oh my God, Bryant. I'm going to kill you," Helmer muttered under his breath, doing his best to divert his eyes from the vile scenes.

The women's lacy bras barely held back their breasts as they moved between the crowd, offering liquor—cheap bottles and top-shelf alike. One of them stopped in between the benches and waved at a guy, half-shrouded in shadows, his face barely visible beneath the hood. He leaned in, his tongue trailing along the woman's bare shoulder before he slid a wad of cash into the waistband of her shorts. She gave him a slow smile and carried on, bottle in hand, eyes scanning for the next willing customer.

"That's him," Bryant said, rushing to the hooded guy, dragging Helmer along.

"What?" Helmer said, his eyebrows narrowing. "That's the guy you're talking about? He looks like a runaway felon."

Helmer watched Bryant's hurried steps, his energy palpable, like a man on the run. But Bryant was quiet, not really at will to provide any answers. Helmer's eyes shifted to the men betting money on their fighters, with another question lingering in his mind. "Bryant, what are we really doing here?"

The fight club was filled with smoke as the audience blew their cigarettes. It was also packed with drug addicts, gang members, and homeless boys trying to make a living to survive. Usually, a place like such had a Don ruling everything inside. Helmer only wished he could leave before any incident and that the head of the club wasn't present. The last thing he'd want was an unnecessary confrontation.

"Just relax, man," Bryant said, "don't act like you haven't set foot here before."

"That's exactly why I'm asking why you brought me here."

"Go with the flow, okay?" Bryant said. "Now, stop with the questions."

Helmer reluctantly nodded and then observed what Bryant meeting the guy was about. He stood behind Bryant and let him do the talking. Bryant wasn't afraid, even though the neighborhood wasn't the safest. Cops barely drove through the area, and unless it was about a life and death matter, they avoided it at all costs. Yet, he didn't feel estranged from these kinds of people. Helmer wondered since when he has been coming back there, although they had both decided in the past to never go to such a place ever again.

"Give me the same ones I asked for years ago," Bryant requested, handing the birth control pills to the guy.

"Another try to be a father?" joked the guy, taking the pills. "Another try?" Helmer frowned, wondering if he heard the guy correctly. "You have tried to be a father before? You and Sonie never talked about this."

"I'm sure that wasn't his fiancé," the guy said. "That was a couple of years ago."

"Nina," Helmer realized. "Like this couldn't get any worse." "Listen," Bryant said, looking back at Helmer. "Nina had a miscarriage. We were both trying at the time—"

"I thought you said you two weren't serious," Helmer opined, losing track of his best friend's love affair, not knowing whether to offer his comfort or apathy for just finding out about this.

Bryant groaned, palming his face. "We're here to help you, Helmer, not to be lectured."

"How much do I still not know about you?" Helmer asked, genuinely concerned about what more he could find out about his friend.

Bryant ignored him and shifted his gaze to the guy who gave him a large blister pack full of white pills. "These are identical to the ones in the bottle. Fill it up, and I wish you the best of luck."

"Wait, you're switching my wife's pills?" said Helmer, his eyes widening in surprise. "Bryant, I-I can't do this. That would be wrong..."

"Do you want to be a father? Yes or no?" Bryant said, proceeding with his plan.

"These are effective from the first dose," the guy said, interrupting the tension between the two.

"Perfect!" Bryant whispered, taking the new pills.

"I'm not sure about this," Helmer said, reluctantly taking the pill bottle.

"I promise you, this will get the work done," Bryant said, tapping Helmer's shoulder.

"By the way, are you taking any refills this week?" the guy asked, interrupting once again. He couldn't pick up on social clues, and he seemed intoxicated. His eyes were red, and his pupils dilated. Something seemed wrong even with his voice, and he wasn't the quiet type either. "Later. Not now," Bryant said in a dismissing tone, trying to shut the guy up.

"Later?" Helmer frowned, taken aback by Bryant's behavior and coded interaction. "What you got going on? What is this guy talking about? And who have you tried getting pregnant? Nina?"

"Helmer, you ask too many questions. Take the pills, and let's go."

Helmer pushed Bryant aside and directed his attention to the hooded guy. "I'm curious; what else do you sell?"

"Helmer…" Bryant said, worried he might find out.

"Well, I sell stuff that helps people have a good time. Are you good now?" The guy giggled and opened his jacket, exposing his sealed blunts and drug inventory.

"Tell me I'm dreaming," Helmer said, taking a step back, processing what he had just seen. There was no way his best friend kept this from him that long. "Wait! So, you're back on that crap? You relapsed, and you haven't even gotten yourself help, yet you're talking about me needing to seek medical attention?"

"I told you I don't have the best ways to cope with crap that happens in life," Bryant said. "I'm not like you." He shifted his gaze, avoiding Helmer's eyes. "Now, drop it! Because I am not going to discuss my life choices with you. And everyone gets stoned once in a while. What's the problem?"

"The problem is when you have a history of drug addiction, Bryant, you stay the hell away from it. You don't even breathe near it, ever!" Helmer scolded, giving Bryant's shoulder a push, hoping that would wake him up to the gravity of the matter. "You have an amazing life, a perfect job, and your parents. Me, I have nothing to hold onto. Be goddamn grateful! Coming here to get a sniff of that damn powder is not the way to appreciate what you have and those who care about you."

Maybe Bryant couldn't help himself to stop the toxic ways to handle his own problems. He was the one making everyone laugh, yet no one seemed able to cure his inclination to destroy himself. Moreover, the one person who could make him smile was the one who made him cry.

"You said you got nothing to hold onto..." Bryant shook his head. "No, Helmer. You got a family, but me, I have nothing. My parents are already advanced in age and it's only a matter of time to receive some bad news. And Sonia wants nothing to do with me. So, I absolutely have nothing to hold onto other than the company. Now, are you done judging me? Honestly, is living not enough as torture? Any more questions you wish to ask?"

"I do," the guy said, backing away, his face wrinkling in panic. "Why are we being circled?"

"And by us calling for trouble, I think you were right," Bryant said, noticing a group of gunned men, heavily built. "We definitely did."

Helmer formed a fist, holding his spot. "Holy hell. I know these guys."

CHAPTER 13

Make A Fist

FLASHBACK

The phone rang. It was Bryant calling, checking on Helmer, making sure he didn't lose an eye this time. Every beating felt like it was his last; The violent spankings and ice baths for punishments had gotten worse. Helmer wanted the abuse to stop, but he didn't know how to. He wasn't a toddler anymore. He shouldn't be getting beat past his teenage years, yet there wasn't much to do about it. Mr. Jean was paying for his school and brought food to the table. Who could ever rise against the hand that feeds them? It seemed impossible.

"I have 2 minutes," said Helmer, picking up the phone, his voice frantic. He couldn't keep calm nor understand why his body was shivering as much and slowly growing numb. He dropped by his bed, hoping he'd be relieved from the discomfort. "He hit her. He hit her, Bryant."

"Hit who?" asked Bryant on the phone, while making sure he didn't make any noise to not get his best friend in trouble. Mr. Jean could hear. He was near, and getting caught in the dark telling his best friend what was happening behind closed doors in his home would be chaos.

"Gladice," said Helmer through a gasp. "My father hit her. He had too much to drink, so she was trying to stop him from hitting me. Then...he punched her. I must do something."

"You should've called the cops," advised Bryant, the anger building in his voice.

He always wanted Helmer to run away from home, but that wasn't an option. Helmer had a special bond with Gladice; he'd never agreed to leave her behind, at the hand of his father, who beat anything his hands fell upon.

"Listen," Bryant resumed, "I met a man who promised to help you. He's a doctor—a therapist, to be exact—and his name is Elvino. But here's the catch: he's not a regular doctor. He might be the person who will make sure that your father never beats on you ever again."

"What's his number?" Helmer asked, pressing the phone to his ear.

***

The men started to shout, gritting their teeth and circling around. Their arms seemed like they were carrying the strength of a bull, and so were their necks. Their voices sounded like deep waters, terrifying and intimidating. They approached closer and pushed Helmer into the cage, where they held the fights.

The audience, surprised by the unexpected match, made way for a bulky bald man to get inside the circle. The bettors started to hype the bald guy, throwing money around and betting on him and some on Helmer.

"I can't believe it," Helmer realized, shifting his head to Bryant who got pulled out of the circle. "It's a trap! What were you thinking about bringing us here? You dumb fu—"

Helmer's words interrupted as the man shoved his head into his lower abdomen. Helmer tried to counterattack, but the bald man's hit felt like bricks. He felt his intestines churn up from the effect, and before he could even get ready to block the second blow, he got punched in the face.

"C'mon punk," said the man, laughing, overtaken by pride and inciting the crowd to cheer him on. "You don't walk into a tiger clan and don't get preyed on. And the Don told me not to be gentle with you." "The Don? Who are you talking about?" Helmer asked, shifting his gaze to Bryant, shaking his head in pure disbelief. How could his best friend bring him back to that place with these people? He knew those guys, their lifestyle, and definitely who trained them to fight. That was what most of them did for a living, and those who didn't weren't as honorable either, for they were almost inhumane in their practices to do what their mentor expected of them.

"You shouldn't have hit me," Helmer said to the bald man, his body shaking with anger. He needed to unleash all this rage somewhere, and the occasion was now present. He wasn't thinking anymore. He walked toward the guy and hit him under his chin, then attacked his left knee, knuckling him to the ground. It was easy to do it, making it obvious he's done it before. But he didn't stop hitting the man; Helmer kept going, and for some reason, he enjoyed it. Maybe he missed hitting on an actual person, seeing them bleed, and asking for mercy. He was zoned out, unable to hear the men in the background telling him to stop.

"Stop," shouted a man, approaching the circle Helmer was in. All the men stepped back, making room for their mentor to walk through. One of them ran in haste to light up his cigar, watching him in admiration as he paused to observe the bloody scene. He motioned at the gunned men to open the cage to let Helmer out.

"You could have actually killed him, Helms. What have I taught you about your anger?" "Elvino?" Helmer whispered, his body weakening just by being in the man's presence. He dropped to the floor, drawing his hands to himself. They were indeed bloody, something he has sworn to himself to never do again. He glared at Bryant, every muscle in his body fighting to contain the thunderstorm inside. "You set me up."

"No need to be upset at him," said Elvino, inhaling his cigar and getting close to Helmer. "I didn't leave him a choice, to be frank with you. I needed to see you."

"I can't believe you found me."

"Found you?" Elvino cut in, brushing his thick, perfectly shaped gray eyebrows with a casual flick. "Was there ever a day I didn't know where you were or what you were up to?"

"I want to keep away from you," said Helmer, trying to keep his composure around Elvino. Even if he tried to do anything, he'd end up either in really bad shape or with a bullet through his head. The last time he felt such animosity toward someone was when he had parted ways with his father. History was repeating itself, but this time, it was with someone he trusted and who had once given him hope in humanity. "Helms—"

"Don't call me that," raged Helmer, getting up, his voice masked with melancholy.

"Do you want to talk about it in a more private setting?" asked Elvino, lowering his voice and entering the cage. He cupped Helmer's face, his lips pressing onto his cigar. His heart was aching seeing how much affliction his presence had caused, yet he thought of it a priority to get back on the right foot with Helmer, his most beloved foster son and delicate patient.

Elvino stretched his arm toward Helmer's shoulder, trying to take him into a proper embrace like the old times. But Helmer pushed him, which brought a couple of guns pointing toward him, making him instantly regret his lack of control.

"Easy boys! Don't hurt him," Elvino said, gesturing at his men to lower their pistols. "I mean, he was part of this family once. Hurting one of our own is against our rules."

Elvino dusted his cigar before resuming his talk with Helms, just as he used to call him in his younger days. He patted Helmer's cheeks and took out a handkerchief from his pocket to wipe the blood off his knuckles. "Look at that. Your knuckles are bruised. I can tell you've lost practice."

Watching Elvino carefully wipe his hands brought Helmer back to a chapter in his life he never wished to revisit. When he was a teenage boy, Bryant had introduced him to Elvino—a man who swore to look out for fostered kids, providing them with a better life and resources to stay off the streets. But it didn't happen like that, as most of those kids got into illicit practices, including running fight clubs.

"I'll be fine," said Helmer, pulling his hands to himself. "I was fine until I got tricked to come here."

"I swear I didn't have a choice!" Bryant shouted, his voice breaking into a plea. He knew that he had signed up to bring his best friend to meet Elvino, this man dressed like an angel but was the devil himself. "You should thank Bryant because since you guys were kids, he was always the one ready to do what's necessary to keep you alive."

"No worries, I know," Helmer said. "He'd sell me for a penny." "Oh c'mon, he got you this," Elvino said, motioning at one of the men to bring him a briefcase. The guy opened it and showed the massive amount of dollars. There were blocks of them, well stacked and rubber- banded.

"I should've known…" Helmer backed away in complete shock and horror. That money could've come from anywhere or been anything. And worse! Being tied to a crime or any illicit activity. He couldn't hide his disgust or the melancholy that took him captive at that moment. "You booked me to fight."

"And you won," Elvino said. "Now it's your money. I know you needed it for your company. But you wouldn't accept it unless you worked hard for it."

Helmer shifted his head to Bryant, who kept his gaze away from his best friend. "You reached out to Elvino? Really? I will mess you up." "No, you won't," said Elvino in a composed tone. He stepped beside Helmer and lightly brushed his hair. "You hit him; I will tell your wife what you were really doing in Paris after you got married. I mean, doing some activities that your wife would be concerned about if she ever came to find out. And, of course, with me."

Helmer's eyes widened, unable to fathom that his past would get back at him. His eyes were begging Elvino to keep that information to himself. His heart pounded, for he forgot that somewhere out there, someone knew him like the palm of his hand. That's why he was always afraid of Elvino, the man who knew how to pull his strings.

"Oh, you haven't told her. Have you? Let me guess, you fed her the pitiful story of your father, making amends with him. Oh Helmer..." Elvino said, shaking his head. "What's your wife's name again? Magda, right?" Elvino prepared the briefcase and gave it to Helmer, his face warning him to take it. "The man of secrets, who hates secrets never fails to amaze me. You are truly a character. I missed you, Helms. Out of all the boys I've adopted, you've always been the most special."

Perhaps Elvino meant it. After all, he did admire Helmer as his patient and mostly his adopted son, but this man wasn't holy. He was hated and feared by those who truly knew what he was capable of. Elvino was many things, yet being a liar wasn't one of them.

"What do you want? Why are you creeping back into my life? You want to collect for everything you've done for me? That's why—"

"Blah blah blah," interrupted Elvino, chomping on his cigar. He lightly patted Helmer's cheek and smiled. "Still so dramatic. But to answer your question, I'm here to help you. I heard the company is struggling, so I wanted to find a way to give my help."

"He insisted that I tell him how you were doing financially..." Bryant said, trying to explain what he did. But no word could've made him worthy of forgiveness at that moment.

"Okay, the air is tense over here. How about we crack some jokes?" Elvino said, letting out a giggle. He motioned at the men to pick up the bald guy off the ground and clean the bloody mess. "Anyone who finds the answer to this joke gets $25,000. What do you call a fat mom?"

All the guys looked at each other, trying to think of a response. But none of their guesses were correct. This oddly lighted the mood as it took the tension away. Elvino laughed, watching them struggle to get the question right. "No need to kill yourselves figuring that one out, boys. The answer is—"

"Just spill it out so I can go home, please," urged Helmer, annoyed.

"Maximum," Elvino said. "Funny, right?"

The guys processed the joke, and despite their delayed reaction, Elvino clapped for his performance. Cracking dad jokes was almost like a hobby. He knew how to be a father and a mentor at the same time. He was a man of many talents, and although Helmer tried to hide it, he smiled a little.

"By the way, Helms," started Elvino. "That was a lot of anger. You could've killed this guy."

"I defended myself, that's what happened. I didn't sign up to fight, so I'm under no obligation to follow any rules. I'm not a bad person," Helmer objected.

"I never said you were."

"You say you're not here to collect, but I know that you want a pawn, and you're upset that I don't want to be that anymore." Helmer pointed at the men, some holding their loaded guns, others hiding their knives under their sleeves. They all had a tiger tattoo on their necks, reminding Helmer of the one he got on his chest. Helmer knew all their tricks, and it was obvious he used to be one of them. "They're your pawns, and I clearly see that you still hold Bryant by the neck. He admires you so much that it's getting scary."

"How is that wrong?" Elvino asked, his face curious. "I raised those boys, the least they can do is to follow my voice. Don't act like you've never been a follower yourself."

"Except for the fact that I realized I wasn't born to be one," Helmer spat out.

"You've always been a rebel, and I made peace with that. Except, I wouldn't want you as an enemy."

"You're a criminal," Helmer said.

"And what are you?" Elvino frowned, finishing his cigar and blowing it in his face. "Would you swear that you wouldn't have killed this guy if I didn't intervene? This kind of rage has always been your worst enemy, not me. Don't be such a hypocrite!"

Helmer fell quiet, his eyes filled with shame. He cupped his face to conceal his worry and guilt as the man he had beaten up nearly to death surged through his mind. He remembered his rage and intense desire that the guy had stopped breathing. He wondered if he was really Elvino described. A hypocrite. A man with secrets. Or perhaps, a killer.

"Oh, you got nothing to say?" Elvino leaned close to Helmer's ear, discreetly continuing his statement. "You don't have to keep your innocent mask around me, Helms."

Tears glistened from Helmer's eyes, revisiting the most broken parts of himself. Those wounds he covered up but never took the time to heal. "You know Helmer..." Elvino sighed, his face empathizing. "You swear to hate lies, but you lie when it's convenient for you, something I've always taught you not to do. You're a perfect husband, but your heart inclines for a woman who's not your wife, claiming she's just a friend."

"Stop..."

"What is he talking about?" Bryant asked, his tone spiking up.

"Are you sure you don't know? I thought you were smarter than that," said Elvino, glancing at Bryant. "It's obvious the chemistry between the two. The cutie, Sonie, the girl he always had a crush on."

"Stop," Helmer said, his voice softening and looking at Bryant. "Sonie is like a sister to me. That's it."

"If you say so," Elvino said, letting out a chuckle and starting another cigar. He passed an arm around Helmer's neck, as they were about the same height, both strongly built. Elvino looked good for his age, his face barely holding any wrinkles and his white afro sitting on his head as a voluminous crown. He had an earring on his left ear and nose and a tiger ring on his left finger. One would take a hint that he was left-handed. His suit was also impeccably tailored, reinforced with bulletproof material to ensure his protection.

"Like it wasn't enough," Elvino continued. "You told your people you've built your company out of great investments, but you never told them what you've been investing or what kind of business funded your wealth. Or who has always been behind your success all this time, which is me..." He lifted his left hand and showed Helmer his tiger ring with a disappointed stare. "Do you remember who this belonged to?"

Helmer lowered his head, the guilt from his past breaking through his soul once more. His chest was rising, and his body slowly gave in to the pressure. The fear consuming him became stronger, prompting him to let out a few drops of tears. It was like an elephant was sitting on his chest, and he couldn't break free from whatever he did. Helmer was strapped in, having no other choice than to face the affliction claiming him. "Why are you doing this?"

"Doing what?" Elvino asked, lifting Helmer's chin. "You want to break me and reel me back into your clan."

"No," Elvino said. "Let's say I choose not to. What I want is your trust back. You can't keep hiding anymore as I can't protect you like I did before." He opened Helmer's hands and placed the ring from his left finger into his palm. "

"I didn't choose this," Helmer said, his tone defensive. "You did the moment you made me cross a line I could never take back. It's all you!"

Before Elvino could say anything, a young boy appeared, holding a tiny knife, breathing as hard as a horse on a field. "Sir," he called for Elvino's attention and joined both hands to his knees, catching some air. "Someone has called the cops to raid the place, reporting unusual activity. They should be here by early morning."

"Really?" Helmer said, disappointed, as he looked at Elvino and the boy. "Now, you've downgraded to children to do your dirty work for you. I bet he's barely 9."

"He's a spy, and he's well-trained," Elvino replied, dropping his cigar on the floor. "I'll protect him. I always protect you guys. And I suggest you don't judge when you don't know what's happening around here. Now, go home, and when you're ready, we'll talk." He patted Helmer's cheek and made sure he took the money. "You know where to find me." Elvino turned to his guards and the audience, snapping his fingers, ready to give a red notice order. Everyone knew what that meant, as they all got up and started to clean the club and then headed for the cage where

Helmer was still standing. "C'mon, boys! Wash out the blood and drop your guns or any weapons in the underground bunker," added Elvino, dusting his vest and preparing to dismiss. "I need no incidents; send the fighters home, and you know exactly what to say. If you are carrying drugs or anything of that sort, leave now!"

Some of the men cleaned the ground and threw water to wash the blood off. Helmer, out of the cage, looked down at the briefcase in his hand. That money was cursed as if the ghosts of his past came back to haunt him. He wondered what would happen if anyone caught him in such a place. His biggest fear had always been going to prison. And any cop who had been in the south of Chicago long enough, catching the tiger tattoo on him and the ring on his finger, would know what kind of group he used to be part of. Helmer couldn't allow it. He was a changed man, a husband, a dad, and a respectable businessman. He could never allow himself to be in a position to lose any of these privileges. Yet that fear now was well alive, so present that it paralyzed him.

"C'mon, let's go," urged Bryant, grabbing Helmer's arm to move to the exit. He knew what he had done and what the fighting club meant in Helmer's past. Yet, no sorry would be enough, so he did not utter any other words about it. Reaching outside, they got to the car, and Bryant started driving at maximum speed, leaving the neighborhood.

On the road, something kept troubling Bryant until he gathered the courage to ask. "What was Elvino talking about when he mentioned Sonia?" Bryant looked confused and distraught. He was hoping it was just an allegation, but Elvino wasn't the type to lie.

"I can't talk right now," Helmer replied, realizing that his dirty laundry had been spilled. He didn't want to do any more damage to his friendship with Bryant and Sonie. They were dear to him, but the clock was ticking. Questions needed to be answered, and Bryant needed an explanation from him. His silence, however, had already given away his guilt. He was holding onto a secret that Bryant wasn't ready to hear. "A lot happened tonight. I need to go home. And you know you owe me because you messed up—"

"Yes, I get it," Bryant said. "I should've never tried to force you to fight or make amends with Elvino or brought you back to the club. But..." he paced away, his hands briefly brushing through his beard. "I'm having a lot of thoughts right now. I don't know why. I need to understand what Elvino was talking about. Is there something about Sonia that I need to know?"

"You know how Elvino is. He plays around with our emotions," Helmer replied, his voice dropping. "Don't let him get in your head." "But he mentioned her!"

"What about Sonie? She's like my sister. That's it!" Helmer said, his tone dismissive. "And you should be ashamed of yourself for having made a fool out of Nina, knowing goddamn well she nearly had your child, you bastard."

"That's between me and Nina," Bryant riposted.

"No, everything matters here," Helmer objected, peeping a quick look at the rearview mirrors, making sure the road was clear, and they weren't followed. "You know that. And I'm your brother. If there's anything that you needed to know about me or Sonie, I'd be the first to tell you."

"You know, I admit I wasn't always a perfect friend," Bryant said, exhausted from asking Helmer the same questions, knowing he wouldn't get any answers. He didn't want to think anything wrong, especially about his best friend. Even the idea of doubting Helmer upset him. "But that's all I tried to be for you... like today, and I really hope Elvino is not saying what I'm thinking right now."

"Of course not," Helmer snapped.

"I choose to give you the benefit of the doubt. Don't take it for granted," Bryant said, eyeing Helmer. "I admire you. I respect you, and above all, you're the one I trust the most."

"Bryant..."

"I mean it," Bryant emphasized. "Let's go." He gestured at Helmer to go to his car and drove him home. It was a silent car ride, but the deception shared between the two seemed mutual. There was actually no perfect friendship, and theirs was finally hitting a rocky road. No one knew what to expect nor what was left out of the story. Perhaps Helmer wasn't an open book, as Bryant thought. And Bryant was not as cold as he tried to portray himself. But inside, there was a soft boy who acted the silliest to gain everybody's approval and love. The least he expected was to get his genuineness reciprocated.

Helmer reached the mansion and exited Bryant's car, waving at him. Bryant sped off, and by his demeanor, he indeed had a lot on his mind. Could he be angry about Elvino's comment? Could he be doubting his best friend? Or was he only curious about him and Sonie? They have been friends the longest. What could he have possibly missed?

"Hi, sir," greeted Jonathan as Helmer reached the gate.

"Hi, Jonathan," Helmer replied with a nod and rushed inside, hoping to find his wife. He wanted to make sure that he wasn't about to make a mistake by switching the pills. The thought was tempting, but there would be no going back. He got to the room, unloading the events of the day and removing his shirt. He went to the restroom, washing his knuckles and his arms so strongly that he scratched himself. He kept scrubbing, and before he realized, tears were running down his face. Hearing Magda's steps, he splashed water on his face to wash the tears away.

"Hey," said Magda, coming toward Helmer sobbing.

He immediately rushed over to her and wrapped his arms around her for comfort, wondering what was wrong. Maybe he could give her the benefit of the doubt or that she was dealing with something he didn't know yet about. "Come, sit."

He took her to the bed and looked down at the paper in her hand. Magda motioned at him to take it. That was a medical note, her name written on it. "I went weeks ago to a doctor, trying to see if I could…" Magda paused, trying to get her words together, yet hesitant.

"Doctor? For what?"

"I can't conceive," she said, her voice trembling. "I found out today. Helmer, I can't give you what you want. I can't ever get pregnant."

"What?" Helmer muttered; the words hit him like a punch to the gut, leaving him momentarily breathless. "Like… I don't understand. W-What do you mean by you can't?"

"I'm so sorry," cried Magda, barely able to breathe through each sob. "I decided to run extra tests to make sure everything was okay, but then—"

"Then what?" Helmer prompted, his heart racing.

"I can't have children," Magda emphasized, her eyes empathizing with his. "It has to do with my endometriosis condition."

"How come?" Questioned Helmer, frozen on the bed, digesting what Magda said. Maybe that was the reason why she was taking the birth control pills. He was no savvy when it came to women's health, but he surely thought of the pills being some sort of relief. "I'm just trying to understand."

Magda sobbed. "I know."

"Okay, hm... maybe we should leave this conversation for later," Helmer suggested, assuming that his questions were weighing too heavy on her. He rubbed up Magda's shoulders and progressively locked her into a hug. His eyes let out a drop of tear, then another followed, until it became a stream.

The dreams of fatherhood were slipping through his fingers like sand. "Can't" was not what he thought he'd ever hear. He was expecting something bigger, nicer, an announcement precisely, of being a future dad. Yet his gut was telling him to not give up on the hope he still held onto. What about what happened at the party earlier? Could he have been wrong about the pills? Perhaps he had misunderstood.

Magda leaned back and sniffled. "I'm going to the bathroom really quick to freshen up."

Helmer nodded, his fingers slowly letting go of her. "Go ahead."

"Thank you." Magda got up and made haste to the bathroom. While she washed her face, Helmer took the paper and discreetly scanned through it. For some reason, the document looked fishy, as there wasn't quite anything that specifically mentioned the reason why she wouldn't be able to conceive. Then Magda's phone vibrated, and due to the water running, she couldn't hear a thing. Helmer grabbed the phone and sneaked out of the room to take the call, heading to the library. That number was the same as the one at the top of the medical paper Magda handed to him, and surprisingly, a man spoke with excitement.

"Did he fall for it?"

Helmer's heart dropped.

CHAPTER 14

Mask Off

*H*elmer hung up, shaken by the disruptive thought that the man who just answered could be an imposter. He hurried to text the number, and the man replied, assuming it was still Magda.

"Is your husband here? I called, but you didn't say anything."

Helmer gritted his teeth, resisting the urge to call and curse the man out, yet he still wanted to believe that Magda wasn't lying to him. He carefully thought of a reply that could bring the truth out but avoided taking too long to answer so the interaction didn't become suspicious. The inclination to throw the phone to the wall persisted, but that'd unfortunately blow his cover. He wouldn't want Magda to start asking questions.

"Yes, he's here," Helmer replied, annoyed and anxious. "But he's in the shower. Now, what do you have for me, doc?"

"Doc? I wish. Anyways, it's triple this time. Falsifying a document is not a tiny task."

Helmer reached for a chair and sat, his legs slowly giving up on him. He clasped his hands over his mouth to smother the cries he wished to let out. Now, it wasn't just his body heating from the wrath; his heart was also burning inside of him. Not in a good way, more like Magda should be running for her life.

"Ok," Helmer texted, managing to ease down for the sake of his current plan. "Talk to you later. Don't text back. I don't want him to suspect anything."

Helmer tramped around the room, every sentence fueling his rage. It was coming out of him, yet he refused to allow another relapse. He deleted the messages and cleared out the call log, dropped the phone in his pocket, and stormed out of the library. Reaching the hallway, he saw Magda running toward him, worried and frantic.

"Helmer, I was looking for you," she said, catching her breath. "By the way, have you seen my phone?"

"Your phone?" Helmer said, his face confused. "No, why? You usually have it on you."

Magda pushed her hair off her face, venting herself, feeling a medley of worry and fear that Hemer could've found the phone or that the doctor would call and ruin her sobbing masquerade. A doctor, charlatan, imposter, whomever it was on that medical note, she hoped he didn't call yet to claim his payment.

"You know what? I'll be right back. It was a hectic day, and I need a little bathroom break again," Magda said, the same worrying expression plastered on her face. Could she be suspecting that someone had her phone? Well, when you hide things, you can never be fully at peace.

"No problem. Go rest, I'll be right in," Helmer said, kissing her forehead. He watched her leaving, looking like she was in a rush, maybe searching for her phone. That device seemed to carry many secrets and potential information that could turn her marriage upside down. No one could hide forever from their shortcomings; sooner or later, they'd need to face the chaos.

Magda didn't go directly to the bedroom, which gave Helmer enough time to head there. He placed the phone beneath the thick duvet from the bed and exited the room right away. The hall was empty; it didn't seem anyone was watching and less, invading his privacy. Helmer took out the birth control pill bottle and the pills Bryant gave him. He took a deep breath, and after a few seconds of thinking it through and hesitating, he switched the pills. They were identical, just as he was told, and as he pondered on Magda's lies, his guilt dissipated. It was done. The pills were replaced.

Helmer darted through the hallway to head down the stairs and bumped into Marie Lisa.

"Marie," startled Helmer, sliding one arm across his chest.

"Sir," Marie said, greeting him with a nod and carrying on with a large empty laundry bin toward the staircase. Surprisingly, Marie was always at the right spot, right time, and knew every single thing happening in the mansion. That was somehow interesting, yet no one asked any questions. Why?

"Marie," Helmer started, "does my wife know you had her pills?" She shook her head. "I don't think she does, seeing she hasn't asked." "I need a favor," prompted Helmer.

"Sure." Marie nodded. "Anything, sir."

Helmer took out the bottle and handed it to Marie, who took it with haste. "I need you to take it to my wife and make it seem like you just found it. Don't tell her anything about our conversation or that you brought it to me."

"You mean that you had it?" "Yes."

Marie smiled, thinking about the request, an opportunity she perhaps had been waiting for the longest. Who knows? She never seemed that clever; who would ever assume she'd be so invested in such matters?

"What?" Helmer asked as Marie lingered. "What's my share for the favor?"

"That's why it's a favor, Marie. You don't get anything."

"No," she said, raising a finger in the air. "Silence costs, sir. I'm sure you know that."

"What would that be then? How much do you want?" Helmer asked, taking out his wallet, ready to give some thousand bucks if that'd conclude the deal. That was a matter of life and death to him; he really wanted to have a baby and have the complete family he ever wished for. His dream had the potential to succeed if only Marie would keep her mouth shut.

"That's the thing, sir. I don't want money. And this matter between you and Mrs. Dupris ought to hit a rocky road anyway." Marie put the laundry basket on the stair step, excited about her uninvited elaboration on her boss's marriage. "I saw the pills before, well hidden in her drawer. She swore no one would've seen them. Not even you!"

"You went through my wife's stuff?" Questioned Helmer, crossing his arms, annoyed yet invested.

"Yes, I did, and I have absolutely no regrets. I also understood that, after the announcement at the party about having a child, she was hiding the truth from you. Mrs. Dupris never wanted to give you a child."

"How much do you know about this?"

"Way more. But I won't tell unless we get a deal."

"I'm listening," Helmer said, putting his wallet back into his pocket. He had a sense of pride as if he was onto something big, scary, and somewhat deceitful. Nonetheless, Helmer wanted to know who his wife really was and if he could've been fooled all this time.

"I heard you've asked Mrs. Dupris to take her to Paris. I want you to take me there," requested Marie with a satisfying smirk.

"No," Helmer objected. "I'm not taking you on a private trip along with my wife. That's insane."

"Then no deal."

"I'm no longer going to Paris," Helmer said. "Then take me wherever you guys go."

"That would be weird as hell, Marie. What's the intention?" "Simple," Marie replied, a playful twinkle in her eyes. "Making connections. Being present. And who knows? I could use some of your potent influence to make things happen for me."

"Connections?" Helmer said, squinting.

Marie nodded. "What's the harm in aiming high? Dreaming big doesn't make you reckless—it makes you ambitious."

"There's no way I am negotiating this with you, my employee who's also a busybody."

"A busybody who's smart enough to request what they want? It's either that or no deal. And believe me when I say if you don't take that offer, there won't be a second chance to reconsider."

"Okay," Helmer gave in, letting out a sigh. What was he getting himself to? That question made him restless and doubtful. "Well... One trip."

"Not enough."

"What are you playing at?"

"Now, you've upset me. I changed my mind," Marie scoffed, starting to walk away.

"Marie—"

She stopped in her tracks and turned. "See? I've been thinking lately. Maybe being a laundress doesn't fit me. I see me somewhere with an office or maybe somewhere fancy. I'm so tired of being treated like nothing."

Those words seemed like they were rooted deep in her heart for quite some time. To be frank, she had built a reputation that wasn't the most respectable. Gossiper, coquette, spreading out information that was meant to remain in the dark, and at times, she could act quite clumsy. If it was on purpose, then she had already succeeded in deceiving everyone, including her boss—the loving and perfect husband or the victim in his marriage.

"I'll be your personal assistant," requested Marie. "No more laundry for as long as I keep your secret."

"You have no experience to be my PA, Marie—"

"I'm a fast learner," Marie interrupted, "and knowing all the troubles you've been through today, I'll give you until tomorrow to decide."

"And the pills?"

"Don't worry," Marie reassured. "I'm an expert in sneaking stuff through. And as a bonus regarding our deal, I promise to tell you everything that you probably haven't known yet about Mrs. Dupris. Have a great evening, sir."

Marie took her basket and withdrew herself, seeing her boss's ears perk hearing his wife's name. Could Marie really know that much? Sure, she was a gossiper but insinuating that Magda could be living a double life seemed far reached. What could Marie possibly know?

Helmer headed back to the library in deep thought. He was going mad, or maybe he really wanted to save his marriage. However, no matter what he did, all his efforts seemed useless.

Helmer bit his hand, his body contracting from all the anger he's stored throughout the day. He wanted to unleash it, set his soul free. There was a blazing fire within him, sending shock waves to his brain, making his thoughts wilder than usual. His gaze shifted to the door, seeing Magda's shadow approaching. What could she possibly want after all this damage?

She entered and was startled by the sight of him staring intently at her. "I was looking for you. I-I wanted to finish our conversation and hopefully say sorry."

"Sorry?" Helmer puzzled.

"About the news! I never wanted to tell you that at such an inconvenient time..."

"It's ok," prompted Helmer, tired of hearing the sad tale again. Seeing her there, talking softly, and her hips moving at a moderate pace as she walked toward him gave him a wild idea. His breath grew heavy like a growling animal ready to attack. He could no longer hear her apologies nor notice her confused stare. Helmer approached her, absorbed with lust and ferocious fantasies. Helmer's nose scrunched by the scent of her perfume, heightening the temptation to seize her captive against his shirtless skin. His gaze was detrimental, and that made Magda feel as if she was thrown into a lion's den.

"Are you okay?" she asked, wondering what put him in the mood after such a stressful evening.

"I am," Helmer whispered, his arms arching forward and his eyes glued to the opening of Magda's robe, inflaming him even more. His pupils grew wide, like a cat making a mating call at night, hungry and in visceral heat.

"Are you sure?" Magda asked as Helmer pulled her closer, his hand cupping the back of her neck.

"I don't even know," he replied, his breath mingling with hers, leaving no space for air between them. "You have made me so angry that I'm now hungry for you."

"Is this about the conversation we had?" she asked, as Helmer leaned over, his chest pressing against hers.

"Forget our conversation," Helmer said, seizing her lips. "We can finish it in a better way. I want to play a little."

"Play?" Magda said, feeling Helmer's hands freeing her bosoms.

Helmer lifted her, her legs instantly wrapping around his hips. He pinned her against the bookshelf, his eyes warning her that he wasn't about to be gentle.

"Helmer, I-I don't think we should do that."

"Do what?" he asked, gorging on her well-rounded cups.

"Oh..." Magda let out a gasp, captured by an intense pleasure from her breasts. "Helmer, you seem—"

"Brutal? Untamed?" he groaned, sliding the robe off her shoulders. He reached for her breasts once again, exploring every part of her. "I thought you wouldn't mind some roleplay." He ripped her night robe, too eager for her to appease the passion.

"I don't," Magda said, as Helmer slid his hands between her thighs, his fingers toying through her sensitive walls. She whimpered, her legs tightening around Helmer and quivering. She got nailed against the shelf, her head falling back.

"Helmer..." she wailed, feeling Helmer anchoring himself into her. "Go ahead, say my name," he whispered, his speed increasing by the second.

"I'm going crazy..." Magda gasped, her face distorted with pleasure. Her nails dug into his back, instinctively drawing him closer as the passion surged between them. She wrapped her arms around him, her breath shallow, the pressure building within her. Her body tensed, every fiber of her being on the edge, yet he didn't stop. Her legs quivered, the urge to flee overtaken by his steady presence. There was no escape, and still, she didn't want him away.

"Talk to me," he urged, his voice low with yearning.

Seeing her struggle to find words, he was only filled with pride, his hands roaming with possessive confidence. He moved to kiss her softly at the curve of her belly, teasing her with light pecks, before his lips trailed further down. Magda's legs instinctively clasped, but Helmer held them open, his kisses growing deeper as he moved to her thighs.

"H-H-Helmer!" Magda exclaimed.

"That's right. Let go for me…" he murmured, his lips trailing down her body once more. He kissed each part of her with slow, deliberate care, his hands moving to cup her breasts, massaging them with intent. Then, his movements slowed, drawing the sensation out, taking her right to the edge, but never quite letting go. Finally, with a deep, shared breath, they both surrendered to the climax, their bodies pulsing in unison. He lowered her legs and collapsed beside her, barely catching his breath.

Magda remained on the floor, staring at the ceiling until a little smile showed on her lips.

"You okay?" Helmer asked.

Magda looked at him and nodded. "You-You've never touched me like that before."

"Did I hurt you?"

She shook her head, pushing her sweaty bangs off her face. "It felt different and so good."

"I want us to be like this every day, every night, every morning."

"Me too," she whispered.

The night was so good that Magda forgot about all the questions concerning her phone. And just as Helmer requested, every day became a honeymoon. Helmer was on his best behavior, and Magda was completely submitted to him, drawn up to their bedroom, catching up on the absent passion.

CHAPTER 15

Spy

FLASHBACK

"C'mon everyone, let's take a picture," said June, motioning at Allimair and Mr. Brooks to come closer for a neat shot with Magda and Helmer, who just got officially engaged. Everyone was rejoicing about the good news, but Magda longed to see only one face, Richard's. Her eyes wandered around, reading each person in the room, wishing someone would have objected or told her it wasn't real that she was soon to become somebody's wife. Somebody her heart didn't incline for and less, choose.

Overwhelmed by all the happy wishes, Magda left Helmer interacting with their families and rushed to the closest guest bathroom. She stopped and grabbed a small towel, turned on the sink faucet, and placed it under the running water. She raised her head to take a look at the person who had just walked in, and it was June.

"June, not right now. I need a moment."

"You mean a moment away from your fiancé?" he teased, watching her desperate attempt to escape her engagement party. There was her entire family waiting outside in the living room, and Helmer was probably wondering where she was headed. June knew something was tormenting Magda, as she had not even drunk the entire party.

"It's not right. June, I'm lying to this man," Magda said, reaching for a handy paper towel so her tears didn't smudge her mascara and leave any evidence that she was unhappy. She fanned her face, then took a few deep breaths, but only revealed the true reason behind her guilty statement.

"No way," June realized. "It's Richard, isn't it?"

Magda's eyes met with June's in the mirror from over the bathroom sink. The truth was sitting on her face, revealed by her sudden drops of tears and red cheeks. She couldn't answer, and neither did she nod. What she was doing was wrong and immoral, enough to seethe a man's ego to the roof and cause them to go wild.

"You're still seeing Richard," June summed up, holding back from giving a lecture and sermon. But for whatever reason, he felt pity for her and wondered how he could help her fix that situation. As a man, he wanted her to confess to Helmer what happened, and at the same time, the betrayal seemed to hurt his ego.

"Tell me my suspicions are not true."

Magda's face reddened, her head nodding to confirm. "We didn't break up. I couldn't do it, June. Now I don't know what I'm going to do."

"Oh my God, Magda." June sighed, pacing away and lifting both hands to his face.

"I know what you're thinking—"

"No, you don't," June cut in, "this is wrong. That's cheating, Magda!" Magda lowered her head, the tears breaking through, flooding down her face. She was lost and, of course, guilty, too. However, leaving Richard never seemed to be an option, for she'd burn the world for him if that were ever in question. But Helmer, what would he think of it? "Don't tell Helmer," June advised.

"What?" asked Magda, sobbing.

"I would not take you back even after confessing. So, my advice to you is to go to that kid, break it off, and carry on with the engagement like nothing ever happened."

"June, I am scared," Magda emphasized, her voice shrinking even more.

"You have to be! Because somebody's going to get hurt in all of this…"

"He's right!" Mr. Brooks shouted, breaking through the conversation, wishing he did not hear his daughter's confessions. He wanted to give a sermon and be angry, but Magda already had enough guilt eating at her soul. Mr. Brooks motioned at June to leave him alone with Magda, trying to process how he was going to tell her about what he had recently discovered. His face was weary, a few eyebags exposing his lack of sleep. Closing the bathroom door, Mr. Brooks clasped his chest, then spat a heavy mouthful of blood. Despite the treatments, his health didn't seem to improve, and he tried his best to keep it secret.

"Pops!" shouted Magda, pulling Mr. Brooks close to the sink, scanning him through, frightened that her biggest worry would turn into reality. Was her father dying? Was it just a malaise or a scare?

"Mag..." Mr. Brooks whispered.

"What just happened? Do you feel ill? Do we need to call the doctor? I thought he said you'd be fine." Magda said, releasing her racing through in the open while searching for a towel to clean up the bloody spit. She twirled around, bothered by Mr. Brooks not giving an appeasing response. She needed to know what was happening to him. Why did he look as if he had not slept for days and spit his lungs out.

"Mag!" Mr. Brooks grasped Magda's arms. "You don't have to do this."

Magda flinched, hearing her dad's surprising statement. She looked at him from the mirror over the sink and lowered her head, trying to ignore what he said. It was too late; she had already agreed to marry Helmer. Mr. Brooks' treatments were paid in full, and her family was doing financially well since her relationship with Helmer. It seemed that her father would need even higher care now that her suspicions were true. Could she back out? What would be the consequences, then? What would it be for her dad's health?

"You don't love him," remarked Mr. Brooks, his tone remorseful.

Magda turned off the faucet and rang the towel to tap on her dad's face, her eyes agreeing with him yet hesitant to say a word.

"I know your mom has convinced you to be engaged to Helmer, but you don't have to marry someone you can't visualize a future with," emphasized Mr. Brooks, skirting the towel aside so Magda could give him her full attention. His eyes were filled with contrition as if they were telling Magda he was sorry. Mr. Brooks coughed again, which he couldn't hide anymore. His nose started to bleed, and as he glanced down at his palms, he accepted that his health wasn't getting any better. "I am dying, honey."

"What?" Whispered Magda, hastening to help Mr. Brooks clean up. Tears ran down her face, realizing that her suspicions were true. The treatments weren't working, and her wedding day was not that far away. The fear that her sacrifice could be in vain was terrifying and so was knowing that she was hiding something from Helmer for months.

"Stop..." Mr. Brooks said, drawing Magda into a comforting hug, his heart splitting across his chest, hearing his daughter trying to conceal her sobs. "Don't cry. Don't do that. You're a strong woman, and I'm not leaving this world with you sobbing over me. You hear?"

"But how do you know that?" Magda said, tugging at every little string of hope from her soul. She needed it, that light and reassurance that her father could be wrong. She smiled at him, rubbing up her arms to comfort herself. "We don't know that yet?"

"Listen, I'm going to tell you something." Mr. Brooks took Magda's hand and peeked his head outside the bathroom, making sure no one was around. He allowed the water to run in the sink so they couldn't be heard, as what he was about to say was risky and scary. "I know you're still in contact with Richard."

"Father..."

"He's a good kid," Mr. Brooks prompted.

"I'm so sorry," Magda cried. "I know you must be so disgusted with me."

"What I'm disgusted with is not telling you this sooner. Don't marry Helmer, and God forbid you ever have a child with him."

"Why do you speak so disdainfully of Helmer?" Magda asked, arching an eyebrow. "You loved him before."

"I know you're confused," continued Mr. Brooks, "but I discovered some things about Jean. Although he's my friend, I suspect he is not somebody to mingle with, including his son."

"Why do you say that?" Magda asked, wrinkling her nose.

"Jean is tied to an organization in Haiti, one that exploits women, including girls too, treating them like property, demanding favors upon hiring them." Mr. Brooks's voice dropped, as his revelation settled in the air. "He told me while we were having a few drinks. I guess he was too wasted to realize he was telling on himself. Apparently, his son's nanny is one of those women."

"What? Gladice?" Magda gasped. "That's horrible. She's like a mother to Helmer."

"Of course," Mr. Brooks replied, sighing. "Obviously, she can't go anywhere. It's some sort of domestic enslavement system they got going on in Haiti..."

"Even when they come here in the U.S?" Magda questioned, her body tensing, afraid she might discover worse.

"Honey," Mr. Brooks clasped Magda's face. "Sometimes, when someone has been trapped for so long, they forget what freedom even looks like. They become so scared of leaving the cage, that they convince themselves it's the only way."

"Then Helmer---"

"Might take after his father. Maybe not now, but down the line, I wouldn't put it past him."

"I disagree," spat Magda. "Magda."

"Helmer is not a kid; he is a good person and father, the real person you should be angry with is me. I'm the one taking advantage of him; we all are. Helmer is not Mr. Jean. He's perfect." Her voice rose slightly, but she caught herself before it went any louder. "And... That's the only reason why I'm considering leaving with Richard. I don't deserve Helmer."

"Trust me, honey," Mr. Brooks pleaded, "He's the one who does not deserve you. Because believe it or not, it's just a matter of time before this boy becomes like Jean. In such a family dynamic, there's very limited guidance. And for that, I'll come up with a plan to break the engagement."

"But what about Helmer?" Magda asked, the hollow in her chest growing deeper as she thought of the decision she now ought to make.

"I'll speak to him," Mr. Brooks reassured. "Trust me, you're far better off with the kid than this guy. I have some savings; I'll give it to you, and you go as far as you can."

"With Richard?"

Mr. Brooks shrugged. "I'll leave that up to you."

"And why are you doing this, father?" asked Magda, already aware that Helmer and Mr. Jean never had a good father-son relationship and that their family was dysfunctional compared to hers. However, there was never such a thing as a perfect family. It was just impossible to look for perfection in anyone or anywhere. Magda wondered whether judging Helmer based on Mr. Brooks' perceptions alone was a good idea.

"I wouldn't forgive myself for leaving this world, leaving you in the wrong hands." Mr. Brooks kissed Magda's hand and then stroked her face. "Your mother is blinded by money; she can't see what I see. Helmer can't be a good husband to you when all he's witnessed in his life is hate, anger, and a father like Jean. And God forbid you ever allow their blood to mingle with ours. Never!"

"But... now..."

"Now, enjoy the party, then later, go and tell the kid to reach out; we'll come up with a plan."

"Thank you." Magda hugged her father and decided to reach out to Richard about their new plan.

***

Snapping away from her deep thoughts, reminiscing about one of her most emotional moments with her father, Magda reached for her cocktail. She took a sip and got back to her painting, starting to fill the drawing in. Then, another flashback popped into her head, reminding her of his last letters. Could she finally get the courage to destroy them and leave the past for good in the past? That was always the idea, but every time, she would find herself reading them and grieving Richard, that ghost that followed her everywhere, and even in her sleep. A ghost that seemed like it still existed on the other side of the world, longing to haunt her.

She painted the portrait, then left it on the easel to dry, then moved off the stool to go to her closet, the tiny room holding all her secrets. She knelt, unlocking her letterbox, but underneath, there was also a diary—a tiny book that seemed even more threatening if it ever landed in the wrong hands. Magda took a couple of letters and read them, torturing herself even more. It was almost Richard's death anniversary, which, of course, had caused so much limerence on her part. As the tears fell down her cheeks, someone's shadow appeared from the lighting. The door was unlocked, bringing an instant panic upon Magda. Could it have been Helmer? How could she have lacked so much discretion, forgetting to close the door? Her hands shook as the shock moved across her body, crippling her in her spot. She slowly turned her head, and her shoulders dropped immediately. "Marie!"

"Ma'am, I'm sorry for scaring you."

"Crap!" yelled Magda, dropping all her letters inside the box and getting off the floor. Her closet was exposed, and so was her portrait, Richard's beautiful face, well drafted and oiled up. "What do you need, Marie? You know I don't allow anyone to come to this room."

"I-I know..." stuttered Marie, buying herself time to do what she came for—again, at the right time, at the right opportunity. Her eyes traveled to every corner of the room; then she leaned where the curtains hid the other paintings, holding onto a tray with tea.

"Marie, careful," shouted Magda, her eyes widening in terror, seeing Marie dropping her tray and falling off behind the curtain. Her dusty paintings fell off the easels, most being Richard's portraits and some of her deceased father, Mr. Brooks. She ran over, picking up two of the tea-stained portraits. Magda brushed her robe over them in a desperate attempt to save the canvas. But there wasn't much to do; besides, they were her oldest collections. "You...ruined them."

"I am so sorry," said Marie, dropping next to Magda, yet checking out the other paintings as she picked up pieces of the tea glasses from the floor. "I thought I could bring you something to drink."

Magda stacked up the paintings, her body giving off a strange response the more Marie lingered. She wanted her out so she could cry in peace. "You have no idea what you've done. You ruined my collection."

"Oh," Marie gasped. "I'm honestly so sorry."

"These were so dear to me, and you ruined them."

"Is there anything I can do?" asked Marie, insisting to prolong her presence.

"Get out."

"I can clean up the mess if you let—"

"Get out!"

Magda's scream was like a mother bear who had just lost her cubs, her eyes threatening and ready to show her claws. She was a sea of lava that would burn up anything close enough, and Marie was one of them. Raising her head, Magda noticed Marie still lingering to leave, inciting her fury to surge through her. She stood, grabbed Marie, and hurled her out of the painting room.

What if Marie saw something? Maybe her diary, or the letters, the faces on the canvases? Who knows what Marie saw or was looking for. Besides, she was a gossiper, which left Magda's heart faint with worry. What if Marie perceived her closet full of dry roses collections? The painting room was almost like a forbidden cave; why would Marie ever randomly bring her tea on a Friday morning? What if Marie left something in there or told Helmer about the portrait out of plain curiosity? Magda's racing thoughts made her wonder if she was smart enough to keep a tiny room as storage of grief over her ex. Who in their right mind ever does such a thing? She surged through the closet, checked each item, and did the same with her letterbox. Magda counted each letter, then scanned through her diary, and then headed to the paintings, watching and examining them carefully. She dusted them off and made sure the door was locked a couple of times before sitting down across the closet. Magda crawled to the letterbox and searched desperately for her diary, diving back into her wounds, unaware that she was calling for more trouble. Summoning her past and its ghosts could only result in more affliction and obsession.

Magda opened her diary and took her pen, trying to capture this latest event in a few lines to the best of her ability.

September 13th, 2023

Dear Diary,

It has been months since I've come for a few words, but today, something horrible happened. I left my painting room's door open today, and someone walked in. Thought it was my husband, God forbid! But it was one of the personnel. She spilled tea on some of my canvases, my dad's and Richard's portraits. They were my first collections from when they were still alive. I remember telling them how I'd make it big one day, and I got them each a similar portrait to keep. In a few weeks, it'll be their death anniversary. I miss them terribly, and I can only mourn through my art, just like Richard has taught me to do.

Meanwhile, saying his name brings me so much heartache. Richard. I wish I lost the ability to pronounce it, to forget him altogether, for his face haunts me, bringing nothing but torment. He's the face of my sins, a reminder of who I am under the covers once the lights go out.

There are so many things here in this room, including you, dear diary, that I'm desperately trying to hide. But for how long? Maybe I should burn some things, yet I can't let go. Besides, Richard is like a ghost, keeping hold of me, refusing to let me be at peace. My Richard, the kid, as father would call him. I made another portrait of him, with his smile on those beautiful lips of his. Sometimes, I feel so angry that I still miss them. He had hurt me so deeply that darkness claimed me.

I lost the innocent parts of myself, to the point where the word justice had become a curse, a detriment.

I wonder what would happen if one day he miraculously came back from the dead and showed up at my doorstep? Would I still be able to look him in the eye, especially after what I've done the last time we've seen each other? Would he still consider me his Maggie? And if he would, what shall I do? What would I tell my husband? What would become of my marriage? There are so many questions in my head every day that I feel filthy. How can I ever tell Helmer that I'll probably never be able to love him like I loved Richard, a ghost in my past? How can I be sane when I desperately want to see my husband measure up to a ghost? A ghost I created? I swear I'm a monster.

Magda shut her diary and put it back in the box. She sought a rag across the easel, which she used to dry her brushes, and soaked off the tea from the floor. She swept the shards of glasses and pushed them into the dustpan. Sitting on the stool, her phone rang. It was Helmer, causing her to stand, alert and making sure to lock the door. What if he came home already? Magda picked up the call, but her heart rate slowed, realizing it wasn't Helmer speaking.

"*Maggie. Maggie,*" the caller whispered.

Magda dropped on the stool, her legs weakening, knowing her ears heard the voice. Could a ghost resurface to life? Could Richard be stalking her? Did he hear her mention him in her diary? Or could somebody hack Helmer's phone to play a joke on her? June was not the type to joke around that way, nor was he tech-savvy enough to pull off such a move.

"W-Who are you? This is my husband's phone. Please talk. Answer me, please."

"*I saw you going into the coffee shop last week. Wish I could have a chat with you.*"

"Who's speaking?" demanded Magda, her grip tightening around the phone. For some reason, she wanted to hear more from that voice, as it felt familiar and intriguing.

"*Why didn't you take my gift? Why didn't you accept it?*"

"Because I don't know you," Magda replied, the dots finally connecting in her brain. "You're the guy who ran. The roses are from you. The roses I received, the note, and—"

"*Now, let them burn,*" the man said. "*Let them burn. They will burn...*"

Magda hung up, shaking, a terrifying realization overcoming her— the man sounded like Richard. His tone was spiteful. The words left her even more perplexed and frantic, wondering if she was hallucinating. It couldn't be! That man couldn't be a ghost. And ghosts don't exist. He had to be real. Those lines sounded like a threat that someone was coming for her. The stranger was known, and Magda feared for her life, as her secrets were even more threatened to be now exposed to the world. What would it be of her marriage? Her family and their future?

Magda squirmed off the stool and trailed to the closet, as if she were hiding—hiding from a ghost threatening to rise back from the dead. Could it be true? She wondered, lowering her head, hiding away as if darkness could ever keep her safe.

CHAPTER 16

Drawings

The bell rang, and all the students rushed out of class, making their way to the school's hallway. Helmer spotted Sonia from across the attendance office, as she was very involved in the school and the office. She was raising money for one of the clubs by selling snacks and Gatorade to the kids. Sonia had on her business fit-on, afro in a pony with her sideburns curled down. Her eyes locking with Helmer's brought an instant smile on his lips, but he was too shy to show it. Helmer was very subtle in the way he showed his feelings, and he had planned to ask Sonia to prom, practicing his speech, hoping he wouldn't stutter. He had been wanting to ask her to go out since sophomore year, but due to how calculated he was, wanting things to be under control, he chose not to, except the timing he thought was ideal was faulty.

"Hey," said Bryant, nudging Helmer while he was lost in thoughts, watching Sonia. But Helmer flinched, his sides hurting and well covered up so no one would notice.

"What's up?" questioned Bryant, reaching for Helmer's shoulder again, confirming his suspicions. "Don't tell me that scumbag hit you again."

"I don't want to talk about it," Helmer said, walking away, knowing that bringing up his father's name would only ruin his day. School was his escape, yet he had to skip practice due to the scar left on his back, dreading that somebody would see them. He didn't need anyone involved in his family dramas and less with his father. He dreaded being taken to foster care and getting his case messy.

"I told you to keep in contact with the Elvino guy; he can help you," Bryant said, walking at a faster pace to keep up.

"I mean, what about him? That dude is strange as hell, cracks dad jokes all the time and can't keep away from his cigar. I wouldn't be surprised if he's a weirdo collecting kids and selling off their organs on the black market."

"You can trust him. And you have to act before your dad attempts something worse. If you don't hit him back, you'll end up in a hospital." "I prefer that," Helmer said, his voice monotone, remembering how he got in a violent fight with his dad the night before. It became normal at some point, getting beaten and scared each time he'd get home from school.

"Stop being so hardheaded," Bryant coaxed.

"Bryant, I am not you, ok? I don't blindly put my trust in people. They got to earn it."

"I'm trying to help you," Bryant said, concerned and restless, witnessing his friend going through hell yet unable to salvage him. He had already tried countless times to help and eventually introduced

Helmer to Elvino, a man who seemed to have the world under his sleeves. Yet none of those efforts gave any results. Helmer was gradually withdrawing himself socially from everyone and shut the doors to anyone who could potentially make the abuse reach an end.

"By the way, I asked her out," Bryant said, changing the subject to lift the mood.

"Who?" Helmer asked, stopping in his tracks, his heart throbbing with panic.

"I know you've told me not to go for it multiple times, but I couldn't resist."

"Keep talking," Helmer urged, fearing that it wouldn't be the girl he was thinking about.

"Sonia. I asked her to be my girlfriend."

Helmer's head shifted toward Bryant, reading his lips and repeating Sonia's name. It couldn't be her; maybe that was a mistake. "Sonie?"

Bryant nodded, wondering why his best friend was not more excited. But he was too glad to care and too blind to understand what was happening.

"W-What did she say?" Helmer asked, his body tensing. "She said yes," Bryant said, smiling.

"But I don't understand," Helmer said, unable to digest his best friend's confession. The world started to spin around him, keeping him steady in his spot. What was he going to do? The girl he had liked since he was a kid was now standing between him and his best friend. "You dated plenty of girls, and you can have anyone you want."

"That's the point! I don't want them." "Why Sonie?" Helmer questioned, his hand brushing his chest, urging his heart to keep still.

"Because she's different, you know that," Bryant replied, shrugging, yet certain about his decision.

"You dated half of the cheerleading team, and out of all of those, you choose Sonie? Our Sonie?"

"Friends end up dating all the time. Why do you oppose the idea of me and her together so much?" Bryant asked, his tone imposing. "It's almost like you're obsessed with her. Sonie is not your possession; she can date any guy she wants, and that guy happens to be me. That's all!" Helmer bumped Bryant out of his way and started to walk faster through the hall. The easiest thing would've been to be honest and say what was really bothering him, but his ego was always standing in the way. "I need air, and please, don't follow me."

"Did I do something?" Bryant questioned, puzzled by the reaction. "We didn't even finish our conversation."

"Too bad!" Helmer left, moving like a stormy wind out of the school, noticing a Mercedes Benz parked across the entrance. A black man with gray hair stood there, leaning against the car, his legs crossed, and both his arms stretched out, but one was holding his cigar. By the look of his suit and glasses, one could tell he was no ordinary man.

Helmer shifted his gaze to the streets, wanting to send the man a message to stay away. He didn't need a conversation and less, having to explain he didn't need help. He headed to the sidewalk, fixing his book bag as it was too heavy and hurting his shoulder. As he walked, hoping the man had left, someone whistled at him.

"Seems like you need a ride!" the man shouted, one arm securing the car wheel and the other resting outside with his cigar.

Helmer kept his head straight, the man's car riding at his pace. "What do you want? I already told you I don't need help. I'm fine."

"What's your name again? Helmer?" the man asked, entertained by Helmer pushing him away. All he could see was a teenage boy throwing a tantrum, left with no guidance and needing saving. "You know what, I'll call you Helms. My name is Elvino, as you already know. Got a nickname for me?"

"Yes. How about asshole?" Helmer spat, making a stop to put his two cents in. It did look like he had no manners; he was angry all the time and kept to himself, pushing everyone who could be a support away. But what could they expect from a boy whose father taught him those exact patterns? Even if Helmer did fight to be different and immune to the toxicity of his dysfunctional home, at some point, he wouldn't have been able to keep up and that was exactly what happened. "Now leave me the hell alone and stop following me."

"You know what, I like you," Elvino said, laughing it off. "In my career, I've met so many boys like you, yet they all got trained up like stray cats." "What the hell does that mean?" asked Helmer, frowning.

"To start, I have plenty of cats. They're all strays for a particular reason," Elvino replied, as he pulled a polaroid photo from inside his suit. He took out the photograph and showed it to Helmer. "These are my cats. They were very aggressive when I got them, but as I built trust and looked out for them, they softened. I love fulfilling transformations." "You got a lot of nerves comparing me to your strayed cats, respectfully," opined Helmer.

"I like a good paradox," Elvino said, dropping the picture back in his patch pocket. "It was not my intention to offend you."

"Your jokes are lame."

"I agree," Elvino nodded with a grin. "But not my car. It's fast. And I'm sure you'll want to drive it."

Helmer paused, thinking about the subtle offer. "I... I don't know how to drive."

"Oh, what a coincidence. I own six fast cars, and I am one hell of a driver," Elvino said, fixing his shades. "I am sure that'd make me also a great teacher. Don't you think?"

"No one here owns that many cars," Helmer said, his tone easing. "I'd need proof for me to believe you."

"Then hop in." Elvino gestured, parking the car, his gold teeth showing. He looked so intriguing, full of layers, yet so inviting. Everyone felt comfortable around him, especially kids. Helmer saw it, but he questioned why Elvino, a stranger, was so alluring. What about him that made him both enticing and scary? "You may share your location with your friend Bryant if you fear that I might take you somewhere questionable.

The only thing you should fear, honestly, would be my driving 'cause I drive fast."

His humor was slowly growing on Helmer as he stopped refusing the ride. Helmer went to the other side and opened the door, hopping into the passenger's seat. He put on his seatbelt and felt a sting from his sides, but he remained silent, not wanting to draw attention.

"Why are you holding your side?" Elvino asked, his brows forming into a frown, putting the car on shift, intending to give Helmer the ride of his life.

"What?"

"I said, why are you hiding your ribs? You're in pain." Elvino stuck a finger toward Helmer's face, his voice deepening and raising, cutting Helmer's words off before he could even put them together. "Don't try to lie; it is one thing I hate more than anything. Who hurt you?"

"Nobody," Helmer replied, sharply.

"I'll repeat," Elvino started, "Who hurt you?" "I already told you---"

"A lie," Elvino cut in. "How many more are you going to tell?"

"Listen, I don't know you, and I think I'll prefer you stay out of my—"

Elvino suddenly pulled the car to the side of the road, the tires screeching as he parked abruptly. He recalled Bryant telling him stories of Helmer's father's violent tendencies, the bruises hidden beneath school uniforms, the absences that went unexplained. Elvino couldn't bear another lie or vague excuse. He slammed the car door and stormed toward Helmer, his eyes scanning every inch of him as if searching for the truth.

Elvino poked Helmer's rib, causing him to jump in agony, tugging at the car door handle for dear life. Helmer held his breath in and lifted his school shirt. There were different types of scars, and they didn't seem to come from regular beatings. "These wounds look fresh," Elvino said, his face turning rigid. "Your father did this to you?"

"Does it matter?" Helmer replied, trying his best to sit straight.

"It does matter," Elvino said, leaning over to take a closer look at the scars. "What does he use to spank you? These scars can't be from a belt." He dropped his cigar on the ground and stomped it out, wanting to give Helmer his full attention.

"It's... nothing."

"I won't repeat myself," Elvino warned. "What does your father beat you with?"

"The tv cable, and any wires or hardware that hang around the house." Helmer put down his shirt, fearing that he had over- shared about his life. But at the same time, someone besides Bryant knew what was happening at home and the violent loop he was trapped in. "And other times, there's this whip made of dry cow's skin from Haiti that he uses. That's what gave me the scars."

Elvino rubbed his face, and then tugged Helmer's shirt down, unable to look at the scars any longer. Otherwise, he might put a stop to it, and not in the most redeeming way. "Okay, listen to me. What your father is doing to you is wrong. You can't continue to live with him—"

"I can't leave," Helmer blurted out.

"If I do, I won't be able to protect Gladice. He hits her, too, when he's drunk."

"Who's Gladice?" Elvino asked.

"My nanny. She's been living with us since my mom left my dad."

"That's some heavy baggage to carry at such an age," Elvino said, his arm draped on the car's door, fingers tapping against the metal. "I must do something about that."

"What can you do? I don't want to go to foster care."

"Helms, I hate to break it to you, but I'm not a saint," Elvino said, as his posture exuded effortless ease. "I'm not asking you to be okay with living with another family or to run away from home. I'm asking you, would you be willing to fight back?"

"I don't know how to fight."

"I know," Elvino smirked, now his hands patting his suit. "That's why I'm asking, would you be willing to? I'm one hell of a teacher."

***

After finishing his workout, Helmer sat on the bench, stretching his arms. He had his sweatpants on and a pair of sneakers. He was shirtless, with a towel curled around his neck. It was 4:00 in the morning, almost time to go to work, wondering how he was going to enlighten Bryant over Elvino's statement about Sonia. He wasn't ready to have that conversation and face the truth he had always run from; the simple fact that, like everyone, he wasn't perfect.

Helmer patted the sweat off his face and left the gym. Wandering in the hallway, he was nudged on his neck. He turned quickly, nearly striking Mr. Hens with a shove of his elbow.

"Mr. Hens!" He gasped. "I could've hit you."

"I'm sorry, sir," Mr. Hens said. "I-I had something to ask you. It's quite an audacious favor to request, but..."

Although Helmer was annoyed by his stalling, he waited for Mr. Hens to tell him what was on his mind. One of Mr. Hens' shirt buttons popped, which didn't fit him anymore because of his plump stomach. Helmer watched Mr. Hens trying to button his shirt. He wanted to laugh but held back so he didn't make his all-time favorite Butler feel uncomfortable.

"I have to admit that my stomach has gotten stubborn lately," remarked Mr. Hens. "I can't even wear my old pants anymore."

"I always invite you to come to the gym with me," Helmer said. "You know I don't have a problem with that."

"Sir, I truly want to exercise. Especially now that I have my eyes on Ms. Gladice," Mr. Hens said. "You've known her for a long time, so I was wondering if you could give me some help to impress her."

Helmer nodded instantly. "Sure! I'm happy to hear that. Gladice is like a mother to me, and I believe she might give you a chance."

Mr. Hens' face crimsoned just by the thought of it. However, he was concerned about his weight. "She'll probably say no. Yesterday, after she walked your daughter, Ms. Meg, outside of school, she said I look like a distorted minion."

Helmer gawked at Mr. Hens, who seemed to have no hope for Gladice to accept his advances. Helmer put one hand over his shoulder and walked with him, trying to lift his spirit. Nothing he said made sense to Mr. Hens, who desperately wanted to earn Gladice's heart.

"I know I've asked you this before, Mr. Hens," said Helmer. "Do you love your job here?"

Mr. Hens curled his eyebrows in confusion, unsure of how to respond. "I've been working here for more than a decade. I like being a Butler."

Helmer shook his head. "That's the problem! If you want to gain her attention, you have to give her time to miss you. Be out of here a bit; make her wonder about you."

"A bit of mystery?" Mr. Hens summed up.

"Yes, and to start, maybe we could find you new clothes. We will figure it out, but now, I need to go to work."

He headed to his room and flung the wet towel in the laundry bin. He hopped into the bathtub and showered. Stepping out of the tub, he snatched a clean towel from the door's handle to dry his hair. He threw the door open and stepped out with an extra towel wrapped around his thighs. He startled by the unexpected visit of Marie Lisa, who was getting the dirty clothes out of the laundry basket and trying to place something on his bed. Helmer tried to return to the bathroom, but slipped, and the towel slightly rolled off of him.

"Marie Lisa!" he screamed.

Marie's mouth gaped open, realizing she had run into her boss half-covered. The basket dropped from her hands, and the clothes scattered over the floor. Marie Lisa brought her hands to her mouth, watching with no slight effort to pick up the clothes.

"Stop staring at me, for God's sake, Marie Lisa!"

"I'm sorry, sir!" She turned her head, hoping to regain her sanity after being flashed by her boss, who was indeed too good-looking to deny it. "I wanted to start doing the laundry early today, but then I remembered we still had a deal on the table."

"Well, learn to knock before sneaking up on people and scaring the hell out of them before I change my mind." Helmer crawled on his knees as he adjusted his towel to cover himself and managed to stand off the floor. He gripped the laundry basket, collected the dirty clothes, and then dropped them in.

"Does that mean you're making me your assistant?" "Temporarily."

"Not after I give you this," Marie said, handing Helmer a tiny device, a live footage of the painting room, showing Magda inside dusting off her canvases.

"What is this?" Helmer asked, grabbing the device for a closer look and clicking at the images for different angles of the room.

"I planted a camera inside the other day, and I'm surprised I didn't get fired," Marie said, pacing beside Helmer, showing him how to manage the device. She zoomed in and clicked on the screen, bringing his attention to her discovery. "That's a diary. I think if you get hold of that, then you'll discover more than I could ever tell you about your wife."

"Damn, Marie! You're a genius," Helmer said, genuinely thinking about it. He went on and watched the previous videos of his wife, noticing her cleaning a closet inside the painting room. He was always aware of her obsession with that room and her being very protective of it. Helmer respected that space since Magda had held portraits of her father there, but as he looked deeper into the footage, there were tons of portraits that weren't just Mr. Brooks. Due to the quality of the videos, he'd have to get close enough to the paintings to see for sure who it was. But what else would he find getting into that room besides seeing the portraits? As a man, he didn't judge it necessary to look, but his gut wanted him to. Maybe it was time to fully put his curiosity into his wife's art and maybe get a hold of her diary. But wouldn't that be a violating act of her privacy?

"You can leave, Marie," Helmer said, noticing her reluctance to withdraw. Perhaps transitioning from being a laundry lady to a personal assistant sounded already like a big task for her to get more involved in her boss's marriage.

"I wanted to tell you something else, which will be a bit weird," Marie said, fidgeting with her shirt, rushing over to her boss, keeping her voice low. "I went to a store nearby to get a few things when I was on my way to buy this device…"

"No worries, I'll reimburse you," said Helmer, already jumping in to be the hero. Except, it wasn't about money, but rather a comeback, or a scare, or even a prank.

"Sir, I don't need your money," Marie whispered. "Someone crashed into me. I'm sure it was a man. He slipped a piece of paper in my pocket. It happened so fast, I-I couldn't see a face, but when I took the paper, I saw your name written, sir." Marie took the crinkled paper from her pocket and handed it to Helmer. He grabbed it and snapped a finger for her to dismiss, but she stalled longer while her eyes filled with tears.

"Sir, there's something else." Her hands shook as she reached again for her pocket. There was a tiny knife wrapped in a small towel. It was stained with fresh blood and looked like it was used to commit something unholy. Marie stretched it out to Helmer, but he stepped back, eyeing the weapon.

"I'm not touching that! What is this? Why do you have this, and what happened? What's the meaning of all this, Marie Lisa? There's blood on that thing!" Helmer said, now driven by curiosity to read the paper. There were a few simple words. Yet heavy enough to make him worried.

Helmer Dupris.

The rich and perfect guy!

Laying with the lying wife. The burning rose, burning everything on her path.

"This note doesn't make sense. Who would ever send me that?" he asked, stomping around the room while resting his hands on his hips. The note wasn't just about him. It mentioned his wife, with a bold statement on top of it. A lying wife—something that Helmer agreed with.

Marie insisted that he took the knife as she transmitted a warning to him.

"You can't tell anyone, sir!"

"Of course, I got to tell someone. Are you sick? What if it's a psycho running around doing this to people for fun? I'll call the cops, and you'll tell them what happened." He reached for his phone on the nightstand.

Marie Lisa ran and dropped to his feet, bursting into tears. Her shaky sobs smothered her voice and shrunk it into whispers. She folded her hands and raised her head, begging Helmer with pleading eyes to reconsider. "No, don't. Please, sir! It could be dangerous to involve the cops because that person seems to know where you live and probably knows more about you than we can imagine. And I'm caught in the middle of it. Why would he choose me to hand you that paper? It wasn't a coincidence. Something strange must be happening!"

"It's okay, Marie. There's no need to beg me," he said, giving her a reassuring nod. "But I don't understand. It must be a joke or someone at work trying to play a prank on me. That's a possibility."

"I doubt it, sir. My advice to you is that you try to be careful and not take this lightly. There's fresh blood on that knife, and I feel like I'm now involved in something out of my control," Marie said, cupping her face and sniveling.

"Did you touch the knife?" Helmer asked after thinking about her request, judging that her fears and analysis of the situation were valid.

"Yes." She looked at him, squinting as she tried to accurately remember the details. "I didn't know what to do with it."

"I'll keep it somewhere safe since you've come into contact with the blood. God knows where it's from! Keep me updated if that happens again." He helped Marie to stand up and took the knife with a t-shirt, then wrapped it. Marie Lisa thanked him and dismissed herself, keeping her gaze off her boss. Helmer locked his door and looked through his closet for a gray suit, trying not to overthink the note. He hid the weapon and the note under his folded gym clothes from the top of his closet. He matched his suit with an ocean blue tie and shoved the device in his pocket, wanting to keep track of his wife. Now, he had many things to keep secret: forbidden to report what happened with the knife to the cops and playing along to keep himself and Marie safe.

Helmer finished getting ready for work and left the room, heading to the foyer and calling his driver to bring the car. He reached for the device Marie had given him and went through the videos, trying to zoom in on each item in the room. Helmer wondered why he was doing this, treating his wife as if she was involved in a crime, watching her closely painting her canvases. Changing her pills was enough, and he thought that maybe he was overthinking about the diary. People had journals all the time, his wife having one shouldn't be a problem. Helmer thought if he would be worthy of any redemption at all, crossing those lines, which he could never come back from.

He got inside the car and shut the door, not knowing what to expect once he'd reached work. He only hoped that it would be a peaceful day, not wanting his anxiety to get the best of him. Helmer put the device back into his pocket, laid back, and closed his eyes, his mind oddly taking him back to a memory of Elvino, the man who took him in when he had no one. He had not spoken to this man for some heavy reasons, things that were too dark to talk about. He had a lot on his mind, especially Bryant and Sonia whom he worked with in close proximity to avoid taking accountability for what Elvino had said. Sooner or later, Helmer knew he'd have to face the person he really was, the man who wasn't always as perfect as he portrayed himself to be.

Reaching work, Helmer exited the car and waved at his driver before going into the building. He walked slowly, realizing he'd need something to eat, his head spinning. He got inside the elevator and headed to his office, greeting Nina, his secretary. She looked like she was in a hurry to tell him something, but Helmer wasn't ready to hear. He gestured at her to give him a minute to settle in, also requesting some decaf coffee.

"You have breakfast inside," Nina said, "Ms. Sonia left it in there." "Breakfast?" Helmer asked, wondering if that meant that Sonia had forgiven him. He rushed to his office, and on the desk sat some non-dairy biscuits, bacon, and a large plate of pancakes. There was also some tea there, and by the smell of it, it was chamomile. Helmer glanced at the phone, wishing to call and thank Sonia, but he held back, wondering what the intent was. But the food aroma was too tempting not to take a bite. Helmer sat, reaching for the pancakes, and stuffed some into his mouth to appease his hunger. Grabbing the biscuits for a large bite,

Nina walked in.

"Not now, Nina. I am starving," he said, his mouth full and some biscuit crumbs falling on his suit.

"I know; I wouldn't bother if it weren't urgent." She handed Helmer an envelope, her hands shaking. "Someone dropped this off for you."

Helmer stood, hastening to get the envelope, taking a quick scan of Nina's worrying face. Hearing the hesitation in Nina's voice reminded him of Marie Lisa, making a request earlier to be discreet about the note left for him. Would that envelope be connected to what Marie was telling him about? "Who sent this?"

"I don't know, sir." Nina lowered her head and rushed out of the office before Helmer could put a word in.

Helmer tore the envelope and took out the paper. It was a drawing of a woman holding her belly. Helmer read the sorrow in the woman's eyes; she looked betrayed. There was a can beside her, which seemed empty but with a question mark on it. The drawing was unfinished, and Helmer couldn't tell how to read it through. What was happening? Could that person be the same one who sent the note and the knife? What was the knife about, and now that drawing?

Unable to carry on with his day and peacefully finishing his food, Helmer went to Nina, inquiring about the sender. Nina had her head down, rocking herself in her seat and squeezing on a balled-up old sheet. "Nina, is something wrong?"

"Please don't ask me any questions. I want to live, sir!" she replied, keeping her gaze down and taking a couple of breaths. She unbuttoned the collar of her shirt for more air, and as Helmer approached closer to place the drawing on her desk, he perceived a large gauze below her collarbone. It was soaked with blood, looking as if she'd needed a fresh new one.

"Nina, what happened? Please, tell me. I won't share it with anyone, whatever you say." Helmer put the drawing into his pocket. Something was happening, and it wasn't evident yet if he was the one in danger, his family, or anyone close to him.

"I can't! I was told not to describe his face to you," Nina explained. "If I do, he won't miss this time. He'll cut right through me and let me bleed to death."

"It's fine; you don't have to describe him," said Helmer, closing Nina's office door. "But tell me! What did that guy do to you?"

"I was at the parking lot getting ready to exit my car, then I smelled something. So, I put my car window down then I blacked out. And when I opened my eyes, that guy was smiling at me." She brought her hand to her mouth, reliving the terror as she explained it. Helmer bent over, encouraging her to confide in him. She clasped her chest, drawing his attention toward the cut.

"I was tied up somewhere I didn't know and couldn't speak. I guess the drug he had given me was strong enough to keep me quiet. My tongue was heavy, and he took the knife, cutting under my collarbone, giving specific instructions along with threats. I think he's dangerous!" Nina wept, taking a shallow breath before resuming. "He's done this before, I'm sure! He didn't flinch when carving a letter into my skin. Then he wrapped the knife into a towel; God knows what he did with it."

There were too many things to focus on at once, but what Nina said about the knife led Helmer to wonder if it was the same one as the one Marie had brought to him. That was too easy of a guess, making him hold back from asking. "You mentioned a letter; what kind of letter? What was it?" Helmer asked, anticipating an answer.

"B," Nina replied, resting her hands on her desk. "He also expects you to report to an address, but not now. He'll let us know."

"Nina, this is outrageous. We should report this to the police so this guy or whoever he is can be stopped," he said, the hair of his body spiking up. "What he did to you shouldn't be taken lightly."

"Don't call the cops," Nina replied, staring in horror at her phone from the desk. "He's watching. He knows what we're up to, and he does not have any mercy. Only a killer or a psycho would kidnap someone and drug them. The more you cooperate, the safer we'll be since now my mission is to report all your whereabouts in the building to him. He said he'll contact me when he needs to."

"This is absurd!" Helmer snorted. "Does he know I can fire you for this?"

"If you do, someone else will be the next victim. That's his warning to you!" Nina took a tiny device almost invisible to the eye in her desk drawer and stood. She pinned it on Helmer, and the device stayed put, giving off a red light. "Please, keep it on! My life depends on it, and maybe even the life of the next victim."

"What is this?"

"It's a tracker. Don't take it off."

"Nina, I don't—"

Nina walked past him, turning a deaf ear to his plea. Helmer tried to follow her and inquire more about his watcher, but Nina refused to divulge a word. Helmer looked in the hallway, and only the security cameras that had already been placed were seen. There seemed nothing suspicious, and everything was exactly as it was before. Helmer took out the drawing and took a good look at it again, planning to take it home, hopefully hiding it next to the knife. It was another piece to resolve, and one day, he hoped he would. But how come somebody could be able to watch him? Who could that guy be? A guy who seemed to know his wife and threatened those close to him. Was he a stranger or someone who was out for blood? Whoever he was, the cops didn't stand a chance.

CHAPTER 17

Lingering Grief

Magda was in her painting room, destroying some of her old canvases. She stopped at the drawings of Richard and brushed her fingers over them. The three weeks leading up to the date of his death anniversary were gruesome. Magda was used to not sleeping at night and not being a big eater, but recently, these were all she kept doing. Sleeping and eating and hiding from reality. Now, the day was here. The day Richard died, a loss that took a piece of her soul, leaving her unfulfilled and absorbed with grief, and indescribable animosity.

Magda never visited his grave. She didn't show up to his funeral or discuss his death with anyone. She wanted him to remain a secret, a souvenir, and a mysterious case that wasn't worthy of a proper investigation. Richard was also a threat whose silence would make him a potential prey even alive. He had seen different sides of Magda that no one ever knew about, and although he was not a threat anymore, his death was still haunting her day by day. It was the epitome of her sins. Sins that were too gruesome to confess. She couldn't share what happened with anyone, not even June, even though she had been tempted multiple times. Besides, he had decided to go out of state for a few weeks for personal matters he did not divulge.

Magda grabbed a primed canvas and some brushes, pondering on what to draw. She sat, staring at the blank canvas, reabsorbing the affliction when she heard Richard's voice asking for rescue. Her soul was aching just by seeing her old drawings of him, and she made peace with the fact that she'd never get over that grief and tedious guilt. She felt his absence every day and smelled his cologne, even on her bed at night.

Even gone, he owned her; and after that phone call three weeks ago, Magda obsessed over the idea that he was alive. Richard came back from the dead, her mind refusing to believe otherwise. Besides, Magda had her eyes on Marie Lisa since that day in her painting room. That could never happen again, and she made sure of it, taking off the liberties for the personnel to go to her floor. They were only responsible for the 2 other floors, which included the servants' section and foyer. She did not care whether that'd raise more questions about that tremendous change in the mansion and less what Helmer would've thought of it.

Magda started to draw a circle, then added a few extra lines for symmetry, and proceeded to draw Richard. She did this every year for his death anniversary as if it was a way to redeem herself. She could never fully escape from the memories of him, his voice, their walks together, and his awkward laugh. She also remembered how much he had hurt her and the countless tears she had shed because of him.

Each brush stroke speared through her heart and made her give in to the pain. She paused in between sets and then hung the portrait by the stained ones to dry, which Marie had left her upset about for weeks. Going through her secret closet, Magda found the anonymous card from the bouquet she had received two months ago. It wasn't a joke nor a flirtatious note. Someone was after her, and she was sure that it was Richard, the person she loved and now feared the most.

Red, every killer's favorite. She read the note again, pondering over everything that happened the day Mr. Hens had delivered her the bouquet. She wanted to ask him if anyone had dropped by and delivered something. Magda couldn't understand the labyrinth she was lured into. First, it was the bouquet, then the note, then the roses and people playing a part in the act. What did she miss? Yet there she was, waiting for the caller to reach out again, and he never did. He completely disappeared, and even the stalking had stopped. One thing she was sure about was only that the man from the shop was no secret admirer. He looked like he was there to cause harm, potentially to her.

Hoping to put her racing thoughts to rest, she dropped all the letters back in the box and secured them in the closet. She locked the painting room and started to wander off the hallway, hoping nobody would catch her off guard in her mourning.

"Mrs. Dupris," called Mr. Hens, running up to her and taking out his pocket notebook. "Have you decided yet what we should make for dinner?"

"Oh, dinner." Magda sighed, running her hands through her bangs. "Maybe some deep-dish pizzas of different flavors, chicken Vesuvio, and tamales on the side, rice and beans with shrimp gravy."

"Isn't Mr. Helmer allergic to seafood and cheese?"

Magda's cheeks flushed, realizing she always forgot these small details. "I meant gravy. No shrimp and forget the pizza. The chicken will be enough since he has been busier with work these past three weeks anyway."

"And for dessert?"

"Chocolate brownies, a couple of cinnamon rolls, and Gladice's famous Haitian treat," Magda replied. "Helmer loves her kremas cake and sweet potato pudding."

"Yes," Mr. Hens nodded, turning red from smiling at the mention of Gladice's desserts. "I love w-when she makes them too."

Magda, noticing his flush, let out a chuckle before asking, "Mr. Hens, by the way, does anyone else know about the flowers besides you?"

Mr. Hens shrugged. "I'm not sure what flowers you're referring to, Mrs. Dupris."

"The bouquet," Magda said, her eagerness causing Mr. Hens to startle. "I'm sorry... I am talking about the roses from 2 months ago. I was wondering if you've seen the person who delivered them or noticed anything strange when you picked them up. Did you see a name tag or any useful indices?"

"No, ma'am! I don't have a clue, to be honest," Mr. Hens replied. "The bouquet was left in the mail. I saw no one!"

"Are you sure?"

"Yes, Mrs. Dupris. I-I swear." Mr. Hens stepped back, fearing that his unfavorable response could get his head bitten off from his boss's stare alone.

"Okay." Magda sighed. "That's all, Mr. Hens. Thank you."

She allowed Mr. Hens to dismiss and headed to Meg's bedroom. Hiding behind the door, she watched her do homework, her music blasting at top volume. Magda shook her head, her heart letting go of the heavy despondency from earlier. She stayed there observing her daughter, then closed the door as Meg turned so she did not notice her. Magda was not up for a chat, as her weariness was written all over her face and she was not ready either to be asked questions about it.

Magda walked away from the bedroom and went down to the foyer but ran into Marie Lisa, who was carrying a stack of paperwork. She was dressed in a black pantsuit set, along with a gold-colored scarf around her neck, matching her studs and cufflinks. "Marie, what's the suit for? Did I miss something?"

"Oh, I'm sorry... I thought Mr. Dupris had already told you," Marie said, securing the folders on her chest. There was a whole pack of documents in there, tiring her arms out. Yet, this task still seemed so much better than picking up dirty laundry and washing everyone's underwear. She was too smart for that, dressing up in a uniform, pretending to be a regular girl who just gossips around. "We will be taking off soon—"

"What are you talking about? My husband hasn't left for work already?" Magda asked, her eyes scanning Marie's pantsuit. From her stare, Marie could tell she hated the outfit. Besides, since the day that Marie had set foot in her painting room, Magda had been very cautious and kept a close eye on her. She didn't know why, but her instinct was telling her there was something fishy brewing around, and Marie was bad news.

"Mr. Dupris went upstairs to get something. He probably forgot his suitcase. But today is my first day of training, so I'm trying to move at his pace."

"I don't understand," Magda said, her laugh sarcastic. "You haven't done any laundry for days."

"I know," Marie replied, her tone calm yet teasing. "Mr. Helmer said he'd be searching for a new person soon. Maybe it's taking him a bit longer. I'll make sure to remind him."

"W- What are you talking about?"

"I'm his new assistant," Marie said, directing her gaze to the stack of papers she was carrying, hoping she wouldn't have to repeat herself. "How come?" Magda questioned. "You were hired for the laundry room. That's your job."

"That's a bit presumptuous, don't you think?" Marie responded, a sly smile tugging at her lips.

"I don't like this," Magda said, folding her arms defensively. "There's something off about you, Marie. I don't know what it is, but I can feel it." Marie shrugged. "I'm aware," she said, glancing briefly at the documents on her chest. "And unfortunately, I don't think there's anything you and I can do about it."

There were so many changes happening under Magda's nose, yet she had no clue. She wondered why Helmer was making decisions he didn't tell her about, and why would her laundry lady be transitioned to a position she obviously wasn't qualified for? Everything seemed to spike Magda's annoyance, especially Marie Lisa's sudden burst of overconfidence, which made her sound quite condescending.

"Keep playing whatever game this is," Magda said, her voice dropping to a hiss. "But trust me, I'll be the one holding the last card."

Marie's smile widened. "No problem," she said, clicking her tongue. "I just hope you're as good at winning as you think you are."

Magda watched Marie leave and then stormed away, taking the stairs to her bedroom. She wished to have a chat with her husband, yearning for some clarity. Reaching the bedroom, she found Helmer walking out the door. She shoved him in and closed the door behind them. "What is this all about?"

Helmer was holding his briefcase, knowing he couldn't say anything unless he'd be willing to lie. Could he tell his wife about his deal with Marie? That he was watching her whereabouts 24/7, and obsessing with her painting room?

Those past two weeks, Helmer had not slept, neither had appetite due to the burdening awareness that someone out there had sent him a note about his wife. As a man, his mind was running miles, thinking about every possibility that his wife was lying about something big. How come a stranger out there could be shaking his life around, and everybody around him? He felt watched, and he was. Being forced to wear a tracker wherever he was, for the sake of what Nina had warned him about, was like having a gun to his head, unable to defend himself. Could he really tell Magda all these things? Wouldn't it ruin all his chances to find out what she was also keeping from him?

"What are you talking about?" he asked, his voice calm yet showing he was in a hurry.

"How come you randomly decided to make Marie your assistant without telling me?"

"I was busy."

"Busy?" Magda said. "How busy were you crawling in between my legs every day the whole week? Every night we'd be together, and yet you have not said a single word."

Helmer sighed. "Magda, I really have to go to work."

"Work? I'm trying to tell you about how I feel, and you don't even care."

Helmer watched her vent, trying his best not to rush her mid-sentence, his heart aching the longer the conversation threatened to last. But as he tried to make sense of what Magda was saying, he noticed her pausing between each sentence and bursting into tears, something she had not done for a while.

"Are you on your cycle?" Helmer asked, his heart dropping at the thought. It'd only mean that their long nights were in vain. Maybe Magda was right; they couldn't conceive a child, and that sudden realization scared him.

Magda's eyes widened. "Am I on my cycle?" she snapped, her voice rising. "That's all you can think to say? I knew you wouldn't understand." "No, no," Helmer reassured, approaching her yet really needing an answer to appease his worry.

Helmer clasped Magda's cheeks, his stare remorseful. "Listen, I'm sorry. I-I didn't mean to ask that. I mean—"

"Stop," sobbed Magda, skirting Helmer's hands down and pacing away. "I don't understand why you're acting this way. It's so weird. I would almost say that you're treating me like a prostitute. You don't talk to me unless you want to sleep with me or gain something. You don't even pay attention to what I'm saying."

"I am paying attention," he whispered, putting his briefcase on the bed as he sat behind her. "I didn't mean to make you cry." He rubbed her back and kissed her shoulder, knowing it'd tickle, hoping to make her laugh. Knowing she did like it, despite her efforts not to show it, Helmer kissed her repeatedly, wanting a reaction, but Magda had not flinched a bit.

"Would you like me to skip work today?" Helmer asked, his lips close to her ear. He laced both arms around her and sat there patiently waiting for a response.

"No." She sniveled. "I can go to June. I know you really have to report to work. Just be on time for lunch. I'd like us to eat together."

"Ok. I'll call you a ride." He spent a few minutes with her, cuddling and kissing her shoulders until she gave in to his touch.

Magda turned her head, and then their nose touched, inciting them to give in. They kissed, and it was like being strapped on a ship in space, where everything was still and quiet. Their souls interlaced, with strong vibrations shooting through each other, as if they had just touched the heavens. Their eyes opened, bringing them to reality, but each let out a giggle. It was magical, that kind of intimacy. Knowing what their tears tasted like and being able to hear each other's heartbeats and hear the cries of their souls.

"I'm going to make the call now." Helmer got up, grabbing his phone to get her the ride to June.

Magda handed him his briefcase and rushed him out of the room, knowing he had already been late for work. She went to the walking closet, grabbed one of Helmer's joggers set, and put it on. It felt nice, and that slowly drew a smile on her lips, staring into the mirror across the room. The cuddle from Helmer before he left helped her feel regulated and in a better space to think things through. However, the thought that something was brewing persisted.

Magda circled the room, caught in an endless loop of torment. The man slipped back into her thoughts, refusing to let her go. His voice lingered—so familiar, strangely tender when he said her name. Magda longed to hear it again. Was it wrong to want that? She yanked at her hair, disgusted by the idea of falling for a ghost. Not just any ghost—one that might be her curse. She shivered at the thought.

"I can come in?" said Gladice, showing up behind the door with a tray of fruit snacks and sparkling water.

"Of course." Magda waved at her, aware that Gladice could see she was crying.

"Helmer wanted you to have something to eat before you leave, and your ride has just arrived." Gladice placed the tray on the bed and turned around, dismissing herself from the room, until Magda reached for her arm.

"Please, sit with me," Magda said, in a pleading tone. "Watch me eat or tell me a story; I don't care. Just sit with me."

Gladice heard the tension building in Magda's voice as she insistently begged for her company, wondering what could have possibly put her soul through such stress. Gladice glanced around the room and dragged a chair near the bed. She sat and served Magda some yogurt with guava on the side, her inviting gaze encouraging Magda to take a spoon.

Magda reached for the tiny bowl of yogurt then her eyes shifted to a paper. It was a note, the nightmare starting again. A burst of adrenaline spurted through her soul, causing her yogurt to drop on the floor. Her chest cramped with panic. It couldn't be! That note seemed familiar even though she had not even read it.

"Everything okay?" asked Gladice, concerned, witnessing Magda shift to fight or flight mode.

Magda grasped the note from the tray and read it, unable to judge whether it was a good idea or a terrible mistake. The note was tiny but rolled up as if somebody had made sure to hide it there for her to find.

Maybe she was going crazy. That's what she thought for the most part, and opening the note in anticipation, a violent storm of terror took her hostage, refusing to let her mind ease.

How ironic! Wherever you are, I always find you. I miss the satin night robe you usually wear. It looks good on you.

R.

"Oh my God," Magda whispered, the note falling out of her hands. Her body froze from the sudden revelation. That guy was the same one who had sent her the rose bouquet 2 months ago and the same who had called before. She had waited weeks to hear from him, leaving her wishing to hear his voice again, and now, out of the blue, he made an appearance, but this time, in her home. The comfort she's known for a long time, the privacy of her roof. He was watching her, but how?

"W-What happened? You want me to call Helmer?"

"No!" Magda said, sprinting toward the door to lock it. "I need to cancel the ride. I can't go out. I-I can't..."

"What is it?" Gladice questioned, witnessing Magda caught up in a loop of distress, running to every corner of the room.

Magda rummaged through the room, from the drawers to underneath her bed and the covers. She delved into the walking closets, the dirty laundry bins, and the bathroom, but there was nothing. Everything seemed neat, so how was her stalker able to see what she was wearing? God knows for how long this has been going on. So many days, she's been bare in that room, sharing intimacy with her husband, and hiding her pills too wouldn't be a secret anymore.

"I can't be in this room anymore. I'm trapped. No matter where I go." Magda paused, processing this striking discovery, giving in to the tears that kept begging to be released.

"You need help with anything? You are looking very disturbed," said Gladice, getting off the chair by the bed.

"No, sit!" Magda shouted; her voice filled with some sort of urgency. "We're being watched. It's best that you don't move."

"What's happening?" Gladice whispered, confused.

"I'm trapped in hell. That's what's happening." Magda turned off the lights and then slumped in front of the bed, drawing herself into a ball like a frightened cat, keeping her head tucked in between her lap. She finally understood that the note was a threat, drawing her attention to the inevitable truth. Her stalker found her. The ghost, maybe that only existed in her mind as she thought, was just there to haunt her. There was no escape.

CHAPTER 18

Soft Punches

FLASHBACK

Elvino would pick up Helmer from school and then take him to practice at a boxing ring. He'd teach him regularly how to put on a few punches, but no matter what Elvino's efforts were, there always seemed to be something holding Helmer back whenever he had to fight. "You're too soft. Men don't slap; they punch," Elvino shouted, his eyes widening with excitement. He wanted to see his mentee become fearless and more confident. "Try again. Hit me, and don't miss."

"I-I can't." Helmer panted, removing his boxing gloves. He was wearing a t-shirt and a pair of shorts. His shoulder-length sandy curls hung loose, the ends rough and sun-bleached, like threads of seagrass left to dry in the breeze. His soft demeanor seemed out of place in the boxing ring, having a 40-year-old man yelling at him to take a hit.

Helmer's energy slowed down, making him realize he was about to pass out. He needed water and fast. His heart was racing like a rollercoaster ride coming 1000 feet from the sky to the ground. His breathing increased, causing him more panic.

"It's okay," said Elvino, throwing the boxing gloves away and getting Helmer a bottle of water. "Take deep breaths and try to count with me. It'll help distract your mind from what you're feeling."

Elvino sat Helmer down and stooped over, helping him drink the water and breathe through his anxiety.

"I get those panic attacks too," Elvino confessed. "That's why my home is flooded with cats, to be frank with you. They soothe me like magic."

"I don't want to be like my dad, you know?" Helmer said, his heart getting back to normal rhythm. "I fear if I hit you, I'll become just like him."

"You are not him, Helms; you'll never be unless you choose to," reassured Elvino. "Life gives, but in the end, we choose. We're the choosers, so we're really the ones in power."

Helmer sat there for a while, but in reality, he was dreading his daily ordeal, having to go home and face his father. Although his ears grew tired of listening to Elvino's senseless jokes in an attempt to tear a laugh out of him, Helmer started to see him as a shelter and family. But after all, he'd have to face the storm alone.

Helmer stood, grabbed his uniform and water bottle, preparing his mind for what was to come. Home was an arena in which no one knew what exactly to expect, and he just wished that he wouldn't be hit since he had a tiring day. His body wasn't ready for new scars since there were already too many. "I'm walking home today. I need to free my mind a little."

"Listen," said Elvino, pulling Helmer back in before he left. "I know you're not good yet with punches. But if anything would happen to you, I'm one call away. You hear me?"

Helmer nodded, his eyes making all the noise that he wasn't going to. That was a boy who was stuck in a bubble, wondering if he'd ever be set free. Somehow, he didn't want to be free, as he started to be used to the chaos. But deep inside, he wished one day, his father could strike him dead and end it for good. Life became bitter, so bitter that he no longer wished to choose it.

"Thanks for the water and everything," he said, then surprised Elvino with a firm hug.

Adjusting to the embrace, Elvino's arms slowly joined in; then, he patted Helmer's head. "You're welcome, Helms. I'll see you tomorrow after school, and you'll have more intense training. One hundred reps of pushups, no negotiations."

Helmer laughed to himself, then put on his school backpack and took the way home. He couldn't think despite his sincere efforts. But reaching home, he had walked into an outrageous scene that even a boy with soft punches would never have the heart to just stand by and do nothing.

Mr. Jean was drunk, but something was unusual about him that night. Helmer looked at the floor, and there were rolls of white powder and different shots of drinks. He didn't know what they were, only that they made his father become a filth with no morals.

"Gladice," Helmer mumbled, watching his father rip his nanny's dress with force. She was stuck, her back facing Mr. Jean and her head pressing against the wall, hopeless and begging for him to let go. But Mr. Jean only got aggravated even more by her resisting and he hit her. "I have to do something," whispered Helmer to himself, wondering how he could take down that violent man off of the lady who had been the only mother he'd known.

"Tanpri Jean, don't do this," cried Gladice, feeling Mr. Jean's hands invading her private walls. "Think of all the times I've been working for you. I haven't said a word, but not this. Plea—"

Mr. Jean stumbled back, gripped away from Gladice, finally setting her free. She fixed her uniform and ran out of sight, too ashamed to look at the boy she had raised witnessing such a horrific act.

"This will be the last time you'll touch her like this again," Helmer warned, his eyes meeting with his father, who was so inflamed with anger that his stare called for murder. "What? You're mad that I didn't let you finish your filth? I was hoping you'd have some decency or humanity in you, but you got none. Maybe my mother had a good reason to leave after all."

Mr. Jean knelt on the ground, sniffed some of the powder from the rolled paper, and then sniffed a couple of times before getting up. "That's what we do now? Drugs? What? Cocaine? Or God knows what."

"Mais, quel ingrat!" Spat Mr. Jean, his frustration obvious, not needing translation. "You had no reason to mention your mother," he added, smoldering with malice, his accent heavy like a thick fog rolling in over a bay. "No wonder you're such a failure, and a worthless mut just like her." His hands formed a fist then he threw it in Helmer's direction, who didn't dodge in time. "I'll teach you how it's done. You want to square up with me, then show me what you got." He kicked Helmer, and the pain rang through his spine so hard that he could feel his back cracking in half. Pushing through with another kick, Helmer winced on the floor, feeling each hit.

"Non, non…Jean, tanpri…" yelled Gladice, her motherly instinct kicking in. "Jean, please, stop." She rushed back in and stooped over Helmer to spare him from the heavy kicks. Besides, Helmer was not physically strong enough to hit back hard enough. Each hit felt like they were breaking him. "Please. You'll kill him, please, let him go. I'll do whatever you want." Mr. Jean pulled Gladice's coarse strands and dragged her to the dining room. Her agonizing screams didn't stop him, nor did her plea.

"Why don't you tell him the truth? Huh? That it's not the first time I've touched you like this. Se kay gwo manman m' ranmase w wi, Gladice," Mr. Jean pinned her to the table, his hands tightly grasped around her neck. "Tell my son what you are and where I found you. C'mon, tell him you were a cabaret whore I saved from Haiti and added to my charity list."

"You're hurting me," cried Gladice, pressing her legs together, fearing what's to come.

"No, I need you to tell him that I brought you to the U.S. and gave you a second chance in life," Mr. Jean yelled, his spit splattering over her. "You are nothing without me. You are my charity work, Gladice. Nothing—"

A full bottle of wine crashed onto Mr. Jean's head, making him collapse, losing clear vision. Helmer seized him and punched him repeatedly, all his anger and hatred unleashing. He was watching his father unresponsively, yet he kept hitting and grunting with rage.

"Helmer…" Gladice whispered, trying to make the violence stop. Mr. Jean's nose was bleeding, and so were his ears. He was in bad shape, but Helmer only found it gratifying. He had waited so long for that moment that he didn't want it to end.

"Helmer…"

Gladice placed her hands on his shoulder, her pleading voice gradually bringing him back to his sense of reality. Helmer slowed down and dropped on his butt, fitting into Gladice's arms. "It's okay, ti cheri. It's okay. It's over now."

Helmer looked at his bloodstained hands and the bloody mess around him. He had fought back—he'd done it. But at what cost? He hoped he hadn't just become his father.

***

Helmer was in his room, keeping to himself, avoiding contact with everyone. He had put his phone in silent mode, not wanting to be bothered. He had skipped work, escaping all the chaos happening with the notes he had been receiving. There were too many threats and directions to follow, making him feel like a mouse in a cage or a spinner going round and round with no hope of getting anywhere.

Helmer looked on top of his closet where he had kept the bloody knife. He was ruminating about whose blood was on it. The thought that it could've been Nina's troubled him. Who in their right mind would carve a scar into someone's flesh as if they were objects? He glanced at the nightstand, assuming that he had his tracker there, but it was nowhere to be found.

Helmer darted toward the nightstand, looking through the drawers and the bed covers between the pillows. He had remembered turning the tracker off due to his desperate yearning to keep his family out of this whole ordeal, away from the stalker's gaze. Helmer did not want to bring trouble to his home, except that trouble was already in.

"Damn it, I lost it," realized Helmer, a wave of panic moving through his body. He patted himself, then his pockets, praying that his suspicions weren't true, but the tracker wasn't in the room or anywhere. His heart pounded, wondering what would happen next. "Nina. I must call Nina."

He reached for his phone and a puddle of Nina's missed calls flooded his screen. Someone knocked on the door, and Helmer hid the knife in haste, then shoved his hands into his pockets. It was Mr. Hens, coming to announce the arrival of Jonathan who was urgently requesting to speak with Helmer downstairs. Urgent didn't sound good. Helmer's heart raced faster, fearing that it had to do with the same person he had been trying to hide from. He gestured at Mr. Hens, followed him out of the room, then made it to the foyer.

"Sir..." said Jonathan, rushing over to speak to his boss. But what he really wanted at that moment was a heartfelt hug, someone to tell him that everything was going to be okay. His face sank into his palms, a huge lump clogging his throat. "They're gone. They're gone."

"Gone? Who are we talking about?" Helmer asked, gesturing at Mr. Hens to provide some privacy.

"My family," Jonathan replied. "There is a guy who has my son and my wife; he told me to make sure I do as told if I wanted them back."

Jonathan looked around him, his body shivering as if he had seen a ghost or that a bullet would fly through the back of his head at any moment. His face kept warning Helmer of one thing: his days were counted. "He's watching me."

"Who's watching you?" Helmer asked, his ears perking at the tiniest sounds and objects around the foyer. Despite his efforts to act calm, his hands constantly twitched and reached for his chest for comfort.

"The psycho guy," Jonathan said, his voice cracking. "And boss, I'm so sorry. I did what he told me to do." He rushed over to the couch and sat, lamenting over what he did. Jonathan rubbed his face, his wailing breaking through the roof. "Boss, the baby. The baby."

"Damn," whispered Helmer, remembering there was also a baby involved. Jonathan's wife was due soon, and no one knew what would happen to her at the hands of that stranger who was shaking up everyone in his life. Helmer did not have the words to bring Jonathan any relief but sat with him, right by the phone on the coffee table in the living room. "I'm so sorry. I-I don't know how exactly I could help right now." "There's nothing you can do," wept Jonathan, wiping his nose with the back of his hand. His ears longed to hear from the psycho guy just for the reassurance that his family was safe and sound. He wanted to hold his wife again, kiss her belly, and sneak candy to his son as his wife scolded him not to have any. His heart was soaked in despair, leaving his soul too numb to act.

"Jonathan, what did you agree to do?" asked Helmer, his eyes shifting to the phone next to him. His heart dropped; then, the phone rang.

"That's him," said Jonathan, raising his head. "He told me he'd call."

"It's—" Helmer gulped, his face turning a shade paler. "It's him? Are you sure?"

His eyes were wide, unfocused, darting as if trying to find something solid to cling to. He staggered back, nearly stumbling over his own feet, and his breath came out shallow and rapid—like he was suffocating in open air. He stared at Jonathan, his hand slowly reaching for the phone.

"Yes, boss," Jonathan confirmed.

Helmer placed the phone in his ear, his body absorbed with an uneasy sensation. He could hear his pulse beat at a higher frequency in his head and Jonathan sniveling. His fingers tightened around the phone so hard that his knuckles blanched, but he couldn't seem to let go. His chest heaved, trying to pull in a breath that wouldn't seem to come. Could all this chaos be all because of him? As he waited for a response, a sobbing voice released over the phone, a medley of screams and panic.

"That's them," Jonathan realized, his entire frame shrinking. A cold sweat dotted his forehead, feeling the icy grip of dread coil tighter around his spine. He reached over, attempting to get the phone from Helmer.

"Wait," Helmer finally managed to speak again, his voice hoarse, barely above a whisper. He motioned to Jonathan to keep quiet.

"No need to warn him. I won't hurt his family," said the caller, his voice sounding like a robot.

Helmer looked at Jonathan, his eyes begging him to stay still. The voice sent chills through his soul like lightning dismantling a tree to its roots. Helmer stood, anticipating the caller's next sentence.

"I am not a monster."

"Are you sure about that?" Helmer said, yet panicking at the sound of his bold reply. "This man had done nothing to you, neither have I—"

"*I agree; my problem is not with him,*" the caller cut in, the voice monotone yet serious. "*My business is with someone you know. But I can't get to them without your help.*"

"My help?" Helmer said, throwing a look at Jonathan, yet failing to help him ease off. "And who are we talking about?"

"*You'll know soon. But for now, I need you to keep the tracker on wherever you are. However, I have a warning...*" The voice paused, and then a glitch followed until the call resumed again. "*I don't take it well when people choose not to cooperate. There are consequences.*"

"What did you ask Jonathan to do?" questioned Helmer, bracing himself as his knees buckled slightly.

"*I commanded him to place a device under your car. It has an explosive attached.*"

"Explosive?" Helmer gasped, his gaze shifting to Jonathan. He pressed a hand to the wall, using it to support his weight. His hands shook, and they wouldn't stop. His heart kept singing sad tales, yet everything around sounded quiet all of a sudden.

"It's a bomb," Jonathan prompted, knowing what he had done would take his boss a minute to process. He had betrayed the one thing he had always promised to do—the vow to keep those under his boss's roof safe, to protect them above all else.

"A bomb?" Jonathan's words replayed in Helmer's mind, the realization hitting him in relentless waves. His lips moved, but no sound came out, like the air was caught somewhere deep in his throat.

"It's not activated," the caller resumed, *"unless you give me a reason to like you did these past days. You have not listened to my instructions."*

"No, no," disputed Helmer, like a child begging for mercy, fearing punishment. "I lost it. I lost the tracker. It wasn't intentional..."

"Your guard's family will be dropped off at home but with a message. You call the cops; they get blown up."

The caller hung up.

"Let me explain," said Jonathan, rushing toward Helmer.

"A bomb? You agreed to place a bomb in my car?" Helmer stepped a few feet away, biting onto his fist so he did not crash it into Jonathan's face. There was a lot of onload; first, it was about the tracker, now an entire family in danger, then a bomb. Could the caller be exaggerating? Would he really blow up a person if given the reason to?

"I'm so sorry, Boss. I'm not proud of what I've done."

"Please, save it," Helmer said, motioning at Jonathan to stay away from him. He tramped around the couch, then sat, pondering on what the caller told him. "Now, a stranger has access to my home. God knows what he will do next. What is he going to ask from me now?"

Helmer looked over Jonathan's shoulder, meeting his guilty eyes. A few wrinkles surfaced between Helmer's eyebrows as he clenched his fists, struggling to keep his composure. "There is a bomb in my car."

"I had no choice," said Jonathan. "I had to do it for my family!" "I get it, I do, but what about my family?"

"What about your family?" raged Jonathan. "I don't think you understand what it's like, but I have a baby on the way. If anything were to happen to my wife or my son, I'd never be able to live with myself."

"Did you just say I don't know what it's like?"

"If you did, you wouldn't have questioned my loyalty over this matter," Jonathan said. "When you're a dad, you would do anything for your kids."

"And to protect your kids, does it mean to sacrifice another man's family? Now, my home and everything is in jeopardy."

"Let me remind you, I have two kids. Two, and they're at the hands of a guy I don't even know and who is apparently after you, for God knows what!" Spat Jonathan, his voice burning through the air. "If there's somebody who should be mad here, it's me. You dragged me into this mess. You dragged all of us into this mess, not to mention I don't even know if I'll see my family again. If placing a bomb in a car was all it'd take to keep my family safe, I'd do it all over again." Jonathan lowered his head and crossed his arms behind his back.

Helmer's glare made the silence sound like an eternity.

"I know it's not your fault," Helmer said, pacing around and in deep thoughts.

"I have dedicated more than a decade to everybody living under your roof," Jonathan added. "Never have I given you any reason to doubt my integrity. Right now, I'm asking you not to understand but to show compassion because I really need some grace right now, and the best way to do that is to tell me the truth. Is this guy after you?"

The fever from thinking about it came upon Helmer again. His breathing halted, and a jarring memory struck him. "No," Helmer replied, his voice shaky. "Someone else, b-but who apparently I have ties with."

"Who?"

"It was a long time ago," Helmer said, cautious about delving deeper into the mystery. He breathed in, feeling a punch in his gut just thinking about who his nemesis could be. Helmer had smothered away the memories about that person before, so now he wondered why he would want to pull them back and purposely haunt himself.

"So, you know who it is," Jonathan said, eyeing Helmer.

"I'll have to make sure before I confirm," Helmer said, shaking his head. "But I promise I'll find out."

"Wouldn't that contradict what he instructed? I don't want to place my family in jeopardy."

"He'll send them in the evening. He said he won't harm th—"

"He better not," Jonathan interrupted, sitting on the couch. "Because I'll drill a hole into that bastard's head." He took his phone and looked at his lock screen, his wedding wallpaper bringing to him an instant memory of his wife dancing with him at their last party in the ballroom. He remembered staring into her eyes, feeling his baby's little kicks as he pressed his hands on her belly, and how much she felt like home. Now, there was nowhere to turn to but his solitude and his exasperation, having to wait for hours to hold her again.

"They'll be okay," Helmer said, reluctantly sitting next to Jonathan, failing to believe his own words.

"I need a minute."

"Then I'll leave." Helmer knew that certain pains could only be felt and unleashed with silence, away from gaze and judgment. Not every pain required hugs or words to be dissipated; some only required one's acceptance and space to grieve. "I'll go to Mr. Hens in the meantime to get you some water."

Jonathan nodded, his tongue too heavy to form the sentence he intended to. His shoulders dropped, his hands interlaced between his knees, sniveling the first current of tears away. His body was held hostage where he sat, feeling like he had strings drilled into his skin and being pulled in all directions. Strings that were tearing through his wounds, where pain wasn't even a good fit to describe it.

Helmer withdrew to get him the water. But his mind was dangerous, just like a loaded gun. Helmer had ideas about who the caller could be referring to, yet the bomb in question left him anticipating the caller's next move. What if he got pissed and pressed the wrong button? What if his family also gets abducted one day? The chances were growing, and so were Helmer's different plans to get out of that situation.

As he was lost in his streams of thoughts, he bumped into Mr. Hens, rushing out of the kitchen. Helmer asked him to stay and requested some water for Jonathan. "Take it to him when you're done."

Helmer watched Mr. Hens move to the pitcher, pouring water into a glass. He slid onto a stool, unable to shake the prickling sense that eyes were on him. Was there a camera somewhere—watching, recording?

"Sir, are you alright?" Mr. Hens asked, his brows knitting as he noticed the unease pulsing through the house.

"I don't know," Helmer muttered, rubbing the ache in his forehead. "I'm... I'm losing it."

"Would you like to talk about it?" Mr. Hens offered, placing the glass on the counter.

"Listen," Helmer said, beckoning him closer, his tone dropping to a harsh whisper. "I need you to keep an eye on the house—everyone. Especially my daughter and Gladice. You understand me? Make sure they're safe."

Mr. Hens's face tightened at the mention of Gladice, his nod quick and firm. There was something he wasn't asking, but Helmer's strained expression warned him not to. "Of course."

"If you notice anything unusual, you tell me right away." "And Mrs. Dupris?" Hens inquired, raising an eyebrow.

"My wife?" Helmer's voice roughened, his gaze hardening. "I'm still deciding. Now, vodka. Get me a glass of vodka. No ice."

"Right away, sir." Mr. Hens set the water aside, heading to the liquor cabinet. He poured a neat shot, handing it over. "No ice."

Helmer seized the glass, downing it in one gulp. The sting jolted his senses, momentarily sharpening his focus. But the crawling sensation of being watched returned, prickling at the back of his neck. He slammed the empty glass down. "Come with me," he ordered, his voice as tense as a drawn wire.

Helmer led Mr. Hens into the walk-in pantry, pulling the door shut behind them with a quiet click. "I know this seems strange," he said, his voice barely more than a whisper. "But I can't talk out there. We need privacy."

"O–Okay," Mr. Hens stammered, his eyes wide and darting around the cramped space. He couldn't understand why they were hiding in the pantry, but something in Helmer's expression kept him silent.

"I need you to spy on my wife," Helmer said, his words tense and clipped.

"S-Sir. Your wife, but…" Mr. Hens's face paled, his hands fidgeting by his sides.

"I won't take no for an answer!" Helmer's whisper came out like a hiss. His eyes bore into Mr. Hens's, making it clear that refusal was not an option.

"Even if I agreed," Mr. Hens began, his voice shaking, "I couldn't do it. Mrs. Dupris... she's forbidden the staff from going to her floor. It's off-limits. I wouldn't be able to get close. And besides... I don't meddle in family matters."

Helmer's jaw clenched. "So, is that a no?"

The pantry felt smaller, the air denser, as Mr. Hens shifted uncomfortably under the weight of his boss's stare. "N-Not exactly. I'm just—"

"Hens, if you do that for me, I promise you a date with Gladice. It's guaranteed," Helmer said, his voice persuasive yet threatening. His towering figure loomed over Mr. Hens, the intensity in his eyes cutting straight through him.

"O-Okay," Mr. Hens stammered, fidgeting with his sleeves, feeling the heat of Helmer's alcohol-laden breath hovering over him. "I'll do it, sir. I'll help you."

Good," Helmer said, with a sharp nod. "We'll talk more tomorrow. For now, I have bigger issues to deal with. Go on, take the water to Jonathan."

Mr. Hens nodded and then exited the pantry room, hastening to get the water to Jonathan as his boss requested. His belly kept jiggling around as it fully slipped out of his pants, which were not tight enough. He left Helmer inside the kitchen, having a moment to himself, desperately needing a plan. But what kind of plan would be effective against someone he could not see?

As he gulped another glass of liquor, Helmer heard Mr. Hens rushing back to the kitchen. But he paid no mind until he saw Mr. Hens' hand with a splash of fresh blood. Helmer dropped the glass on the table, his heart forgetting to skip a beat. "Sir, we have a situation at the gate. It's a matter of life and death."

Helmer's breath caught, his chest tightening like a vice as the blood drained from his face. His glass shattered against the floor, sending shards skittering across the tiles. He couldn't process Mr. Hens' words fast enough, couldn't move his legs until the sight of blood seared into his mind. His legs jolted into motion, sprinting past the foyer toward the entrance like a man racing against fate.

His lungs burned, and his pulse drummed a deafening beat in his ears. But nothing—absolutely nothing—could have prepared him for what he saw. The world seemed to tilt on its axis, reality becoming distorted and surreal as he stumbled to a halt, eyes locking on the black cargo bags laid out like some grotesque offering.

"Boss, you really have to come and see this," said one of the guards, breathing as if he had seen a ghost, or maybe something just too gruesome to describe.

A strangled cry lodged in his throat as Jonathan bolted past him, his steps frantic and desperate. Jonathan's guttural wail ripped through the silence as he tore open the nearest bag, his fingers trembling so hard they fumbled over the zipper. The sight inside stole the breath from his lungs, and he collapsed forward, his body shaking with sobs that rattled through his entire frame.

"No!" he howled, cradling his wife's scarred and bloodied face in his hands. His tears mingled with the blood that stained his fingers, his voice cracking under the weight of his woes.

"Oh no," Helmer muttered, his vision blurring as his own tears began to spill. "What just happened?"

CHAPTER 19

FLASHBACK

Magda and Richard met again in the woods, trying to decide what to do before it was too late. Richard sat on one of the huge rocks, pondering intensely about Magda's plan. Richard was good at calculating every detail, possibility, and danger, and at times, he'd do things that even felt like déjà vu. As a young man who had little resources, that raised a lot of questions. Will Magda really be able to stick with him to the end?

"What are you thinking?" asked Magda, stepping behind him. She leaned down and placed her chin over Richard's shoulder.

"It is wrong," Richard said, getting off the rock and pacing away from Magda.

"What's wrong?"

"All of it," Richard replied, "You're engaged to that man, and I feel like I'm stealing something valuable from him because of my own selfishness."

"But you know I don't love him," Magda prompted, getting close to Richard and lacing her arms around him. "We can leave and start everything over."

"I get it, and you know I'd cut an arm off for you. I'd do anything, but taking you out of the States before your wedding is insane. It's 3 days away, and you're asking me to pretend it's okay."

"So, what are you trying to say?" Magda asked, crossing her arms and reading the repugnance in Richard's eyes.

"I think we are the ones being selfish here."

"Richard, we talked about this. You can't turn on me now. My dad gave me some of his savings. We will be able to survive off of it for a while until we settle down in Indianapolis. I promise."

"If you really love me, then why not just break the engagement?" Richard asked, staring into her eyes for any signs that his concerns weren't valid.

"My dad told me not to for my protection," Magda replied. "I don't know why he changed his mind about us and thought of Helmer in such a bad light suddenly. It almost felt like the guy was a serial killer. Anyway, whatever the outcome is, I want you in my life. I don't want anyone else; I love you."

Richard went back to sit on the rock, staring at the trees shaking off their leaves. He wondered if he was the tree in Magda's life or the leaf that sooner or later would fall off. He was quiet for a minute, his ears perking at the sound of Magda's feet approaching him.

"C'mon, we can do it," said Magda, pacing around Richard.

"This is cruel," he said softly as if he no longer wished to make a point. "I also don't have the means that this man has or any sufficient resources. I don't want to go to the end of the earth with you living off of your father's savings."

"Richard, it's temporary," huffed Magda. "My father has accepted our relationship.

This should mean something, don't you think?"

"You won't break off the engagement not because of what Mr. Brooks told you. It's because deep inside, you want that comfortable life and everything this guy has to offer. You want to hang on."

"You sound insane," argued Magda. "I don't even know this guy, and my father is telling me not to trust him. Why would I want to wake up next to a stranger and somebody I can't trust?"

Richard rubbed his temples, pacing back and forth. "It doesn't take away the guilt I'm feeling."

"I'm literally leaving this man for you. For us!"

"The night before his wedding," Richard spat, his voice growing hoarse.

"This is the closest date I found for us to go to Indianapolis, Richard," Magda said, her mouth twisting into a pout. " It wasn't on purpose."

"If this man is really as dangerous as your father describes, God knows what he might do when he finds out t—"

"You're overthinking it," Magda cut in, a soft attempt at reassurance that even she didn't believe. She clasped his face and pecked a kiss on his nose. She wrapped her arms around him and then proceeded to sit on his lap. "You got to trust me."

"It's not you that I don't trust, but the guy you're with,"

Richard said, his eyes shutting at the feeling of Magda's smooches. "Like I said, a man can do anything when he's losing the woman he loves."

"Maybe," Magda said, caressing Richard's face. "But you'll be fine.

Helmer won't find out a thing. He doesn't even know who you are."

"Let's hope so." Richard kissed her, putting his concerns at rest.

END OF FLASHBACK

Magda was in the family theater room, her legs crossed over the footstool, watching her favorite cartoon series projected on the enormous white wall. She pressed the large bowl of popcorn to her chest, casting a handful into her mouth. She reached for the plate of guava cakes on the couch and placed it on her lap, and the delicious view of the food eased her uneasiness. Richard was on her mind, the ghost she could never conceal from, and oddly enough, she expected that ghost to find her. But why?

Magda grabbed a handful of cake, buffed some whipped cream on it, and stuffed it into her mouth, along with the popcorn. Her thoughts trailed back to her stalker; what if the theater room wasn't safe either? The thought made her jump off the couch, her eyes scanning through the room. She licked her yellow-stained fingers from the cheddar popcorn and proceeded to turn off the projector. She needed answers, good ones, not just vague, leaving her hanging.

"The guards," she remembered. How could she not think about this possibility for all this time? Who would really be the best to tell her who dropped the bouquet 2 months ago or who has been delivering the notes? Magda exited the theater room and took the stairs to the foyer. She didn't want to cause any suspicions nor afford to have Helmer find out about her stalker.

Magda arrived at the gate and greeted one of the guards, her eyes traveling around as if she was being followed.

"You're okay, Mrs. Dupris?" asked one of the guards, reading the frantic expression in Magda's eyes.

"I'm okay," she said, though her eyes darted away, her lips pressed tightly together. She probably didn't want to ask questions and find out. Some things were better to be left alone and buried in the dark. Except, her stalker didn't leave any room to ignore the fact that she was in danger. A huge one that was slowly transforming into a trap, the type of trap where one feels so threatened that they have no choice but to turn wild, just like the past–things she never talked about.

"Are you sure? You look a bit flustered," said the other guard. "Would you like to call your husband and let him know you're not well?" "No," Magda prompted, knowing that would ruin her plan. She had everything under control, or she thought so. "I'm just feeling a bit dizzy.

But I needed to ask you guys something." "Anything, ma'am," the guards said in unison.

"I wanted to know if there's anything strange that you have noticed lately."

"Strange how?" one of the guards asked.

"I don't know. Like, a bouquet delivery, some notes, or anything at all that you would have noticed from the house's camera footage." Seeing the guards a bit dumbfounded, staring at each other and shrugging at her question, Magda didn't seem to have much hope left. She needed to know, for the uneasiness of not knowing what was broiling around was pure anguish. "I need the footage of whoever has dropped by the house in the past 2 months. Every single person, no exceptions."

"Wait, you might be right," one of the guards said, thrusting a finger forward. "But I don't think it'd be strange. There was a boy who delivered a bouquet 2 months ago—"

"That bouquet, yes," Magda said in haste, her hands shaking and nearly clasping the guard's arm, to inquire about his statement. If he had seen more than the bouquet, he could enlighten her about the odd events of those past weeks. Nonetheless, she understood that her stalker wasn't only in her head; he was present and maybe more than she realized. "Tell me about the boy. What did he look like? What was he wearing? Did he talk at all? Have you done anything to talk to him?"

"W-We don't know." the guards shrugged as Magda kept urging them to tell her more. "Actually, it was a boy, so we didn't question anything. He handed the flowers in front of the gate, then left, and we radioed Mr. Hens to come get it."

"That's probably the boy from the coffee shop, the one I saw with June," Magda muttered, the pieces falling into place. "Nothing is a coincidence... It's all connected."

"Jonathan might be able to tell you more. He's been working overtime lately, watching the cameras closely," one of the guards added. "He seems the right one to ask."

As they turned their heads in the dark, they noticed two flashlights coming slowly toward them but swaying through the roads. "Wait, Miss, please step back," the guards said, shielding Magda and cautiously reaching for their pistols, for they couldn't identify what was coming toward them. "This is private property!"

Then, a multitude of muffled sounds reached the guards, making them hesitate to point their pistols. As their eyes adjusted to the voices, they felt a horrible wave of shock. "That's Jonathan's family."

"What?" Magda whispered, puzzled at the guard's statement. "What are you guys talking about?"

"Please, stay here," the guards suggested and then radioed Mr. Hens.

"Wait!" Magda said, holding onto them. "Whatever we talked about today, do not say a word to my husband! I know he's your boss, but what I am doing right now is to protect him and our household. I need you to trust me and pay attention to the cameras more than ever. I'll pay whatever amount. I demand your discretion on this. Please!"

"We will ma'am, but right now, we got to inform Jonathan. It would really help us if you could call an ambulance or the cops."

One of the guards headed inside to inform Jonathan about his family arriving at the mansion in a horrible state while the other attended to them.

Jonathan's family was delivered as the caller had told Helmer he would, but he left some details out of the story. Jonathan's family were blindfolded, their mouths heavily taped, walking in unsteady steps with their arms strapped all around with a wired cord. They looked dehydrated, as they could be seen about to collapse as they walked desperately, hoping to find shelter.

"Oh my God. Who could do such a thing?" Magda said as she rushed over to get a closer look. There was a large cut carved under Jonathan's wife's neck, still fresh and spurting blood.

"She's losing consciousness," realized the guard, securing his arms around Jonathan's wife before she dropped to the ground. He caught her and held her there while pressing the side of his shirt over the large cut while shifting a glance to the boy who passed out in Magda's arms. "For God's sake, what the hell happened to them?" As he reached for the tape to remove it, the guard got pulled back. It was Jonathan, wanting to confirm his worst fear. What happened to his wife at the hands of his abductor?

"Baby... Oh my Lord, baby," whispered Jonathan, a stream of tears flooding up his face. He dropped to his knees and leaned over his wife, his arms slowly swaddling her up. "Give me a minute." He couldn't even manage to hold both his wife and his son, for holding one was too overbearing. It was too much of a shock and distress for his heart, which was slowly beating at the moment.

"I'll check around the area and the cameras," the guard reassured, patting Jonathan's shoulder. This provided little yet ineffective comfort to his grieving partner.

Jonathan nodded at him and directed his focus back to his wife. Her skin felt damp and lifeless, and the heavy mascara watermarks under her eye bags revealed possible torture and no sleep. Jonathan traveled her eyes to his wife's belly, his heart racing from the terror to find out if the baby was okay. He touched her belly and then rubbed every quarter of it, tears streaming down his face. He wanted desperately to say for sure that his family wasn't tortured, yet all evidence showed possibilities that the baby might have been affected.

Hearing Helmer's footsteps behind him, Jonathan let out a whimper. "He said he wouldn't hurt them. I don't understand, what have I done to have such a thing happen to my family? I spend my days providing safety for you and your home while I can't even provide the same for my family. I failed them."

"I-I don't know what happened," said Helmer, aware that no words could alleviate Jonathan's guilt and agony at the moment. "I thought he wouldn't hurt them either."

"You know why?" Jonathan said. "Because that's what psychopaths do. They tell you what's in their minds but do the opposite."

They both understood that this guy from the shadows was not a normal man. He was the face of fear and everything that would cause one to go mad. Helmer stooped over and noticed the cut under Jonathan's wife's neck, then felt butterflies in his chest. It wasn't the sort of feeling that one feels when happy or ecstatic. It was rather what one feels when reason and freedom feel scarce and knowing that their world will soon come to an end.

Helmer removed his shirt and placed it on the cut; he did not seem to want to stare at it any longer, for the cut was deep. "He drugged her," Helmer realized. "That was what happened with Nina."

"What are you talking about?" Jonathan asked, his hands desperately waiting for a baby's kick that would never come.

"Hold on," Helmer said, removing the shirt to check the cut. He took out his cell phone and turned on his flashlight. It was a letter.

"Wait, is that…"

"A letter," Helmer confirmed. "U."

"That's a psycho!" raged Jonathan, looking over at Magda on the other side with his son. "Please, stay with her."

Jonathan left Helmer with his wife and rushed over to Magda, who was still holding his son.

"He's breathing fine," Magda reassured.

"Have you called an ambulance yet?" Jonathan asked as he took his son from Magda. He stroked his son's cheeks and hugged him tightly, grateful that he could carry him again.

"I tried, but for some reason, the call wouldn't go through," Magda replied, reaching for her phone, intending to call again.

"But there's a perfect internet connection here," Jonathan opined, gesturing at Magda to try once more.

"Okay, I'll—" Magda's face dropped, noticing a rose petal fall from underneath the boy's shirt. The world stopped instantly, leaving her in a realm of turbulence. It couldn't be what she was thinking. Magda palmed her forehead, feeling the hot wave of panic surging from the depths of her soul. The nightmare was repeating. The rose was back.

"Mrs. Dupris, please hurry," urged Jonathan, seeing her boss's wife lingering.

"Y-Yeah, Yeah. I'm calling right now."

Magda dialed 911, but from the sound in the phone, it wasn't the cops or a dispatcher. She walked away from Jonathan and her husband, pressing the phone to her ear. There was a glitchy sound until the person responded. "Maggie."

"It's you," whispered Magda in a disappointed tone. "The guy who sent me the bouquet, a-and the notes. D-Did you do this?"

"*I think you know the answer,*" the caller replied. *That is not so different from what you did years ago. Everything you touch leaves a scar on it.*" He didn't use a generated voice to hide; he allowed her to hear his voice once again.

"There's no way," Magda said, too absorbed in the caller's voice to hear his statement. "You... you sound just like him."

"*Like who?*" He taunted.

"Richard," Magda whispered, feeling the old wounds split open. "Why are you doing this? What do you want? What's with the roses and that voice you put on? Did somebody ask you to do that?"

"*I want to see you.*"

"What are you after?" she demanded, her voice rising. "Why are you tormenting me? Why hurt the people I care about? You've attacked my house. You didn't even spare a child and a boy. Who are you?"

"*Does that mean you're afraid of me?*"

"I don't even know who you are," she said, her voice trembling, "but I have this awful sense that I know your face."

"*Elaborate,*" He urged, quite amused.

"Because monsters don't need a face," she said. "Cruelty is all they are."

"*I'm the opposite,*" He objected. "*I was made a monster. I wasn't born one. I had a face, then they took it from me, so I decided to add fear to it. Because fear is an amplification of one's passion and obsession. Tell me I'm wrong.*"

"You're not making any sense."

"*Then tell me my voice doesn't do anything to you,*" he pushed, his tone soft and maddening. "*That it doesn't stir any curiosity—so much that your soul aches for my longing. Tell me I'm wrong.*"

"You...You are wr—" Magda began, her voice faltering.

"That's obsession," he cut in harshly.

"And what good does that do for you?" she finally snapped.

"Closure," he said simply. *"Meet me in two days at the theater on Vincent Avenue. Maybe then, you'll get a glimpse. I'll make sure you see me."*

Before she could say anything, she felt an arm wrapping around her. It was Helmer, concerned and distraught about the whole situation.

"You're okay?" he asked, making sure to keep a close eye on her.

Magda nodded, glancing at the phone, relieved that the caller hung up just in time. "I'm fine."

"Who were you on the phone with?" Helmer asked, taking a quick look around and anticipating her answer.

"No one, but I was trying to call the cops—"

"The cops?" Helmer said, his eyes bulging out of his face from the horror. He tried his best not to look restless, but his breathing betrayed him. Short gasps escaped his lips the more he thought about it. What if the caller found out someone called the cops? "Tell me you didn't call them."

"I did."

"For God's sake!" Helmer shouted. "Why didn't you call me first? Now, I have to check on our daughter. We need to give her utmost protection, and you, then Gladice..."

"Helmer, the call didn't go through. Why are you so flustered?"
"Me flustered? No, I'm concerned. Because you see what happened tonight with Jonathan's family, that could have been us, you or me or our daughter. We don't even know if we're safe here anymore..." "Helmer, what are you talking about? Is there something you're not telling me? What is it?" Magda inquired, realizing that there could be a possibility

that she wasn't the only one being stalked. What if her husband was too? Or maybe he was a target, along with everyone under their roof. Magda watched him speak, her eyes reading the drops of sweat forming on his forehead. Could he be worrying about something more? Could the caller have called her husband too? Those questions were taunting her and causing all sorts of turmoil inside her brain.

"Did the cops say anything? What did you say? What happened?" continued Helmer, holding onto Magda, keeping her away from the gate. "Helmer, is there something you're not telling me?" she asked, causing him to go quiet.

CHAPTER 20

Pancuronium

*H*elmer stayed up the entire night in the emergency room, anticipating updates about Jonathan's family. They had rushed to the hospital due to Jonathan's concerns about not feeling any movements from the baby. Jonathan was silent for hours, looking toward the hallway, hoping the nurse or somebody would come with some updates. He watched a nurse escorting a little boy in a wheelchair into a room as he was bleeding. Seeing the scene made him plunge back into deep thoughts, fearing that he might walk out with heart-wrenching news. Nothing he was seeing made him feel any better, and having his family back untouched, safe and sound was all that could give possible relief.

"They'll be alright," Helmer said, as he saw Jonathan slowly becoming restless.

Jonathan nodded, acknowledging Helmer's concerns, and stood to shake off the weighty fear sitting on his chest, giving him the urge to vomit. "They... They have to be. I'm really hoping they are."

Helmer's gaze shifted between Jonathan, who was pacing back and forth, and the sterile, fluorescent-lit hallways of the hospital. He scanned the faces around him—the nurses at the reception desk, the patients waiting quietly in their seats, even the security guard leaning against the wall. Any one of them could be watching him and working for psycho man who had been haunting his life these past weeks. The soft murmur of voices and the echo of footsteps in the hall did nothing to ease his nerves. He had learned by now that the threat could be anywhere, hiding in plain sight.

Helmer took a deep breath, but it felt shallow, each inhale a struggle against the tightening fear clawing at his chest. He didn't dare relax. Not here. Not now. Not when the shadows seemed to stretch longer in this place of supposed safety.

"I swear these people don't give a damn," said Jonathan, glaring at the receptionist typing information in the computer, looking calm and unbothered.

Jonathan rushed over to the lady at the desk and repeatedly rang the tiny bell by her computer. "Hey, would you mind telling me what's going on with my wife? I've been sitting here for 18 hours, and nobody has said anything."

"Oh," the lady at the front desk startled, stopping to chew her gum, her hand slowly reaching for her phone. Assuming that she was about to call security to escort Jonathan out for the disturbance, Helmer stepped in.

"Wait, please. We're sorry." Helmer apologized, pulling Jonathan off the desk. "He's just very stressed right now…"

"I'm not stressed; I need answers," Jonathan riposted, skirting Helmer's arm away. He walked a few feet from the desk, moving back and forth, his hands on his hips.

"Listen," Helmer pressed, his voice strained, redirecting his focus toward the front desk lady. "I would really appreciate it if you could say anything to ease our minds. My friend hasn't slept at all, neither have I."

"I'll see what I can—" the lady began.

"Do it now!" Helmer spat, his voice cracking through the air like a thunderclap. His hands clenched the edge of the desk, knuckles white, and his eyes were fierce. The woman flinched, instinctively leaning back, her eyes wide. One of the security guards by the entrance started moving toward him but paused when the doctor finally appeared in the hallway.

"Doctor!" said Jonathan, rushing toward him. The man was of average height, with kinky white hair and glasses steady on his button nose.

Meanwhile, the security guard stopped Helmer, gave him a warning, and left him and Jonathan to interact with the doctor.

"S-Sir..." the lady at the desk swallowed hard, calling for Helmer with a wary expression. "If you don't mind, I have a few more paperwork for y-your friend to sign."

"Okay," Helmer muttered, turning toward her, trying to gather himself, his breaths ragged.

"And you're Mr. Jonathan Amari?" the doctor began.

"Yes, I'm her husband, and the boy is my son," Jonathan replied, following the doctor's questions to confirm his identity.

"So far, we've run a few tests, and the baby—"

"The baby, what?" Jonathan asked in haste, his chest rising.

"Is okay," the doctor said, finally giving Jonathan the relief he needed. "And so is the boy."

"Thank God," Helmer said, peeking behind Jonathan, the clipboard with the documents in hand.

"But have you noticed anything odd with my wife?" Jonathan asked, getting close enough to the doctor to whisper.

The doctor hesitated, pulling off his glasses and letting out a weary sigh. His shoulders sagged as he prepared his answer. "Well..."

"Well what?" Jonathan urged.

"We've detected traces of pancuronium and another unidentified substance in her system," the doctor revealed.

"What does that mean?" Jonathan asked, his face turning as red as a bloody moon. "What are those?"

"It's not entirely clear if it was intentionally injected," the doctor said cautiously, "but pancuronium, especially when mixed with other substances, can be incredibly dangerous. It's a paralyzing agent. In the wrong dosage... it can be fatal."

"Son of a—" Jonathan couldn't finish the sentence. He rubbed his face, his hands trembling, before stepping away, trying to cool the fury bubbling inside.

Helmer, seeing the color drain from his friend's face, stepped forward. "And what about his son?" he asked, his tone sharp and controlled. "Was he drugged too?"

No," the doctor shook his head. "We've found severe dehydration and signs of possible hallucinations due to lack of sleep. Nothing indicates drug use in the boy's system."

Jonathan's chest rose as he listened. "When can I see them?" he asked, his voice barely holding up.

"They're stable," the doctor reassured, "but we're transferring them to the maternity ward. We need to keep a close watch and run more tests. They'll be in for a while, depending on what we find."

"Thank you, doctor," Helmer said, pulling Jonathan up gently and leading him toward the front desk. Helmer knew they needed to get through the paperwork before he lost his composure.

"I'm going to kill him," Jonathan said, his voice gravelly and sturdy. "Not if I get to him first," Helmer growled, grabbing the clipboard and thrusting it into Jonathan's hands. "Sign it. We'll deal with him soon enough."

"He's a psychopath," Jonathan muttered, scribbling furiously on the forms. "This ends with me. I swear, I'll kill him."

"No." Helmer's expression hardened. "As far as I'm concerned, he's already dead," he said, his jaw set and voice as cold as steel.

Helmer had to do something, and quickly. But who would he turn to? Could he reason with a psycho who had no limits, not even sparing the life of a baby? Helmer was aware of what he signed up for, but a repeated yet simple question kept taunting his mind. Why? Why would a stranger cause so much chaos? Who was he after?

"I'll get you something to eat," Helmer said, heading out of the emergency room. Reaching out, a soft breeze hit his face. It felt like a hug, and a nice glass of whiskey helping him to decompress. How could life change in such a blink? What about the days when everything seemed easy and normal? Not having to worry about his family being taken hostage, or his close ones being blackmailed, and a bomb going off. Helmer went off to the cafeteria and scanned through the different lunch options; then, someone bumped into him. "Hey, watch it," he said, brushing it off, as he was too hungry and preoccupied to think. He moved to the high protein bowls section and stopped by to place an order.

A man was standing by Helmer. He had a heavy coat on, his face fully covered, except for his nose, which allowed air to flow. Two tiny holes, about the size of his eyes, allowed him to see through his thick black face covering. He was not tall nor looked brawny enough to draw attention. But his mannerisms did, and the fact that he barely spoke when he stopped next to Helmer to order. He stood there and stared, his face looking ahead at the server.

"Go ahead," offered Helmer, not minding delaying his time on the line.

"Are you sure?" said the guy taking the orders. "I mean, you were here first."

"It's fine. He can order."

The man, his hands fully gloved, placed them on the glass counter and looked at the options. He pointed at the jalapenos and lifted a finger, signing that he needed one scoop.

"One? Only one?" the server asked.

The man nodded slowly, then proceeded to take out some cash from his coat and placed it on the counter. He paced one inch away so Helmer could place his order. He watched Helmer carefully but his observation due to his mask was discreet. Helmer didn't seem as much of a stranger to him, wondering how one could be so kind and yet so unpredictable.

The man stayed close to Helmer enough to sneak a paper into his pocket. Sneaking stuff in seemed an unmatchable skill, and so was the way he made people feel about him.

Helmer stepped aside, wishing for some personal space, and then finished up his order. He got two family-size platters of chicken vesuvio with vegetables and a vegan rainbow cone on the side. Helmer watched the man before the server could hand the jalapenos to him. The man was making haste to leave, moving in a zigzag pattern across the cafeteria room.

"Odd," Helmer said to the server, "he didn't even wait for his order." "Not everyone is okay in there ," the server joked, pointing at his head. Helmer, hoping to make a call, reached for his phone. When he pushed his hands into his right pocket, he felt something. A paper. One tiny piece of paper. Helmer pulled it out immediately, yet was hesitant to find out.

Helmer unwrapped the folded piece of paper and read.

"Onto the next."

R.

The paper slipped from his hand, falling to the floor without a sound. But the message on it rang loud in his mind. R could be any name. But there was one that immediately came to Helmer's thoughts. His chest cracked, as if an earthquake had torn through the pavement. Every cell in his body ached, hardening, ready to shatter. His hands shook, growing numb. He was like the tiger drawn on the cave wall—powerful, yet helpless.

His gaze drifted across the cafeteria, trying to make sense of how the note had ended up in his pocket. And then, a thought struck him, shuddering through him with a force that rattled his very core.

"That was him. That was the psycho man," Helmer whispered to himself. "He was here."

His eyes came back to the server packing his order. But whatever the guy was saying didn't seem to stick, for Helmer's mind was lured into a loop of turmoil. He was being stalked. Where could he be safe then, for everywhere seemed like a trap or a nest for the psycho man to find him?

Fresh memories of the man standing next to Helmer earlier revealed something. He didn't stay for his order. He didn't wait for it. So, was he even there to order? Helmer ran from the pickup line and sprinted across the cafeteria, heading to the door. He reached outside, then continued running, going to the parking lot. Maybe the psycho man had a car or could be walking miles to stalk people? Would he have people working for him or with him? What exactly was he on?

Reaching the parking lot, Helmer saw a glance from afar. He was there. The psycho man, looking straight ahead at him. He had his coat on, arms loose on his side, hands gloved to the elbow. He had heavy boots, wearing all black like a warrior wasp, ready to sting a target.

"Please, don't leave," Helmer shouted, hoping the psycho man would stay a while to chat. Maybe not as close, but at a considerable distance to hear him at least.

Helmer approached slowly, clutching at his throat, fearing that his words wouldn't release themselves. Why come in the daytime? That was some boldness Helmer had never seen. In fact, he has always preferred darkness, for it was comforting, the only place he could truly be himself and safeguard memories of his past.

"I-I finally meet you," Helmer said, out of breath. "I needed to ask you. Why? Why his family? Why me or my home? Who are you after?"

"Call me R," the man said, his lips not moving an inch. His voice sounded artificial and low, with a subtle glitch.

"R, as you allow me to call you, I wish to know what you want. I need answers," Helmer said, his voice slightly strained. "I need to know."

"It's nothing personal," R replied.

"Nothing personal? You are hurting people I care about. You couldn't even spare a baby in your malicious schemes, not to mention you asked my guard to place a bomb in my car."

"A non-activated explosive, to be correct."

"Why? Please, tell me. And what could Jonathan's family have possibly done to deserve such treatment?"

"They haven't done anything," R replied, the light in his eyes slowly dimming off.

He adjusted his coat, his stare steady and somewhat cold. "You have." "Me?" Helmer asked, shrugging. "I don't understand. I have not met you even once in my life."

"I fear we have," R corrected. "I was expecting you to have a better memory."

"You are not okay," Helmer said. "You need help. I don't understand what you're up to or what you're really after."

"You know what I want."

Something tightened in Helmer's chest, an ache he never thought to feel. That was worse than panic. R's message was like a subtle warning: he was ruleless, and his next victims weren't going to be spared.

"I'm still not following."

"You have something that's mine," R said, looking straight at Helmer.

"And what's that thing you're talking about?" Helmer asked, fearful of the answer.

"Your wife," R spat out.

"I beg your pardon?" "That's what I want," R said firmly.

"You're sick. She-she's my wife. Do you understand what you're saying? You can't request somebody else's wife; that's not how reality works."

"I make my own reality. I don't follow the order of things."

From the look in his eyes, he wasn't joking. "You are really deranged, maybe more than I thought."

"I want her," R repeated. "That's what I want from you."

"I can't even process what you're requesting. In what way exactly? I can't…" Helmer paused, taking a few steps back, his heart rate increasing by the minute. He couldn't tell if he was bothered or offended or that he wished to seize that stranger guy and beat the life out of him. His hands formed a fist, but he held back throwing them, not knowing what the aftermath would be. "Do you know my wife? Have you ever seen her before? I need answers."

R stared at him but barely made an effort to answer. He was not a chatty man, and neither liked to explain himself. Confessing those brief parts of his life seemed enough and was more like a warning than a chore. "What if I did? And... why ask if you are not even ready to find out?"

"I want to find out, and now! Because if all this goddamn chaos you're spreading is about my wife, it better be for a good goddamn reason, and that sounds more than personal to me."

"Do you truly want to know who I am?" R said, stepping slowly toward Helmer. "Do you wish to see my face in daylight? Will you be ready to fight the dark?"

Helmer approached R, knowing his urge to crash his fist into his face was growing, robbing him of clarity. "At this point, I wish we get to the bottom of this and that you leave my family alone. That's what I want." The composedness of R awakened something in Helmer, which he had tried to keep asleep for years. The urge to fight, but like a deadly one, where it's either life or death that'd be on the line.

As Helmer's arm swung toward R, a white powder blew in his face, blurring his vision instantly. Helmer paced backward, his head growing heavy, making him see R double. He stooped down, one hand reaching for the ground for support.

"No worries, I won't hurt you today," R said. "But soon. And just so you know, I always get what I want."

"You're crazy," Helmer panted, his eyes fluttering with the sleeping effect from the powder.

"This drug should be wearing off in a few minutes, and then you'll be fine," R said. Then he headed out of the parking lot, vanishing completely, leaving no trace behind, as he'd always managed to do, no matter the time or place.

A lady rushed toward Helmer, assuming he fell and needed assistance. "Sir, are you okay? I was just about to get to my car when I saw you."

"I-I am fine. I just need a moment." Helmer held his head; the drug was still strong and taking time to wear off. The person helped him stand and offered to get him something to drink. But Helmer was thinking about R's request, which sounded like a warning. How could he be so audacious to ask for his wife, what was legally his?

"Thank you, ma'am," Helmer said, still feeling the tight sensation in his chest.

"You're not well," the lady said, her voice reducing to a whisper. "I'll call for help."

"No," Helmer mouthed, his body slowly growing numb. His eyes got blurry, and he eventually fell to his knees, barely able to lift his neck. "I'm...okay."

"No, you're not," the lady said, "I'm calling help right now."

Helmer saw the lady's blurred shadow moving away and talking on the phone. He was limp, as if the drug was eating away his soul. He dropped on his side and then his eyes fell shut.

CHAPTER 21

Spirals

In the morning, his alarm went off, but his eyes refused to open. His head throbbed, heavy like a battle-worn shield. A sharp cramp in his neck anchored him deeper into the bed. He inhaled slowly, his eyes finally adjusting to the room. The curtains were drawn back, and sunlight pierced his sleepy gaze. He groaned, squinting at the clock. Had he been asleep for hours? Days? Then he saw Gladice's arm reaching over to shut off the alarm.

"Good afternoon, ti cheri," Gladice's voice rang out, a smile stretching wide across her face. "I'm so happy you're finally awake. You scared us!" She pressed a hand to her chest, her expression softening. Then Helmer saw Meg peeking out from behind Gladice, rushing forward with a jump.

"Meg, your dad is sore. C'mon!" said another voice—Magda's.

That voice. Helmer's stomach churned, his jaw tightening. The memory of another man's words, another man's claim on her, flooded back like poison. He tried to tell himself it was a nightmare. But no, it was real. His encounter with the psycho man wasn't some delusion. He felt Meg's arms wrapped around him, and he closed his eyes, wishing his tangled thoughts to settle.

"Meg, your dad needs rest," Magda said, her voice soft yet firm.

Helmer's eyes snapped open, his arms tensing around Meg. "I'm fine. No need to send her away."

"I'm not. I was just suggesting that you—"

"I said I'm fine," Helmer cut in, his voice cold and unyielding. "How are you, old man?" Meg asked, pressing the back of her hand to his forehead, then to his cheek. "You terrified us. You looked...you looked like you weren't even breathing."

"That's true," Magda added, moving closer to the bed.

Was that worry in her eyes? Or guilt? Helmer wondered, scanning her down. "Would you mind leaving Meg and Gladice with me for a minute?" He asked abruptly, his tone more cutting than he intended.

"What? You don't want me here?" Magda's face tightened, but Helmer didn't soften his gaze.

"I just need a moment to decompress," he said flatly. "From me?" Magda asked, the edge of her voice quivering.

"Dad, you're burning up," Meg interrupted, her concern clear, but Helmer barely registered her words.

"I'm fine, pumpkin," he muttered, but his eyes were still on Magda, tracing the lines of her face, the curve of her neck, lingering on every detail. Her skin, slightly darker, caught his attention. He watched her movements carefully—every shift, every breath. Her skin was intact, maybe a bit tanned up. He noticed every little spot, then a subtle flush of color below her ear stopped him. Helmer's eyes narrowed, his breath halting as he squinted, trying to see more clearly. A hickey, maybe? He flinched as he spotted one below her ear. But no, he shook his head rapidly. It was his touch. His shoulders relaxed, but his hands stayed clenched, the tension still simmering beneath his skin.

"Meg, I need to speak to your dad. Leave us," Magda requested. But Helmer's reply was swift and sharp.

"Not now," Helmer insisted.

"What do you mean?" Meg said, her eyes boring into her dad's. "Is everything okay? Mom had been up, watching you."

Magda bit her lip, carrying a bowl of cold water. "I don't know what it is with you, but I thought it'd do you good to freshen you up a bit."

"Gladice will do it," Helmer said stubbornly, catching the way her eyes lingered on him—was that pity? His hand gripped onto his skin, the burning sensation invading his body.

Magda's smile faded, her brows knitting. "If that's what you want." She handed Gladice the bowl, the rag dangling loosely over the edge. Her gaze lingered, pleading for him to say something—anything—that would allow her to stay. She only saw the resolved expression in his eyes. Magda's eyes dimmed, her shoulders sagging as she turned to walk out.

Meg's gaze darted between her parents. Gladice gave her a slight nod, urging her to follow. "I'll come back to check on you," Meg said softly, pressing a kiss to her dad's cheek. She lingered a second longer, sensing the feverish warmth radiating from Helmer's skin. Her smile was small, hesitant, before she slipped out after her mother.

"Now…" Gladice sat, with the bowl in hand. "What is it? You're tense, and sound very rude to your wife." She rang the rag and dabbed it onto his face. "She's been wor—"

"I don't want to talk about Magda right now," Helmer interrupted, his eyes darting toward the door.

"Where are the guards? Call them—I need to speak with them." "The guards?" Said Gladice, following Helmer's eyes toward the door. "Why do you need them? You need to rest, son. You just wo—" "Who brought me here?" he asked.

"A woman," Gladice said, "She found your wallet and followed the address."

"Oh… I remember."

"Stay put," Gladice whispered, holding him down as Helmer struggled to rise. His body was weak, barely responding.

"Just get the guards! And don't leave the house. Keep the doors locked, watch Meg for me," he pleaded, his eyes glassy.

"Son, you're scaring me," Gladice said softly, putting the bowl of water to the side.

"No, listen to me!" His voice cracked, his gaze darting to the corners of the room. "Watch the house. Okay? Be careful." His voice transformed into a whisper. "I need to tell them."

"Pitit, stay still," Gladice pressed, holding his trembling hands. She patted his arm, "Tell them what?"

"To check the cameras. To watch the house," he replied. "Please, help me get up."

"But—"

"Please," Helmer insisted, stretching his arms out to Gladice. "Jonathan. I have to check on Jonathan. The psycho guy must still be around the hospital."

"Ki psycho guy?" Gladice asked, her attempts to soothe him falling away like dead leaves. She approached Helmer, braced her arms around him, and sat him up. "Ah, you losing it, son."

"You wouldn't understand," Helmer muttered, grunting. "I'd rather you don't know, to be honest."

"Son," Gladice said gently, bending to support him, "you need to lie back down and rest. Let me help." She reached to lift him, but Helmer shifted back, using the headboard to brace himself.

"It's fine," he said. "You shouldn't be straining yourself. I don't want your knee to give out."

"I won't be able to relax unless you eat something," Gladice said. Her eyes flickered with a quiet insistence. "You've been asleep for hours."

"I know, but..." Helmer stopped, catching the unspoken plea in Gladice's gaze and let out a resigned breath. "Alright."

Gladice called for the servants, who soon arrived with a tray. The rich aroma of the pumpkin soup she'd prepared while he slept mingled with the delicate steam rising from a cup of tea. She sat beside him, and as Helmer settled, his head rested against her shoulder. She didn't move, only let her hand rest on his, the slight smile curving her lips.

"You always know what to do," Helmer said, briefly closing his eyes. "Every mother does," Gladice answered, a playful warmth in her tone. But as she adjusted her grip, her fingers grazed his forehead, and the smile faded. A shadow crossed her face as she felt the heat beneath his skin. "You're still burning up, ti cheri."

When the servants arrived, she waved them off after they placed the tray on the nightstand.

"You know, you could be nicer to the servants sometimes," Helmer teased, a half- smirk tugging at his lips.

"And you could be a bit more cooperative," she replied, gently easing him back. She scooped a spoonful of soup and brought it to his lips.

"I honestly don't feel like eating." "You need to," Gladice insisted, not softening. "Back in Haiti, I made it every first of January. I'd lose sleep preparing it." "Hard to know what it's like back there. I've never been. Not that my father would've cared to take me anyway."

Gladice stiffened, her gaze dropping to the floor as memories of Mr. Jean surfaced. "I know. He was, unfortunately, not a kind man. But it's not worth dwelling on right now. The country is overrun by gangs and violence. You're honestly better off here."

Helmer finished the soup, then reached for the tea. Gladice held it, blowing on the surface before offering it to him. "This should help you relax."

Helmer frowned as he sipped. "What do you mean?" "Just something to help you rest," she said, her tone even.

"Why would you do that?" Helmer asked, shifting off the headboard. "I can't fall asleep right now. I need to stay alert... to keep an eye on you—"

"And you will," Gladice said softly, patting his forehead. "After you've rested."

She rose from the bed and carefully tucked the sheets around him, pulling them up to his chest. "With the tea and the heat, you'll sweat that fever right out."

Helmer hesitated, his lips pressing together, but he didn't argue. "You'll be fine," Gladice said, her voice gentle but sure. "You're not alone. I'm here."

Helmer hesitated again, then spoke with a slight shift in his tone. "You know, I think I'd like some more tea. Can you get me another cup?" Gladice's eyes hardened. "Tea? You barely wanted this one."

"I know. But... I'd need you to get it for me," Helmer persisted, his voice quieter now. "Please?"

After a moment, Gladice nodded and left the room.

The moment the door clicked shut, Helmer slowly climbed out of bed, his movements stiff. He limped to the edge, casting a glance at the door. With a brief, practiced motion, he made it to his closet, finding the shape of a safe. He entered the code with unsteady hands, the lock yielding. Inside was a rifle—military grade, cold, looking back at him. He missed the weight of it, the solid grip that he hadn't touched in far too long.

He slid it under his bed, close to the headboard, his breath tight and shallow. No one knew about this safe as one would've thought it was to keep his money secure. But there were times when certain things called for more extreme measures. And his family's safety—his own sense of security—demanded it. Psycho man was out there somewhere, and someone would have to stop him. Or perhaps, it would be a rifle. And his wife? Could she have something to do with all of this? If that were true, he knew he'd become that man—a man who fought demons no one else could see, even if those demons looked a little too much like the people he loved.

Helmer settled back, the mattress dipping under him. He kept his gaze fixed on the door, waiting for Gladice to return.

CHAPTER 22

Broken Trust

Time was ticking quickly for Magda. She had a deadline to follow if she wanted to discover who her caller was. Vincent Avenue, across from the theater, would be the destination. She had to think, as she only had a few hours left for the evening to settle in. But why had her husband become so distant, so withdrawn? Had she caused this? Was it something she's done?

Magda sat around the table, taking a few bites of chicken, but chewed slowly, watching Helmer not touching his plate. He was pensive, his eyes glued to his wedding band, and for minutes.

"Are you okay?" Magda asked, wondering what the long stare meant. She'd give everything to read his mind at that moment. She feared whatever he was thinking about, and she only hoped that her caller would have nothing to do with it. "I figured you had a bad day."

"Yes," Helmer said blankly, his eyes still locked on his wedding band.

"If you're still worried about Jonathan and his family, they'll be okay," Magda said, with a slight smile. "You're a good friend."

"Thanks," Helmer said, taking his arms off the dining table. "He's been servicing our family for more than a decade. I owe him that."

"But there's something I don't understand. Why didn't you call the cops?" Magda inquired, her eyes piercing into Helmer's soul, trying to read him through. She had tried to call the cops, and that didn't go well, for it only referred back to the caller, the stranger in question. Could the same have happened with her husband? "You looked so upset when I told you I did."

"There's no reason," replied Helmer, looking at Magda, his eyes scanning every quarter of her body. His eyes traveled to her lips, chewing slowly her food and going down her throat. He thought of some things that were not as honorable, and the feeling of rage surged through him again.

There was another man out there probably looking at his wife the same, desiring every piece of her as he did. He hated that thought. He felt his blood growing hot and his palate requiring the taste of her. He watched her carefully, studying her hands going up to her hair, fixing her large clips to keep her pony in place.

What was happening to him? Helmer couldn't understand. Why was his wife looking even more beautiful, fertile, and youthful? He cocked his head to the side, seeing her straightening herself and her dress. He pushed his chair and rushed over to her. He could smell her sweat, her natural scent, igniting the desire in him.

"Hmm... What are you thinking about?" Magda asked, watching Helmer bending over, lowering his eyes to her chest. He secured his hands under her arms, scooped her off her seat, and placed her over the table. He pushed the dishes aside to make space and seized her lips. They had been teasing him for a while; now, it was time to compensate.

Magda looked at him, giving in to the pleasure, not knowing if he wanted to play or was just angry. "You look at me like a beast in a cage." Helmer bit her lower lip as he stared into her eyes. "Not for long.

I'll rip the cage any time. You are mine, Magda Dupris. No one else's." He slid his hand under her dress and swiftly parted her legs.

"Helmer..." Magda mumbled. "That's right," he grinned, "I like when you say my name." "Helmer," Magda muttered, tightening her arms around him and allowing her warmth to mingle with his.

"Say it again," Helmer said, his eyes shutting at the response of her touch, what he had craved for days. His head slid to her chest where her heart was, and he somewhat felt peace. But peace wasn't what he needed. Rather, it was answers to questions that kept tormenting his mind. Has any other man ever kissed those same lips he adored kissing? Were her bosoms round and plump, with that satisfying firmness to them, have ever pleasured any other man than him?

Helmer glared at her, afraid of his intrusive thoughts. It was in his nature to be that angry, but something was taunting him to transform into his old self. Almost, perhaps. But he wanted to, so much that as he kissed her again, he bit her.

"Helmer," Magda said, her head tilting slightly, realizing that the man who was standing in front of her was someone she barely recognized. That ferocious passion in Helmer's eyes, made him look like a tiger ready to attack and perhaps kill his prey.

"You're not yourself," Magda said, unable to retain from touching his back, his well-built muscles, pushing the dirty girl out of her.

"I hate to say it that way, but it's time that you see the real me," Helmer said, his breath blowing on her. He lifted her chin and pulled her closer, causing her back to arc voluntarily. "I hate, hate, hate, and hate to be taken for a fool."

"What are you saying?" she asked, sensing her abdomen aching and wanting some of him. Hearing his voice lowering into a hoarse tone and the way his firm hands scooped her waist made her realize. She liked it when he was angry, and going unhinged like a wild cat.

"Do not test me," Helmer warned, grabbing Magda's hand, his eyes looking for her wedding ring. "Careful."

A stomp was heard, causing Magda to startle. Helmer fixed her dress in haste and called out Mr. Hens who accidentally interrupted their fervent session, trying to run out of the dining room with failed success to go unnoticed. A tremendous rose bouquet covered half of Mr. Hens' face. Helmer, seeing the roses, gestured at Mr. Hens to approach, then threw a glare at Magda. His eyes had danger in them, passion, and something just as similar as repugnance.

"Who's this for, Mr. Hens?" Helmer asked, his voice composed yet daunting.

Magda hopped off the dining table and glanced at the rose bouquet. If her heart could speak, it'd tell her to bury herself alive or vanish. She didn't order any flowers, and neither would June send them. He was not that sentimental; neither was he a flower person. Odd? Maybe not, since her eyes gave away that she might have an idea about who sent them.

"These flowers were delivered," Mr. Hens said. "I assume they were for you, Mrs. Dupris."

"Who are they from?" Helmer prompted, the words leaving his mouth even before he thought of saying them.

"I-I ordered them," Magda said, clearing her throat but still glued to her spot. She couldn't allow any wrong moves in case Helmer noticed how nervous she was.

"Is there a card attached, Mr. Hens?" Helmer asked, disregarding Magda's reply.

"I-I don't know, sir."

Magda wished Mr. Hens would just shut up and leave; he wasn't helping. "It's for me—"

"Put them on the table, Mr. Hens." Helmer interrupted. "You may be dismissed. Thank you!"

Magda reluctantly reached for the bouquet, her hands obviously shaking as Helmer's eyes scanned them. She felt her hands burning from Helmer's stare alone. Her heart refused to remain still. She noticed it finally. A card!

"There's a card attached," Helmer commented. "Why are you looking so flustered for some flowers that you ordered? Shouldn't you be excited?"

"I am excited," she said. "It's you who needs to tell me what's going on. First, you don't want to eat; you're quiet; you want to touch me, then change your mind, and then start saying random things. Perhaps you are hiding something."

"Me?" Helmer frowned, his face burning from the effect of Magda's words. "How can you even talk? Those lips of yours utter nothing but poisonous lies, and you deliver them with so much charm and serenity that they undeniably sound true. How do you do this?"

Helmer, not giving Magda a minute to maneuver and think of an answer to escape from the truth, grabbed the bouquet and pulled the tiny card. He wished he had not read it. For God's sake, his face twisted with loathing. His blood was not just hot; it was like a furnace within him. His breath grew louder as he turned to take a glance at Magda. His eyes were wide with seething tears. Helmer dropped the card on the table and paced away, avoiding staying too close to her in case his demons would get the best of him.

"What? What is it?" Magda asked. If only she knew. It'd have been better for her to stay quiet. Her voice was pure torture to Helmer. An agony that he wished to stay out of his ears.

Magda's heart pounded heavily as she cautiously reached for the card, seeing the same unrecognizable face from earlier when Helmer was angry.

Mine.

R.

She could run, but running didn't seem to be a great option. By the look on Helmer's face, Magda knew he dared her to. "I—"

"Caught you in your lie," Helmer began, his breathing loud and heavy. He circled the table, clutching at his hair until the silence taunted him to an extent. He grabbed a fork and thrust it into the table, causing it to shake and the pitcher to spill.

"Helmer..." Magda gulped, yet not knowing what to say. She tugged at herself, trying to ease the tension of not knowing what was behind her husband's mind.

Why hold so much anger? And most importantly, were tears in his eyes? "Helmer, I-I didn't lie."

"I can't believe you're doing this to me, Magda," he said, trying his best to speak through the painful tightness in his chest. "Tell me—where exactly have I failed at my duty as your husband to deserve this?"

Magda's lips parted, her eyes letting out a few drops of tears, knowing her husband was not the type to show such emotions. No words came to mind, but she was actively listening, wondering if she had broken a part of him by keeping her caller a secret.

Magda brushed her arms, soothing the spiked hairs from her body. "What have I done?" She muttered, hoping she had not said it too indiscreetly for him to hear. She couldn't afford to fuel his rage.

"I give you everything you want," Helmer continued, his voice growing raspier. "I bend my morals for you. I do whatever it takes to keep our family together, to take care of you. I even bought those goddamn tickets to Paris for your paintings—because I want to see you win, to see you happy, doing what you love."

"I know that." A sob escaped Magda's lips.

Helmer's words woke something in her, perhaps her conscience which she almost forgot having one. His tears were like needles in her ears, sending chilling vibrations to her body, making her shake continuously. She felt his torture and heard the screams of despair for the truth. Magda didn't want to hold it back any longer. Her mouth itched from keeping shut. She had now to choose between her caller and her husband. Who, then, would it be?

"And now, you're lying to me." "I'm not lying—"

"You are, Magda. You are!" Helmer roared, pointing at the roses. "This shows that you are hiding something from me." He grabbed the flowers and tossed them into the garbage. "It's the psycho guy. He knew you'd be here with me, so he sent the note on purpose so I could see it."

"He?" Magda said, her voice shrinking. Her eyes discreetly searched for the sight of the bouquet. She wanted to take one last look at the flowers, perhaps touch them, to make sure they were the same she had received two months ago.

"If you utter one more lie, I swear I'll do something I regret," Helmer said, walking towards her slowly. "Who sent this bouquet? Who's R?"

"I don't know wh—"

"Do not lie to me!" Helmer raged, the veins on his forehead warning Magda that she was better off telling him the truth.

"I don't know. I swear! I don't know." Magda whimpered, burying her face in her palms, her reflexes growing stronger as Helmer got closer. "I started to receive some notes, calls, and the roses. But I honestly do not know who they could've been from. I swear I'm not lying. I'm not lying, Helmer."

"If so, why keep it from me?" he asked, his heart frantic for an answer. But his soul was slowly letting go of the steam. For the first time, Helmer heard sincerity in her voice and seeing that he had caused her to fold in terror made him step away. He didn't want to alarm her anymore.

"I was scared, and I feel that this guy is dangerous," Magda elaborated. "I wanted to protect our family."

That thought was familiar, for it had been an active concern of his too, for a while. But why would psycho man do this? He was in Helmer's mind, his workplace, his home, and now in the midst of his marriage. How could Helmer stop this man who seemed like an impossible threat? Clearly, the psycho man was trying to seduce his wife. Perhaps he knew her.

"I am telling the truth, and I hate that you doubt it," Magda said, getting the courage to approach him. In fact, he seemed to be easing off a bit, and his tone was less of a threat. Magda reached for Helmer's hands but was startled by him pacing away again.

His eyes held no more warmth nor passionate sparkles when looking at her. His face was a damp and rigid surface, numb to whatever she was saying. Magda insisted on trying to convince him, but that was like testing his patience. He didn't want her near, maybe just now or not ever.

"Please," he said, telling her to keep away. "I need to get out of here and get a breather."

"You don't believe me," Magda said, her eyes begging for him to consider her plea.

"A trust broken twice can never be repaired," he said, turning away from her gaze. "I don't think I can ever give that to you again."

His words reached a part of her heart she'd never known existed before. It was like a knife stuck in her throat, disrupting her breathing. Yes, Magda forgot to breathe and how to speak, and the guilt was pouring out of her, for her tears started to rain down her face.

Her soul sank when Helmer turned away to leave, not saying anything else. Magda needed just one more word to show he didn't mean what he said. She finally understood that a lie wasn't just a scheme—it was a slow-acting venom, sinking in deep and hurting long before its true effects were felt.

What could she have said anyway? She had no proof of who the caller was—only speculation. Unless she went to Vincent Avenue, like the caller instructed. That chance might never come again. She had to go. Without thinking twice, Magda dashed out of the kitchen and rushed downstairs, unsure if she was about to make a mistake or find a way to prove her innocence. Reaching the foyer, she felt someone's presence. She hoped it wasn't Helmer, for that would ruin her plan to meet her stalker.

"Going somewhere, Mrs. Dupris?"

Magda turned, and that was the last voice she wished to hear during the night. "Marie. How convenient! You always find me when I'm in the middle of something."

"My apologies," Marie said. "I hope you're not still upset about the painting room's incident?" She was wearing her pajamas, with her long brown braids down her shoulders. She was composed, maybe more than usual, staring at Magda and expecting an answer.

"I am, and I also can't fully understand yet..." Magda replied, her tone urgent. "How or why you have gotten a job you're barely trained for from my husband? There's no way he has hired you to be his assistant just because he felt like it. It must have been for a particular reason—"

"You're right," Marie cut in. "There might be a reason. However, I must correct you on me having no experience." She got closer, her hands in her pockets. "Mr. Dupris's secretary trained me, and I've picked up most of the things in a week's time. I'm doing so great that it almost felt like I belonged there. In an office with great AC, a nice view, free snacks, and an amazing, wonderful boss."

"Why do I feel like you have an agenda with my husband?" Magda said, squinting, reading Marie's face. But there was nothing apparent to reveal Marie's thoughts or intentions.

"Everyone has an agenda," Marie said, a smile appearing on her lips. "Just like you may have one. Obviously, you're running off and trying not to be noticed."

"Excuse me?"

"I always knew people have seen me as less," Marie said, moving her hands up to her hips, her stance growing more defiant. "But never have I thought you'd think I am so clumsy that I wouldn't catch onto your little games." She paused, playing with her braids. "And what about me makes you feel so disappointed working in an office?"

"There's something about you," Magda said, hesitant but careful with her words. She wouldn't want Marie to tell her husband that she was sneaking out of the house. Neither have her prying into her affairs nor asking more questions. "One day, I'll discover what it is."

"Perhaps you don't like that I'm working with your husband," Marie teased, her smile growing into a mischievous chuckle. "He's not ugly to look at."

"Listen..." Magda walked up to Marie, her eyes seething at her taunting comment. "Whatever you are doing, try not to provoke me. You may have my husband's favor now, but I rule this home, and God hears me. I'll mess you up if you try to interfere in my marriage again."

"I'll tell him that you went out," Marie said, pouting her lips. "And of course, if you don't mind, it's fine too. Have a great evening." Marie Lisa turned, walking away, looking at Magda from the corner of her eyes. She knew how to get what she wanted, and Magda was the last person she'd be afraid of.

"Wait," Magda said, her voice weakening. "Marie, don't tell him." Marie walked back to Magda. "That'd mean I would be allowed to ask something in return—"

"You're bribing me?"

"I don't bribe," Marie objected. "I negotiate." "And what is it that you want?" Magda asked.

Marie hung her arms out, taking a deep breath. "You smell that? Peace. That's what I'm bringing you right now. So, I expect the same. All I'm asking is that you're nice to me."

"That's it?"

"For now," Marie corrected. "That way I'll know you're not trying to put crazy thoughts inside your husband's head about me. I love to work with him."

"You're so insufferable," huffed Magda, considering Marie's proposition. "But I swear to God, Marie, if you go and try to be messy and tell my husband, I'll make sure you never get to tell him anything ever again."

"I like a good threat," Marie said, with a slow nod. "Except, they don't work on me. Now, go on. I won't tell him a thing. I promise!"

Magda looked at Marie up and down, shaking her head before walking away. She sneaked to the back of the house, called a taxi, and took her leave from there.

Marie, seeing how clever she could be, smiled to herself. She rushed to the stairs, searching for Helmer. She checked every room until she found him in the bedroom, sitting on the edge of his bed, lost in thought.

She didn't bother to knock—recklessness growing with the power she held from all those secrets. "Sir."

Helmer didn't respond, showing no signs of engaging.

"No worries," she said. "I don't need anything except to tell you that Mrs. Dupris has just left the house."

Helmer's head snapped up, his frown deepening. "My-My wife?" Marie nodded. "She told me not to tell you—"

"Where?" he demanded, jumping to his feet. "Where is she going?" "She didn't say," Marie shrugged. "But if you hurry, you might catch her. She's leaving from the back, so I assume she called a taxi."

Helmer quickly pulled on a t-shirt and grabbed his keys, but before he could rush out, Jonathan appeared in the doorway.

"Jonathan? What are you doing here? You're supposed to be at the hospital."

"I know," Jonathan said, stepping inside, his gaze shifting toward Marie. "I needed to pick up a few things to change. They're planning to discharge my wife in a few days."

"Good," Helmer said, his shoulders tense.

"I'll take my leave," Marie said, quickly.

"Actually, Marie," called Helmer, "tell Mr. Hens to get me a key to my wife's painting room. And do it quickly. I need it ready when I get back."

"Right away, sir." Marie left, and Helmer immediately dropped himself in front of the bed, reaching for his rifle.

"This bastard got me, Jonathan. Now he's trying to get to my wife," Helmer said as he carefully pulled his loaded rifle toward him.

Jonathan's eyes widened. "Boss, this is—"

"What I'll use to put a bullet in that dirtbag's head."

"Whoa, whoa, whoa, no." Jonathan stepped back, taking in the gravity of the situation. "Do you even know how to handle a rifle, boss?"

"Only one way to find out." Helmer snapped the rifle open, inspecting it with a grim determination.

Seeing the tension in Helmer's grip, Jonathan pulled a smaller gun from his jacket. "I think you'd be better off with this one. It's less conspicuous."

"Good," Helmer took it. "Because I never miss a shot."

"And I don't care where you're going," Jonathan said, "but you're not going alone."

Helmer nodded, gesturing for Jonathan to follow. What lay ahead was too dangerous to turn back from. His mind was made up, and murder was the only option left.

CHAPTER 23

Apparition

Helmer and Gladice joined Elvino in his foster home following the assault with his father. He had done a great job of keeping his head down and staying out of the way. He'd avoid certain areas of the mansion as instructed by Elvino. There were plenty of antique decor pieces and countless frames of expensive cars on the walls, including pictures of boxing, which seemed unconventional, like caged rings. But there was a side of the walls that spiked Helmer's interest as it was more textured, full of abstract patterns, with an afro painting at the center.

Helmer approached the wall and then brushed his fingers over it. Seeing a crack in the corner, he stuck his finger near it; then the wall slid open. It was a door.

"No way."

Hesitant to walk in and alarmed by the secret door opening, Helmer threw a glance through the hall. No one saw him. He walked in then the wall swiftly closed behind him. It was a room full of guns and fancy jars of bullets. Helmer had never seen anything like this before, and less, guns of all sizes and shapes. They were real, and Helmer wanted to make sure his eyes weren't tricking him to believe so. He approached slowly and stopped in front of one of the shelves. He took one of the rifles and scanned it before brushing his fingers on the bullet hole. Reaching for the trigger— his youthful instinct tempting him to test it out— the door abruptly opened. Elvino came with angry eyes.

"What are you doing? Get away from that thing." He shouted, rushing over to Helmer, his eyes widening in terror at his attempt to pull the trigger. "Goddamn it, don't touch it… Don't. This one is loaded." He carefully took the rifle from Helmer and unloaded it. "Damn it,

Helms. I told you to avoid this side of the residence." Elvino said, his arm landing across his chest.

"You have guns here," Helmer whispered, his face flushed with terror.

"You were not supposed to come here," Elvino reminded.

"And you were not supposed to have a room full of guns," Helmer opined. "Doctors don't carry those things to such an excessive amount, I'm sure." Helmer paced away from Elvino, his hands unable to keep still. His breathing increased, making him more aware of his heart speeding.

"You simply weren't supposed to come here," Elvino said, taking the rifle from where it was and placing it somewhere more secure.

"Well, I need an answer because if I don't, Gladice and I are leaving. Who are you?" Helmer inquired, not knowing that this was not going to be the only time he'd touch a gun. He was not aware that if you touch a pistol once, you might do it again, and maybe countless times.

***

Helmer sat in the passenger's seat, his hands frantically holding the gun. He couldn't wait for whatever was coming, and he did feel as if he was about to discover something big. Something he could perhaps never recover from. He had decided to take a different car than the one his driver usually drove him in, not wanting to be suspicious as he and Jonathan followed the taxi Magda was in.

"You good, Boss?" Jonathan asked, his eyes focused on the taxi, so they did not lose sight of it.

The road was not as crowded, which made it necessary that they kept at a considerable distance to not be noticed. Jonathan waited for Helmer's reply, slowing down his driving and readjusting the rearview mirrors.

"I'm fine," Helmer replied, his tone crisp. "Keep driving." He placed his arms on his lap, his eyes on the road, not blinking once. He wouldn't want to risk not figuring this whole ordeal out with his wife and that man terrorizing people for the fun of it. Helmer wasn't being tracked, as he had decided to keep away from the car that the psycho man had managed to compromise.

They were getting close, and Helmer's chest cramped with discomfort, a subtle panic progressively taking over him. He tapped his feet incessantly, each second dragging on like a decade. Helmer lowered the car's window and allowed the chill air to hit his face and ruffle through his hair like a soft caress from his wife.

The idea of her spiked him again. If she had lied about not knowing who the psycho man was, there wouldn't be anything left of their marriage. He couldn't fathom someone else touching her, making love to her maybe better than he had. He envisioned Magda running to another man's arms, and that wouldn't just hurt—it would ruin him.

"Wait! This is Vincent Avenue," Helmer said, noticing the large street sign. "I think this is where they are heading." He looked at the gun. It was time. Magda's taxi stopped. Finally, the truth would come out. That was all Helmer had hoped for, and burning from impatience, he removed his seatbelt. "Pull over, Jonathan. They're at the avenue!"

Jonathan locked the car's doors and pulled the windows up, worried that if he let Helmer out, he'd do something terrible. He slowed down, about to break, but hesitated. "I-I think we should wait for Mrs. Dupris to step out of the taxi first. Otherwise, she might notice us and mess up our plans."

"I don't want to wait," Helmer snapped. "Let me out."

"I can't," Jonathan said, his tone speculative. "You don't seem to be in your best state of mind right now. Are you sure we're only here for psycho man?"

"I don't feel like talking right now," Helmer replied. "Open the door."

"I fear I can't do that."

"Open the goddamn door, Jonathan! I won't say it another time."

Jonathan looked ahead, across the theater; then his eyes shifted back to Helmer. "I can't yet because there's someone there. Look!"

Helmer glanced through the windshield, squinting to make sure he was not hallucinating. The psycho man was there, by the theater, right at the corner of the street. He had his black coat and cargo pants on, his face fully covered, and his huge boots up to his knees. Even the street dogs hid from him, and that was no exaggeration.

"I'm killing this scumbag tonight," Helmer said, tugging at the car leather, still attempting to get a better view to confirm that it wasn't an apparition. It was R, and he stood in the street staring at the car that Magda was in. "Actually, move a bit closer."

The taxi's lights flashed R, revealing something else: the psycho man's boots were covered in a red liquid; they looked stained, and although it was from a distance, Helmer inferred it was blood.

"Okay, now stop," Helmer shouted, noticing Magda bolting out of the taxi and hastily tipping the driver. Despite all his reasons to be upset, he feared that maybe his wife was telling him the truth and she was perhaps being blackmailed or lured into a trap. Seeing her head turning in the psycho man's direction, Helmer hurled over the steering wheel, pushing Jonathan over to unlock the car's doors. He had to find out what was happening and the reasons behind so much mystery involving his wife and that man he'd never recognized, not even with a mask.

"Boss, wait," Jonathan said, trying to ease Helmer off before he headed there.

Helmer snapped out of his grip and bounced out of the car. He kept wondering why his wife, despite all the danger, would decide to still see that man. Was her heart leading her up to the psycho man? Helmer saw Magda taking her shoes off and shoving a couple out of her way to get to the man. People jostled against her, but she squeezed among them, not wanting to lose sight of her target.

The psycho man noticed Magda coming in his direction and started to walk away. He was tempted to take a full scan of Magda to see her worried face, which only made her more beautiful. The psycho man sped up, which slightly turned into a jog, then a full run, drawing Magda closer to where he needed her. Magda followed him, her eyes solely on him and nothing else, determined to catch up with him. It wasn't going to be like last time when her caller escaped before she and June could figure out who he was.

"Boss, wait..." muttered Jonathan, running after Helmer as he increased his speed. But due to suspicions of being seen, Helmer ran in between a few people on the street so his trail wouldn't be noticeable. Jonathan mimicked Helmer's strategy to not get caught, but his heart grew restless, seeing Helmer grasping tighter the pistol he gave him.

"Boss, let's not do anything you'll regret," Jonathan said, his eyes refocusing on his boss's wife fleeing out of their sight. The trap was set! Helmer was not powerful enough to face what was ahead. The sooner he realized that, the better.

Helmer spotted Magda through the large crowd coming out of the theater and sprinted among them to catch up with her. He wanted to call her name, tell her to stop being a fool, and not try to catch up with the psycho man. Would she listen? The answers were always a maybe. Nothing was certain, and less, the reason why the psycho man would be so obsessed with his wife. Was it lust? Or insanity, proving a point that Helmer had no clue about? Whatever it was, Helmer had no intention of leaving his wife at the mercy of the psycho man and ignoring the idea that she was the one in danger the most.

Meanwhile, Magda didn't stop nor look back. She wanted to know the truth and see if she was imagining things about her conclusions about the psycho man. Her heart stomped against her chest. Her legs were numb from the fear that her target would leave without a chance to talk to him. She crossed the other avenue, ran past the bus stops, and reached the pathway close to a gas station. There stood the psycho man, the mysterious stalker whom she could no longer deny dying to see the face of.

"Please, don't run from me," Magda said, her voice cracking in distress, seeing that she wouldn't be able to catch up with her stalker. Psycho man stopped, hearing Magda begging him to. He turned slowly, knowing that he was being watched. His plan was to meet with her alone, but being aware that she wasn't, made him hesitant to show his face.

"You told me you would show me what you look like," Magda reminded, standing across from him. "Or do you just enjoy torturing me?"

Hearing her words, he couldn't help looking back. Seeing her beautiful face and the sadness covering it as a thick film, the psycho man faced her, looking dead in her eyes, those soft eyes of hers, warm and charming like a dove's. The psycho man's gloved hands slowly reached for his face, his chest rising, aware that he was about to give away his identity. He pulled his mask up to his chin, taking in a deep breath, knowing that he could be seen as hideous and making Magda run out against her will. Who wouldn't be afraid of a face that almost looked like burnt playdough?

"Please," Magda whispered, her voice dressed in warmth and softness. She wanted the mask off, and seeing the psycho man so shaky and reluctant made Magda itch to get closer to him. Perhaps it was to hold him and even remove the mask herself.

The psycho man pulled the mask higher up, exposing the left side of his face, looking like a huge rash dotted with holes.

"It's ok," Magda reassured, seeing his hands shaking.

The mask was now off, and time had stopped. Everything felt still and like a dream. The sounds of cars and the joy of the city became like a whisper around them. Magda's eyes grew wide in terror yet in melancholy. Short gasps found their way out of her closed lips instead of the words she wished to let out. She couldn't think because there was a sea of thoughts drowning her at once. She had so many questions, and the biggest one was if this encounter was real.

There she stood, staring at the psycho man, unable to move any more steps even though she yearned to. The tears fell on her face; they were hot, burning her cheeks. Whether it was shock or pain that she had suppressed for years, all those feelings resurfaced, trapping her between her past and the present.

"I..." the psycho man said, letting out a word out of the countless ones he wished to say. His eyes were meant to hunt Magda, and so was his face, but he could not tame the inclination to worship her beauty. His gaze was obstinate in focusing on her, caressing her cheeks as to soothe them. But at the same time, he was upset at himself for even looking at her that way, for he had one mission, which was to hate her. So much that he could turn off his softness toward her and eventually bring her to face her worst fear: justice. Nonetheless the reality caught up with him, that no one had ever the power to simply switch off their feelings.

Some feelings could dwell forever if not controlled, and even torture lovers to their very deaths.

Magda attempted to approach him, hesitant but not hiding her yearning to see his face closer to touch it. But psycho man paced away, afraid that her touch might make him lose focus. His plan wasn't to be weak but to create chaos and spread terror. Now, he was getting the taste of his own medicine, seeing his target getting so close to him. The psycho man ran, and Magda followed him, not wanting to miss this chance to indulge in that moment.

Her foot stepped upon a shard of glass that hobbled her. Magda fell, and then a voice reached her. "Magda!" shouted Helmer, rushing over, along with Jonathan, to Magda's rescue.

"Maggie," the psycho man whispered, watching Magda on the pavement.

"Richard," Magda mumbled, wanting to say more words, but her body numbed as she saw that she was being followed. Her husband was watching her, and she wondered how she had no clue.

A crowd circled her, and their voices sounded like murmurs in her ears. She was out of breath, her head spinning as if the world was crashing upon her. How come Helmer was there? She swore that Marie Lisa would never snitch, but then she was in a loop of drama involving her secrets and her past, putting her marriage at stake.

The psycho man, the stalker who was no longer a stranger, wanted to be the one rescuing her, but he had to remain in the shadows. He couldn't approach much closer, aware that Magda's husband was near, knowing that he could be unpredictable. Besides, for Magda, it had to be delirium or that she was too dizzy to see clearly. The truth was that the ghost came back to life. Her eyes needed to go shut to escape that new set of reality. She remained frozen on the ground until her heart halted when she heard the gunshot from among the crowd. Helmer shot the psycho man. The bullet hit his arm, which made him stagger from impact.

"No! Richard!" Magda screamed in terror, hoping that he could escape from her husband while it was still time. The psycho man held his arm and managed to keep running, escaping once again.

"Boss, please, your wife needs you," Jonathan said, discouraging Helmer from running after the psycho man, afraid that he might actually kill him. He didn't want him to have blood on his hands due to anger. But his reasoning succeeded as Helmer handed him his gun and rushed to Magda with his blank and angry eyes.

CHAPTER 24

A Surprise

There were drips of blood on the pavement as the psycho man progressively escaped. Magda watched him go, bracing his arm and unable to put his mask back on. Her eyes could not get off from where the psycho man was since he was no longer a mystery. He was not a psycho but rather someone she had grieved and resented for half of her life. She had seen his face just as she remembered it despite the burns and gruesome scars. He was still the person she could never fully let go of, but there was one question irking Magda: was he real? Magda closed her eyes, fearing it was a hallucination, as the dead don't usually come back to life.

Magda felt Helmer tugging at her arms and pulling her up so she could stand. She was unsteady due to the glass embedded in her foot. Helmer shifted Magda's head toward him, making her spine shiver like a frightened cat. She forgot that part where she'd need to explain why she was there at Vincent Avenue. To know the right words to say or to figure out how to put her husband's heart at ease. To be fair, Magda could barely process having seen a ghost. Or was he?

"You said a name."

"What?" Magda mumbled, feeling Helmer's nails digging into her skin as his grip around her got tighter.

"When I shot him, you said a name," he said.

"Helmer—" Magda paused, the words forming in her mind but hesitant to come out. One wrong answer seemed threatening. She didn't want to take the risk. The fire within her husband's eyes warned her not to. It was not safe to lie, nor being on the streets with him alone as people started to scatter, seeing that she got assistance.

"What was his name?" Helmer asked, gesturing at the people to continue clearing the way to give him privacy.

"I—"

"You swore you didn't know him," Helmer interrupted before Magda could put a word in. She had, at the moment, already rehearsed tons of scenarios in her mind, but it seemed that they would be of no use.

"I didn't," she managed. "I-I really don't know him."

"I'm not buying it," Helmer said, his breathing progressively growing loud. The delicate freckles, and the tiniest muscles of his face had transformed into something menacing and gruesomely scary. There was nothing but darkness in his eyes. They were no longer looking at Magda with the same hunger and passion. "I was watching you out there, and I saw something between you two. That's why I didn't want to interrupt too soon."

"I was scared," Magda said, her lips involuntarily trembling.

"Scared?" Helmer leaned in, grazing his knuckles on her face and then across her shivering lips. His nose squished, holding back the couple of words he wanted to say. Being that close to Magda was the opposite of delight. Saying her name didn't taste as good, and neither did the sight of her face.

"Helmer," a chilled gasp came out of her lips. "You, your nails, they're hurting me."

"You weren't scared," he spat, his eyes scanning her from forehead to toe. "It wasn't fear that I saw."

"Boss," Jonathan said, "I'm sorry to interrupt, but I'll go get the car closer, so Mrs. Dupris won't have to walk—"

"She can walk."

"I'm sorry?" Jonathan said, his voice low yet concerning.

"I said my wife will walk," Helmer repeated, through gritted teeth.

Jonathan nodded quickly, not willing to make a point in the midst of their heated conversation. He stepped aside and thought of paying close attention to Helmer, whose voice was echoing on the streets, drawing attention.

"Since you said that you were afraid, being scared is not sneaking out of our house to come meet a psycho. Do you know what he's done to Nina and Jonathan's family? He's obsessed with you, and still, you came here alone to look for him?"

"I didn't come here to look for him," Magda protested.

"Oh, so you didn't? You magically have decided to come here at this time?"

"Y-Yes," Magda replied, her eyes bulging out of her face, seeing Helmer reach for the pistol from Jonathan who got caught unaware.

"Stop lying to me!" Helmer yelled, the pistol right under Magda's chin. He stopped at her eye level, making sure she understood that he was not joking. He meant every syllabus, and something that Magda wasn't aware of was that he'd used guns before, and he was very familiar with pulling a trigger in someone's face without flinching.

"Boss..." Jonathan whispered, seeing Helmer's finger teasing the trigger. He feared that he could let it go, for his posture showed that he had decided to do what most would call evil and monstrous.

"Stay out of it, Jonathan," Helmer warned, unaware that people started to stop around the corner to watch. He moved the pistol around Magda's face, then pressed it into her forehead. "You're playing such a dangerous game, and you don't even know it. You have no idea what I can do to you right now. Not even the devil would be able to stop me!" Magda's eyes fell shut, her lips quivering. She couldn't move. Her body was still numb. She had never known what it felt like to have a loaded gun in her face. The thrills racing throughout her blood, making it warmer than usual, or the flashes of one's entire life hitting you at once in a second. "H-Helmer." "Tell me why you came here," Helmer demanded, his tone sharp.

"I only came because..."

"Yes, I'm listening," urged Helmer, leaning his ear closer. "I'm listening, Magda. You came here because what?"

A couple of girls were by the theater, recording the scene, while others were taking pictures on their phones. Jonathan, noticing the ordeal, approached Helmer cautiously and warned him to take his marital chat in a more private setting.

"Open your goddamn mouth!" Helmer shouted, pushing for an answer from his wife, paying no mind to Jonathan's suggestion.

"Helmer," Magda whimpered, "Jonathan is right. We are causing a scene. They'll call the cops."

"I don't give a damn about these people nor the cops," Helmer replied. "If it'll take me going to jail to get the truth out of you, I will. Why have you come here? Did he threaten you? Did he try to blackmail you with something?"

Magda opened her eyes, encountering Helmer's seething gaze. She shivered, and before she realized it, her face was drowned with tears. Her ears couldn't handle his thunderous voice, which became so uncanny and unfamiliar to her. It was so different, and Magda never thought the little girl within her could ever come out and wish to hide from anything. There was an underlying sense of danger in her husband's tone that made her body clutch at itself. For the very first time, she's known true fear.

"Answer me!" Helmer insisted, his hands shaking and tempted to seize her cheeks.

"Boss, please, I think we should go." Jonathan hesitantly laid one arm over Helmer's shoulder, which wasn't enough to settle him down. "Please. Please, I beg you. Let's get out of here." Jonathan slowly reached for the pistol from Helmer and took it away from him. But seeing his boss's face, the quarrel wasn't done, and he only wished to be able to stay close to monitor Helmer's next move.

"C'mon," Helmer said, hurling Magda over his shoulder, carrying her to the car, and passing the judgy eyes on the streets. He settled Magda in the backseat and put on her seatbelt while ordering Jonathan to take them to the nearest hospital. He sprinted to the other side of the car and got in, sitting next to her. He leaned over and raised Magda's leg above his knee, taking a close look at the bloody glass stuck in her foot. "If I remove it, it'll start to bleed. So, we'll wait."

Jonathan removed his top shirt and handed it to Helmer in the back. "Just in case."

"Thanks." Helmer spread the shirt on his lap and settled Magda's foot back on it. He relaxed his back, then focused his eyes on the road. Helmer feared that one look at her could seethe him off once again, and it'd be catastrophic. Jonathan was able to calm him once, but would it always be as effective? Helmer was terrified by his thoughts, the things he wanted to do. He couldn't stop picturing the psycho man with Magda, whom she seemed to know more than she admitted.

Magda swept her arm off her robe and reached for Helmer's hand. Her fingers slowly managed to greet his, only to see Helmer jerk a few inches away from her. Wondering when she had become something so repulsive, Magda reached for Helmer's hand again for any signs that it was all in her head. Her husband could not even handle a single touch. God knows what it was like having her sitting next to him.

"Please," Helmer whispered, pulling his hand to himself and eyeing Jonathan, whom he caught looking from the rearview mirror. "Want to say something?"

"No," Jonathan shook his head, caught in his indiscretion. "But we should get to the hospital in 2 minutes."

Magda looked at Helmer and then at Jonathan, wishing to speak to him, but she remained quiet, which was smart to do. Her voice was the last thing Helmer wanted in his ears right now. She wondered whether she was the reason behind all the late chaos around her. Did she feed the psycho man's delusions by coming to meet him? The big question at that moment was: Did she just ruin her marriage in one single night?

Jonathan pulled into Saint Anthony's Hospital. Helmer removed Magda's seatbelt and placed her foot on Jonathan's shirt. He got out of the car and opened the door for her before carrying her to the Emergency Department. A patient care representative greeted them, and after answering a few questions, they put Magda in a wheelchair and escorted her to get immediate care.

Helmer went in with her, yet Magda was not close to feeling at ease. Noticing Magda's fearful look, the nurse asked, "Ma'am, please tell me. Are you nauseous?"

"No," Magda grimaced. "I simply feel a tightness in my foot. It hurts..."

A sobbing lady caught Magda's attention. The lady walked by her son on a stretcher whose body had severe burns and stabbing marks below his abdomen. He was unconscious, and from his state, everyone could tell he wasn't going to make it. The burns reminded Magda of Richard and the wounds on his body before the fire. Actually, they reminded her of his face right before he got shot. If only she could've gotten much closer, and their interaction wasn't disrupted. She could then confirm if it was really him. For there was no way she could explain how he was alive.

"Is there any paperwork to fill out?" Helmer asked the nurse, his voice monotone, unable to empathize even if he'd forced himself to.

Before the nurse could answer, the front desk lady gestured at him to come get the documents to fill in.

"And after that, will my wife be discharged the same night?" Helmer asked, flipping the pages for him to sign.

The nurse looked at both of them and sighed, eyeing Magda hard enough to show her empathizing gaze. "It depends, sir."

"Well, I hope it won't take long."

The Doctor came and greeted them. He examined Magda's wound and then ordered some tests. Thankfully, the wait time was not as long as they expected, and the doctor came back, calling them in. He checked Magda's vital signs and performed all the necessary basic procedures to make sure she had no possible fractures. Magda's ribs were fine, but she had bruises on her elbow from the fall. Magda was confused when the Doctor's forehead wrinkled as he reached for her stomach.

"What happened, Doctor?" Helmer asked.

"I will wait for the results to make sure that the baby is fine before proceeding. I'll step out for a minute!"

"Baby?" Magda whispered, her eyes growing wide and a jittery laugh escaping her quivering lips. She brought her hands to her throat, attempting to mask her suspicions as Helmer locked the door.

Helmer pulled the wheelchair Magda sat in toward him, watching tears forming in her eyes. All of his anxiety was slowly dissipating. He stared at her, then at her stomach, with the pure inclination to touch it, to see if it was real. Did he just hear he was about to become a father? He could hear his heart drum in his ears, wondering whether it was excitement, shock, or confusion. He had chosen to have this baby, the only thing he had ever wanted, but now with a woman he might hate forever.

"What did you do to me?" Magda asked, her voice trembling as her skin prickled under Helmer's piercing gaze.

"What did I do to you? You're really asking that?" Helmer's nostrils flared, his jaw tightening.

Magda blinked, her hands tightening on the arms of the wheelchair. "I don't understand—"

"Understand what? That I caught you in your lies?" His voice was sharp, cutting through the silence like a blade.

Helmer's lips twitched, torn between a smirk and a snarl. He couldn't settle on either. Odd, wasn't it? His head felt adrift, like it was stuck in a storm cloud, swirling with anger and disbelief. His thoughts collided as he realized that when dreams turn sour and the fantasies someone has clung to dissolve, it doesn't bring peace but chaos.

"I've found them," he said, his tone low and deliberate. "The birth control pills you swore you never touched."

Leaning down, Helmer placed a hand on the armrest of her wheelchair, his fingers curling with barely restrained rage. His other hand cupped her face, his thumb pressing into her cheek. His touch wasn't tender; it was a warning. His grip tightened just enough for Magda to swallow hard, her breath catching in her throat.

"You lied," Helmer spat. "That's all you do. You lie!"

Tears welled in Magda's eyes, spilling over as she struggled against the pressure of his hand. The crimson flush rising to her cheeks startled Helmer for a moment. Was he hurting her? His gaze dropped to his other hand, now gripping her thigh, his knuckles white. He released her abruptly, stepping back as she gasped for air.

"You're losing your mind," Magda whimpered, her voice cracking.

"Choose your words carefully," he said, his voice strained, trembling with restrained fury. "Lie to me again, Magda, and I swear no one will save you."

Magda's hands gripped the arms of the wheelchair. "Where did you find them?"

The words left her lips before she could stop them, and she immediately regretted it. Helmer's posture shifted, his shoulders squaring, as he loomed over her.

He leaned in, his breath hot against her ear. "It doesn't matter where I found them," he whispered, his voice seething. "They shouldn't have been here in the first place."

Straightening himself, Helmer began pacing away, his boots clicking against the floor in a steady rhythm that made Magda flinch with every step.

"I was torn," he said, his voice icy. "Torn to find out you've been lying to me for years. Now I see it clearly. This is who you are. A fraud who married me for my money. A liar who made me believe a child was mine. And let's not forget—Meg is the daughter of your ex's brother."

Magda's sob broke through her lips; her body curled in on itself as Helmer's words lashed at her like a whip, each syllable striking harder than the last.

"Now I wonder..." Helmer continued, eyeing her. "If you've ever told me the truth about Ricks. Was it really rape, or did you willingly sleep with him?"

"You're being unfair," Magda muttered, as tears streaked down her face. She was too numb, too disgusted with herself to fight back.

Helmer snorted, his laugh humorless and sharp. "You can't talk.

Can you?"

He grabbed the bottle of pills from his pocket and threw them into her lap. "You made me believe I was the problem. We spent years seeing doctors, running tests—tests you paid to falsify! And for what? To keep me in the dark?"

Magda's mouth opened, and no words came. Her hands gripped the bottle, her gaze dropping to the pills spilling onto her lap.

"You had my phone," she said finally, her voice wavering. "You—you spoke to him."

Helmer nodded, his lips curling into a bitter smile. "The charlatan you paid? Yes. I'm surprised you didn't figure it out sooner."

Magda's fingers tugged at her robe, her mind racing. She felt trapped, like a bird in a cage with nowhere to fly. Her thoughts spiraled as she considered the life growing inside her. A child. She was going to have a baby—a child in a world of lies and chaos.

"What did you do with the pills?" Magda asked, glaring at him.

Helmer moved behind her, placing his chin on her shoulder. His hand brushed her hair aside, his breath warm against her neck.

"They got switched," he replied. "A good Samaritan gave me a replacement. Fertility pills. Same color, same size, with a little side effect where you couldn't resist me. And oh, Magda, you didn't. You begged for me, and we had such a good time. Didn't we?"

Magda's tears fell freely now, her body contracting as his words cut deeper than any blade. She looked down at her stomach, her hands hovering over it, unsure if she wanted to touch or reject the life growing inside her.

Helmer stepped back, his eyes softening for a moment as he watched her anguish. But the warmth was fleeting, replaced by the cold resolve in his voice.

"Now you have to care for two lives," he said. "And let me be clear. You will have this child, whether you like it or not."

Without another word, Helmer stormed off, unlocking the door and stepping out, leaving Magda alone in the suffocating silence of her despair.

CHAPTER 25

An Awakened Past

School was over, and Helmer had to report to practice. He had not noticed Bryant anywhere. Helmer called, yet no response; he checked in the school's office and CSI, assuming that maybe Bryant had gotten into detention. Helmer saw no signs of him until he went to the auditorium and noticed Bryant sitting in the back row by himself. "Bryant," murmured Helmer, a sign of relief swirling out of his lips, rushing to his best friend. He sat next to him and noticed that Bryant had not let out a word, staying still and pensive. "You good?"

"Someone set me up," Bryant replied. "They sent a blonde girl up to me and she kissed me right at the moment Sonia reached the hallway. I tried to get the girl off of me, but it seemed already too late when I did."

"Y-You mean…"

"Sonia broke up with me," Bryant explained, turning his head toward Helmer. "But you know I wouldn't cheat, right? She didn't even want to hear it. She shut me off and called it quits."

"I see," Helmer said, blinking repeatedly and struggling to look his best friend in the eye. "And do you know the girl, or was it random? I need details so I can see if I need to do something."

"You should talk to Sonia for me. She will listen to you." The desperation in Bryant's voice and his pleading eyes were haunting. Bryant placed one arm around Helmer's shoulder and drew him close. "Please, talk to her for me. I can't imagine what one day without her will be like. The only thing I know is that it'll destroy me. My soul is in complete torture, a solitude that feels so foreign I can no longer go on about my day. I can't—"

"It's fine," Helmer cut in, keeping his gaze low, knowing he couldn't reassure Bryant. "I'll talk to her. Where is she?"

"Probably with the cheerleading girls at practice."

"Ok," Helmer said, getting up, his mind filled with muddling thoughts. Staying there with his friend would only torment his conscience, which he couldn't afford to let happen. "I'll let you know how it goes."

Before Helmer withdrew, Bryant caught his arm and thanked him, something Helmer did not see coming. He didn't need to be thanked or any gestures of gratitude. In fact, he deserved none.

Helmer squeezed his eyes, concealing the discomfort from his friend's crestfallen confessions. He ran out of the auditorium and made his way to the school gym, where the cheerleading girls would normally practice. He searched for Sonia and saw her sitting on one of the benches along with a few girls from the group, and judging from a distance, Helmer noticed she was not well.

"Sonie!"

"Not right now," said the girls from the group as they shielded Sonia, whose eyes were red from crying. "She does not wish to speak with you, nor your cheating ass homeboy."

Helmer said, "Sonie, please, I need to speak with you."

Sonia turned her head toward him and wiped her face, which was of no use for the tears that refused to cease. "You guys are liars. I should've known. All the girls from the school were all over you two. How could I even fathom that I'd be any different?"

"Actually," Helmer said, approaching her despite the judgy stares of the cheerleading group. "I can't believe he did that to you. I would have never imagined Bryant doing such a thing. I swear I had no clue he'd been seeing that girl. It was wrong, and I do not condone what he has done to you."

"Prom is one day away, and this nigga decided to cheat," said one of the girls.

"I know," Helmer said. "He's... He's a character. But I would hate for Sonie not to go."

"I'm not going," Sonia emphasized, sniffling.

"No, you don't have to ruin your moment because of him," Helmer objected, scooting down close to Sonia.

She shook her head. "I can't go. It's too late to get another date and—"

"Not if I'm available," Helmer said, his eyes meeting Sonia's. For a minute, the group fell quiet, and there was only the sound of Helmer's heart racing from taking such a risk. "I promise if you do go with me, you'll have a great time and forget about what happened. Bryant does not deserve you, Sonie. He never has!"

It was a choice to pick his own feelings over his best friend's, and that was what most would call the cruelest betrayal. But he wanted Sonia. He had always dreamed of having her to himself. So much that the aftermath of such a risk never seemed to matter.

***

Helmer stepped out of the elevator, his shoes clicking sharply against the polished floor. Eyes flicked toward him, curious, assessing, as he pushed forward without a glance. He hadn't been in the office for days and would've wished to be at home to make sure his family was safe.

His mind was a storm, caught between what had already happened and the threats looming ahead. He had confronted the psycho man—a man obsessed with his wife, who had escaped despite his efforts to stop him. Helmer hadn't wanted psycho man to walk away; if anything, he would have gladly carried his blood on his hands. But now, there was an enemy on the run with no limits to how far he would go to harm those Helmer cared about.

And then there was the baby. A new life was on the horizon, reshaping everything, and undoubtedly his marriage. Had he gone too far? His actions might have bound him even tighter to Magda, tethering him to a marriage he wasn't sure he wanted anymore. Magda—even her name felt like a spear, gutting him strip by strip.

Divorce? No. That word didn't sit well with him. Divorce would make him turn into his father—bitter, broken, and cruel. He could never be that man. He wouldn't turn into someone violent, lashing out at his children, becoming someone they feared.

The more he thought of Magda, the more the ache in his chest grew, sharp and relentless, like a headache that wouldn't ease.

Helmer reached Nina's desk, but she was not there, though he proceeded to settle into his office first. Going in, he found Nina placing a bin full of documents on his desk. There was a lot of work for him to catch up to and questions he'd have to answer after what he had done to the psycho man. And he did not think his actions through, until he remembered that Nina or anyone close to him could suffer the consequences.

Helmer braced himself, walked in, and stopped Nina in her tracks before she reached the door. She did not seem to wish to chat or even be in the mood to greet her boss. Nina laced her arms around her as if she was giving herself the hug no one thought of giving her. She needed it, that reassuring feeling that she was no longer in danger and that the man whom she didn't even know what he was after would not abduct her again and torment her. She was the first victim, though her fear could not be compared to anyone's. Having her skin carved, watching it happening, seeing her blood spurting out, yet unable to feel a thing or move. That was like looking death in the eye and unable to save one's soul.

"Nina," Helmer said, pacing behind her. "I-I wanted to know if you were okay."

"Are you sure?" Nina replied, her tone ice cold.

"Yes," Helmer said, nodding his head. "I genuinely would like to know how you are doing, especially after last night. I don't know yet if you are aware, but I had tried to—"

"Defy him? I know," Nina said, her face blank, not giving any clues as to whether she was upset or angry. She reached for her scar, the only greeting she's remembered from psycho man, then breathed in. "I know what you have done. You tried to kill him, knowing well it'd only put my life or anyone else here in danger."

Helmer flinched, his heart pumping faster. Why couldn't he have just run after the psycho man and get the job done? That was all he heard from what Nina had said. He missed his shot, almost rather, and that left a distasteful look on his face. "Has he reached out? Has he done anything to you? Please, tell me."

"You've awakened a monster, Helmer, and he won't stop."

"That's why I was trying to stop him," Helmer said, his tone turning firm and invasive. "What I had done last night was for all of us, and whatever he got going on, I swear to you it'll end with me."

"Well, he hasn't called. This can't be a good sign," Nina said, pacing around the room and lifting her hands to her face. Her head was going to explode from trying to put one and two together. She didn't know what was coming. Actually, no one did. Psycho man was in the shadows, probably hungry for blood. Or perhaps he could give up haunting them after Helmer's deliberate attempt to kill him. Or, going back to the shadows would only empower him even more, fueling his darkness.

"He is coming for you, me, and whoever you are attached to the most," Nina said, seeing that Helmer was in deep thought, wanting him to say something. Her body was restless the more she thought of the situation at hand. "He's very unpredictable!"

"That's it!" Helmer said, his face showing a sudden light of hope. "He is unpredictable. And just so you know, you get to kill the monster easier when he's asleep."

"Okay?" Nina said, scrunching her face.

"We have to beat him at his own game," Helmer continued. "We can't be predictable. So, I will need us to work against him, something he'll not expect."

"W-Work against who?" Nina snorted, shaking her head. She took a step back, watching Helmer so sure of himself that she assumed he'd lost his mind. There was no way they could plan against a man who seemed to be terror itself. "Doing that will only cause him to hurt more people."

"Look around." Helmer sighed, seeing that it'd take a bit more effort to convince Nina. But who could blame her? Helmer had no plan yet, and he had not even been consistently coming to work due to his fears about showing up. His face looked sleep-deprived, and he had hired Marie Lisa, whom he had Nina training to work in the office. There were too many decisions that seemed too incongruous he'd been making while away, which affected the workflow, and everything in the office, for Nina to even consider his idea as logical.

"I think you're afraid." Nina said. "We all are. You don't see the end of this, me either. But this is not a good idea."

"Trust me, I know what I'm doing."

"No, you don't," Nina said, boldly raising her voice. "Because a few days ago, he had promised to hit his next target, and I fear it's somebody you really care about."

"And who would that target be?" Helmer asked, his body tensing as he waited for an answer. He had plenty of names on his mind, and surprisingly, there was one he could not stop thinking of. He hesitated to say it, fearing that this name wasn't his wife's. She should be the first on his mind, or at least their daughter, and even Bryant. Gladice came to mind but for a brief second. But he didn't have to guess anymore. The phone on his desk started to ring. Helmer gawked at Nina, whose face crunched with terror.

"It might be him," Nina whispered, glancing at the office window and then at the ceiling. She felt him everywhere, even without any proof of planted cameras or trackers. R was watching one way or another. Nina gestured at Helmer to take the call, which he hesitated to do, wondering if last night was a mistake. Would shooting R cost somebody's life?

Helmer approached the desk, his arm reluctantly reaching for the phone. He placed it in his ear and listened. There was no longer the baffled sound anymore or the glitch. R's voice was clear. The psycho man was stepping out of his hiding shell, and that had to be either him backing away or testing Helmer's defiance.

"Hi," R said. "You must be so disappointed. I know that feeling. You shouldn't have missed."

"Why are you calling? What is it that you want?" Helmer asked. "Oh, I thought I was clear about what I wanted. You've seen it too. You caused such a big scene that now, you've upset me."

"If there's anyone who should be upset, it's me."

"I understand what it feels like," R said. "Watching your woman go to another; probably someone you'll never measure up to, and who has so much control over her."

Helmer walked to the window, his voice shrinking. "What is it with my wife that you want? Do you know her?"

"More than you think," R replied. "But I don't kiss and tell." "You're such a goddamn psychopath!"

"It takes a psychopath to recognize his match," R hinted. "We are no different. I was hoping you'd recognize that."

"What are you talking about?"

"I know your little secrets," R teased, his tone sounding amused. "And even those you don't know about yet."

"I have no secrets," Helmer said, his voice high-pitched but still shaky.

"Are you that good man you portray yourself to be?"

Helmer paused, processing R's question, the psycho man who seemed to not be as crazy as he seemed. The last time Helmer had heard this question, it was from Elvino, his foster father who knew him better than his own self.

"Have you ever been in love, Mr. Dupris?"

Helmer froze, his heart skipping a beat. He pressed the phone harder to his ear, hoping not to miss this one out. He wanted to hear the psycho man's last words. Not because he cared about what he had to say, but rather who he was going after next.

"Secrets. Secrets," R said. "You once took what was mine; now it's my turn."

"What are you talking about?" Helmer questioned.

"You mean who?" R teased. "What is she again? Your associate? She's beautiful. I've seen her bring you tea in the morning, even when you don't show up..."

"Sonie," Helmer whispered, the words rushing out of his mouth before he could hesitate to repeat her name. The sweet name of that girl he'd loved since his high school years.

"Oh, you know who it is," R snickered. "At least you see now who I am talking about."

"What do you want with her?" Helmer asked, leaning away from the window, feeling a rush of adrenaline. If only he had wings to shield Sonia from whatever was coming her way, but he couldn't run fast enough. He had to find Sonia.

"Let's give it 15 counts, and then—"

"Then what?" Helmer cut in, his body overheating with impatience. "Boom, boom, Boom..."

"Damn!" Helmer sprinted to the office door, and Nina, apprehensive about what was said on the call, followed Helmer down the hallway.

"What happened? Helmer!"

"I have to get to Sonie," he said, running. There was a countdown on the phone.

"One, Two, Three..."

It kept going, leaving Helmer in an anguishing panic. Was it a bomb? Was the psycho bluffing? The faster the count, the faster Helmer ran, barely feeling his heartbeat.

He got to the elevator, the door delaying to open. That number of seconds sent a violent shock throughout his body, which tempted him to let out a cry. He held it in. He couldn't let out that tear yet. No, what mattered was to get to Sonia.

Helmer trotted to the emergency door and took the stairs, heading to the floor Sonia was on. He rushed through the corridor leading to her office. He tripped. He couldn't believe it; it wasn't the time to fall. His face distorted with despair, horrified that he wouldn't make it there before R finished his count, for God knew what.

"Sonie," he shouted, getting up and letting out a short gasp, so that he wouldn't choke on his words. "Sonie, get out of there."

"Nine, ten, eleven..."

No one came out of the office. Helmer wasn't even sure Sonia was in there. His chest cramped from not knowing. He got to the door and pulled it open, seeing her standing by her window. Sonia raised her head to acknowledge him, only for Helmer to see a red dot under her neck.

"Helmer?" she whispered, puzzled at the horrified look on his face.

It was a red light, looking like a laser, pointed at her neck. Sonia still had no clue. She was staring openly at Helmer running toward her. Helmer tackled her to the ground, then a gunshot erupted. "Sonie!"

She lay flat on the ground, not moving an inch. Helmer moved off of her, lifting her back so he could take a better scan of her neck. It was intact. He pressed his fingers to her wrist. She was breathing. He heaved a sigh of relief and then clutched against her, hugging her tightly. He did not even realize it, but his tears fell on her chest, bringing her eyes to open fully.

"Oh, Sonie. You scared me," Helmer said under his breath, brushing his hand over her full round cheeks.

"Helmer! What—what just happened?" Sonia gasped, her hand clutching her head from the jarring impact. "Why did you push me?"

"Are you okay? Did I hurt you?" Helmer asked, his hands steadying her head, scanning her for injuries.

"I think so," Sonia said, her voice unsteady. Her fingers found Helmer's shirt, clinging to it as she looked at him. "But you... you look like you've seen a ghost!"

Helmer sighed. "Maybe I have. C'mon."

Helmer gently cupped her waist and sat her up. He glanced at the window, then across the room, and finally noticed the bullet hole in the wall. The psycho man wasn't joking. He indeed tried to get his payback, and it was obviously not going to be his last attempt to make Helmer's life a living hell.

Just as he reached for Sonia's arm to help her stand, the door creaked open. A teenage boy, dressed in a sharp suit, hesitated in the doorway, his eyes darting around nervously.

Then Nina appeared behind him, wringing her hands. "I'm so sorry, Ms. Sonia. He insisted on seeing you. He said he's family."

Sonia's breath hitched, her legs trembling beneath her. Her gaze flickered between Helmer and Nina before landing on the boy. Her lips parted as if to speak, but no sound came, seeing the chapter of her life she'd kept secret for 17 years had come to light. Something she had fought to never happen, ever.

"Yes," the boy giggled, shaking his head at Nina's comment, realizing she hesitated to say the reason for his visit as he told her earlier when she found him in the hallway. "But I'm sorry, that's not just my family." His eyes gleamed as he looked at Sonia. "That's my mom."

CHAPTER 26

Penance

Helmer and Sonia started dating after prom. That night, they shared their first kiss, and Bryant didn't have a clue. He did not go after Helmer told him that Sonia would've preferred not to have him there. To maintain his friendship with Bryant, Helmer asked Sonia to keep their relationship secret, and they kept it that way for a long time, even throughout their college years.

"You're telling me that all these fight clubs belong to Elvino?" Sonia asked, watching Helmer kick the punching bag, then giving in a few knee strikes. He turned and gestured at her to hand him his water bottle.

"Yeah," he replied, panting, "and soon, I'll be taking the lead.

There are already two he has placed under my name. That's what happens when you're a good fighter. The world would give anything to have you on their side."

"Right," Sonia said, forcing a smile. "But don't you think it's time to take a break? I mean, you've been doing this for quite some time now."

"He didn't force me."

"Exactly!" She nodded with haste. "You choose to fight, and it's not even for the money. You love it, and you can't get away, not even for a day."

"Believe it or not, that's my way to repay Elvino for everything he has done for me. Those clubs are what give him the power he holds, all this fortune that people in the city can only dream of." Helmer gulped down the water and then ran some on his face. He handed Sonia back the bottle and pointed at his chest. "What do you think of the tattoo? I'm part of the fighting team now."

"It's cute," Sonia said, shrugging. "It's a nice tiger."

"Just cute?" Helmer snorted. "Not even sexy?" he teased, pulling her close. "Why do I feel like you're not excited?"

"I don't know, Helms," Sonia said, scanning down Helmer's bandaged hands and bruised knuckles. They were nearly ruined from fighting, yet he didn't seem to care. "I'm worried... Having random men betting on you for some bucks is not a life." She looked at the fresh tiger tattoo and ran her finger over it. "When I saw you fighting the other day, I barely recognized you, and I thought you were going to pass out."

"Look, I do not want us to fight," he said, lifting her hands to his lips and kissing them. "So... I'm just going to ignore what you said. I trust Elvino. And he likes you. He has even asked when we'll take it to the next step—"

"I'm scared," Sonia confessed. "What about Bryant? Elvino caught him taking a pot the other way. I think he's onto that stuff."

"That's why we can't tell him about us yet," Helmer said. "I will when it's time. Right now, I need to find a way to help him stop hanging out with the Patterson Brothers. They're the ones influencing him to do these kinds of things."

"Who are the Patterson Brothers?" Sonia asked.

"Elvino forbids me to talk to them, but he said they are as powerful as him in the fighting business," Helmer explained. "I don't know much. But when it comes to Bryant, he also has a lot going on with school. We have finals next Week." Helmer added, pecking a kiss on Sonia's nose. "So, we'll worry about him later." He playfully bit her shoulder. "You know what? You should kiss me more."

"Not with this sweaty face," she teased.

"I don't care." Helmer pulled her tighter and looked into her brown eyes. He could see the future in them. That was what love was supposed to feel like. Escaping one's reality with one glance. And they had that. "You know what? I can't wait for the day we have our own little family and settle down somewhere in Paris." He took her index finger, brushed it lightly across his lips, then drew it into his mouth and gently sucked on it. "We will give our child everything we didn't get to give ourselves growing up."

Feeling the warmth of his mouth on her finger, Sonia gave in, no longer bothered by the dampness of his skin against hers. "I'm sure we will be the best parents in the world. Our child will have love, peace, a safe home, and an amazing dad who happens to be the love of my life."

"You mean that?"

"Helmer," she clasped his face and rubbed her thumb against his cheek. "I know you're worrying about becoming like your father, but I promise you're not like him. You'll never be him."

***

As the silence in the room lingered, Helmer leaned toward the boy, looking at him carefully. The boy's head was full of curls and seemed very well maintained. He had freckles and subtle dimples when he smiled. His skin was also interesting; his complexion was lighter than Sonia's.

"Hey, what are you doing here?" Sonia said, finally managing to put a word in. She clasped the boy's cheeks and then drew him briefly into her arms. "How did you end up here?"

"I don't know," the boy said. "Grandfather's driver told me he was instructed to bring me to see you."

"Grandfather?" Helmer said, appalled by the boy's statement. Or maybe he was too confused about the scenery to think clearly. "Who is that?"

"Oh," the boy glanced at Helmer, ready to explain. But Sonia stopped him, knowing he wouldn't know to be discreet. Sonia clutched at his shoulders and motioned for him to accompany her outside.

"Wait, what's your name?" Helmer shouted while waving a hand at Nina, not to dismiss yet.

"Christopher, sir," the boy replied, stopping in his tracks before Sonia could take him out of the office. Now, she'd be bare in the open, her secret no longer covered up. Sonia's heart was racing, and having the boy and Helmer in the same room was the biggest fear she had unfortunately ever experienced.

"Helmer, it's not the time—"

"May I ask how old you are?" Helmer questioned the boy, dismissing Sonia's statement. He needed answers and quick, for his soul kept alerting him of his speeding heart, hoping he wouldn't face a panic attack. He brushed his arm over his chest repeatedly as he waited for the boy to reply.

"Seventeen, sir."

"Stop answering!" scolded Sonia, growing impatient with Helmer's instigations. Her shouting only triggered her headache from the fall earlier. She grimaced and held the back of her head, wondering if she could manage that pain and the fact that her son had been discovered. Sonia was wishing for many things: first, that the word would not spread in the office. Second, that she would need to explain herself, and third, that Nina, who was still standing by the door watching, would be discreet about it too.

"No need to shout at him," Helmer said, his gaze softening and unable to shift away from the boy. "I was the one asking the questions."

"Well, he knows better!"

"Nina, take the boy to the lobby outside my office," Helmer ordered, lifting one hand toward the door. "His mom and I need to talk—"

"We have nothing to talk about," Sonia cut in, hoping to rush out of the office.

"If you do not wish for me to make a scene, then I think we do," Helmer said, his voice subtly threatening. Seeing this, Nina rushed the boy out of the office and took him away.

Sonia moved to the opposite side of the room and crossed her arms, avoiding his longing stare. "What?"

"What?" Helmer snorted at her question, refusing to believe she'd be so oblivious as intended to be. "You-You have a son."

"And why should that be your business?" Sonia said, raising her head, her furious eyes meeting his.

"It is my business," Helmer said, walking toward her. "Sonie, he's 17."

"And?"

"We need to talk about all this," imposed Helmer.

"About what exactly?"

"You know what," he insisted, reflecting on their history, all the years they had kept their relationship in the dark, and promises made to each other.

Sonia hunched over her desk. "I have no idea."

"Does Bryant know?" Helmer asked, seeing he wasn't going to get any word out of her, even if she was tortured to death. There needed to be something stronger to make her talk, and perhaps bringing up Bryant could.

"He never has to know," Sonia replied, her face firm and resolved. She wasn't giving in to his instigation, and neither was willing to take the fall for something they both did. "And you will make sure to keep this to yourself just as the times you've asked me not to tell him about us."

"Sonie, this is different," Helmer groaned, pacing back and forth in the office. There was no hope to reason with her, and that made his soul ache with despair.

"Different how? Helmer, what you saw has—"

"Everything to do with me," Helmer cut in. "This boy has my freckles and even the dimples. I-I don't know if you noticed, but he even talks like me, walks like me, and his facial structure—"

"Please, drop it," Sonia interrupted, moving toward the door, intending to walk out of the office. "This is my personal life, and despite being friends, you do not have the right to pry into my life."

Helmer darted toward the door and locked it. He stood in front, staring at Sonia's terrified face, apprehended by what he was doing.

"Except this is not your life we're talking about but ours. And I want to know who the father is, or else no one is walking out of this damn office."

"Helmer, let me out," Sonia said, her voice demanding yet giving off her sudden fear of him acting a fool. A fool, indeed, was all she could think of. Her heart was shrinking in gloom, watching him beg for the truth. Sonia knew that this truth could only break him, and she wasn't ready to witness it. She wondered what their lives would've been then, but probably more chaotic, secretive, and forcing them to be on the run. She didn't want that lifestyle, the fighting clubs watching him almost half dead, and his bond with Elvino, whom he was ready to do anything, absolutely anything for.

"You've hid this from me!" Helmer said, his voice thundering across the room. "That explains all the traveling and family abroad you could never tell me about."

"Helmer..."

"Who's the boy's father?"

Sonia swallowed, feeling her gut churning and her legs giving in to the numbness. "It's not your business."

"Who is it?" He pinned her against the door, securing both arms around her. He wanted her stuck, in panic mode, and absolutely vulnerable. "Please, tell me."

"No." Sonia shook her head. "Helmer, I only wish for you to go back home to your wife, and Meg. Forget about me, or the boy whom you barely know, and the past. Why do you wish to revisit it so badly?"

"Because that's all I really got of you," he said, his voice growing shaky as he swallowed back a tear.

"You-you have bigger fish to fry," Sonia said, attempting to squirm away from his hold. "The company needs a deal, and I've decided to call Mr. Will. We only need your signature to complete it."

"You what?" Helmer let go of her, freezing on his spot from disbelief. "What sense would that make? This guy disrespected you."

"It does not matter. You need to let go of your pride, and for that, I'm letting go of mine. I know you would have agreed to take the deal if it wasn't for me."

"We no longer need this money. Bryant and I managed to find something else? And now Christopher—"

"Is my son," Sonia cut in. "Yes, I have my secrets too, and you are the least to judge. I need you to open this door because I have plenty of things to do."

"I don't care," Helmer riposted, his voice barely audible. "Helmer..."

"I do not care," he repeated, his voice now rising at a more potent volume. "I don't give a damn about anything right now! I was the first to ever touch you, Sonie. The first, the only one, I'm sure even now."

"Oh, so you're bragging about that now?"

"His age can't just coincide with the time we were together," he reasoned. "Something must have happened."

"Perhaps something did happen, but I won't be the one telling you."

"Keeping something like this from me would be just as hating me,"

Helmer said, wondering how long he'd be able to hold back tears. "I told you so many times, I confided in you how much I wanted to be a father. Actually, we both wanted that. It's unimaginable to think you, out of everyone, would punish me to such an extreme as to withhold the only thing I've ever wanted away from me."

"I am not the one to blame. You did this!" Sonia replied, her voice breaking. She didn't know her reason for melting into tears, whether for not elaborating on the matter more as she wished to or the fact that she was breaking him apart. "And I know," she added, taking a deep breath. "It hurts to relive those flawed chapters of our past. The imperfect Helmer who had deceived me, his best friend, including himself, and even the life he'd promised us. But you have to let me be, and pretend this had never happened, just like before."

"You hate me." The tears came; Helmer couldn't fight them any longer. He was standing there, barely breathing or existing. He was a pinch of dust in the air, vanishing in seconds. He was numb, so much so that he couldn't feel the tears wetting his collar. Each breath he drew was agony, and all he wished was for it to end.

"I will never hate you," Sonia reassured. "You hate yourself, and it's time to stop using me or anyone as a mirror."

Processing Sonia's words, Helmer managed to lift a foot. Then the other. They were heavy, as they did not want to let her go. Despite their ordeal, all Helmer heard was that Sonia didn't hate him. His Sonie could've never hated him, no matter what. He cleared the way, allowing her to open the door to leave.

"By the way," Sonia turned, looking at him, her soul wrenching as she saw his glassy eyes. "If you really want to know why I haven't told you, I'd suggest you ask Elvino."

Helmer's head shifted to the door. "Elvino?"

She left. The door was now open. In a mere moment of taking all in, Helmer looked at the wall, where the bullet drilled a hole in, reminding him of his new goal: taking down psycho man. But yet, he couldn't take the boy out of his head. He needed one more glance at him and perhaps have a chat with him to confirm his suspicions.

Helmer rushed out of the room and headed to the elevator to go to his office. Needing to get out of there so badly, he pushed all the elevator buttons at once which only delayed him more. After a minute, the door opened, then he spotted Elvino, in the lobby greeting Nina. Helmer darted toward Elvino, the sounds across the room dying around him. It was silent as he pulled Elvino toward him.

"Oh, Helms—"

Elvino's sentence was cut short by Helmer's fist slamming into his face, followed by another, and then a sharp knee strike. Helmer grabbed Elvino by the collar, shaking him before slamming an elbow into his ribs. Elvino staggered back, his vision blurring, but Helmer wasn't done. He charged again, too fueled by anger to stop, until a shove from behind forced him back.

"Stop! Hands off, pal. That's my grandfather!"

The voice snapped Helmer's focus; it was Christopher, his finger pointed at him, telling him to back off.

"Christopher!" Sonia's panicked shout filled the hallway as she rushed to her son. She placed both hands on his face, trying to steer him away. "Baby, what are you doing? This is grown folks' business."

"He touched my grandfather," Christopher retorted, shaking free from her grasp and heading toward Elvino, whose split lip dripped with blood.

"Your grandfather?" Helmer's voice came low, his gaze shifting from the boy to Elvino. Something about the way the boy moved, the way his fists clenched, tugged at a memory Helmer couldn't place. "What does that mean?"

"Simple," Christopher said, gripping Elvino's arm. "This man may look old, but he raised me. And let it be the last time you ever lay hands on him."

Helmer's eyes locked on Christopher's knuckles—flushed red, callused, but not bruised. His mind flashed to his years of training with Elvino, his hands taped and raw from countless strikes.

"You've been trained," Helmer said, his suspicion audible.

Christopher's eyes narrowed, but he said nothing, turning his focus back to Elvino, who coughed and waved him off.

"We should leave," Elvino rasped, wiping the blood from his lip. "I see I'm not very welcome here."

"We only came for my mother—" Christopher said, his voice firm as his hand steadied Elvino.

"Perhaps there was someone else for you to meet," Elvino interrupted, his gaze lingering on Helmer. "I fear he just blew it."

Helmer's chest tightened, and before he could press further, Sonia stepped in, her voice quavering.

"Please, Helmer, not now."

She placed a guiding hand on Christopher's shoulder, nudging him toward the door alongside Elvino.

Helmer watched as they left, his mind racing. Christopher's build. His eyes. The way he carried himself. Something about him felt unnervingly familiar. It was almost like watching the younger version of himself.

And then, just for a moment, Christopher glanced back, his stare holding Helmer's. It wasn't fear or anger—it was something deeper, something unanswered.

Helmer swallowed hard, his fists clenching at his sides. He had to see that boy again.

CHAPTER 27

*I*t was the night before the wedding, and the plans were already finalized. Magda had to meet Richard at a party and leave before dawn. T hings didn't happen as planned, and that, too, led to consequences.

"Have you seen Richard?" Magda asked the guy serving the drinks.

She looked everywhere for him, and he could not be found.

"No," the guy answered. "But I think his brother shall be here soon to take you home."

"Home? What do you mean- by home? Whatever we had planned must happen tonight."

"I'm sorry, I don't know." The guy shrugged, handing Magda a letter. Magda took the letter and went to one of the guest rooms to read it.

She sat on the twin bed in the room then turned on the nightstand light and started to read.

Maggie,

For so long, I've been thinking it through, but I couldn't do it. There's a part of me that feels like I'll never measure up to what this guy can offer you. Besides, it wouldn't be fair to leave while we both know your father is slowly dying. I do not have the heart to take you away from the life you could have and deserve. Neither would it be right to take you away from Allimair, your mom. You're all she got, and we spoke yesterday. She offered me a generous amount of money to let the wedding be, and no worries. I declined it! She discovered our plan, Maggie. And for other reasons, I cannot proceed with our plan. You're better off with that man, Dupris, the charming and perfect guy. I am not perfect and I'm barely standing on my own financially. I got evicted, me and my brother, and so we've been staying with a friend. I couldn't tell you because I wasn't sure you'd understand. It'll take years for me to be able to provide you with half of what you need. I'm so sorry! You'll always be my Maggie, the love of my life, my sun and my moon at night, my muse. My reason to keep going and the only rose I've ever held and loved.

From Richard to Maggie.

Desperation is as dangerous as deception; both can drive a person to lose their mind and do the unimaginable. Magda felt both, and she was stuck, knowing she wouldn't be able to escape that wedding. He could've told her about his decision way before, but Richard hadn't. Magda had her stuff packed, and she'd sneaked out of her house. Allimair would've noticed by now, and indeed, she knew. That's why sometimes it was believed that moms could not be fooled, and Magda figured that out too late.

She ripped the letter, not even having the time to grieve Richard and the life they could have. Turning her head to her right, she saw a bottle of tequila and chugged it down. At last, her emotions were unleashed; she was feeling that anger, and her heart was shattering inside of her.

She continued drinking, hoping to gather the courage to walk out of that party without Richard, the one who bailed on her at the last minute. Feeling lightheaded, Magda went to the door of the room and opened it, only to see Richard's brother entering in a hurry. "Ricks?" Magda muttered, seeing him double due to the alcohol effect. "I'm surprised you still came. R-Richard bailed on me."

As Magda looked up at him, squinting to see him more clearly, there was something in Ricks's eyes that made her uneasy. His gaze, dark and determined, was as though he had come for something other than to bring her home. "I-I want to call my mom for a ride. I hope it'll be okay with you..."

While attempting to put another word in, Ricks's lips crashed onto hers. Magda couldn't understand where such boldness had come from, or how that kind of lust had found her. That was her lover's brother. Something like that happening had never crossed her mind, not with him—not in this way. She tried to make sense of the situation, but her thoughts were clouded, tangled in the uncertainty of his intentions.

Ricks kicked the door closed, moving swiftly, and scooped her into his arms, carrying her toward the bed. Magda's heart raced as her thoughts scattered. She wanted to scream, to push him away, to demand answers, but her body betrayed her, her arms instinctively latching around Ricks's shoulders. Then the thought struck her. What just happened?

"H-Hold on, hold on..." Magda stammered. "Richard.... is your brother. I-I don't get it."

Despite hearing his brother's name, Ricks leaned in for another kiss, oddly finding her beautiful and alluring. Then Magda lifted her knee, shielding herself.

"Wait!" Magda said firmly, shoving Ricks away. "I think we should stop. It's not right."

"What's not right?" said Ricks, crouching down over Magda, trapping his arms around her.

"It's wrong," Magda said, trying to push him back, but failed due to him weighing into her. "Please, think of your brother."

"What about my brother? Richard does not want you," Ricks said. "C'mon. You've turned me on."

"No, no, no, please. Stop! Please," Magda begged, her voice cracking into a wail. She felt his hands press against her mouth, silencing her, though no one would have heard anything due to the loud music from the party outside. Slowly, her eyes fluttered, the alcohol taking its toll, already leaving her at his mercy.

***

It was 2 a.m. Magda couldn't sleep. She kept thinking of her baby, envisioning her stomach growing round and sturdy in a couple of months and indulging herself in her pregnancy cravings. She finally understood the reason behind her monstrous appetite and constant fatigue throughout the past weeks. When it came to timing, she wondered if it was right. Her marriage was being held by a thread, and she wondered whether to hold on or simply accept it had failed. Protecting her baby could also be challenging, with Richard being alive. Magda was still refusing to believe it was him, and she needed one more meeting to see him close enough to make sure it wasn't a hallucination. She needed to see R, the psycho man her husband seemed determined to kill.

Magda needed safety and somewhere to hide, but every action must be now calculated. Maybe she could convince her husband to start everything over and leave the country for a while. But knowing how upset her husband was, that wasn't an option. Helmer would've never agreed, neither Meg, without a proper explanation. He had even canceled their anniversary trips and never mentioned the painting exposition again.

Carrying her stake alone seemed the best option to keep her family out of danger. Nonetheless, if anything happened, Magda was resolved in her heart to leave the country with both her kids, even if it meant without Helmer. She couldn't tell him that R's obsession with her could have nothing to do with lust but rather revenge. She had done some things to him after he had sent that breakup letter. Magda wasn't ready to share that with Helmer. Maybe June? He was out of town, so it wasn't an option. That wasn't a matter to discuss over the phone. It was too risky.

Magda walked out of her bedroom, heading to the painting room. She noticed the face she least wanted to see, Marie Lisa's, coming from the hallway. "Marie!"

"Mrs. Dupris," Marie said, greeting her with a hand wave. She had her office outfit on, ready to dismiss herself.

"Now, wait a minute," Magda said, dragging Marie forward as she tried to walk past her. "We need to talk."

Marie glared down at Magda, feeling her grip deep in her flesh. Marie wished that Magda got the point already. She wasn't the type to back out with threats, and neither liked to be assaulted. "You're hurting my hand," she said calmly, waiting for Magda to let go.

"What are you doing here? I thought I made it clear I didn't want any of the personnel on this floor," Magda reminded, pulling her hands to herself. "You should be fired for this."

"You can try to," huffed Marie, lightly brushing her blouse.

"Your impertinence grows stronger every day. What is your plan here?" Magda questioned, closing the space between her and Marie. "And... I thought we had a deal. We agreed that you wouldn't say anything to my husband, yet you ratted on me."

"No." Marie shook her head. "I simply had to pick a side, and it was your husband's. It wouldn't have been fair to keep this secret from him. Would it? After all, I owe him a lot; he supports me, and he loves my work."

"What kind of work? Don't tell me you're also blackmailing him." "Would you be surprised?" Marie teased. "When one has leverage, they must use it."

"What do you have on my husband?" Magda asked, her eyes briefly assessing the way Marie's bust pressed against the fabric, the shape accentuated by the blouse.

"Won't say," Marie said, waving a finger up. "The question is, what would you give me so that I can tell you?"

"I swear you'll leave this house before you know it," Magda threatened. "You're such a bitch!"

"Bitch indeed," Marie nodded. "You also fit that description."

Magda reached for Marie's hair and pulled her by her two French braids. Marie's head snapped from the pull, and she let out a giggle, seeing that she pushed her mistress's strings hard enough for a reaction.

"You're so sick."

"I am." Marie pushed herself from Magda and patted her hair, hoping her braids didn't get messy. "Yet I thought rich folks had more manners than the lower class."

Magda approached closer. "Listen, I need you to go and pack your stuff, and leave by early morning, even before anybody can see your filthy face."

"I can't do that," Marie said, sighing.

"Excuse me?"

"I can't do that," Marie emphasized, watching the defeated expression on Magda's face. "I warned you to be nice to me, so you failed my test. Now, it's my turn to make a request."

"And what leverage would you have to make any request from me, Marie Lisa?"

"I thought you'd already figured it out." Marie clicked her tongue, pacing around Magda, amused even more by her leaning in to listen. "Why do you think I'm here? By the magnificent and mysterious painting studio of yours? Or should I say where you keep secrets about a famous guy named Richard?"

Magda froze, her face turning crimson. She blinked but could barely keep eye contact. There was no way Marie knew about Richard. No way that she got to her painting room, where all her secrets were piled up.

"No need to freeze, no worries," Marie began. "I haven't given your husband the journal yet. Or the letters of that guy who seemed so in love that he was planning to run away with you before Mr. Dupris's wedding day. Oh, and it got canceled, because your momma bear convinced Helmer to postpone it."

"You…" Magda paused, struggling to build a sentence due to the pressure building in her chest. "You went through my stuff."

"Oh no, don't think so lowly of me," Marie reassured. "I had permission to do that. Your husband asked Mr. Hens to find him the painting room's spare key so he could know what was hidden in there."

"H-Helmer asked this?"

"You know, sometimes, jealous men can be just as dangerous as a seething fire. That shouldn't be surprising. Don't you think, Mrs. Dupris?"

Fire. That brought Magda back to a lucid flashback of the fire that supposedly killed Richard. She didn't want him to die, and she honestly desired to help and save him from there. She couldn't, and after all, she had to run from the fire scene fast before she could be seen. Why would Marie know about that? Did she dig enough to find out?

"You said fire. Is there a reason in particular you've mentioned fire?"

"Maybe yes, maybe no," teased Marie through a chuckle. "But listen—at first, I wasn't going to ask for any money. After this little incident between us, I've changed my mind."

Marie leaned in, her voice lowering. "And if you can do that for me, I'll give you the journal and everything you want to put your hands on it before Mr. Dupris does. What do you say?"

"How much are we talking?" Magda questioned. "Since I am very considerate, let's settle for $200,000."

Magda thought of the offer, her mind so full that it felt like exploding. "That's a lot to ask, Marie. I don't have that sum."

"That sounds like your problem, not mine," Marie said, her tone unfaltering. "It's either this or no deal."

How would she even get that kind of money to Marie? The question broiled in her mind, as that sum was all she had in her savings, accumulated over years when her painting business still thrived. There was no way she could ask Helmer for help without arousing more suspicion. He'd start asking questions that would lead far too close to secrets she wasn't ready to reveal. As much as it stung to submit to someone like Marie, this felt like a necessary evil.

"Bring me the journal and the letters, then I'll give you the money," Magda settled.

"Perfect," Marie said, nodding. "I guess I'll see you later."

As Marie left, a text notification flashed on Magda's phone's screen. She opened it and saw a few question marks with nothing else written. She told herself it was a scam. After deleting it, a private number called. She picked up. No one answered. She hung up the phone, and the person called again. She asked who it was, but there was only the sound of someone clearing his throat.

"I know it's you," Magda said. "No need to hide anymore." "Maggie," the caller replied.

Magda's pupils grew wide. Her body shivered, yearning for a hug.

The panic had held her voice hostage. "Richard."

She wished it was a dream. It was him. Something wasn't right; how come he was alive? Her heart was jumping out of her chest.

She had flashbacks of screams and a daunting fire. She hated the brutal memories, and Richard's voice kept making it worse.

"How's your arm?" she asked hesitantly.

"I can't feel it for now, but it's manageable," he replied. "Listen, I'm sorry about your foot. It wasn't my intention to cause you any harm."

The hairs on Magda's body spiked up; she was not afraid, rather perplexed and curious. Why would he apologize when she was the one who needed his forgiveness, or had he forgotten what happened the day he was supposed to die?

"I need to see you," she blurted out. "Alone. Once again, please."

A few days ago, she would've sworn it was a random psycho playing tricks on her, now she was calling him by his name. Magda's thoughts slowed as he lingered to answer. It'd be the right time to meet, for Helmer wasn't home yet. Despite Richard not talking for seconds, his voice seemed like a seed planted deep in Magda's ears. She could not run from it nor wished to stop hearing it. It sprouted at each breath she exhaled, and it felt like torture that he kept hesitating to respond.

"Please, allow me to see you! Did you send the roses and the killer note? Was everything from you?" asked Magda. She pressed the phone harder to her ear and rested one hand over her frantic heart. If Richard had sent the first note accusing her of being a killer, it would mean he believed she was the one who tried to murder him—and in the cruelest way imaginable: by fire. That thought brought terror upon her soul, which desperately needed mercy.

"Please, I need to see you. I'm begging," she emphasized, hearing his breath rising on the phone. "I need to know. How did you survive? How come you're alive? And—"

"The old house," he said quickly.

"What?"

"I'll be at the old house, waiting for you." "I'll come right now. May I..."

The call dropped.

Magda knew where he was, and she'd be alone with him. The nerves rushed through her; then, she unknowingly clasped both arms across her belly. That part she nearly forgot about: she was pregnant.

Why did that need to happen now when she had to deal with so many things at once? All her suppressed rage toward her husband came back, making her care less about whether he was safe and sound for not being home yet. She couldn't even think of them sleeping next to each other, being in the room breathing the same air. However, it was better to keep their marital affairs away from the gossiping personnel due to her learned experience with Marie Lisa. It was better to be safe than sorry.

Magda walked to her closet and put on a red dress, the first that came into sight. She threw a beige jacket on with it and a scarf on her head, covering her hair so she'd not be as recognizable. The air in the room was a gush of toxic smoke in her face; she was overtaken with a rush of dread along with excitement. Magda burst out of the room, hoping no one had seen her head to the back side of the mansion. She reached there and noticed two other guards, who greeted her with a concerned look.

"Miss," they said in unison with a head nod.

"Who are you?" Magda asked, not recognizing those two faces despite her efforts.

"Oh, we're new here," they confirmed. "Mr. Dupris hired us a week ago."

"Technically, yeah," one of them added. "We only had to finish out some paperwork so we could officially start, and today we'd—"

"Funny how he didn't even have the decency to tell me." Magda broke in. "Anyway, not a word of my leave to my husband. Understood?" The new guards looked fearfully at each other and then nodded, wondering why on earth their boss's wife would leave their home at such a dark and inconvenient hour. "Understood, ma'am."

"Get me a car, and fast," she ordered. "I need you two to take me to the woods."

CHAPTER 28

Fallen Rose

The chills started to sprout in her stomach, giving her the urge to throw up. Magda clasped her mouth, taking a deep breath before speaking to the guards watching her concerned.

"It's fine," she said, her voice robbed of any slight confidence. "You two may leave. I shall depart from here."

The guards looked at each other, perplexed and preoccupied by her request. "Mr. Dupris told us to watch over you and to protect you from anything that may arise."

"Then you two shall keep discreet about this little trip," Magda said, "since you have failed to follow those very specific instructions by driving me to nowhere in the middle of the night." Before the guards could object, she hurled the car door open and sprinted out, horrified yet enthralled by what may come. She was about to see the man of her youth, the one who once made her whole and who had taught her what hate felt like. Or, more supposedly, a deception and heartbreak she may have believed to finally be able to find closure for.

The woods were quiet, as the moon led Magda's way. She was eager to get there, and reaching the door, it all became real. The clog in her throat merely allowed her to breathe, and so did the butterflies in her stomach. Magda, managing to find a bit of courage, opened the door, then her eyes slammed shut. She wasn't ready for any inconvenience, surprises, and less to see him face to face, Richard, the face of her past.

"Have no fear; you may open them," he said.

Magda's eyes slowly opened, and there he was across the room, looking at her.

"Richard," said Magda firmly, finally convinced.

It was him, flesh and bones, a few feet away. He had his mask off, revealing freely the gruesome parts of his face, which didn't frighten Magda one bit. After all, why would she? More than anything, she could not judge what he looked like.

"I... I am so—"

"Later. Let's talk later," he insisted, gesturing at the floor so Magda could take notice.

A trail of petals led Magda to a dining table in the center of the room. She noticed a bottle of champagne on the table and a pair of wine glasses by the red and gold dishware. The place was warm, setting a welcoming mood.

The house looked completely astonishing from the last time she remembered it. That house where they used to meet, escaping Allimair's insistence for their relationship to discontinue, and Mr. Brooks's lectures. That house where there used to be only them against all odds, and where they had first confessed their love. The shivers took over Magda's body as she approached the table, hesitant to be in awe, for the scenery didn't feel real. She was expecting it all to vanish in seconds and for Richard to no longer be alive.

"I know it's a lot to take in," Richard said, "but you shall find all the answers you're expecting after our dinner."

Magda could not hear a word but only noticed his bandaged arm under his coat. Her eyes would not move away from him taking his coat off, revealing his refined three-piece black suit. She had never seen him in a suit before, making him appear strangely appealing despite his scars. How could he afford such clothing?

Magda didn't dare to ask, fearing it'd be offensive. She worried about something bigger, the limerence his presence would leave her soul in, and the longing to breathe in his cologne. That scent was new, but it was where she stood, pulling her toward him even without moving a foot.

"Maggie?" Richard whispered, seeing that she got distracted.

It wasn't on purpose, but how could she not? She was watching him walking so elegantly toward her while he stared at her lips. She couldn't tell whether he was provoking her or not.

"Yes," she said, her voice unintentionally shaky, aware that he had noticed. "You-You look different, at least tonight from the last time."

"Thanks," he said, a smile spreading across his lips. His words were short, precise, and somewhat charming. "So do you. You're still such a ravishing rose, the one I've ever held and longed for."

Magda stared at him, surprised to realize that his words could still make her body tingle. She clutched at herself, her lips parting slowly.

"Are you all right?" asked Richard, seeing her silent.

Magda nodded, turning her head away, no longer sure if the danger came from him or herself. Her mind spun with thoughts she shouldn't entertain. She was burning to an extent where sanity was foreign to her. Perhaps it was the depths of Richard's voice that subtly sounded like poetry itself. She wondered what he was doing here, her cheeks red from the thought.

Classical music played softly in the background, candles flickered in every corner, and a feast was laid out on the table. The air smelled of lavender and roses, and she caught sight of a small sculpture in the corner—a piece of her, carved in ivory.

"This is for me?" Magda asked, keeping her trembling hands clasped tightly at her sides. She glanced at the golden candles and the margarita-filled pitchers that served as centerpieces, her gaze never settling in one place too long. The alcohol, just the sight of it, gave her the urge to puke. She had to hold back. Richard should never know that she's pregnant. Her baby wouldn't be safe. And she remembered her husband's warning very clearly. She had no business putting their baby in danger. "Yes, for you," Richard confirmed, showing her the scrumptious meals on the table. He stepped into another room and returned with a bouquet of red roses. "And these," he added. "It's not a date without flowers."

"A date?" Magda said, hesitantly taking the bouquet. What was she doing here? What was all this? She had come to confront her stalker and put this ordeal to rest. But Richard wasn't just a stalker. He was the shadow of her sins, the embodiment of a past she couldn't keep buried, no matter how hard she tried.

She looked into his eyes; they were empty at the start, then showed warmth as she reached for his face. The truth was she couldn't help it. She placed her hand on the untouched side of his face, and watched his eyes fall shut. He had not felt such a tender touch for a decade, if not more. The bouquet slipped from Magda's grasp, landing on the table as she leaned closer. Her palm found the scarred side of Richard's face, and she froze, feeling its coarse texture beneath her fingers. His eyes snapped open from her touch; he had missed it. The silence spoke the pain between them so eloquently that words would be mere distractions. Her other hand joined the first, trembling as it moved over his scars.

Her chest brushed against his, feeling the storm in her heart. It was his breath, warm and uneven against her cheek, that broke her resolve. "Wait," she stammered, her voice barely audible. "I-I thought you were dead." S he pulled back, her hands hovering near her face. "I swear, I thought you died. I saw it."

"Obviously, I survived," Richard replied with a sardonic edge. His voice softened, dangerously so. "Shall we dance?"

There was so much to discuss and questions to be answered. Magda could not hold still. How could anyone ignore the absurdity of it? This man had a funeral, a burial, a death certificate, yet he was here in that room with her. And was it wise to come alone? To meet her ex-lover while carrying her husband's child? Her hand instinctively moved to her belly, a futile attempt to shield the life inside her. She had to leave— now. As Richard extended his hand, asking her to dance, she froze.

"I was hoping to spend the night with you," Richard said, his hand beckoning hers.

"The night?" Magda questioned, her widened eyes revealing her panic.

"Richard, I…" Magda paused, wondering whether he really had not noticed her wedding band or had simply decided to ignore it. "I can't… I'm married. I shouldn't even be here—"

"Seeing me?" he cut in. "I know. Or else he might try to kill me." "My husband was bluffing the other night," Magda said hastily, her hands instinctively moving to shield her stomach, the gesture subtle but not lost on Richard.

"Bluffing?" Richard's laugh was low, almost pitying, as he leaned closer, his breath grazing her ear. "No. He meant to shoot me. I know jealousy when I see it."

Magda took a step back. "I'm sorry, but you can't talk," she retorted, her voice sharper now. "You've hurt so many people."

Richard's lips curved into a mocking smirk. "But I don't kill." "And Helmer has?" Magda snapped, her words faster than her thoughts. "If he had, I'd be the first to know." "Does he know you're here with me?" Magda's throat dried. She couldn't answer.

Richard stepped much closer, his nose nearly brushing hers. "He doesn't, does he?"

"Richard, I…" Her words faltered as his knuckles tilted her chin upward.

"Let's dance," he requested, pulling her hands into his, and leading her gently to the center of the room.

"Richard," Magda whispered, "what are you doing?"

"A dance," he repeated, stretching her arms out and sniffing her neck. He saw the shivers forming on top of her skin, robbing her of all possible reasoning. "Don't resist this. It's just a dance."

Magda's eyes fell shut, feeling his arm leading her to the right and then to the left. They were dancing, and he was gentle. His fingers skimming through her back as if she were an instrument made her gasp. Was it a request for something that she knew she could never provide? Whatever it was, Richard's fingers tugging at her skin were tempting, and such touch could be catastrophic. Her chest pumped, knowing the danger hanging over her head; their lips were close. Too close for a married woman. They both stilled when Richard's breath moved across her shoulder, lingering as it grew hotter. "I..."

"You what?" Richard muttered, holding her tighter, his lips less than an inch from hers.

"I..."

"Tell me," he whispered, his knuckles tilting up her chin.

"I have to leave!" She pushed herself away, breathing hard as if she had run a marathon. "I can't do this to Helmer. I-I love my husband. I shouldn't be here."

"Then why have you come?" he asked, keeping his gaze on her, his arms crossed behind his back.

"For closure," she replied. "To make sure it was really you.

But I see now that I was right to worry. Your intentions aren't good."

"And why would that be?"

"You know why," Magda replied, pacing away, her eyes searching for the nearest exit. "We didn't leave things on good terms the last time we saw each other."

"So, closure, huh?" Richard repeated, removing his gloves with deliberate slowness. His scars came into view, raw and jagged, the skin stretched and uneven. "Or... is it to see if I want revenge?"

Magda's heart jumped as her gaze fixed on Richard's damaged hands. The skin was rough, chewed, and covered in scabs, so different from the softness she remembered before the fire. The sight churned her stomach. Anyone would want revenge for what had been done to him, and she wasn't special. That thought clung to her as she stood in this old house deep in the woods, away from home and her husband. She should've told Helmer. She could perhaps reach for her phone discreetly to call him.

"I remember I couldn't use my hands for months, nor move without feeling my body tearing and peeling apart," Richard said as he noticed Magda's eyes getting teary. "You have no idea the kind of pain you have put me through."

"Richard, I don't even know where to begin," Magda said, her voice weakened by a sob. "I didn't know what I was thinking or doing that day. I was upset with you! I was hurt."

She braced herself, her arms instinctively wrapping around her stomach. This baby—barely formed in her womb—was nestled in the chaos she had created and willingly walked into. She was a mother, and the realization that she was at the mercy of a man she had hurt—a man she had hoped would remain buried—ignited every instinct to flee.

The realization clawed at her as Richard's gaze darkened, his presence growing more precarious.

"I felt abandoned, Richard! You left me," her voice broke, trembling as her words spilled out. "I had nowhere to put all that rage. Nowhere! I didn't know what to do. I am so sorry." The tears poured in streams, flooding her face, her lips quivering. "I've been carrying this guilt for so long..." Magda continued, "I am a horrible person. I failed you. I failed us! Please... please, forgive me."

FLASHBACK

After the night with Ricks—Richard's brother— Magda woke up bare in the room, her eyes barely adjusting to the light seeping over the bed. She saw a shadow, barely, but once she heard the voice, she knew it was Allimair. Magda rubbed her eyes, clearing her vision progressively, then noticed her mom rushing to the bed toward her. Allimair snatched the covers off of her, exposing her breasts.

"What are you doing here? It was supposed to be your wedding day today," said Allimair, furious, even more as she noticed Magda cupping her boobs. "And what the hell are you doing here in this room? You were with him, weren't you?"

Magda's face flushed, her senses and memories of the night before coming right back. Her eyes widened in terror, moving slowly down her breasts to her legs. She was truly naked, and she could not deny what happened the night before was real.

"Thank God I spoke to your future husband, and he agreed that we postponed the wedding until the end of the week," ranted Allimair, too absorbed in her disappointment to notice her daughter bursting into tears. "I had to lie for you, telling him you were sick and making up a bunch of stories which I don't even think sounded credible. Yet you were here sleeping with this boy! What were you thinking? Richard is a nobody—"

"Ricks raped me."

"I can't believe you—" Allimair paused, slowly processing what Magda said. Her ears didn't want to believe and, worse, accept it. Her angry gaze shifted to Magda and then softened as she took a step forward. "What did you say?"

"Ricks, Richard's brother," Magda confirmed, hugging herself. "He raped me. He raped me, Mom."

"So, it's not even the boy, it's his brother? What the hell, Magda? What do you mean he raped you?" Allimair said, upset and unable to digest that new information. "You know? I found out about your sneaky plan to run off with the boy, and I told him to stay away from you, but never have I imagined something like that to happen."

"I-I don't know what to say." sobbed Magda.

"No, you need to. Because it's so messed up," Allimair raged. "What am I supposed to do now? This guy has brought nothing good into your life, and here I am, having to hear that his brother is even worse. What should I do?"

"Maybe… Hold me?" A louder sob broke out of Magda's parted lips while she tried to place some pillows over her chest. "Just hold me?"

Allimair sighed, her heart drenching into a pain she never thought possible to feel as a mother. Those cries from her daughter woke up something in her and placed some dangerous thoughts in her mind along with the chaos. Allimair hastened to sit next to her, and then her arms reached for Magda, scooping her against her chest.

"I'm so sorry." Allimair caressed Magda's head and allowed her to express her agony. But there was one thing about her. She was a momma bear. She could do anything for her family and that situation with Richard had truly pushed her buttons. "No worries. We'll press charges so Ricks or whatever his name is can pay for what he's done."

"They both hurt me, Mom," Magda said, her voice cracking as her nails dug into her palms. "But Richard... may he burn for what he's done. He broke me in a way no one else ever could."

***

Richard's darkened gaze was eating away Magda's soul. His silence clung to the air like a storm on the brink, each second a torment she couldn't endure. "Don't leave me in the dark," she pleaded through a sob. "How did you survive? What happened? Why wasn't I... Why wasn't anyone told you were alive?"

"Should you be surprised at not being informed?" Richard said, pulling a chair out for her to sit.

"What do you mean?" Magda asked, her steps hesitant as she lowered herself into the chair. It'd be foolish to upset him.

"That scent," Richard said, sitting down. He pulled some of the dishes and fixed his plate. "Your perfume, I missed it every single day. I mourned the sight of you, your caress, the way your hair danced between my fingers when you lay in my arms."

He poured himself a glass of wine, the crimson liquid swirling as he tilted the glass to his lips. After a slow sip, he set it down and fixed her with a look that felt like it could pierce her. "It's crazy," he continued, his voice dipping to a dangerous whisper. "That same perfume was there the day of the fire. The day of my demise, to be precise."

Something in his voice made Magda's heart uneasy. His pupils dilated as he spoke to her, and a smirk kept making an appearance at the corner of his lips. He fidgeted with his fork and his knife, but it wasn't anything like a play or nervousness. He was in deep thought, and that could be either a good or a bad thing.

"And since then, Maggie, I've learned one thing about you," Richard resumed, as he leaned closer. "You're the monster I mirror because you're the last face that has haunted me to this day." He cleared his throat, reaching for the pitcher and pouring her a glass of margarita, his eyes never leaving hers.

"Funny, isn't it?" he added, cutting into his steak with unsettling precision. "You've always blamed me for our relationship falling apart, but never once have you pointed a finger at your mother."

"You don't know that," Magda retorted, her voice tense as she slid the glass aside. Her hand lingered briefly, steadying herself. She couldn't drink it, and she was hoping that Richard would not notice.

"Oh, I do," Richard objected, reaching for his wine to wash down his throat before going for another piece of the steak. "You just said I abandoned you, not that Allimair threatened my life to let your wedding be."

"S-She did that?" Magda froze, her fingers tightening around the edge of the table. "You told me that she offered you money, and you declined it."

"No, she threatened my life and my brother's," Richard said, his smirk dissolving. "And I know you found out somehow."

His face straightened, not any lines in sight. That face sent shivers down Magda's spine. That face was no longer the innocent, sweet boy with the baby face she had once adored. Helmer was right. Her husband's warnings about Richard being dangerous began ringing loudly in her ears. She should have told someone where she was going. Anyone. But no one knew.

"I-I didn't know that," Magda stammered, her fork trembling in her hand. She hadn't touched the food. The margarita's smell made her feel ill, and then she realized why Richard was staring at her like prey.

"This is something similar to pancuronium," Richard said calmly, lifting a pocket square to his face, pressing it against his nose. "It will put you to sleep."

"Wha-What are you saying?" Magda said, her vision weakening as her eyelids grew heavy. Her voice turned into a whisper, and her hands immediately reached for her belly. "My ba—"

Her words could not form a sentence from Richard's sudden grasp of her neck. He lifted her and knocked her onto the table, her back breaking the pitcher used as a centerpiece. Magda's eyes widened, the grip of death tightening around her, just as in her nightmares. She did not see it coming, and neither could she fight back when she was pinned down against her will, barely breathing.

"I wanted to do this for years," Richard, or the psycho man she had underestimated, said through gritted teeth. Magda's body moved helplessly under his devilish hold. "You have no idea," he continued, his teeth clenched and grip tightening, "how someone can love you and hate you with the same intensity."

Magda's eyes fluttered shut, her blood rushing to her head. Her hands wandered on the table, desperately looking for something to get him off of her. Her breathing slowed, leaving a scarier feeling and shock throughout her body. Her fingers managed to squirm through the plates—the ones that didn't fall from the impact—and there, she felt something. A utensil? No, she didn't care what it was. Magda managed to grab it, and from the shape, it was a knife; then she hurled it into his arm.

Richard let go of her neck, and she slid off the table, feeling the pieces of glass in her back, leaving her in an indescribable agony. She clasped her throat, still struggling to breathe, but something was telling her that she didn't have much time to move. Magda had to run. She had no choice. For her baby, at least, she had to make it out of there, and fast. Magda reached for the table for support to stand, and she managed until she felt a grab on her leg. Terror came upon her once again, and she fell. Magda clasped her stomach, tears running down her face. She got pinned down again, her body pressed to the floor.

"I should've warned you that no one runs out of this place without feeling a little bit of pain. Something I've known thanks to you." Richard covered his nose with his vest and splashed a thumb of powder onto Magda's face. He released her and watched her crawl desperately, trying to escape. Like a snake letting its prey wander off to its death, he allowed Magda to reach the door. Soon, her movements slowed, growing sluggish, and then her shoulders crashed onto the floor.

CHAPTER 29

When Darkness Wins

It was a celebration night for Helmer as Elvino had placed 2 other fight clubs under his name. Those clubs were huge resources of money, and of course, with places like those, the associations were always questionable.

"I promise I can win this fight. Let me get inside the ring," Helmer insisted as Elvino showed him his assigned fighters, being twice the size of their opponents.

"It's your night; I don't want you near this ring," Elvino said, adjusting his cigar and gesturing at his bodyguards to light it up. "With this money, you can fund the company you wish to build with your friends. Trust me, we're winning tonight."

Helmer looked at the opponents' side, and the two men placing their bets were nervous, chatting between themselves. Helmer couldn't put his hands on it, but something seemed fishy. The environment, the way that the fighters from the opposite side looked so composed, and some bettors were eager to place their bets gave it all away that something bad was boiling underneath. Helmer ignored his intuition and took a seat, watching the fight start.

His fighters were doing well, which brought him huge excitement, shouting and proudly reacting. Then he noticed the two men who were chatting earlier getting up and gesturing at Elvino, who immediately followed them. Helmer pretended not to notice so Elvino wouldn't know he'd followed along after. As Helmer was getting up, he overheard someone saying something that made his heart stop. "There will be bloodshed tonight."

Helmer adjusted his ears, discreetly listening. And one of the young men continued, "Someone must warn the Don. And quick before it's too late."

"The Don?" Helmer whispered to himself as he continued to listen. "The Patterson Brothers just left with him—"

Helmer didn't wait for another word. He bolted down the bleachers and signaled Elvino's bodyguards to stop the fight and send everyone home. He grabbed one of the guards' guns and before anyone could react, he sprinted toward the back. Elvino was more than just a business partner; Helmer felt a strange sense of responsibility toward him, something that ran deeper than he could explain. Elvino had trusted him, and Helmer had no intention of letting anything happen to him, not tonight.

When he reached the break room, he slowed his pace, hearing Elvino's voice. Helmer peered inside, spotting one of the Patterson Brothers with a gun pointed at Elvino. Helmer's pulse quickened. Every instinct screamed at him to act. He wasn't sure what exactly was going down, but he couldn't wait to find out. The thought of Elvino being hurt—especially after all they had been through—was unbearable.

Without thinking twice, Helmer darted inside and pulled on the trigger. The noise of the shot deafened him, his ears ringing as one of the brothers crumpled to the floor. His heart raced, and for a moment, the room seemed to start spinning. Did he just...shoot someone? His hand shook as he lowered the gun, staring at the man on the floor.

Elvino quickly regained control, attacking the remaining brother when Helmer's mind reeled. Some of his guards rushed into the room, taking over the scene. They moved fast, checking on Elvino, and securing the area. Helmer barely registered them, his thoughts still racing. He watched the Patterson brother he shot on the floor, and Elvino checked his pulse, only to affirm what Helmer feared.

"Don't tell me..."

"He is dead," Elvino confirmed, motioning at the guards to take the body away. He rushed to Helmer, seeing him clasping his chest. "Helms, it's okay—"

"Get away from me!" Helmer pushed him. "Or should I call you Don Elvino now?"

"Helms, it's not what you think," he said quietly, taking Helmer's gun from his shaking hand. "Please, just let me explain."

"No!" Helmer recoiled, his mind spinning. "I should've known who you were. I should've seen it. All this time, I've been blind, caught up in whatever game you were playing. And ..." His voice cracked as the panic rose. "I should've listened to Sonie. It's like she knew you were hiding something."

"She... She told you that?" Elvino asked, his voice strained.

"It's clear you've done this before," Helmer spat, his words sharp. "You're not even shocked. How many times have you—"

"You're overthinking it," Elvino interrupted, attempting to step closer.

"What am I going to do now? I have blood on my hands." Helmer cried, tramping back and forth across the room. "I killed someone. I-I don't want to go to jail."

"You're not going to jail," Elvino reassured. "All you need to do right is to listen to me."

"I don't want to listen to you and trust you, for that matter," Helmer said, his hands trembling uncontrollably as he tried to steady himself.

"Well, if you care about Sonie, that girl you're with, you'd better start paying attention. She might become a target now."

"Sonie?" Helmer sniffled, his chest tightening at the mention of her name. "What do you mean?"

"You need to let her go," Elvino commanded. "Take the money from tonight, fund the company, lay low for a while, and start everything over."

"And how the hell am I supposed to do that?" Helmer sniffled, eyeing Elvino for further directions. "I love Sonie—"

"Then you'll let her go," Elvino interrupted, his eyes hardening as he motioned for his bodyguards to drag the other Patterson brother out of the room.

"Where are you taking him?" Helmer asked, his eyes following the man being seized at gunpoint and about to be taken away.

"Helms, I need you to focus…"

"Please, no more killing," Helmer pleaded, his gaze fixed on the brother, whose eyes were wild with grief and rage. "I didn't want this. I didn't want to kill your brother, I swear I didn't."

"Hey, focus," Elvino growled, yanking Helmer's head toward him with a firm grip. "You think you're the good guy here? You won't last another day if you keep acting like one. That man will come after you and your little girlfriend, too. You want that?"

"No," Helmer shook his head. "But no more killing. Please, just this once."

Elvino looked at him, his gaze hard, before taking the gun—the one Helmer had used to kill the Patterson brother—and slipping it into his pocket. "Fine. But understand this. No more mercy after today. Keep the gun. It'll remind you that whether you like it or not, there's evil out there, and sometimes, we do what's necessary to survive."

"And Sonie?" Helmer asked, his voice shaking.

"Like I said, you forget about her," Elvino repeated, his tone firm. "You go find a new girl, get married, have a kid, and whatever helps you keep a clean profile." Elvino gently wiped the tears from Helmer's face. "Sometimes, it helps to be perfect."

"You're insane," Helmer muttered under his breath.

Elvino remained stoic, his eyes cold. "I know. And that's exactly what will keep you alive."

***

It was a long day for Helmer. He had contacted the local executive protection agencies to look for more bodyguards. He wanted Sonia and

Nina to be safe, so he insisted on reinforcing security within the company. He met with the IT Department to increase their cybersecurity systems and upgrade their cameras around the building. Despite his rebellious acts against the psycho man's instructions, Helmer refused to consider calling the cops. Perhaps involving them would not have been such a bad idea, and still, he decided to take care of the matter on his own.

The evening came upon him, holding interviews with a few candidates; none seemed to be the right fit. Some of the men were well-muscled and tall, but Helmer looked beyond their appearance. They didn't give the right answers to his questions. He liked to look for perfection in people, even too much at times. He kept trying to tell himself not to be picky. However, his family's safety and his friends were at risk. Even though he needed protection for his household as soon as he could, he wanted to make sure he hired the right men for the job. He also thought of Meg, having her homeschooled so she could not run into the same dangers everyone had recently.

Feeling his body crack with fatigue, Helmer went out of his office. He watched the janitor clock out and waved him goodbye; then, he saw Sonia coming toward him. He was surprised that she was still in the building, but she was on his mind anyway. And mostly the boy since the last time he's seen him.

"Sonie."

"Helms," she whispered. "Listen, I'm sorry for not having told you about my personal life when it comes to Chris—"

"Who's the boy's father?" Helmer interrupted, his voice tight with urgency.

"What?" Sonia froze, her heart skipping a beat. She hadn't expected him to ask again. She should've prepared, but the question hit her harder than she anticipated. For a moment, her mind went blank.

"Who's the boy's father?" he repeated. "I need to know." "I-I"

"Oh my God, Sonie," Helmer breathed, his voice dropping low. "Please, don't tell me that what I am suspecting—"

"W-What could you... be suspecting?" Sonia broke in, scratching her forehead.

"You're nervous." Helmer's gaze hardened, his tone glacial. "You don't get nervous unless there's something you're guilty of."

Sonia's chest rose, and her eyes refused to meet his. The words she should have said felt locked in her throat. She prided herself on always being eloquent, but here, in this moment, she couldn't respond to a simple question about her own son.

"I'm... I'm not guilty of anything."

"I don't believe you. This boy knows Elvino, Sonie."

Sonia's throat tightened. She swallowed hard, her gaze dropping to the floor, her fingers wringing together.

"He called him grandfather," Helmer continued, his voice tightening. "He looks..." He trailed off, his thoughts tangled. He hesitated, unsure if he was seeing things or if his suspicions were valid. But then the boy's face came to him clearly, looking so much like him. "He knows how to fight. He's protective over Elvino, exactly how I used to be. What exactly are you hiding? What is all this about?"

Sonia's fingers clenched, her hands growing cold as they fisted into the fabric of her slacks.

"Nothing specific," she replied, her voice rough.

"Elvino corrupts people, Sonie. You have no idea what he's capable of," Helmer pointed out. "He has no mercy. Once he gets inside your head, it's too late. Do you understand that?"

"I-I do." Sonia's voice quivered slightly, keeping her head down. "He's not good for the boy. You need to get him far away from him."

"I disagree," Sonia corrected, her voice firm despite the nervous tremble in her hands. "Elvino is the one who has kept this boy sane. Like I told you before, if you want answers, you need to go to him." "No..." Helmer shook his head. "It is not like you to say such nice things about Elvino. What did he do to you to keep you close? What threats did he make? What did he say to you?"

Sonia's chest tightened. She stepped back slightly, hands trembling but never releasing her grip on her slacks. "Helmer..."

"Please, tell me," Helmer urged, his voice rising slowly. "Why the hell are you close with him? What has he promised you?"

Sonia paused, gathering herself, her eyes shifting away as she exhaled sharply. "Honestly, if you truly care to know like I said before, ask him directly." She looked back at Helmer, her eyes hardening. "One thing I've learned, and you should too, is that secrets destroy trust and ruin us. We need to do better, Helmer."

He stood still, her words lingering in the air. "How?"

"You want me to start telling the truth?" Sonia said. "Then let's begin with Bryant by telling him everything about the past we've been hiding."

"But you want to tell him now? You two are not together anymore."

"Helms," Sonia continued, taking a step toward him, her hand brushing gently against his face. "I spent weeks blaming Bryant for his mistakes. How am I any better if I hide behind mine? I need to take responsibility. This is the right thing to do."

"No," he whispered, his voice barely audible. He pressed her hand more firmly against his face. "Sonie, he'll hate me."

"Not if you tell him before I do," Sonia whispered, giving him a nod. "I trust you."

"O-Okay," he said hesitantly. "C'mon...I'll walk you out."

Helmer took Sonia to her car and watched her leave. Then he dove back into his thoughts. He was tormented by their last conversation and finding out about Christopher. Helmer was curious; he needed answers, and maybe seeing the boy again would confirm everything he needed to know. Being under the influence of such pressure, Helmer took the elevator and headed to the floor where his bodyguard parked. He called Jonathan to come pick him up in front, for he had to go somewhere he never thought he'd visit again. Helmer had to look ordinary so as not to draw attention.

"Boss, you ready?" said Jonathan, seeing his boss looking at him in deep thought.

Helmer nodded, getting into the passenger's seat. He looked at Jonathan again, wondering if what he was about to ask was even appropriate.

"You okay, Boss?" Jonathan asked, pressing on the gas to exit the building.

"I need your clothes," Helmer said.

Jonathan stared at him, frowning and concerned. "My clothes?" He was wearing black shades, a navy T-shirt, and khaki pants, which looked completely different from what Helmer usually wore.

"We're swapping clothes," Helmer explained, reading the worried look on Jonathan's face. He needed a cover so people wouldn't recognize him. He could not trust anyone else besides Jonathan, and he would need someone with some fighting skills in case things escalate where he thought of heading.

"Boss, I'm sorry, but what exactly do you have in mind?" Jonathan asked.

"I'm going somewhere deep in the south, and no worries, it shall not take too long," Helmer said, his head shifting to the back of the car and noticing a blue cap between the seats. "I'm borrowing that too." He reached and took it, then motioned at Jonathan to make up his mind about the clothes. Jonathan grunted out of annoyance, knowing he didn't have a choice, and stopped the car.

Once they swapped, Jonathan got back inside the car and asked where they were going. Helmer gave him the address, and they drove there, sitting in complete silence. Helmer was too absorbed in his thoughts to notice that Jonathan started to worry once he realized the neighborhood they were headed to.

"Boss?" Jonathan whispered, his eyes fixed on the road, increasing his headlights. "I don't know if you're aware, but these areas are known to be dangerous."

"I know," Helmer replied, his gaze directed at the car mirror, anxious that they'd be followed. It would be the last thing he'd wanted, for they would discover that other side of him, the part of his past he'd tried to conceal from for more than a decade.

"If I'm not mistaken, there's a Mafia Don who lives around here," Jonathan added. "No one knows his name, but he owns the streets. He's very powerful. I don't think being here is a good idea at all."

"I know."

"Boss, I don't think you understand—"

"I do understand, Jonathan," Helmer cut in. "Just do your job."

Jonathan fell quiet and asked no more questions even though he knew he was making a point. He was trying to protect his boss, and at that moment, he wondered if there was more to his reaction. Why was he so composed about it? Helmer didn't look shocked. Somewhat, he was aware of what that neighborhood was about, and that made Jonathan uneasy.

The car pulled into an isolated parking lot crammed with motorcycles and old cars, just as Helmer directed. In a matter of seconds, they were surrounded by a crowd of men with beards and tattooed arms. Some were young, with colorful bandanas around their necks, their half faces covered in black ink. Others were carrying heavy, loaded rifles, making Jonathan squeak where he sat.

"Boss, what the hell is this place?" Jonathan asked in a low tone, his head slowly shifting toward Helmer.

"Turn off the engine and do everything I do," Helmer told him, getting out of the car. Jonathan turned off the car and got out, sticking his arms up along Helmer.

"I am here to see Elvino! I'm not armed," Helmer shouted.

The men approached him but then noticed his face. His voice had already sounded familiar.

"Oh wait, it's Helms," said one of the armed men. "Elvino's son." "Holy hell! Helms, is that you?" another one added, pushing his firearm to the side to pull him into a hug. The others seized Helmer into an embrace as well and slammed hands with him. "We missed you, punk."

"Me too," he said hesitantly, knowing that Jonathan was observing. "And who is he?" one of the men asked, his gaze shifting to Jonathan.

He got closer and patted him down, making sure he wasn't a threat. "He's a friend," Helmer said, telling them to back off and let Jonathan off the hook. The guys looked at Jonathan up and down, smacking their gums in his face.

"Where is Elvino?" Helmer asked.

"Inside, he was waiting for you. I'm sure you'll remember your way in."

Helmer went inside the house, and there stood Elvino from a distance, feeding his cats. His hands were bloody, which gave away that he was taking care of some unfinished business in his basement. Elvino, smooching his cats, finally noticed Helmer walking toward him.

"Helms? Oh, I knew you were coming, but not so soon," Elvino said, kissing his cats once more before letting them go. He walked toward Helmer, who attempted to hit him again, but Elvino dodged and struck him in one hit. He locked Helmer's head between his knees and kept him still. "I allowed you to make a mess out of me the other day so you can let off some steam, but don't get it twisted. You can't beat the master."

"Let go of me," grunted Helmer, struggling to get himself free from Elvino's headlock.

Elvino let go and stood, taking a handkerchief from his satin blue pajama set and wiping his hands. They were still bruised and bloody. "You want a drink?"

"No, what I want is the truth," Helmer said. "What happened with Sonie? Who's that boy who defended you the other day? Why did he call you grandfather?"

"Okay, first of all, you're suffocating me," groaned Elvino, walking away to the staircase leading to his basement. "It's too many questions at a time."

A scream echoed from the basement. It was a man's voice in pure agony. "Who is this downstairs? What are you doing?" Helmer asked, following Elvino along. The basement was full of blue lights, and it was damp compared to the rest of the building. Elvino negotiated his business affairs and had his main fight rings in that house. It was huge and filled with torturous activities.

"Oh my God!" Helmer said, covering his mouth, fighting the urge to puke. There was a guy whose hands and feet were nailed into the wall, the flesh nearly poking out. He was grunting in pain, barely able to breathe through the agony. He was disfigured, his body covered in scars, and his hair hung in a machine above his head, pulling his hair out when he refused to cooperate. "I knew you were a sociopath, but not to that level."

"Well, that depends on what he did," Elvino said, grabbing a bin of heavy metals and sharp tools. He dropped some of them on the large ceramic table across from the guy and pointed at the drill machine. "Do you see this? You won't like it. It'll hurt like hell. So, tell me who commanded you to drive my grandson to that building."

"Grandson?" Helmer whispered. "Are you talking about Christopher?"

"Yes," Elvino said, turning his head to face Helmer. He crossed his arms and leaned his back against the table. "This driver took the boy to your company. I only knew because I had a tracker in the car, and I'm very attentive when it comes to him."

"So, you didn't take him there," Helmer summed up.

"My dear loyal driver is working for someone who commanded him to take the boy to you, for God knows what. And he won't tell me who hired him to play such tricks on me." Elvino sighed, knowing his only way to get answers was through torture. But the guy on the wall was dying, and even through his agony, he refused to give any intel.

"Why are you so attentive to the boy? What makes him special?" Helmer asked, almost in a begging tone. The last time he'd seen Elvino so protective over someone was when he adopted him. When he became a son to him and had to save him from his abusive household. That boy had to mean something deeper.

"Helms, I meant to tell you a long time ago, but I couldn't," Elvino said, scratching his arms, unable to stay still as he spoke. "After what happened with the Patterson Brothers, I made it a mission to keep Sonia protected because I knew out of everything in this world, she was everything you ever cared for."

"What did you do after you tore us apart?" Helmer asked, a feverish sensation growing through his body. "You always have schemes no one sees coming." The answers he'd been anticipating were coming, but he was unsure about being ready for them. Helmer let out a shaky breath and pushed his hands into his pockets.

"Not long after you two broke up, she came to me, saying she was expecting," Elvino confessed, scrunching his nose so he wouldn't allow himself to cry, knowing how much it'd hurt Helmer finding out.

"She..." Helmer paused, a sob forming under his breath. "She was pregnant?"

Elvino nodded, shamefully lowering his head. "To summarize, she did have the baby."

"I don't need your goddamn summary right now," Helmer said, his voice tearing into a louder cry. "Whose idea was it to keep this from me? You or her?"

"Helms..."

"Tell me!" Helmer cried out, the tears flowing before he could even catch himself breaking apart.

"I did," Elvino replied, knowing Helmer deserved the truth.

Helmer's legs numbed out, and he only figured it out as he could not stand straight. He secured both arms on his knees, bending for some balance. His heart had never known such intensity of pain before, so much that it simply went silent. He couldn't explain how one could have the universe crushing their chest, leaving them barely breathing, and still looking alive. He wasn't alive. "So, you took it all from me. Everything!"

"No, I gave you a better life," Elvino replied.

"You took more than you gave," Helmer snapped. "You manipulated and forced me to leave Sonie; then you took a life we could have together, besides causing me to be a criminal like you."

"You are not a criminal, Helms."

"I am!" Helmer raged. "I killed someone. For you! I knew that those fight clubs were illegal, yet I asked no questions. I looked up to you and eventually wanted to be like you. Do you know why? Because I had a void inside. I needed a father, and you came disguised as one, only to ruin my life and do me much worse."

Elvino couldn't hold it in, the tears came. He hated crying, but those words pierced him. "You might be right. But all I ever wanted was for you to be better than I was. I failed, that's it. Because no matter what someone may do, they can't give what they don't know. I wasn't raised with a father, so that's why I had to make something out of myself. Do you know why? Self-pity doesn't take you anywhere; it only keeps you in a loop, where you're just as miserable and acting like a damn victim."

"What did I do to deserve this?" Helmer mumbled, weeping heavily.

"I raised your son, and I told him a lot about you," Elvino said.

"What you don't understand, since the day we've shot the Patterson Brother, it's been war. They dug into everything about you, so having you away and Christopher in Paris had helped to keep you both safe."

"So, Christopher is my son?"

"I think you know the answer," Elvino confirmed. "It only takes a few minutes with him, and it'll give it away. And you should be proud he can hold his own."

"You could've told me about the pregnancy," fumed Helmer. "You could've let me be part of my son's life. Obviously, you forced Sonie to hide it from me."

"I didn't force her," Elvino objected, "I did what was necessary."

"Necessary?" Helmer scoffed. "Like manipulating her? How did you even convince her?"

"She found out the Patterson brother who survived sent someone to track her down. A scoundrel from the club who bet big. He's been dealt with."

"I guess you killed him?"

"You had a better option?" Elvino shot back, snorting. "He knew you from the club, from our circle. Once I made it clear you were away, the tension eased. And I gave Sonia the option: Go to Paris and have the baby, or tell you the truth and decide together."

"You gave her that choice?"

"But you were busy with that new girl," Elvino said, dismissing him. "Magda?"

"Yes," Elvino nodded. "Once Sonia found out you were seeing her and taking care of her father, she decided to protect your son and move on."

"She moved on," Helmer snorted. "You say that as if you didn't have a hand in it. Your words are so enticing, even where they're false." Helmer stared at Elvino, his gaze tinged with pity. How could Elvino stand there, so composed, as if he had no pulse? Could he be blind to the destruction he'd caused in a young man's love life? How could he not see the damage he'd done? "Did you at least tell her why we couldn't be together?"

"Sonia knew. I was honest with her," Elvino responded, smoothing out the small wrinkles in his pajamas. "She felt it was best you start fresh, away from this life. To her, you having ties with me was already collateral damage."

Helmer sighed. "You sat there and watched me go through with a marriage I didn't want, just for the sake of being off the hook."

"Would you have preferred a life on the run? Unstable? Always risking it all?" Elvino's voice hardened. "Let me tell you something. Love isn't meant for people like us. One wrong move and you're a target. Love blinds us, and family... family makes us prey." He reached for his cigar and lighted it. "Keeping you away, no matter how hard it was, was the best decision I ever made. And you should do the same for your son. Do you think I never fell for someone? I did. But for her sake, I stepped back. Sonia will thank me one day, and your son will too."

"For so long, I've been wishing for a kid, and this entire time, he's existed. I miss 17 years of his life, and for that, I'll never forgive you." Helmer said, then heard his phone notifications. There was an exclamation point, and he hoped it wasn't a virus or scam. But he thought it safe to check in case it was psycho man, and it was.

"There's no way," Helmer whispered, the little strength from his knees giving up. He dropped to the floor, watching the video of his wife and the psycho man dancing together, being so close to kissing. "It's him."

"What is it, Helms?" Elvino questioned, seeing Helmer in harsh distress.

"That's her ex."

"What are you watching?" Elvino approached and saw the video. It wouldn't be an allegation saying that Magda was cheating. They did look close and maybe got intimate after. "So, that's your wife and—"

"Richard. I-I think that was his name." Helmer gripped the phone tighter, so much that he could crush it. And before he thought of hurling it to the wall, a live message popped up. It was Richard, or psycho man, the ghost Helmer never thought would resurface. "That's impossible... How?"

"*Oh, if you're watching this, I have something that belongs to you,*" said the video, then Richard continued. "*No worries, I didn't kiss her. I mean, I didn't want to. But...*"

Richard shifted the camera toward his bed and Magda was there asleep under the covers. He touched her face and grinned.

"*I might touch her, though. She's sleeping right now; I don't want to wake her up.*"

"Son of a bitch!" Helmer breathed heavily, his heart sinking and reminding him it was troubled.

"*Did you know she has a tiny mole right below her cheeks? I'm kidding; it's between her legs, right where she'll invite me tonight. I hope it's not too much information. Goodbye, Mr. Dupris*".

The video ended, and Helmer threw the phone away. "I have to kill this guy."

"Who is he?" Elvino asked.

"Nobody, okay? Give me a minute to think," Helmer replied, his voice seething. "I should've shot him dead in the street when I had the chance. How could I have missed? Now I'm starting to think maybe it was him who got Christopher there to warn and spite me."

"Are you sure?"

"Get me the tools," Helmer told Elvino, getting up and shifting his angry gaze toward the man on the wall. "This man will have to tell me who hired him to mess around with my son."

"You'll torture him?" Elvino realized.

"Not if he tells me what you've been trying to get out of him this entire time," Helmer replied, with a nod. "Time to find out who's after my son."

When Monsters Meet

Magda's eyes fluttered open, adjusting to the lighting from the ceiling. Her head was crushing from the effect of the drug; it took her a while to realize that her body was limp. She was unable to move or feel any of her limbs, for that matter. As her vision cleared, she noticed a shadow from the wall. Then she realized it was a room, and she wasn't dreaming. Richard was there, and she had not managed to escape. She watched the shadow move, assuming that he was behind her. Magda whimpered, calling for help, yet feeling nothing responding in her body. She watched Richard poke above her and sit her up. He had to place pillows around her to keep her in place, which gave away that the drug had not worn off.

"Hi, Maggie," Richard said, placing a tray on the bed. He reached forward and kissed her forehead despite Magda's efforts to protest. "Trust me, I won't hurt you."

"You tried to kill me," Magda said. "Did you forget? You said you wouldn't hurt me, yet you did..." She paused, still feeling her throat sore and visualizing him squeezing her neck. It was painful to swallow, and from the feeling, her neck was swollen.

"I know," Richard admitted, taking a piece of guava cake from the tray and crushing it. "Sometimes, I tell people what they want to hear. You can't blame me, can you? After all, you taught me that. To lie, to be deceitful, and to torture others. A little pain doesn't hurt anybody, does it?"

"Why can't I move?" Magda asked, feeling her skull creaking from pain.

"Because I can't trust you," he said calmly, taking a tiny spoon of the crushed cake to feed it to her. "You might run away. Or worse, set me on fire."

"Richard, I didn't try to kill you. I swear—"

He shoved the spoon into her mouth mid-sentence and watched her gag. Magda spat the food in his face, and aware that she'd upset him, she started crying. She was already in pain, not able to make any use of her body, and defying him would only call for more torture.

Richard laughed and grabbed a tablecloth to wipe his face. He saw her helpless, and he thought, why not play a little? He removed the covers from her and grabbed a fork. He let out a giggle, seeing Magda's eyes extending in fear, not knowing what he was about to do. "You know, you have no idea what I would like to do, seeing that we're alone. I mean..." He grazed the fork across her collarbone, then moved it to the strings keeping her clothes in place. Magda let out a cry, watching but unable to do anything. Richard freed the robe off her shoulders; then, there was her bra left exposed. He lowered the fork to her cups and looked into her eyes.

"Should I lower it?" he asked, his excitement showing. "No, please, don't," Magda begged.

"Why? I have touched them before, even while you were with your husband," Richard commented.

"He wasn't my husband," Magda objected, her voice hoarse and sounding painful due to her throat hurting from speaking.

"Yet, you were with both of us," Richard said, moving the fork further down. "All I wanted was that you would've chosen me, and you still didn't."

"I couldn't, Richard. You know that. Helmer was paying off my dad's treatments—"

"No," he corrected, dropping the fork, seeing her believing her lies. "You never truly wanted to abandon the guy and what he had to offer." "You're wrong, because I was willing to run away with you, and then you bailed on me."

"I didn't bail. I told you," he riposted. "Your mom sabotaged everything and made it seem that way. The night was sabotaged."

"What do you mean?"

Richard took a piece of napkin and wiped Magda's face; then he reminisced on what happened the day of the fire that nearly took his life. Never had anybody tried to give his case proper investigation, and so he wanted to finally find a voice and tell his side. He knew how the things exactly happened, but he could never do that as a ghost. Sooner or later, he'd have to come to light. "I want justice, Maggie. Justice, that's why

I'm back. And this will start with you and everyone who was involved in my murder."

"Who do you think was involved?" she asked, shakily. "Where should I start? It wasn't only one person."

F L A S H B A C K

It was the night that Richard was supposed to run away with Magda that he received a visit. Allimair rushed into the tiny apartment with fury. She opened her purse, took out a huge sum of cash, and threw it on the small coffee table across the broken TV. "Here, take this and disappear from my daughter's life."

"Ma'am—"

'Take it and leave our family alone," Allimair said, her tone threatening. "My daughter is marrying this man, and he's the love of her life. Take the sum or I'll make sure you and your brother's lives become a living hell. And... I have done it before. I heard about your eviction."

"You knew? So, you caused it?" Richard asked.

"I mean, you were late on payments, so technically, I didn't. However, I may have played a part," Allimair admitted. "I swear to God, if you insist on brainwashing my daughter to run away with you, I'll destroy you, whether by hand or by death. Let me tell you, it's never good to play with fire. It might burn."

"Well, in that case, I hope you have the gut to tell your daughter that you are the one who had sabotaged tonight and be okay with her heartbreak. And I am not taking your money."

"Only an idiot would decline such a sum," Allimair said with disdain, taking back her money and heading to the door. She left, and then Richard was alone, needing to make a decision. He believed Allimair's threats; she was everything, except a liar. She wouldn't bluff, and it had been months since she had tried to keep the pair apart.

Everything was ready for their departure, and Richard had decided to back off, fearing that his brother could have something happen to him. He sent Ricks to give Magda more insight into his decision, not having the courage to tell her himself. The letter was a rip-off, and he knew that she was going to be devastated—so devastated that she found him where he lived days later.

Magda got inside, claiming she only wanted to talk. She needed closure, maybe not the best kind, for it didn't end as Richard saw it happening. She talked about the letter to him, though Richard avoided telling her that it was because of Allimair. He didn't want Magda to hate her mother, and less, because of him. But amid their heated argument, Magda had pulled out a bottle and splashed a liquid on Richard's face, making him scream in agony. He stepped back and then tried to hang on to something for support, unable to process what was happening to him. He felt the liquid drop on his hands, and he screamed louder. "Maggie! Maggie. What is this? What is this liquid? It's burning. My face is burning."

"I trusted you. You bailed on me," Magda said angrily, her voice sounding as if she wanted to cry. "And now, because of you, I have to live a life I didn't want. Now I have no way out just because of your selfishness."

Richard dropped to the floor and heard the bottle break. He felt an impact on his back, toppling him. "My mom has convinced Helmer to push the wedding, and now I have to marry him. You denied me the life we could have together. You… you hurt me more than anyone ever has. Why?"

***

Magda recalled the horrible thing she had done, remembering that everyone, including herself, had a darkness in them. She had seen Richard's face even haunting her dreams before, but this time, he was real, sitting in this room with her.

"You burned my face with that acid. You took so much from me that night, and you tortured me," Richard said, his voice revealing the pain and betrayal he had continuously felt for years. "I didn't even understand what was happening to me. I kept calling your name, and surprisingly you meant to do what you did."

"Richard, I am so sorry…"

He assembled a handful of cakes and pushed it into her mouth, then clasped his hands over her face. "You hit me behind the head before you rushed out. Now, it's so satisfying to see you go through a little bit of pain, which is not even close to the level you've made me endure."

Magda tried to spit out the food. She had no other choice but to swallow. The food felt like sharp knives sliding down her windpipe, confirming that her throat was still inflamed.

"Don't worry though. I am not going to torture you past your limits," said Richard. "I'm just trying to feed you."

"You're crazy," Magda whispered, letting out a cough.

"Having acid thrown at you and being nearly killed by someone you trust, being forced to live in the shadows fearing for your life, will do that to you," Richard explained. "After minutes of trying to move from the floor, I smelled something. A burnt smell. Then I started shouting. I couldn't see anything... I was confused."

"Richard, I am sorry," Magda cried, looking at him, her eyes begging him to believe her. However, her words, no matter how much she dressed them, sounded vain. "I admit it. I was mad at you; I was going crazy. The wedding was approaching, and I almost had no choice. Then—"

"Then what?" Richard cut in, impatient to hear her next sentence. "And it better not be a lie because then you'll know what torture is."

"I lit a fire... I put it out right before it seethed off. Then I ran," Magda said, her face sinking. "After about 10 minutes if not more, I was at a good distance. Some people started to bump into me; I looked back, and saw smoke going up the sky. I didn't think twice; I ran back to you, only to see the flames raging."

"You set the fire," Richard said. "I was there shouting your name to help me, and then I saw a glimpse of you across the apartment in that window, standing between the bushes. You ran!" he added, his face tense from remembering the scene. His body grew rigid, visualizing the burn scars and excruciating pain he had to endure from that night, which lasted for years. "You didn't want to get caught. That's why, when it comes to monsters, it makes two of us."

Richard took some water from the tray and forced it down Magda's throat, then wiped her mouth. "And no worries, I won't touch you unless your body is willing for it," he teased. "You scream, I numb that mouth of yours. So, pick your battles wisely."

The last thing Magda remembered was putting out the fire. She had left running, so she wasn't seen, realizing what she had done. Coming to her senses, Magda realized that she had assaulted, tortured, and attempted to murder the man she loved. Maybe that made her worse than a monster, for love didn't stop her from choosing such a dark side. She couldn't judge anymore, for she was now in the same pit. Magda wished that her coming out alive from that house was still possible, for she still didn't know in what way Richard was looking forward to justice. Was it through torture? Having her confess and go to jail, something she had feared for years? Or what if he'd accidentally killed her baby? Should she even tell him?

"What exactly do you wish to accomplish keeping me hostage here?" Magda asked, gathering a bit of courage.

"I am still deciding," Richard replied, admiring her fearful eyes. They were grand and beautiful, but he didn't say it. "Now that you're fed, I might take you for some carving art session."

"Carving art? Meaning?" Magda asked, her heart leaping. Was the torture not enough? Being exposed in front of her ex, his eyes on her like she was fresh steak on a plate. Thank God her belly wasn't obvious— she was still early in her pregnancy—but the thought of something happening to her, or worse, to her child, sent a wave of shaking panic through her body.

"You will see. There won't be any pain, I promise," he reassured, taking the tray off the bed. "You messed up badly, Maggie. You took a piece of me that died in the fire, my identity, my name, my future, everything."

"So did Ricks," Magda spat. "Or won't you point a finger at him too? You didn't care to check on me, not even after he went to jail for what he'd done."

"I did not condone my brother's actions," Richard replied, his eyes briefly showing warmth. "I never thought he would do such a thing to you. I blamed myself... many times, actually. I should never have involved him in our business, never asked him to take you home. I-I only wanted to make sure you were safe."

"Obviously I wasn't. And you..." a sob broke through her voice. "You couldn't even tell me to my face. You broke up with me in a letter, Richard."

"With reasons," he objected, "and you did not try to understand me either. Instead, you attempted to take my life."

Magda closed her eyes, the weight of his words sinking into her soul. Was she truly a monster? A shudder ran through her as the question echoed in her mind. "I know."

"You don't know," Richard grunted. "Those burns have stayed with me. They reminded me of you each time, and not in a good way."

"What can I possibly do to make you spare me from whatever you're planning?" Magda asked, a quiver tinged in her voice.

"There's nothing you can do," Richard replied. "I show mercy when I choose to. No one tells me what to do."

Magda swallowed, her throat tight. "Then tell me. What happened that night? How did you survive?"

"Ricks had already been charged with assault, so he wasn't at the apartment," said Richard, thinking about his brother. "I hated him for what he did to you." He breathed deeply, the memories of the fire creeping in. "But our friend—the one who owned the apartment—was there sleeping in his room with a girl. They were both wasted, too much to hear my screams when you came…" He added, then paced around the room, reenacting the tragedy. "It was interesting that after you left, two men came in and left me half dead as if they were told to come and finish me off."

"What? T-That wasn't me," Magda stammered, shaking her head. "I swear."

"It could've been any of you," Richard said. "You, Allimair…"

"My mom wouldn't!" Magda broke in, her tone sharp.

"I'm not so sure. She threatened my life."

"She's all talk. But she would never do that to you," Magda said, her gaze following Richard, moving around the room.

"There were others at the crime scene," Richard continued, stroking his hand on his burn scars. "And yet, no one bothered to look into my case."

"Everything you're insinuating about my mom can't be. She wouldn't have the power to influence your case—"

"That's right!" Richard clapped, then pointed a finger toward her, excited about her reply. "Now, you're getting it."

"What are you getting at?" Magda said with narrowed eyes.

"Who else would find it beneficial to have me killed beside you or Allimair? Think!"

"I-I don't know, Rich," Magda said. "I don't even know the entire story to connect the dots."

"Connect them then!" he shouted, losing patience. He had held his composure enough and seeing her so clueless hurt him even more. She couldn't see his point nor the direction he was going. The truth was simple. It was a name, one killer in question, someone who would have deliberately burned him that night.

Magda startled, shaking, and hiding her face through the pillows from the bed's headrest. She wanted to hide so badly and at least hug herself, but she couldn't.

"But..." Richard resumed. "The girl from the apartment wasn't so wasted after all because at the time that the fire started, she came out of the room coughing, and then she ran to me. She was very petite, and all I remember is that I couldn't stand on my own. The two men nearly broke my back and my knees." Richard exhaled, unloading the pressure from his chest. "I told her she had to find us an exit window of some kind so I could not even be found to be rescued. She asked me why, and I told her that some people were trying to kill me. Eventually, she dragged me to one of the guest rooms, which had a ladder going up to a window. By the time we managed to figure out how to open it, the smoke was everywhere, choking us. We could barely breathe."

Richard sat back on the bed, the memories still fresh in his mind. He wanted some human touch as he told the story, which made him realize he was alone. He was a cold being, which happened against his will. Tragedies change people and he was the testimony of that. "She struggled to help me up, and then we both realized we had to go back for my friend. But it was too late. Some of the things were already falling and melting apart; we could barely see through the fire. I wasn't much help. I caught her hand and begged her not to go back for him."

A tear ran down Magda's cheek, noticing how much she wanted to hold him. Was she the monster who had caused such a tragedy? She was still wondering whether it was the truth that she had successfully put out that fire. Or would her mom, with her ambitious yearnings, allow herself to go that far? Who else would've attempted to kill Richard? Although the answer seemed so near and clear, Magda couldn't find it.

"So, the girl helped you out of the apartment?" Magda asked.

Richard nodded. "We jumped out of the window then she helped me to hide in the woods. Before the police and firemen appeared, we were already from a good distance. I lost my friend and my hope in humanity."

"I'm so sorry about your friend…" Magda empathized.

"He was wasted, and he died because some devilish people were after me. That's it! It was my fault and the least I can do is to make sure he also finds justice."

Magda's heart dropped, seeing the depth of the destruction she'd caused. The man she once loved—broken beyond repair. She had shattered him. She was the reason for his downfall. And now, he couldn't expect anything less than cruelty from her. "Are you planning to kill me?"

"I could never," Richard replied. "Even though I think of doing so many times. However, you will know the pain. You have no idea!"

"What do you mean?"

Richard stood and picked her up from the bed. He walked out of the room and took her to a garage. It was filled with warm lights and paintings. All sorts. Then Richard sat her on a chair and strapped her so she would not fall.

Something came to Magda's attention. There were also pictures of her house on the walls and Polaroids of her in the shower. Seeing them left her baffled and more horrified. He had been watching her inside her home for years. And it wasn't even the end of it. The garage had plenty of videos—cameras placed in each corner of the Dupris's house—and short footage of Meg doing homework.

"How did you—"

Magda fell silent when the garage door swiftly opened, and she saw the woman coming in. If she had poor heart problems, Magda would have a stroke.

"Hi, Richy, I'm home." The woman walked in briskly, wrapping her arms around Richard in a tight embrace.

Magda's stomach twisted as the woman turned her attention to her. "Hi, Magda. Or should I say Mrs. Dupris?"

Richard, clearly savoring the shock on Magda's face, gestured dramatically. "Maggie, I present to you the girl who saved me from the fire, Marie Lisa."

"Marie?" Magda whispered, her voice barely audible. This was the woman who had been working inside her home, the nest that held her family together. Yes, there had been some issues, but never in her wildest thoughts did Magda imagine seeing her here, in this place, in the middle of the woods, at the height of her misfortune. Her breath was trapped in her chest, refusing to release.

CHAPTER 31

The Mastermind

Magda wanted to vanish in the air, for the sight of Marie Lisa filled her with contempt. She had been fooled all those years with Marie living in her home and not catching her sooner. How could she have missed it? So many times, Magda had bumped heads with Marie, annoyed with her gossip and prying indiscreetly into people's affairs in the house, yet she never thought once that Marie would be connected to Richard. Or maybe she did not pay attention enough to see what was happening right under her nose in her own home. "Marie."

"I know you have questions," Marie said, seeing the disappointment on Magda's face. "What can I say? It's nice that I don't have to hide anymore."

"I should've known," Magda said. "Something has always been fishy about you."

"I agree." Marie nodded, moving toward the center of the garage room, gathering a bag that Richard had hung from one of his empty easels. "Sometimes I made it so obvious, and you still have not noticed anything. I don't know how either you or Helmer could have missed it."

"Let me guess," Magda said, throwing a glare at Marie and then at Richard. "You two are—"

"No!" Marie corrected. "We're not together. Of course, if that worries you. Besides, it doesn't happen every day to have a married woman care so much about their ex."

"Why?" Magda asked, her eyes bringing Marie's attention toward Meg's pictures in the garage room. "Why my daughter? What would be the motive to make her also a target?"

Marie snorted, shaking her head at Magda's question. "Isn't she Richard's niece? Don't tell me that you forgot you've also slept with his brother."

"You told Marie about Ricks?" Magda asked, her eyes piercing Richard's.

"Why wouldn't he?" Marie interjected, seeing Richard hesitating to answer. "Richard doesn't owe you anything. You almost got him killed, and we did lose someone very special that day. My boyfriend at the time was so drunk that he couldn't have saved himself even if he thought about it... I also couldn't save him."

Marie took a moment, heaving a mourning sigh before proceeding. She took the bag from the easel, grabbed one of the half-filled paint buckets, and sat facing Magda. As she emptied the bag, a hot tool—similar to a drill—and carving knives dropped to the floor, making Magda's body clench with terror.

"You do know I didn't do it, right?" Magda said, her yearning to hug her stomach growing intense. "I didn't."

Magda's voice did not show any certainty. She was the kind to believe her lies, but this time, she swore to tell everything she knew. Magda had destroyed Richard's face, to the point of no return, and started a fire that was meant to take his life.

She had gathered some dry leaves and lit up a match, letting the tuff burn. But she stomped it out and ran before getting caught. After all, she would've been charged, and that was a heavy concern. A hurt woman could truly destroy a planet, but Magda was willing to destroy her entire world just because she couldn't have it to herself—Richard.

"Then who set the fire?" Marie asked, composed yet her eyes glowing with devilment. "Honestly, who would? Richy had no enemies but your mom. So, if it's not her, then who?"

"How am I supposed to know?"

"Oh my God!" Marie glanced up at Richard with unbelieving eyes. "Is she truly that blind? She is still so clueless."

"She is." Richard nodded. "Maybe we can bring the truth to her so she can hear it herself."

"How?" Marie asked.

"Her husband will come for her," Richard said. "I know it. Magda was not alone when she came."

"Oh no, the guards," Magda mumbled, realizing that Richard had thought everything through. Coming here to meet him was his plan all along, and she was that mouse in bait, luring others along with her. If only she had told Helmer, she could have avoided that situation. A thought hit her, shaking her to the core.

"He knows I'm here," Magda said out loud, trying to get confirmation that her suspicion was true, although she desperately wished that it wasn't. "Helmer does, doesn't he?"

"Of course he does," Richard replied, the malicious beam extending on his cheeks. "I mean, did you think we would meet alone? I made sure he watched us. We danced, held each other, and nearly kissed. Have we not?"

It was like a knife stabbing her repeatedly, recalling her being in proximity with Richard. She hated herself. So much that whatever was waiting for her in that garage room would be more relief than torture. Magda longed to be tortured, punished, and made to vanish. She recalled Helmer's last warning about the baby although she was very upset at him. She did put that baby in danger, and she saw no way out. It could only result in a disaster of her walking out of that room damaged or dead. "You tricked me."

'I didn't," Richard riposted, bending his knees to speak to Magda at eye level. "I didn't threaten you or put a gun to your head to come here. So, what's the blame for exactly?"

"You wanted to break my marriage apart from the very beginning. Why? Why not just punish me?"

"You'll know, soon," Richard replied, briefly stroking Magda's cheek.

"And he still loves you," Marie added, bothered by Richard's demeanor changing around Magda in the room. His voice was softer, and knowing him, he held back from his malpractice to make her pay for what he was accusing her of.

"I don't." Richard straightened himself up, glaring at Marie.

"Then stop acting soft and do what you got to do." Marie pointed at a portable table across the garage room. "Let's finish the job."

"What job are you guys referring to?" Magda asked Marie, then turned her gaze toward Richard. "Richard! What is Marie talking about?" Richard gave Marie a nod, and then he pulled the table and set it up near the center of the garage. Marie grabbed some gloves that were among the tools and put on a pair, shifting her gaze to Magda. "It's sad that neither you nor your husband know much about each other.

Anyways, it shall take a little time for him to find out some things about you and Richy's story."

"So, that's what you were up to?" Magda said, a quiver rolling out of her lips. "To sabotage my marriage?"

"Your marriage was hanging on a thread, and we barely touched it," Marie said, gesturing at Richard to help her lift Magda to put her on the table. "So, learn to self-reflect sometime. It helps to not be delusional." "Let go of me. Let go of me..." screamed Magda, watching the pair turn her on her stomach. Her back was facing the ceiling, and then she heard Richard bring Marie the tools. "Please, I am begging. Let me go." "Too late, you shouldn't have come." Marie unhooked Magda's bra, brushed her hands on her back, and proceeded to drop a sanitizing liquid on it. "No worries, I'm very good at washing things clean.

Richard was also a good teacher."

"You. Are. Insane." Magda said, her face hurting from moving too much as if she could free herself from what was happening.

Richard turned his face away, then moved to a corner, avoiding to watch, haunted by Magda's helpless whimpers. The one thing he didn't expect to happen occurred: his heart was melting for her, and he felt tempted to tell Marie to stop what she was doing despite it being his original idea. "I'm going outside to watch the cameras in case—"

"No," fussed Marie. "I want you to watch. This lady caused your friend, or should I say my boyfriend, to die. The least you can do is to watch her bleed. And she's not in pain."

"For now," Richard said, "you know she'll be hurting after the drug wears off."

"Not our problem. It's even better that she'll also live with that scar for the rest of her life, just like us." Marie grabbed the carving knives and drew an "R," taking the entire surface of Magda's back. She powered the hot tool, allowing it to be as hot as lava before going to the next step. But she paused, her eyes in awe, watching Magda's back flooding with blood, so much that she could barely see the lines of the carved letter. "This is so satisfying."

"You cut her deeper than the other ones we've marked before," Richard opined, hoping that Marie would back out, seeing the thick and large letter on Magda's back.

"Like I said, even better." Marie took the hot tool and drilled it inside the letter lines, burning it to seal it off and stop the bleeding. Richard covered his mouth and paced further away.

"I-I can't believe you are letting someone I've fed and sheltered for years do such things to me, Rich," Magda cried, hearing the loud sounds of the hot tools going inside her flesh but still not feeling anything due to the drug.

"Oh, by the way, Richy doesn't do those steps," Marie divulged with a grin. "I do. Remember Jonathan's wife? Do you really think Richy had the guts for this? He's still a kind-hearted man, unfortunately."

"What?" Magdawhispered, struggling to process Marie's confessions. "How did you think Richy could've gotten access to Jonathan's family? And not only that, I've also done the same to Nina, your husband's secretary. She was a pain in the butt; I barely touched her."

"So, Richard didn't lie," Magda said. "He didn't hurt those people. It's been you the entire time because you know them. And you're feeding Rich that hate speech to spite him against me, so much that he nearly suffocated me to death."

"See? Now, you're upsetting me." Marie raised the tools' temperature to the max, then dipped in the letter, bringing a shock to Magda and making her scream. The drug was no longer strong enough to fight that intensity of pain.

That still wasn't sufficient to hear Magda painting in agony. Marie needed more, and she wanted to reach the limit. She wanted Magda to break and beg her louder to stop. Marie picked up a can by the painting bucket and asked Richard to open it. He couldn't, due to Magda's scream growing more intense, consuming every corner of the garage. The sound crawled under Richard's skin, twisting his insides until he doubled over. He threw up.

"Marie, you're going too far," Richard said, gagging. "This is acid." "Don't you want justice?" Marie hissed, throwing him a glare. "There's a thin line between justice and revenge," Richard opined.

"This is not the way."

"It. Is. The. Way." Marie grabbed the can and opened it herself. "She'll know the pain we both felt all those years."

Marie dropped a heavy amount of acid in the crack of Magda's back.

Magda squirmed, wailing her guts out. She could not stop shrieking, and there was nothing to do. It was like the acid had reached her heart and burning it instead. There was no accurate description for such searing physical pain. Magda's thoughts flickered to Richard, to how he must have felt after the acid attack. The burning sensation as though his flesh was being chewed and consumed by flames. That bitter disbelief at how one human could commit such a monstrous act against another. And then came self-pity, wondering how she had ever allowed herself to end up in such a situation. Even breathing was like labor; her throat, raw and inflamed, burned from the relentless screaming and crying.

"Marie, that's enough!" Richard said, grasping the can of acid away. "No, you need to see that you care too much," Marie fumed, giving Richard's shoulder a shove. "I had put my life on the line for you the night of the fire. I saved you, and I sacrificed my guy for you. I sheltered and fed you, kept you away, hidden so no one could come and hurt you, only to thank me back for treating me like I'm a monster?" "I didn't say you're a monster."

"You didn't have to," Marie said. "Well, it was your idea that I go to the Dupris's house and work there, giving you intel and placing all those cameras, trackers, and even sending those stupid notes. So, you can't back out now. It wouldn't be fair to me or you. Now, give me back that acid."

"No, please, please, Marie," Magda wailed. "I'm sorry. I am the monster. I hurt Richard. I destroyed his face. His life, and even took someone from you. I can't change the past but only the present and the future. Please, tell me what I can do so you can forgive me, because yes, it's my fault. I am the monster."

"Wait, did you just realize that?" Marie said, listening to Magda's pleas.

"Please..." sobbed Magda. "You are right. I caused all this. And I am sorry. Please forgive me! I know I deserve to die, but please, spare my baby. Spare my baby, I beg."

"Baby?" Richard muttered, his eyes searching for Magda's belly.

"I thought you'd noticed," Magda whispered, her tears streaming uncontrollably. When would the pain stop? It wasn't just her body in agony but her mind, her motherly instinct, her hope—all unraveling at once.

"Not that I'm surprised, but that's amazing," Marie added, her voice annoyingly bright with excitement. Yet, there was something beneath it, something cold and calculating that neither Richard nor Magda could quite pinpoint. "Helmer wasted no time after finding those birth control pills, I suppose."

"I guess you knew," Magda stifled, her eyes darting between Richard and Marie.

"I know everything," Marie confirmed. "Like I said, I was often not as discreet, and you still haven't noticed. Starting with catching me in your bedroom, the painting studio, and my meddlings with your husband. Honestly, I thought it was a matter of days to blow my cover."

"I no longer care, Marie, what you did," Magda said. "All I want is my baby spared from this. Please."

"Hm not so quick..." Marie said, her lips curling into a quick smile. "If I didn't spare Jonathan's wife's baby, why would yours be an exception?"

"You..." Magda panted, her skin crawling, laying there like the earth's crust, an earthquake-ridden ground, fissures splitting her composure wide open. "You would hurt my baby?"

"Not directly," Marie replied, shrugging casually. "I'm sure hurting the momma will."

"Marie, no, no, please. I will do anything..." Magda swallowed her sob, hearing Marie getting the acid back and spilling it onto her legs. It reminded her of the first time she had gone through labor. Magda's eyes were bulging out of her face, and when she vomited, she nearly passed out. She had wished they had given her something to sleep, but she witnessed it all, powerless and away from home.

"Marie, honestly, that's enough," Richard intervened, stepping past her. He got himself a towel and cleaned out the blood from Magda's back. He turned off the tools, threw them on the floor, and told Marie to discard her gloves in case she had second thoughts. "You won't touch her again. So, go and find us our next target before her husband arrives. He shall be here soon, as I mentioned earlier. Maggie was dropped off when she came here, so it's guaranteed that whoever did will bring the husband to us."

"You're calling her Maggie. Really?" Marie sneered, tossing the gloves aside. She walked toward the garage door, her movements sharp. "I'll get going. Let's hope it's the last time you get in my way."

The door slammed shut. Marie was gone. And still, Magda could feel no relief. The drug was wearing off slowly, and she just knew by her fingers moving a bit. She would not be able to sleep on her back for a while or months due to the damage. She was damaged goods, discarded on the shore. A sinking boat, Magda, saw no escape. She could only moan, shout, scream, and weep in her misery.

"I-I deserve this," lamented Magda as Richard turned her over to sit her up. "That's why I will not hold this against you, Rich. Look at me! I'm damaged now. Isn't this enough justice for you?"

"I'll get you something for the pain," Richard said, ignoring Magda's comment. "It won't affect the baby, I promise."

"Rich, I'll do anything, but please forgive me," Magda insisted, her eyes greeting Richard's. She watched him covering her up and looking at her stomach. "And the baby—"

"I don't want to talk about it," Richard cut in. "Does it bother you?"

"What difference would that make?" he replied. "You love your husband, and that's a good thing. You love him, right?"

"I do." Magda nodded. "I am aware that the way we left stuff was not the best, and I deeply regret it. I truly need your forgiveness, Rich, so I can finally be at peace." She bellowed, the drug wearing off even more, and the acid still burning her skin.

Richard carefully lifted her off the table and placed her back in the chair. Without hesitation, he dropped to the floor, quickly rummaging through the items that had spilled from the bag. His hands stopped when they found a seringue set and a bottle of medicated drops. He grabbed them both and rushed back to Magda, gently taking her arm.

"It's to numb the pain," Richard explained, seeing the worried look on Magda's face.

"Are you sure it won't harm the baby?" she asked.

"Yes," Richard replied, cleaning her arm before drawing the sedative drops into the syringe. He motioned for Magda to take a deep breath and then inserted the needle. She flinched, but he quickly pulled it out. "Done."

"Are you planning to harm my husband?" Magda asked.

"If it comes to it, yes," Richard replied, wiping an alcohol pad on her arm before applying a tiny bandage.

"Why? He has done nothing to you," Magda said, her eyes tracking Richard's hand briefly hold her arm. "I don't harm the innocent, Maggie."

"Then why are you after him?"

"You can ask your husband when he comes later," Richard said, his tone calm but firm. He knew one thing about Magda. She wasn't ready to discover who her husband truly was.

Naked Truth

Helmer was that man who couldn't judge his wife for having a past, for he had one too. A dark one, so obscure that he was also afraid of it. Having it come back to the surface was not expected. He had always been careful with everything in his life and overly strategic with whatever he wanted. That was the thing with being so perfect. It doesn't always last. At some point, he could mess up and leave trails behind, which would lead to him and his family. Sooner or later, Helmer would have to tell someone about him being just as flawed as everyone and even more than Elvino, the man he swore was the devil.

Helmer was in the basement, hitting the life out of the guy on the wall for an answer. He wanted to know who was after his son, Christopher, and the rage in him, knowing that his wife was still out there in bed with the psycho man, left him manic. Helmer did not even notice how his hands were swollen from hitting the guy on the wall.

"R," the guy said, spitting a mouthful of blood. "T-That was h-h-his name."

"Tell me more!" Helmer ordered, threatening the man with another blow.

Elvino intervened, shoving Helmer aside to prevent an unnecessary bloodbath in the basement. Not that Elvino cared whether the man lost an eye or not, but he had never seen that side of Helmer before. Even as a mafia Don who had witnessed and committed worse, Elvino couldn't help but feel that maybe he wasn't as ruthless as he thought.

"You hit him enough. And he just told you who it is. That's all he knows!"

"Yeah, while you couldn't even get one word out of him," barked Helmer, wiping the dots of blood from his forehead. He moved to the tiny sink from the basement and washed his hands. He rubbed them viciously, so much that he scratched himself. There was still the guy's blood on him, and he wondered why go that far. Did he need to? Or was it just an excuse to allow his inner thirst for violence to reach satiation? Whatever it was, Helmer sensed a detachment toward his humanity. He hit the guy multiple times before he broke out a word, and the scary part was that Helmer seemed to enjoy it. There was an assortment of emotions he could barely sort out to make sense of yet. As to why he hated himself for it, and also why it was a relief to finally be able to hit on someone.

"What is it with this R guy?" Elvino asked, watching the distressing expression on Helmer's face from the square mirror above the sink.

"I told you he's my wife's ex," Helmer replied, keeping his gaze in the mirror. He saw the monster within him roaring, tired of being retained. He had fought it for so long that he had forgotten it still existed somewhere. That monster or guilt he had suppressed for many years was present, staring back at him. It only took Helmer a few seconds to remember he was not as perfect as he tried to be.

"You know..." Helmer started. "Once you kill someone, I wasn't aware that it also takes a piece of your soul which you never get back no matter how hard you try to retrieve it." He rested his hands on the sink borders, still looking at his reflection. "And as weird as it is, your mind wants you to do it again."

He thought his eyes were simply tingling, but then a few tears slipped free. Helmer sniffled, unable to withstand his reflection in the mirror. He hated it and wished that his life wasn't so controversial. He turned his gaze away from the mirror and paced a few steps back. Helmer noticed Elvino's empathizing stare and his arms loose on his sides, undoubtedly eager to hold him in his arms. Even though Helmer could have used some comfort in that moment, he declined it.

"I had blamed myself so much for what happened," Elvino said, putting the tools away. "I never wanted you to know what it felt like to hold a gun, ever. Neither make a living out of fighting nor have ties to my lifestyle. I know I failed you, so I don't even know how to comfort you..." He paused, grasping the courage to issue the apology he had waited years to make. Helmer deserved it, and Elvino knew that all the events that occurred in Helmer's life were nothing but unfortunate. Helmer had an abusive father, which was nearly life-threatening, and then he had known him as his foster father, which also ruined his life. At least, that's what Elvino thought, and there was nothing more painful than failing a child to be better.

"You think I blame you for what happened at the club that night?" Helmer said, approaching Elvino before resuming. "When I shot that guy who was trying to kill you, I would've done it a million times if that meant to save your life. The truth is I couldn't lose another father." Helmer started helping by putting the tools away and cleaning up some of the messes on the table. He noticed the stupefied expression in Elvino's eyes as if he had never expected to hear such words from him. "I couldn't lose you. And I insisted on joining the club, because I was a hell of a fighter. So damn good at it that I couldn't help but make something out of it."

"It's not that it's going to make me feel better, but I appreciate you calling me father." Elvino cupped Helmer's cheeks and hugged him. Helmer didn't resist. His arms slowly moved upwards, giving in to the hug, and to his surprise, a smile crept across his face. "But..." Elvino said, turning toward the guy on the wall. "I'll call up the boys so they can come to clean him up and the basement."

"I guess I'll leave you to it then," Helmer said, walking toward the staircase.

"Helms, wait." Elvino approached him, sensing an unusual heaviness in Helmer's voice. He didn't know why, but he couldn't allow Helmer to leave without sorting some things out first. "What you said about your mind telling you to do it again, are you sure nothing had happened at all besides the accident with the Patterson brothers? Have you done anything that I don't know about yet?"

"No," Helmer replied bluntly.

"Are you sure? Your eyes are telling me otherwise." Elvino knew Helmer too well to be satisfied with a simple no. Elvino already knew, but he wanted to hear the confirmation from Helmer himself. He didn't want to make any assumptions and not give him the benefit of the doubt because, after all, everyone deserved that. "You feel guilty about something, and I don't think it's about the Patterson brothers. Who is it?"

"What?"

"Did you kill someone else?" Elvino finally asked.

"Wh-What the hell! Why would you—why would you even think that?" Helmer's voice was shaky, with no slight certainty in it. He wasn't even sure of his answer. He sounded as if he was trying to convince himself that he had never done such. He was a respectable man, a loving, somewhat possessive, but a loving husband. A friend who was always there when needed, yet he couldn't think of himself as loyal.

His heart skipped a beat, recalling briefly that he'd have to come straight with Bryant sooner or later. He'd have to tell him about Sonia and his son, Christopher, a discovery that had shaken up his life all of a sudden. Helmer clasped his chest and leaned against the staircase. No, he wanted to believe he wasn't such a bad person. At least, that comforted him.

"You're lying," Elvino said. "You haven't changed. Since your high school days, you have had that sneaky tendency in you. I may be a lot of things, a maniac, a murderer, or whatever they call it, but I don't condone lies. That wasn't something you learned from me."

"I'm not lying..."

"You are," Elvino insisted.

"I'm not. I told you I didn't do anything," Helmer spat, his face glowing red from the abrupt interrogation. He didn't think that he'd look so nervous. But it was Elvino, the man who fathered him and knew his weaknesses like a few lines in a glossary book.

Helmer swallowed, his legs eager to leave, and he tried to until Elvino pulled him into a chokehold, locked in and unable to escape. "Helms, you're not getting out of here unless you tell me what you did."

"I-I told you," Helmer said, struggling to get himself free from Elvino's hold as if he had forgotten all the tricks he was taught. "I didn't do anything."

"This guy who's after you… The R guy—"

"He's not after me," Helmer broke in, grunting. "He's after my wife. He's obsessed with her. I told you he's a psycho."

"How do you know that?" Elvino let go of him and Helmer staggered away, dropping onto one of the stairsteps.

"It's not hard to put two and two together. And he told me himself. They might be sleeping together right now for all I care." The rage was back, thinking about the video he had seen earlier. Magda in bed with the psycho man.

Helmer did not give it a thought that maybe it was a farce to spite him or a ruse. He believed it, and there was nothing he hated more than the fact that he was still calling her his wife.

"This psycho knows where I live, where I work, and has abducted people I care about. It's like he's on a hunt; he placed things around for me to find to spread terror. He blackmails everyone, and for some reason, he doesn't leave you a choice but to do what he says. I don't even know where to start about the things he's done."

"I don't understand," Elvino started, shaking his head. "If he's only after your wife, why hurt people you care about? This sounds like a personal matter to me."

"Why would that be?"

"You tell me!" Elvino yelled, his soft gaze growing threatening. "You take me for an idiot; I've been running the streets of Chicago for years, and I know what personal dealings are. You know damn well this R guy is after you for whatever mess you've done that you won't say a word about. Look! He has even located your son. Think for once, does that look normal to you?"

"No." Helmer lowered his head, feeling bare and exposed. It was a relief that it was by Elvino and not by the world.

"Christopher was in Paris; that's where I kept him hidden, and no one except Sonia knew about him. She'd visit often, but she was very discreet."

"Of course," Helmer said. "That's why she kept traveling back and forth and pretending to visit family. I knew something was off, yet I didn't trust my gut."

"She did what she had to do," Elvino objected. "She was protecting your kid. Don't be a prick. I don't know where she got the strength to make such a sacrifice for the sake of keeping you safe, but I respect her for it, and you should too."

"Yeah." Helmer nodded. "The guy nearly shot her in her office. My heart almost stopped, you know? Christopher came in right after I pinned her to the ground and saved her life."

"The R guy? He did that?" Elvino asked, connecting the clues.

"Yes," Helmer replied, rubbing his hands together in deep thought. "He's dangerous. I don't know how he's been hiding in the shadows that long and not getting caught."

"Helms, how do you know this R guy?" Elvino stood closer to the step Helmer was sitting on, his tone invasive.

"Does it matter?"

"To me, yes. Because he knows where your son is," reminded Elvino, leading Helmer's attention to the gravity of the situation. It was now a matter of life and death. People close to him, old or young, rich or poor, were in danger because of him.

"It does not matter because I'll find him, and I'll kill him," Helmer said.

"What the hell did you do to that guy, Helms? You know him."

Elvino paced around the basement, knowing that his realization wasn't an exaggeration. Yet Helmer still decided not to say anything. Maybe it was due to shame or regrets. Helmer still cared about how he would be perceived if he had confessed all his mistakes in the past. And he cared especially how Elvino would see him.

"Sonia insisted that Christopher come to visit her here and spend a few days because we needed to give him some type of normalcy. It honestly was like the days with you staying with Gladice, your caregiver," Elvino continued. "This child has known solitude for too long, so I gave him a break from his caregiver and agreed that I have him here close by. But the driver who I hired"— Elvino pointed at the guy on the wall— "to pick him up from the airport, took him to your company building instead. I received a call, and it was Patterson."

Helmer's face dropped, his eyes dimming with panic. "When you say Patterson—"

"The brother of the guy we killed," Elvino replied, coming close to Helmer and sitting next to him. "He told me that the boy is with his father. It might be the last time he—I mean you— sees him. So, whoever that R guy is, he has ties with Patterson and his group."

"Oh no," Helmer whispered, his chest tightening, barely allowing him enough room to draw a breath. "That's how the psycho guy knows so much about me. He knows. He knows everything."

"Yes, and that means, just like they have allies, you need your own. Me, the boys, us as your family," Elvino said. "Now, go get your wife's daughter out of that house and everyone you care about. Because the Patterson group wants revenge, and unfortunately, they found your trails."

"That's why you're back, that you wanted to get into contact with me?" Helmer questioned.

"Yes," Elvino said, giving Helmer a double pat on the cheek. "I can't afford something happen to you. And the same goes for Christopher."

"Where do I take my family then?"

"Take them to my villa," Elvino advised. "They'll be safe there."

There was a question sitting in the back of Helmer's mind. He had too much to lose if something went wrong. His family, friends, reputation, and having to allow the monster within out of captivity. What was going to happen to him then? What was his life going to be like? "What if... What if something happens to someone I care about in all this? What do I do then?"

"There's nothing you can do other than to protect them the best you can now. And if something does happen, you'll know you did everything you could," replied Elvino from his own experience. "Does Bryant still have no clue about you and Sonia?"

"She wants me to tell him," Helmer replied. "Tomorrow I will, but it will be hell."

"At least you'll be honest," Elvino said, peeping Helmer's phone across the basement. He went and took it for him, and surprisingly, the screen didn't break all the way. "Bryant will come around, I'm sure of it. He'll find a way to forgive you."

Helmer took his phone back and dusted the tiny pieces of the screen glasses off. There was an incoming message, and he tapped on the notification, hoping it wasn't the psycho man again. His heart was not ready for another surprise, and the last thing he wanted to be updated on was his wife being in another man's bed. But the surprise was bigger. Scarier. It was an image of Magda, barely covered, with the huge R letter on her back and her burned legs. She looked lifeless in the picture, and from the deep cuts, Helmer inferred she was tortured. "I can't believe this," he whispered, standing up. "What is he doing to her? I must find her." Helmer trudged up the stairs and exited the basement, with Elvino following him along.

"Helms, wait!"

"I can't. I have to find my wife."

It was happening; the psycho man was after him, and he got his wife to make him suffer a little bit. Unfortunately, it was just the beginning.

CHAPTER 33

Face Of Fear

*E*lvino accompanied Helmer to the parking lot and discreetly asked some of the guys to go into the basement without giving many details due to Jonathan watching. Elvino had not talked to Jonathan but simply waved at him and took Helmer aside, worried about what he had in mind. He was heated, enough for him to make another mistake.

Magda's image was on his mind; he pictured her screaming and probably being in so much pain that she lost consciousness. Helmer thought maybe that was when she was placed under the covers from the video. Or perhaps she was drugged. Helmer was thinking it through, every detail, every word that psycho man had said. However, that did not stop him from being upset at her for being there alone with him, willingly walking into his trap. There couldn't be another explanation unless she was being blackmailed since it was one of the psycho guy's most effective methods to lure his victims in.

"Listen, whatever you do, let me know. Don't act based on emotions right now," Elvino whispered to him, his hand resting on Helmer's shoulder.

"I hear you," Helmer said, "but right now I need to go."

Moving closer to his car, he got stopped by one of the guys in bandannas and tattoos. "Helms, next time you come around, let's party, all right?"

"You never know; we might finally knock you out in a match in the future," added another one, bumping fists with Helmer.

"Right, except I win every time," Helmer replied hesitantly, due to Jonathan watching him. He motioned at the guys to cut their act and got back into his car with Jonathan. "I'll drive us."

Jonathan nodded, switching to the passenger's seat and allowing Helmer to drive. The ride was silent and awkwardly uncomfortable. Then as Helmer put his blinkers to turn to an opposite street, he felt something pressing into his ear. He froze, pushing onto the brake, stopping the car instantly. "Jonathan," he whispered, watching the gun pointed at his head. "What are you doing?"

"No, Boss. You tell me right now what we are doing and who you are," Jonathan said, his hand shaking as he moved his gun up to Helmer's face. "It's obvious you're in some funny business, and so are those guys. Because I am done helping you unless you come clean and stop pulling me into your schemes."

Out of everything that could have happened to ruin his night even more, it was his bodyguard deciding to put a gun to his face. Rather, his second hand, the guy who was paid to protect his life. Helmer tightened his grip around the wheel and straightened himself, his nerves refusing to appease. "Jonathan, lower your gun."

"Or what? You'll try to kill me like the psycho man?"

"No," Helmer replied, his tone low and shaky. "But that could grant me enough time to go and save my wife from that psycho. He's holding her hostage."

"You're bluffing."

"Have I ever?" said Helmer, stretching his phone out to Jonathan, gesturing at him to take a look at the image still on the screen. Jonathan slowly lowered the gun off his boss's face and sat back, staring at the shocking image.

"Damn boss, I'm sorry," Jonathan sympathized, then handed the phone back. He was too ashamed of his actions. He barely thought of what consequences there would be for pulling such a move, and he assumed that the only thing he could expect was to get fired. He fell silent, trying to be on his best behavior, wondering if he overreacted. That still didn't explain why he felt so uneasy around Helmer.

Jonathan wondered even if his concerns were valid. But obviously, if he had gotten no answers, he'd have to abandon his job, working for a man he barely knew. Jonathan wanted to protect his family, and maybe not working for the Dupris anymore could give him immunity.

"I still wonder how she got there, you know?" Helmer said, breaking the silence, driving, and adjusting the rearview mirrors. "I'm so mad right now. I want to save her, and at the same time, I'm upset because she's pregnant, dude. She's pregnant! She's carrying my baby right now, and I—"

Helmer stopped, a shiver shooting through his body and his voice breaking. He didn't want to cry. It was enough tears for the day, and he consoled himself, assuming that the baby was fine. The baby had to be; that's all he kept telling himself and wanted to believe. "And she's married to me. So, why the hell would she go there alone? And with my baby! The goddamn disrespect." Helmer banged his hand on the steering wheel, and the car went to a halt as he braked too hard, almost catching a red light.

"Do you get what I mean?" resumed Helmer, failing to see the concerned look on Jonathan's face. "I mean, you're married. Imagine your wife goes and meets her ex in a house alone. What–What would you think? Would you be okay?"

"Hm…no—"

"Exactly!" Helmer yelled, putting the car on shift, then heavily pressing on the gas. "Who in their right mind does that? I honestly thought they started banging or something. Because why? Why would she go there? Honestly! What the hell? That's my wife. You understand?" Jonathan hung onto the handles above the car window, preparing himself in case the car abruptly stopped again. He looked at the road, then at Helmer, who was still upset. All he wanted was to go back home safely and hoped that they wouldn't end up in an accident.

"Boss, you're a bit unhinged right now, and I honestly want to go back to my wife in one piece."

"Your wife, right," Helmer said, nodding aggressively, then giving Jonathan a brief side-eye. "She's a gem. Meanwhile, mine was supposed to be home right now, but her behind is God knows where."

Jonathan said no other words, realizing that even breathing loudly got his boss more worked up. He sat peacefully, barely moving, but his heart was racing. They made it home, and Jonathan pushed a breath of relief and exited the car, shaking the tension from his legs. Then Helmer took out an old business card from his pocket and wrote an address on it. "Take Gladice and my daughter to this address, Jonathan. Do so right away. I have to take care of some things."

Before Jonathan could ask any further directions, Helmer ran through the gate and got inside the mansion, eager to get to Magda's painting room. Mr. Hens had left the door unlocked for him, and the spare key inside, on one of her dusty shelves. Though Helmer would've never really cared to go there until his doubts about his wife's loyalty became a concern.

As he stepped inside, he darted toward the easels, where Magda's oldest collections were, and stopped, his arms dropping by his sides as he stared at the paintings. The disgust in his eyes was lethal, seeing that they were mostly of her ex. Not any type of ex, but Richard, who had her to his mercy. An ex who also could potentially harm their baby.

A box peeping from the creak of the closet—the doors an inch from being fully closed—caught Helmer's attention. He approached it cautiously, yearning to find out what was inside. Helmer opened the closet and noticed plenty of dried flowers, cards, including notes. He brought his knees to the floor, and he felt something underneath. He pressed a fist on the surface, then tapped his knuckles on it. There was a shallow sound, almost like a book's cover snapping shut. Helmer stood away from it, then realized it was under a carpet. Sticking his hands underneath, Helmer pulled the book out, or rather, his wife's journal.

His heart raced, but he was more curious than sorry. He dropped on his buttocks, barely drawing a breath in before reading.

June 11th, 2008

Precious diary,

Would the heavens ever forgive me? I just told two men that my love only belonged to them. But what can I do? I can barely choose between my heart and my head. Helmer is a kind guy. He cares for my family, and he might be the key to a new life. On the other hand, there's Richard, the guy I can't breathe without. Yet, he can barely breathe on his own. How will he even sustain me? Maybe my mom is right. Love is not always enough. Love does nothing but hold us from the life we deserve.

Helmer slammed the journal shut, breathing out. His wife marrying him for his money was not foreign to him. He had always known that Magda was seeing him and Richard at the same time but reading the cold confirmation in black and white was a slap to the face. It also reminded him how jealousy was something dark and powerful—so powerful it could turn him into someone he despised. Helmer flipped the pages. There was no need to relive that part.

August 23rd, 2008

Precious diary,

I decided to do the right thing. I'm running away with Richard. I'm choosing him. But never mind. I'm a horrible person. I'm standing a guy on his wedding day who genuinely wants to marry me. I feel like a snake. I just told Helmer that I can't wait to marry him, and here we go, I'm abandoning him. Honestly, do I even have a choice? My dad told me he had some illegal dealings that I should worry about. Of course, I don't believe any of it. Helmer is perfect, exactly why I have to leave. He deserves someone better, who loves him, without a divided heart. Mine is already taken; there's not even a piece of it to share. I know Helmer will never forgive me, but that's me doing the right thing for me.

Helmer was pushing himself to read more, but each word was like a shard of glass slicing through his skin. Each time he read Richard's name, his gut twisted. Helmer flipped a handful of pages, skipping to the middle, wishing for a different script that didn't involve him being made a fool out of.

August 28th, 2008

Dear Diary,

Something horrible happened. Richard stood me up. He decided not to follow up with our plan. Then, at the party, I got too much to drink... I don't even recall everything that happened when I was in that room alone. As I was preparing to leave, Ricks, Richard's brother, came in. He kissed me.

"What the hell," whispered Helmer to himself, regretting having ever opened this journal, finding these things out, which Magda never fully opened up about.

I was confused and tried to reason with him, but to no avail. I had never caught him looking at me with so much lust before. But you never know what's in somebody's heart until it's too late. I guess I had to learn the hard way, for I couldn't stop him.

A knot formed in Helmer's chest, each word harder to absorb than the last. He stared at the page, wondering how much more he could take. His throat dried, and he wished he could've been there to protect her, despite his pride telling him otherwise. Helmer massaged his temples, trying to shake off the growing panic, and forced himself to continue reading.

In the morning, I found myself naked in the guest room, my mom bursting in, telling me she knew my plans all along. She managed to convince Helmer to push the wedding, but what got me crushed even more was that Richard never thought of reconsidering his decision. He did not try to reach out after finding out that I was pregnant by his brother. I think he was disgusted, to be honest. This man hurt me so much that I started to loathe him.

Helmer had left me right after we walked out of the courthouse to Paris, which worked for me, as my mom suggested that we hid the pregnancy from him. Around 2 months or so, I was dealing with a lot of stress. I was angry, so I decided to see Richard. I went to where he stayed with a friend that night. They were drinking. That was their way of celebrating soccer games. I pretended to want to talk then I attacked him with acid. He lost vision, and I hit him in the knees, knocking him clean off his feet. After he fell, I ran so I wasn't caught. I could have easily been charged with attempted murder. But I didn't stop there. I tried to set the apartment on fire. What a horrible monster I am! I'm a killer. Diary, I killed him and his friend. I killed them. I burned them both!"

Helmer shut the journal and tossed it away. The monstrous side of humanity was all too familiar to him. He finally understood, and that left him restless. The drawing popped into his mind, connecting the puzzle to the story in the journal. The pregnant woman was Magda, and that can on the floor was what she attacked her ex with.

"The acid. It was the acid," Helmer whispered to himself, slowly processing the events. "That's why he's after her. He wants revenge. I need to do something right now. What should I do?" Helmer proceeded to open the box and found piles of letters from Richard. Old love letters. None of that mattered anymore. All Helmer kept thinking was his wife committed a crime, and she was now in potential danger. Above all else, Helmer could lose his baby, the dream he had held onto forever.

Reaching for his phone, his eyes caught someone's shadow coming toward the painting room. It was Bryant rushing in toward him.

"Finally, I found you. Jonathan told me where you were," Bryant said, greeting Helmer with a shoulder bump.

"What are you doing here? I hope nothing happened…"

"I mean, I haven't seen you for a while now," Bryant said, his eyes subtly scanning the room, wondering when his best friend was a fan of art. Sure, his wife was a painter, but Helmer was never that interested and not enough to be piling canvas and cleaning around that late. "You don't come to the office, leaving me flooded with work."

"I'm sure you're not so flooded, as I have a trainee to help out," Helmer said, his tone dismissive.

"You mean your laundry lady?" Bryant huffed. "Let me remind you. She's a trainee, which means she can't hold on her own yet."

"I know." Helmer sighed with no effort to object. His mind was foggy. He wanted to find Magda and protect his baby, but he didn't even know where she was. He wondered if the psycho man had done more than what the picture portrayed. Was the baby hurt in any form? If anything would happen, Helmer could somewhat find comfort knowing he did have a son somewhere. Nonetheless, he barely knew the boy and it'd take time to build a relationship with Christopher. Helmer wasn't present in his life; he didn't watch him grow up, nor did he get to teach him anything. On the other hand, his baby seemed like a second chance to be a father and a better one at that.

"What's going on? Did your wife get you to do some crazy chores to get laid or something?" Bryant asked, his eyes scanning the room. "Coochie blackmail is a real thing. Ain't no shame in that, by the way."

"Can you not?" Helmer said, giving Bryant a side-eye. Having his best friend there brought his soul some serenity. Helmer was grateful, but Bryant being there for him at such a time only pained his soul, wondering if in his life he had ever deserved such friendship.

"Since I'm already here and you obviously can't chase me out, do you mind serving me some whiskey? The hardest liquor you got!" Bryant said, his head already facing toward the painting room's door to go to the house's library. Helmer followed Bryant to the library since this latter knew his house like the palm of his hand. But Helmer had to tell him the truth, that he hadn't been honest with him.

"Bryant, wait!" Helmer said, stopping in his tracks. "What?"

Helmer breathed out, his heart pounding. "I have something to tell you."

CHAPTER 34

Silent Past

Helmer didn't know where to start, whether the beginning or that he had a son he never knew the existence of. Maybe that could get him some redemption, but it was scary that his hopes were minimal. There was no way Bryant would forgive him for something like this. He kept thinking, was it really the right timing for this, now that Magda was abducted and his family had to flee to be safe?

"Okay, it seems that whatever you have to say can wait," Bryant said, interrupting Helmer's trail of thoughts. "I need that liquor." He continued to walk, and Helmer hesitantly followed along, perplexed about his lack of effort to insist that Bryant listened.

They got to the library, and Bryant found the whiskey bottle. He poured himself a glass and sat where the piano was. Helmer grabbed the whiskey bottle and gulped it down his throat. Bryant stood, proceeded to grasp the bottle from him, and gestured at him to sit.

"You're good? Only a man in distress would grab a whole bottle of liquor and shovel it down their throat like it's water," said Bryant, awaiting a response. "You've been acting strange lately! What's going on? I'm worried about you, man."

"C'mon, get me a glass and fill it to the top," requested Helmer, directing his focus on the whiskey bottle.

"Not until you tell me what's going on with you. And what is that you desperately wanted to tell me about?"

Helmer sat, feeling the liquor warming his nerves. Seeing how concerned Bryant was with him and his family, he couldn't help wondering, what if his best friend didn't have to know about his son? What if he could manage to keep Christopher hidden? Helmer couldn't outweigh the consequences, and telling his best friend could affect not only their relationship but their business partnership, their brotherhood, and the trust between them. "There's a guy out there terrorizing everyone close to me, and he has even hurt Nina and Jonathan's family, Marie Lisa, and now my wife," Helmer explained.

"What do you mean your wife?" Bryant asked. "Magda's not here?" Helmer shook his head. "It's her ex."

"Holy hell!" Bryant flinched, knowing what that meant.

The past was more alive than ever, and his best friend was in a serious situation. Old secrets were always a threat to the present, as they reminded them of their old selves, their mistakes, the habits they left behind, and things they could never take back. Now, those secrets were making an appearance to remind Helmer he would not be able to hide for too long in the dark. To save his wife, he'd need to face the shadows.

"That was exactly my reaction," Helmer said. "He knows where I live, where I work, and everything. And... I found out he may have ties with the Patterson group."

"Patterson? The one whose brother you killed?" Bryant whispered, the hairs on his body spiking up. That shiver running through his soul let him know how much trouble there was on the table. "How could something like that happen? Didn't your wife's ex die? And how does he know where you live?"

"This psycho has dirt on everyone. He blackmails them and asks them for intel," Helmer replied, scrunching his nose. "But the irony is these people are endangered because of me. For the first time in my life, I don't know what to do, Bryant. And Magda's pregnant! The plan worked." Helmer stood and got a glass of vodka before returning to his seat. If something happened to that baby, he could never forgive himself. He tricked his wife into having it, and she was now at the end of a man who was obsessed with getting his revenge, torturing and abusing her. Helmer gulped the whiskey and restlessly pulled at his hair.

"Okay, hold on," said Bryant, pacing behind Helmer's chair. He slammed both hands onto Helmer's shoulders, attempting to give him some reassurance and solace. "No need to stress out, man, it won't help us. Have you thought of reporting what has been happening? Maybe involving the cops now would be a good thing."

"No, no, I-I don't want the cops involved," Helmer said, shaking his head. The last thing he wanted was to get law enforcement into that affair, knowing it was a personal matter. He had to figure it out on his own, and with such things, someone—either him or his wife—could potentially not come out of the ordeal alive. "It's not a good idea. You know why."

"Helmer—"

"People like us can't go to the cops, Bryant," Helmer said, his voice dropping.

Helmer stood and started to walk toward the library door. He desperately wanted to go to his room after the drawing and the bloody knife. He wanted to see what clues he'd possibly missed and anything that could help lead him to his wife. Helmer stopped by his closet and took the knife and drawing from where he hid them. He showed them to Bryant and leaned in, looking at the details highlighted in the drawing. "This drawing had been the answer all this time. Magda had done things to that psycho. Now he wants revenge."

"What?" Bryant squinted, trying to understand Helmer's analogy. "What could she possibly have done—"

"He's after both of us, Bryant. That's it," Helmer interrupted, hastening to keep up with the rushing thoughts flooding his mind. "Each person he abducts has a letter carved on them, like a tattoo. The 3 letters recently have been B-U-R. We're missing one more, and that's his next victim."

"Hold on, you mean that guy carves things into people's flesh?" Bryant asked, needing to confirm he heard his best friend right.

Helmer nodded, looking for a pen to write the letters down on the back of the drawing sheet. He didn't realize it before, but when he accidentally placed the drawing sheet upside down on the nightstand to write, it gave the shape of a letter. He lifted it to the bedside lamp, and the light created a shadow, making the letter clear enough to see it.

N.

"That's it," Helmer whispered, now adding the last letter to the rest. B-U-R-N. "It makes sense. It relates to the fire in the journal." "What's that? Burn? Like…a joke burn, a second or third-degree burn, or what?" Bryant asked, his mind whirling as Helmer tried to give him a logical answer to appease his curiosity.

"Would you stop asking me questions I don't have answers for?" Helmer rolled his eyes, urging his best friend to help him brainstorm the possible scenarios and odds of the drawing.

"I will kill this guy, I swear to you," Helmer said, anticipating who the next victim would be. It could be anyone close to him, and he wished that he would stop the psycho man before any incidents occurred.

"Then listen to me," Bryant said. "Let's go to the police station and report everything. That way, you have cover. We fear the law, but sometimes that's the only thing that can save us."

"We'll waste time," Helmer pointed out.

"Fair point," Bryant conceded with a nod. "Then send some of the new guards to file the report. Have any witnesses call in and give their statements. Cover your bases."

"Did you get high today?" Helmer asked, staring closely at Bryant. "In a moment like this, you choose to be a jerk?" Bryant grunted, palming his face. "No. I'm clean."

"Just wanted to make sure. Let's go!" They darted out of the room and took the stairs, heading to the house gate. The two new guards were there, tormented as they saw Helmer coming their way. They lowered their heads, rubbing their hands. It was their new job, and they had already made a mistake they couldn't repair, no matter what.

"What's going on?" Helmer asked urgently.

"Sir..." One of the guards said, gawking at the other one, not knowing where to begin. Words tangled in his throat as he hesitated, as there was no way to sugarcoat their failure. "We... we took Mrs. Dupris to an abandoned house—"

"We're so sorry, Boss," the other guard blurted out, clasping his hands together like a silent plea.

"Hold on..." Helmer froze in his spot, his brain racing to process the words, but they collided in chaos. "You did what?"

"Okay, you stay back, I'll handle this," Bryant said quickly, stepping in front of Helmer as if shielding the guards from an impending explosion. He raised a hand, signaling his friend to calm down, though his tone was firm and cutting once he turned to the pair. "You two took your boss's wife somewhere? Alone? An abandoned house? Is that what you're saying?"

The guards nodded silently. "Yes, but we... we didn't know what else to do," one of them stammered, his voice trembling under Helmer's piercing glare. "She asked us—"

"Asked you?" Helmer interrupted, clenching his jawbones. His body was overpowered by something bigger than rage. Like a riptide pulling him further from shore, his thoughts thrashed, heavy and unwieldy, sinking clarity beneath the undertow. There was fire in his eyes, and the guards took a step back, expecting him to explode at any second. "The woman I explicitly instructed you to keep safe, to keep indoors, and not allow one step past this gate? You took her to God knows where without even the decency to warn me? Is that what you're telling me?"

The other guard flinched. "Sir, your wife insisted, and she... she threatened us. We felt like we didn't have a choice."

"I don't give a damn!" Helmer yelled, his hands eager to grab the two guards by their necks. The thought made him feel like an animal. He didn't like the feeling, but the fighter in him always begged to come to rescue in times of stress. "You could've called me. Or done otherwise, you punk."

Seeing the guards about to open their mouths to make further objections, Bryant stepped in between them and Helmer. "Don't say any words. You wouldn't want to upset him more," warned Bryant, fisting Helmer's chest so he could back off and retain composure. "What we're going to do now is you two are going to give us the address you dropped Mrs. Dupris's wife off at and go to the police station so you two can report her missing. Deal?"

"Deal," the guards nodded. "We're so so—" Helmer took the words out of their mouths with a double punch. He couldn't help it. He recognized they both made a mistake, though they couldn't both have it easy without having a taste of his type of redemption first. His fists.

"I told you," Bryant added, proceeding to pat the guards' faces. He got the address from them and looked it up on his phone's map. "Damn. She's in the woods? That's miles from here!"

Helmer placed a hand on Bryant's shoulder, his tone more urgent. "Okay, so let's move." He pointed sharply at the guards, his eyes hardening.

"And you two... Go make the report right now. We'll handle the rest when I get back."

The guards nodded, still visibly shaken, and hastily turned to carry out Helmer's orders. Bryant grabbed his fast car, motioning to Helmer to hop along. Bryant sped out of the mansion, leaving the gate, and taking the road. He kept an eye on Helmer in the passenger's seat, wishing to find a way to uplift his spirit. "You know, I am not a father. I aspired to be one. I can't say that I know exactly how it feels, but I know the fear it brings. How much you start caring about that little human…"

Helmer slowly shifted his gaze toward his best friend, hearing the cracks in his voice. "Are you referring to Nina's miscarriage?"

He nodded. "When I found out, I was scared but happy. I thought of this baby for so long, yet one day, Nina found out that I restarted talking to Sonia." Bryant paused, taking a breath before continuing. "We had a horrible argument at her house, and although I kept telling her to stop and not run down the stairs, she didn't want to hear it. So…"

"She fell," Helmer inferred, his eyes full of empathy.

"That's why she took months off from work," Bryant continued. "It was to recover, and the therapy helped. Elvino comforted me a lot, too, at that time. I had caused her miscarriage, and even when I tried to make things right, she didn't want to have anything to do with me."

"That's understandable," Helmer said. "She was broken, Bryant."

Bryant nodded. "I know."

He increased his speed, doubling past a few cars so that they could get to their destination faster. He felt the warm drops of tears running down his eyelids. He hated it, aware that Helmer wouldn't let him live to see him in tears.

"You're crying," Helmer said, moving his head closer to see if he was hallucinating. "Damn right. You're really crying."

"Stop, there must be some dust in the car," Bryant said, blinking repeatedly.

"Right," Helmer teased, allowing the light humor to ease him off. "Well, I'm sorry Bryant. For everything I judged you about. I was not a good friend."

"Of course you were. We're not perfect," Bryant said, his voice steady as he glanced at Helmer. "And you'll be my best man."

"Your best man?" Helmer asked in haste, his ear twitching at the sound of it.

Bryant let out a laugh. "I'm sorry for breaking the news with no heads-up, but yes. I'm proposing to Sonia next week."

"Oh yeah? That's... That's beautiful. I mean... congratulations. You deser—" The sudden ring of Helmer's phone cut through the moment. Sonia's name flashed on the screen, bright and glaring.

Helmer stared at it, his thoughts racing. Was it about their earlier conversation? Telling Bryant the truth? Or maybe something about Christopher? He shifted in his seat, the silence stretching longer than it should.

"Go ahead, answer. It might be about work," Bryant said casually, redirecting his eyes to the road.

"Hmm... Yeah. Y-Yeah, you're right," Helmer stuttered, clearing his throat as he reached for the phone. "What else could it be, right?" His forced chuckle did little to hide the unease as he finally swiped to answer. His heart dropped hearing her voice.

"Helmer, there's an intruder in my house. The electricity has been cut off! I tried to call the cops, but I can't reach them," cried Sonia on the phone, her voice shaky and unsteady yet loud enough for Bryant to hear.

"Baby," Bryant said, panicking.

"Where exactly are you in the house? Tell me. I'm with Bryant right now. Where are you?" Helmer asked, motioning to Bryant to make a detour.

"I'm hiding in the closet," replied Sonia in a whisper. "I'm scared. I couldn't reach Bryant for some reason."

"Listen to me carefully, Sonie! Try not to make any noise. We'll be there soon!" Helmer said, keeping her on the line as they drove faster to get to her place.

"There's someone at the door trying to open it. Please, guys, do something—"

Her voice was glitching, and a scream followed on the phone. Then the connection was cut off.

"Damn it! Sonie? Sonie! Answer me."

"Don't tell me you lost her," Bryant said, snatching Helmer's phone. The call had indeed dropped. Bryant let go of the phone, fidgeting with the seatbelt, distracting himself from the worst scenarios playing in his head. He wondered, why Sonia? She had never hurt anybody, and now, she was in possible danger, and only God knew the fear she was going through. Bryant imagined it, her screaming like that was pure agony.

"It's okay; we'll be there in a few minutes," reassured Helmer, failing instantly to do so. There wasn't much chatting during the car ride, and they both felt that fear of losing someone close. Time was running out, and so were their worrying hearts. They could barely breathe through it all.

Reaching Sonia's house, they parked the car and immediately ran ahead to the entrance. It was pitch-black inside, dead like a cave. No sounds or signs of life. They used their phone's flashlights to guide the way, and the door was open, the doorknob broken, almost like someone had forced their way through.

Helmer stepped onto the patio as Bryant hesitated to proceed, their shoes smashing the pieces of glass on the floor. There was blood! "Don't stop. We have to go in," encouraged Helmer, gripping onto the last strings of bravery he had left.

"Holly hell, Helmer. What if... What if that's her blood?" Bryant said, shaking.

"Let's hope not. We don't wish for that to happen." Helmer grasped his gun and hurried to bolt himself in, gesturing for Bryant to follow. The thought that his best friend could be right sent waves of aversion to his brain, and his fingers were eager to dig a bullet into whoever was behind this. He didn't want to allow his emotions to drive him mad, but he was surely getting there.

"Okay, let's see." Bryant followed along cautiously. He briefly closed his eyes, allowing pictures of Sonia's smile to fill his brain, which brought him immediate solace. He was desperate to hear Sonia's voice or any signs that she was still inside. He made sure to keep thinking of her, and that gave him his strength back.

Helmer and Bryant went completely inside, taking small steps toward the living room, and everything was neat. There was no one. They proceeded to move to the bedroom where she was supposed to be. Scanning across the bed, they saw her lip gloss on the carpet and everything from her dresser overthrown. The closet doors were broken, hanging unsteadily, on the verge of falling off. There were no signs of her, but Bryant still had hope of finding her. He had to, and quickly, before his world fell apart.

Helmer clasped his chest, worried that something horrible had happened to Sonia. He ran out of the room and made his way to Sonia's kitchen. He took two tiny knives from a case, stuck one into his pocket, and handed the other to Bryant.

"Sonie! Sonie, please tell me you're here," Helmer shouted, keeping an eye out, adjusting his gun and posture. "We need to hear you."

A hard compound object hit behind Helmer's head. Helmer wobbled back, and his elbows slammed onto the kitchen counter. His phone dropped, and his vision struggled to stay clear after the hit. Someone grabbed and punched Bryant before he could make any use of his knife, knocking him flat out. He lost consciousness; then Helmer heard something splash in his face. Pancuronium. It was too late when he finally realized what was spreading in the air. The psycho man's drug. His eyes flickered shut, and then he progressively lost his balance despite his ill efforts to hold onto the kitchen counter. And he passed out.

CHAPTER 35

The Choice (Part One)

*H*elmer's eyes flickered open, slowly adjusting to the bright lights flashing at him. He heard a pair of boots moving toward the chair he was strapped in, too weak to make a move. Every attempt to stand up failed, as a heavy chain kept his feet pawned to the ground. He tried to make use of his fingers, but they were numb and stiff. He traveled his eyes around, and the walls caught his attention. They were covered with old drawings, blood stains splashed across them. His vision was still blurry, and the blazing heat emitted purposefully from the garage unraveled his thoughts. He couldn't make sense of where he was, only that he was in serious trouble.

"Water... water... please," Helmer whispered, his head dropping backward. His bones felt like they were being crushed, cracking piece by piece inside his body. His face throbbed, swollen as if stung by a swarm of bees, and each swallow sent a wrenching pain through his throat.

"The drug should wear off soon," said a voice, approaching Helmer's chair with a rusted cup. "We'll need you in your senses for our little session."

"Bryant... where's Bryant?" Helmer questioned, his voice as thin as a whisper lost in the wind. As his eyes continued adjusting, he saw his captor's face. "You!"

"Oh, you recognize me? That's good." Richard raised the rusted cup to Helmer's lips, begging for hydration. Although he had not trusted what was in the cup or its appearance, Helmer took a sip. He hissed, spitting it out. It wasn't water but unfiltered vinegar, burning down his throat.

"You may call me Richard if you like. It's not like you don't know my name," Richard taunted, taking slow, measured steps around Helmer. "And, surprisingly, I won't need to leave any marks on you. You're the last piece of my puzzle."

"W-What do you mean?" Helmer asked, his eyes widening. "Simple. Burn Helmer Dupris. That's it." Richard's grin stretched as he reached the heater, cranking the dial. "All your 'loyal' people? They were just pieces of my plan, leading you to me."

"Where are they? My wife and my friend? Or Sonie. What did you do with them?" Helmer questioned, his eyes moving toward the garage door. It was creaking open. Could it be the cops? The thought brought him a livid smile, only to disappear, realizing who was coming in. "Marie! Marie Lisa?"

"I know, shocker," Marie said, dragging Magda along with Sonia. They both had devices restraining their hands, with duct tape sealing their mouths. They took gentle steps, obeying Marie's command to kneel on the floor facing Helmer. They looked at him, afraid for his safety, and hopeless that any of them would make it out alive.

"What-What does that supposed to mean? What are you doing, Marie?" Helmer said. "Did the psycho force you to do this? You don't have to turn on me because you're afraid of him. Please, let these women go. You know them. They've always been good to you; I've been good to you. I-I don't understand."

"I know, soon you will, when I start torturing them," Marie said, kicking Sonia in the back, making her grunt with pain on the floor and falling forward onto her palms. "But you're here for something big, Mr. Dupris."

"I don't know what you're talking about," Helmer said, seeing that Marie had sided with the other side, despite his best efforts to deny it.

"Oh, you will soon know when I start beating up your lass," Marie said, grabbing Sonia by her thick braids, pulling so hard that one could see her eyes building out of her face.

"Let go of her! What the hell are you doing, Marie?" Helmer shouted, unable to say much from where he sat, at the mercy of his deranged opponents. "You don't have to do this. If you're being forced—"

"Do I look like I'm being forced to you?" Marie snapped, pulling Sonia's neck backward, annoyed at Helmer trying to talk her out of her malice.

"I should've seen it," Helmer said. "Everything makes sense. This psycho guy knows everything that's happening in my house. So, it was you all along giving him intel."

"A guy whom you owe a big apology to," Marie replied, directing his finger toward Richard. "It's him you need to beg."

Richard put on a wired belt on him, giving off a red laser light. He put on his coat, looking heavier than usual. It seemed to be carrying some things that Helmer wasn't too knowledgeable about. He got close to Helmer's chair to tease him. Helmer attempted to move, hoping that the chain and ropes keeping him immobile would weaken. Such a hopeless thing to do, and the more he moved, the tighter the ropes around his neck got. "Knowing that you were coming, I had to take precautions. I also placed 2 bombs on me, and my coat is full of explosives. One wrong move, we all blow up. I die, and so do your two ladies right here."

"Which means you can't kill us," added Marie, circling Magda and Sonia on the floor.

"Oh my God," Helmer gasped, his eyes widening. "The knife. So, the knife was—"

"Mine," Marie replied, with a mocking nod. "I know… It's a lot to digest. But look, we hope that you choose wisely, otherwise, we all get blown up. And we need you to tell your wife who you are."

"I'm not following you," Helmer said, feeling the drug leaving his system. He moved a finger, then another, until he felt his hands. Only to wish he could crash them into Marie's face for being a traitor. "I don't even know why I'm here."

"You don't?" Marie said, her tone sarcastic. "No worries, I have a good remedy for people with short memories like you." She stared at Helmer for a few seconds, him unaware of what she was going to do. Marie hurled a slap across Magda's face, causing her to drop to her side.

"Magda," Helmer blurted out, still confused about Marie hitting his wife, the hands that fed her for a while. He couldn't understand how someone could be so deceitful, although that sounded familiar. "Look at your wife; she's beautiful, isn't she? I found out she's expecting your child…"

Hearing this, Helmer's mind was filled with worry. He did not announce their pregnancy, but of course, Marie knew everything. That was the last thing she couldn't figure out. "No, no, no, please. Marie, I'll do and say whatever you want. Don't hurt my child."

"The baby? You want to keep this baby alive?" Marie sneered, pulling Magda by her hair and dragging her on the floor, her burn wounds being grazed so they would hurt.

"No, please," Helmer begged. "Ask me questions. Anything! I'll answer."

"Good, you're catching up. Tell your wife what that tiger tattoo on your chest is about," Richard ordered, grabbing a pair of scissors to rip Helmer's t-shirt free. He took a tiny piece of mirror and reflected the area so Sonia and Magda could have a clean look. Helmer was quiet. The words wanted to come out but got stuck, as they might've condemned him.

"You don't want to talk?" Richard said, breaking the glass. "Me neither; I'm not much of a talker." He dug the piece of glass into his flesh and sliced it through. Helmer screamed, the drug wearing off, leaving him to feel every ounce of pain.

"What are you doing? Stop. You're hurting him," cried Magda on the floor along with Sonia.

Richard ignored them, grabbed a chair, and sat, waiting for Helmer to speak. It was the first time Helmer would ever open up about his past, and it was no longer going to be a secret. Exactly what Richard wanted, for the perfect guy to be reduced to just an ordinary, well-calculated, and twisted businessman.

"When I was a kid, my dad used to do horrible things to me, especially when Gladice would step out to pick up groceries," Helmer said, not even knowing how he'd find the courage to relive his trauma. But he had to, for his wife, his baby, and Sonie. "Sometimes, he'd beat me until I'd black out."

"Black out?" Magda bellowed, hearing Helmer's confessions. "You never told me these things."

"I couldn't," Helmer said, avoiding looking in her direction. "I-I was not proud of my past. I also feared you'd see me differently."

"How could I have seen you differently?" Magda asked, her genuine interest making her forget the excruciating pain. Her body still pulsed with the remnants of scars, swollen and etched like bloody art on a damp, uneven wall.

"He never liked to talk about it," Sonia said, looking between Magda and Helmer.

Wait! You knew about this?" Magda snapped, surprising herself for a second. "I'm sorry; I'm just shocked you know things about my husband that I don't."

"Magda—"

"No, Helmer, don't interrupt me," Magda snapped, struggling to maintain her balance on her knees. "How come I don't know these things about you? How long did she know that? Or no, let me rephrase. What else does she know that I don't?"

"Maybe more," Helmer said, his voice dropping lower, like the calm of the night.

"Okay," Magda said, her breath growing heavy, warning him she could pop off at any minute. "Go ahead. I'm listening."

Helmer looked at her, then took her hesitant nod as permission to resume. "I needed to do something if I wanted the abuse to stop... Hell! My dad was never going to. In my high school years, Bryant introduced me to a man named Elvino. He was also a doctor, a clinical psychotherapist, to be precise."

"I-I remember him," Magda urged. "What happened to him?"

"He taught me to fight, and I fell in love with it," Helmer reluctantly replied. "The lessons gave me that feeling of control and the power that I lost, so I wanted to make a living out of it."

"Of fighting?" Magda asked, with a brief shrug.

"Yes." Helmer nodded. "One day, my dad was drunk, and he hit me. I walked away, and then he turned to Gladice, my nanny, and started doing things that were very inappropriate to her. She couldn't stop him, and he kept on trying to get her to consent to what he wanted to do. That was when I lost it, and I nearly killed him."

Helmer wished for the drug to stay longer in his system to numb him from replaying such things in his head. Yet no words or anything could comfort such pain, no antidepressants, nor therapy. He shut his eyes and leaned his head back, continuing to divulge the dark side of his story.

"So... you protected Gladice," Magda summed up, an uninvited tear running down her eyes.

"All the rage that built within me for years had broken free that day," Helmer resumed. "Later on, Elvino took me into his foster home, and I got adopted. I thought so highly of him and wanted to make him proud so much that I turned a blind eye to who he really was."

"Tell us who he was," Marie urged.

"I-I can't," Helmer shook his head, a few tears running down his face. He didn't want to remember. It was too much to process all over again. The way he trusted and got enthralled in a world he never thought he would.

"No problem, I'll help you." Marie kicked Sonia from below her abdomen. And headed to the tool bag, powering on her carving metal drill. She left it to be as hot as she wanted it while watching Helmer, expecting a word from him. Yet he gave nothing. No words. Marie, annoyed by his refusal, took the hot tool and told Richard to hold down Sonia.

"Sonie, no. Stop! Don't hurt her, I'm begging," Helmer cried out, still assuming they were bluffing to get him to talk. Until they carved the N letter on her stomach and sealed it with the hot stool. Sonia couldn't do much, and neither Magda, for they were still weak due to the pancuronium.

"I'll tell you. I'll tell you," whimpered Helmer, seeing he didn't have a choice. He was watching Sonia scream and crying hopelessly from the excruciating pain. Each scream was a bullet shot in his vessels, making him wish he was dead. But Magda was also watching how moved Helmer was as soon as he saw Sonia being truly helpless. "I found out Elvino was a Mafia Don."

"What? He's from the mafia?" Magda whispered, staring at her husband. "I don't understand..."

"His group was the tiger clan," Helmer interrupted, despite the chaotic question clamming inside Magda's head. Was he really saying those things? "They were great fighters, bringing him money at his fight clubs and doing whatever he couldn't in broad light. And-And—"

"And what?" Magda asked, her eyes blazing red. "And I was one of them. I joined him."

"When? Tell me," urged Magda.

"Shortly before we got married," Helmer replied, trying to jerk himself in the chains.

What's the tattoo about?" he asked, caught in her sphere of thoughts. "The tiger tattoo is an oath I took, and they sealed it on me. Bryant has it too," Helmer explained. "We got it around the same time. Due to some unfortunate circumstances, I had to walk away from Elvino for a while and handle my business somewhere else."

"In Paris," Magda said, coming to the rough realization that she never knew her husband as much as she thought. She was wrong. She wasn't the only one with secrets. And his were darker. "That's what my dad was warning me about."

"Yes," nodded Helmer, his face reddening.

"You told me you were there for your father's business."

"That wasn't a lie."

"It was a lie!" Magda yelled out, raging. She clasped her belly, feeling nauseous from the overstimulation. "And you-you blamed me and my pregnancy with Meg for so long, for everything except yourself. You're also a damn liar. Do you know that? You're just a better one, I guess."

"The truth is neither of us can point fingers, Magda," declared Helmer, heaving a sigh.

"You have no right to say these words," Magda barked, shaking her head aggressively, her heart turning a pound of ice inside of her. Never had she thought someone's body could get so cold despite being numb. "I should have believed and trusted my father."

"Now," Richard resumed, motioning at Marie to proceed with the last plan. "Tell your wife and your cute bestie over here what you had done 15 years ago."

"I didn't do anything," Helmer said firmly.

"Tell us where you were after the wedding got postponed."

"What wedding?" Helmer asked.

"Your wedding," Marie repeated. "The first one your mother-in-law convinced you to cancel."

"I don't know what you mean," Helmer said.

Richard looked down and walked over to Magda, his eyes moving to her belly. Helmer's heart stopped. He saw those eyes. He recognized that sort of malice. "Don't hurt her. I'll tell you, please."

Richard bent over, his hand grazing over Magda's belly. "I'm all ears."

"I was in town."

"Where exactly in town?" Richard asked, lifting an eyebrow.

"Why does that matter?" Magda asked, wondering where Richard was going with his questions, which she found offensive and very impertinent. What about her husband bothered Richard so much to torture him?

"Your mom had paid me a visit, offering me money to leave town without you, which you already know," Richard replied. "But I also had another visitor that day, and after 2 months or so, everything changed."

Helmer snorted. "I don't know what you're talking about."

"Your choice then. Unless you elaborate." Richard stepped onto Sonia's hands, meaning to crush each finger. Her agonizing wails weakened Helmer's resolution to not say anything further. Her being in so much pain because of him was the burden he would carry with him to the grave. He hated himself for it.

"I did. I came to see you," Helmer admitted, his breath ragged. "What did you do when you came to see me the first time?" Richard asked, stepping off Sonia's fingers.

"I told you to leave town and offered you a higher sum than Allimair's."

"And I refused it," Richard added, throwing a glance at Magda on the floor. "Because this woman right here, I didn't think of her having a price. I loved her."

"So did I," Helmer shot back, his eyes briefly stopping on Magda. "No, what I saw was control," Richard said. "Someone who considered her love as a winning or losing game. We both know what you felt for her wasn't love. It was lust and perhaps a plan to cover up your double life."

"You don't know what you're saying," Helmer objected, his own words tasting hollow.

"You threatened me that night," Richard continued, his voice cold and sharp. "I let her go. I walked away. And yet, you still saw me as a threat. Now..." He knelt slightly, leveling his gaze with Helmer's. "You're going to make a choice. Pick who dies. Your wife, or your ex. "Who's your ex? Sonia?" Magda demanded, her confused gaze shifting to Sonia and then Helmer. "I-I don't understand. What is Richard talking about? Helmer?"

"What a dilemma," Marie said, snickering as he made both women straighten up onto their knees, enjoying the little feud between them.

Sonia had not said a word, facing the part of her life she never wanted to resurface.

"Shut up, Marie!" Helmer yelled as Richard cut out the ropes to set him free. But there was the chain, still holding him back. He had to calculate his moves. He could fight, but he couldn't risk attacking Richard due to the threat of being blown up.

"By the way," Richard said. "We tied your best friend next door; he is watching us live. It must be so upsetting for him to find out what kind of deceitful friend you are."

"Who brought us here?" Helmer asked. "It couldn't be Marie. She wouldn't be able to take both me and Bryant here."

"Soon, you'll know," Richard replied. "It seems that you have more enemies than you can count. Our third ally will soon come after you, but he decided to let me have you alone for now."

"Who is it?"

"You know who. But do you know that your wife is a killer?" Richard said, taking the gun that Helmer was carrying from his cargo pants. "She tried to light me up. She set the fire. She's a cold-blooded murderer. And now, if I am to choose, she's the one to die."

"No. No." Helmer shook his head, his eyes searching for Magda's belly. That little belly he had always dreamed of seeing growing and holding. "She can't die."

"Why not?" Richard pointed the gun at Magda's head, pressing it into her ear. Magda gasped, glancing up at Helmer, and tugging at herself. She anticipated the sound of the trigger, clacking against her skull. One twist of his finger could end her baby's life. Magda squeezed her eyes shut, the mere seconds of her counting turning into a wail of despair.

"My baby. Please. You'd also kill my baby," Helmer pleaded. "She must die!"

"She shouldn't."

"Why not? She's a killer," Richard hissed.

"She is not."

"Why not? What are the odds? Why can't she? People hide who they are all the time," Richard opined, the gun moving to Magda's forehead, making her tremble.

"Magda wouldn't do that." Helmer shook his head. "She might be a liar, a manipulator, or whatever you call her. But she can't be a murderer."

"That's true," Richard said with a sly smirk. "Maggie can be a lot of things. Why should murder be an exemption?"

"Because it is an exception," Helmer replied sharply.

"Why? Why Helmer Dupris? Why would it be, then? Tell me. Who else besides her could have done it? Could've tried to kill me?"

"Me!" Helmer confessed. "I did it. I did it. She didn't set the fire. I did."

The Choice (Part Two)

Magda's head snapped toward Helmer, her eyes searching his lips. Perhaps she hadn't heard him correctly, and those words were a mistake. Her gaze begged him to say something, to take it back, anything to prove that he had spoken out of spite or desperation. Stress could do this to someone, make them feel like a captive, saying things they didn't mean.

"I did it," Helmer confirmed, keeping his eyes averted. He couldn't bring himself to look at her. No, he couldn't believe the words were coming out of his mouth either. They were never meant to be said out loud, much less to strip him bare in front of the two women who mattered most in his life.

"Helmer," Sonia mouthed, joining her gaze to his.

"I was jealous of you, Richard," Helmer continued. "I hated you. I felt humiliated when I found out Magda was still seeing you. My ego got in the way, and I lost my mind."

"You lost your mind knowing that she chose me. Because you are an animal. A monster, Helmer Dupris," Richard said, lowering the gun from Magda's head. "You were raised like one, so I can't blame you. Now I'm going to give you the chance to choose your bid for redemption."

"How? How did you… How did you find out about Richard?" Magda asked, a lump in her throat, making her words barely audible. "Answer me. I deserve to know."

"At our engagement party. I noticed when you followed your father to the restroom. I didn't mean to overhear your conversation, but I did," Helmer explained. "I was hiding behind the door, hearing him asking you to escape the wedding. I heard the plan about you running away with Richard. So, I got curious and followed you one day and watched you meet with him in the woods."

"Days before the wedding," she whispered, the memory coming back to her. "You saw us."

"So, I have had a few men following you since that day, tracking every move. When you went to see him, they saw you coming out of the apartment and lighting up the fire. They called me while I was in Paris, and I ordered them to reset the fire and burn everything."

"It wasn't only him inside, do you know that?" Magda said, trying to make her husband realize what he had done. "That was his best friend's apartment, and he died. That was also Marie's boyfriend—"

"Which we can save the tears for," Marie cut in, the cameras in the garage picking up movement from outside. The cops were coming. The lights of the cars flashed, and she froze in her tracks. "Hold on… Did you call the cops?"

"I-I didn't," Helmer stammered, the blue and red lights slipping through the cracks under the garage door, casting eerie shadows that stretched across the floor, flickering like a warning.

"Somebody did," Richard told Marie, grabbing the key to the chains, following the last step of their plan.

"Now, they've done pissing me off," Marie shouted, tugging at her braids. The cops? What a curse word. Who called them?

They set Helmer free, and Richard stretched out the gun to him. "Remember, you shoot me or attempt anything with Marie, we all blow up. You shoot one of these women, we're even."

"I'm not doing this," Helmer said, looking at Sonia and then at Magda. "You can't ask me to do this."

"Helmer, save your baby. It's okay," Sonia said, urging him to listen to her.

His shoulders dropped. "No, I can't."

"What do you mean you can't?" Magda simmered, watching him hesitate. "Helmer, you forced me to have this baby. You can't bail on us now. You must save our child."

"Quiet! Please be quiet. I'm trying to think," Helmer cried out. "Just shoot," Sonia said. "I forgive you."

"No, Sonie."

"Take care of Christopher!" Sonia whispered, her brown eyes squinting as she fought back tears. If it came to saving Helmer's life, she'd sacrifice her own without a second thought. Her face, flushed and streaked with tears, was like roughened sandpaper, each drop a mark of sorrow, composing its own mournful melody. Her lips, trembling, finally broke with a sob. It wasn't supposed to happen, not yet. Helmer would be delayed in doing what he had to do.

"Who's Christopher?" Magda asked, furrowing her eyebrows.

"My son," Helmer replied, deciding to be honest in case something would happen to him. He didn't want to keep this a secret from his wife or his best friend, whom he was aware would hear that.

"What?" Magda asked, her face distorted with confusion.

His son? What kind of curse was this? Magda blinked—once, twice— her gaze riveted to his, as if combing through the hard planes of his expression for any flicker of deceit, any cracks betraying a cruel joke. None. His eyes held, steady as stone, his mouth set with grim conviction. The truth hit her like a blow. Her breath caught, knees threatening to buckle as the world tilted, the ground dissolving beneath her feet. What had her husband just said?

Sonia gave Helmer a signal and hopped onto Richard, and bit him to buy Helmer some time. But Helmer shifted the gun to the corner of the garage room. He pulled on the trigger with no hesitation, and the bullet escaped, making the room silent. Marie was shot in the head and immediately dropped dead. "Magda, run!"

Seeing her lingering to escape, Helmer yelled at her, and she crawled out of the garage to leave.

"Helmer," Sonia whispered, wobbling backward, holding onto a knife stuck inside her neck. Richard stabbed her using a knife he had hidden in his coat. Sonia dropped to her knees, holding on to the knife, barely breathing. Her oxygen was low, and all she could say was, "C-Christopher."

Helmer froze, every muscle locking, as if trapped beneath water, struggling for air. His usual confidence shattered, leaving only a hollow stillness. His eyes fixed on Sonia, distant, helpless—like watching a plane plummet from the sky, and he was too far away to reach it. His heart raced, but all he could do was stand there, helpless. A fire sparked deep inside him, a fury far stronger than the helplessness eating away at him.

"I'm going to kill you," Helmer grunted, seizing Richard's neck. His fists flew, each punch harder than the last, the beast within fully unleashed. His hands carried the strength of many men, and every fighting instinct kicked in, guiding him straight to Richard's pressure points. Helmer squeezed, watching Richard's face turn red, swelling as if it might burst.

"G-go ahead. Kill me," mouthed Richard, his teeth drowned in a bath of blood.

"I should've killed you when I had the chance to," Helmer growled, as the blood from Richard's mouth splashed in his face. His hand wandered beneath Richard's ribcage, and with a savage twist, he applied pressure, dislocating one rib, then another. Richard screamed, bones cracking beneath Helmer's grip. But he didn't stop. His hands moved to Richard's throat, squeezing until Richard's eyes began to glaze over, the blankness creeping in as a drop of blood trickled from the corner of his mouth.

In the distance, the wail of sirens grew louder, but Helmer barely registered them. His fingers loosened around Richard's neck, and for a brief moment, he hesitated.

"I-I knew," coughed Richard, his throat raw from the near strangulation. "I knew you were a monster. You... you're a monster."

Helmer stilled, his lips twitching, putting his thoughts together. "I am," Helmer said, with not quite a nod, but a resolute tone. His hands fell to his sides as Richard gasped for air, his ribs shattered, and his body broken. "I just wish you never poked me awake."

He crawled to Sonia, her back against the wall, and her knees knocking against each other. Seeing her eyes—despite the fear and sadness in them—there was no hate. She still didn't hate him.

"Sonie." He kissed her cheek and held her hands. "Sonie…" His lips trembled uttering her name. It struck something in him, so deep that a gush of tears escaped, breaking through in a torrent. "I'll-I'll take care of him. I'll take care of Christopher."

"C-Chri…" she mouthed, despite the struggle to form the words, her eyes almost begging him to hug her firmly.

"It's okay, I know. I know," Helmer said nodding, his whispers breaking through sobs. "I'll be there for him. I-I promise. And I'll tell Bryant everything. I'll be better, just like you always wanted me to be."

Helmer slowly moved her off the wall, then sat behind and cuddled her. "I'll hold you. I know you want me to hold you…"

Her warm form grew cold in his arms, though Helmer held on tighter. "By the way, I loved it when you still used my coffee pot. Or making me tea. And scolding me. And for being the first one to have ever said that you loved me. Flaws and all. Sonie. My Sonie."

Her movements slowed. Her legs stretched. She was no longer breathing. Helmer removed the knife from her neck and tightened his arms around her, wailing.

***

The cops had taken Richard away. Bryant was rescued, though too crushed to even speak. He remained silent, until Sonia's burial. Everyone gathered to bid their farewells—Magda and Elvino included, with Christopher standing somberly by his side.

Magda kept her distance from Sonia's grave, watching as the company personnel laid down white lilies and extravagant bouquets. Though she had known Sonia for years, the truth of her hidden child with Helmer twisted Magda's heart. She couldn't bring herself to approach the coffin. Her shades stayed firmly on, her veil draping over half her face, hiding the dry ache of her expression from the small crowd.

She startled at the sound of approaching footsteps behind her. It was Helmer. His presence loomed like a broken branch, crashing to the ground and shaking her to her core. He stood there, silent, fumbling for the right words. She didn't need him to say he was sorry. Not now. Not anymore.

"I-I…"

"No need to say it," Magda interrupted. "I know."

"I didn't mean to hurt you," Helmer murmured. "I didn't know about Christopher."

"It's not really about your son, Helmer," Magda said, her voice brittle yet sharp. "The problem is the lack of accountability from you. Honestly, you betrayed my trust just as much. You forced me to have a child—"

"With reason."

"Exactly," Magda shot back, her head shaking in disbelief. "No accountability. You see things only through your lens. No matter what I say, I'll always be the one at fault."

"I didn't say that."

"You didn't have to. I see it," Magda said, her words like a punch to the chest. "The way you looked at her. It was as if the world crumbled around you when she was in danger. You've never looked at me like that."

"Magda, Sonia is—"

"The mother of your child," she spat. "The girl you loved."

"I..."

"You don't love me, Helmer." "I do," he argued.

"No," Magda said firmly, her hands clasping her stomach. "What you have for me is control. You don't want to let me go, but all we do is hurt each other. It's a cycle..."

"I don't understand," he muttered, his hand reaching toward her face, unsure whether he could still touch her.

"I want a divorce!" Magda blurted out, her voice shattering the air.

"What?" Helmer's voice cracked.

"You heard me," Magda said, her tone resolved. "And I'm not staying at Elvino's villa with my daughter, either. Not after knowing how corrupted he is. I need him far away from us."

"Magda, I don't think you understand what you're saying," Helmer said, stepping closer. His hands reached out, gently clasping her arms as if trying to anchor her, to stop her from drifting further. His eyes searched hers, desperate for anything to indicate she didn't mean it. But her gaze was empty. No light. No emotion.

"Please," he whispered, his voice softer now, nearly breaking. "Think about this."

His greatest fear had materialized. Divorce. Fifteen years reduced to ash. The home he'd built, demolished to its foundation. The woman carrying his child, walking away. He also had a son who would remind him of Sonia, his very first love. It struck him like lightning. His father. Had he turned into that man? A failed father figure, a husband incapable of holding his family together? The thought pierced through him, a searing pain that refused to relent. Would he let bitterness consume him, as it had consumed his father? Would he use his darkness to shield his pain, only to make others pay for it in the end?

There's nothing to think about, Helmer," Magda said, shrugging his hands off her shoulders. She didn't expect it, but the sting of tears began gathering in her eyes, blurring the sharpness of her resolve. "I am tired. And I know you are too. Me walking away doesn't mean that I hate you."

"But no, Magda…" Helmer objected, his voice barely audible.

"Why? Why now?"

"Because," she said, her voice soft but steady, "this is the only way we don't end up hating and resenting each other." Magda folded her arms across her chest. "I'll stay over at June's apartment for a few weeks until I find my own place. He's still out of town. He's worried, but I told him to finish up his trip."

The mention of June, the simplicity of her plan, the calm way she laid it out—all of it left him hollow.

"I think Christopher needs you. You should go to him," Magda said, gesturing toward the boy. Helmer hesitated, his feet rooted to the ground. Magda sighed and turned, her figure retreating into the distance, her posture resolute.

Helmer's gaze followed her for a long moment before shifting to his son. The boy's presence was a cruel echo, a reminder of Sonia—her face, her voice—all buried six feet under. Helmer left Christopher with Elvino, as he could barely hold his own. Yes, he had survived this tragedy, but his mind and heart were in that coffin, so much that comfort wasn't something he knew anymore.

"If you don't mind," Helmer said, cautiously approaching Bryant, as he remained motionless by Sonia's grave. "I'll wait here with you."

"I think…" he finally began, his words dragging. "I think I can forgive your petty high school schemes to get with her and the fact you didn't know about Christopher." Bryant bent down, his eyes glued to Sonia's name on the headstone. His voice grew shaky, though he steadied it with a deep breath. "But knowing she died because of your ridiculous jealousy and carelessness? That, I can't forgive. I didn't even have the chance to hold her hand or say goodbye. I was strapped in a chair in some basement, forced to watch… Discovering things I wish I never had."

Helmer's head dipped. "I don't have the right words, Bryant. But I want you to know I'm sorry. You're my brother—"

"Were," Bryant corrected, his fingers grazing Sonia's name on the headstone. He straightened, his body tensing as he adjusted his sleeves and turned toward Helmer. "I'm going to approach the board," he declared, his voice as firm as steel. "We'll put it to a vote between me and you. Whoever gets the numbers becomes CEO." He took a step closer, his tone dripping with finality. "So, I'll see you at the company, Helmer Dupris."

"B-Bryant," wept Helmer, watching his best friend walk away. He sank to his knees, consumed by his grief and yet another loss to process. Amidst the suffocating sorrow, his family was safe now, including Christopher, the boy Sonia had entrusted him to protect. Yet that small solace couldn't rival the void left behind. The greatest loss of his life lay beneath a cold headstone, unresponsive, unreachable.

Helmer sat by the grave, rocking back and forth, his fingers grazing the name etched in stone. He muttered softly, his words blending with the chilly breeze. A hand suddenly rested on his shoulder.

"Helms," Elvino said, his voice quieter than usual as he lowered himself to sit beside Helmer. "I'm sorry. Losing someone you cherish like that... it's a wound that doesn't heal."

"No," Helmer replied, his voice hoarse, his sniffling breaths labored. "The worst thing wouldn't be losing her. It would be going back to the man I used to be. The one I hated and swore to leave behind." His gaze darkened; his fists clenched against his thighs. "I don't have a choice. I'm going after Patterson. And everyone who stood with that psycho." He paused, his eyes simmering. "When I find them, I'll make them all pay for her death. One by one."

To be continued...

*F*rancesca Pierre, born in Haiti, began her journey into writing at the age of 15 after immigrating to the United States. Adjusting to her new environment and mastering the English language, she enrolled in ESOL classes during high school. It was within these classes that she discovered her voice and developed a passion for storytelling.

Francesca's early works ranged from heartfelt poems to compelling short stories, eventually culminating in the creation of novels.

She believes that every individual possesses an innate ability to tell stories—an untapped reservoir of creativity waiting to be explored. "We all have stories to tell; it's about finding the courage and the means to tell them," she says, underscoring her deep conviction in the transformative power of writing. For Francesca, words serve as the ultimate medium for conveying emotions, experiences, and imagination.

Her debut novel, Silent Past, was conceived shortly before the global outbreak of COVID-19. However, the pandemic marked a difficult period in her life, forcing her to pause the project. Confronted with her own childhood traumas and the weight of isolation, Francesca embarked on a two-year therapeutic journey that profoundly reshaped her understanding of herself and her craft. Emerging from this darkness, she resumed writing Silent Past, channeling her personal healing into its narrative.